PRAISE FOR
SUZANNE BROCKMANN

BORN TO DARKNESS

"Bestseller [Suzanne] Brockmann takes readers on a pulse-pounding ride with the first installment of her new futuristic paranormal series. . . . The drama pulls readers in from page one."
—*Publishers Weekly* (starred review)

"A thrill ride of a series-launcher . . . Brockmann's winning tale, part romantic suspense and part science fiction, will leave readers eager for the next in its series."
—*Booklist* (starred review)

"Romantic suspense superstar Brockmann shifts gears and kicks off a new futuristic series, Fighting Destiny. *Born to Darkness* features all of Brockmann's patented fast-paced action and emotional punch. This series is off to a rip-roaring start!"
—*RT Book Reviews* (four stars)

"Enthralling reading . . . High-octane action kicks the book right into can't-put-it-down territory. . . . Brockmann's latest is darkly thrilling, and as romantically diverse as it is gratifying. Seductive, suspenseful, surprising."
—*USA Today*

"Action-packed and sexy."

Reviews

BREAKING THE RULES

"In the powerful sixteenth Troubleshooters title, Brockmann masterfully weaves the stories of the four Gillman siblings into a single narrative that reaffirms the importance of family."
—*Publishers Weekly* (starred review)

"At long last Izzy Zanella gets his due. . . . Fast paced and filled with emotional land mines, Brockmann gives her readers a great story full of old friends and new adventures."
—*RT Book Reviews* (4½ stars)

"The action is relentless and the passion runs deep."
—Fresh Fiction

HOT PURSUIT

"Brockmann continues to use her patented style of weaving intersecting story lines around a number of different protagonists and relationships. Like an excellent chocolate, a Brockmann book never disappoints."
—*Romantic Times*

"The action grabs you and drags you along. . . . [*Hot Pursuit*] will immediately grab your interest."
—*Romance Reviews Today*

DARK OF NIGHT

"Provides real chills . . . a true Brockmann master-piece!"
—*Romantic Times*

"Once again Brockmann neatly blends high-adrenaline suspense and scorchingly sexy romance into an addictively readable mix."
—*Booklist*

"Brockmann fans will cheer."
—*Publishers Weekly*

INTO THE FIRE

"Another sure-bet winner from the always reliable Brockmann."
—*Booklist*

"A multilayered tale that includes emotion, romance, action and pulse-pounding suspense . . . Readers will root for new and old romances and worry about what the future holds for other characters—a trademark of Brockmann's that increases fan anticipation for the next book."
—*BookPage*

"*Into the Fire* is lucky number thirteen for fans of this ever-popular series. . . . [Brockmann] juggles multiple story lines while keeping the emotional quotient intact. . . . [Her] thrillers make you think and hold your breath!"
—*Romantic Times*

"A jaw-dropping 'conclusion' suggests more fireworks ahead."

—*Publishers Weekly*

FORCE OF NATURE

"Intense and packed with emotion, this book is truly a force of nature!"

—*Romantic Times*

"Brockmann deftly delivers another testosterone-drenched, adrenaline-fueled tale of danger and desire that brilliantly combines superbly crafted, realistically complex characters with white-knuckle plotting."

—*Booklist*

ALL THROUGH THE NIGHT

"In *All Through the Night,* Suzanne Brockmann strikes the perfect balance between white-knuckle suspense and richly emotional romance."

—*Chicago Tribune*

"For the holidays, Brockmann gifts her readers with the culmination of a long-delayed love story—that of fan favorite Jules Cassidy. Of course, in true Brockmann style, this wedding tale is packed to the gills with plenty of danger, bombs, terrorists, and stalkers. But, most of all, it is a satisfying love story."

—*Romantic Times*

"A winning, innovative runup to Christmas from the bestselling Brockmann."
—*Publishers Weekly*

INTO THE STORM

"Sexy, suspenseful, and irresistible . . . [This] novel has all the right ingredients, including terrific characters [and] a riveting plot rich in action and adventure."
—*Booklist*

"Brockmann is an undisputed master at writing military and suspense fiction [with] action, danger and passion all rolled into one."
—Curled Up with a Good Book

BREAKING POINT

"Readers will be on the edge of their seats."
—*Library Journal*

"An action-packed and breathtaking thriller."
—*Romantic Times*

HEADED FOR TROUBLE

HEADED FOR TROUBLE

A Troubleshooters/Navy SEAL Team 16 Anthology

SUZANNE BROCKMANN

BALLANTINE BOOKS • NEW YORK

Headed for Trouble is a work of fiction. Names, characters, places, and incidents are the products of the author's imagination or are used fictitiously. Any resemblance to actual events, locales, or persons, living or dead, is entirely coincidental.

Copyright © 2013 by Suzanne Brockmann
When Frank Met Rosie copyright © 2007 by Suzanne Brockmann
Thoughts on When Frank Met Rosie copyright © 2007 by Suzanne Brockmann
When Alyssa and Sam Met the Dentist copyright © 2004 by Suzanne Brockmann
Waiting copyright © 2005 by Suzanne Brockmann
Sam Takes an Assignment in Italy copyright © 2007 by Suzanne Brockmann
When Jenk, Izzy, Gillman, and Lopez Met Tony Vlachic copyright © 2007 by Suzanne Brockmann
Interview with Tom and Kelly copyright © 2006 by Suzanne Brockmann
Trapped copyright © 2007 by Suzanne Brockmann
Conversation with Navy SEALs Mark "Jenk" Jenkins, Dan Gillman, Jay Lopez, and Irving "Izzy" Zanella copyright © 2006 by Suzanne Brockmann
Interview with Kenny and Savannah copyright © 2006 by Suzanne Brockmann
Home Is Where the Heart Is, Part I copyright © 2008 by Suzanne Brockmann
Home Is Where the Heart Is, Part II copyright © 2013 by Suzanne Brockmann
A SEAL and Three Babies copyright © 2013 by Suzanne Brockmann
FAQs Answered: Interview with Suz copyright © 2006 by Suzanne Brockmann
Valentine's Day copyright © 2006 by Suzanne Brockmann
Glossary of Troubleshooters Terms copyright © 2006 by Suzanne Brockmann
Shane's Last Stand copyright © 2012 by Suzanne Brockmann
Excerpt from *Born to Darkness* copyright © 2013 by Suzanne Brockmann
Excerpt from *Do or Die* copyright © 2013 by Suzanne Brockmann

All rights reserved.

Published in the United States by Ballantine Books, an imprint of The Random House Publishing Group, a division of Random House, Inc., New York.

BALLANTINE and the colophon are registered trademarks of Random House, Inc.

This book contains an excerpt from *Do or Die* by Suzanne Brockmann. This excerpt has been set for this edition only and may not reflect the final content of the forthcoming hardcover edition.

ISBN 978-0-345-52125-5
eBook ISBN 978-0-345-52126-2

Cover illustration: Greg Gulbronson

Printed in the United States of America

www.ballantinebooks.com

9 8 7 6 5 4 3 2 1

Ballantine Books mass market edition: May 2013

For Jules and Robin.
For Sam and Alyssa.
For Tom and Kelly and Max and Gina and Izzy
and Jenk and Tony and Gillman and all the others
who have so completely come to life that readers
frequently email to ask me how you're doing.

And for the readers who believe.

CONTENTS

INTRODUCTION

I started writing my sixteen-book Troubleshooters series in 1999. I've covered a lot of ground in the years since then, creating a large stable of characters—some of whom have insisted on being recurring, showing up in book after book, and some of whom who have faded gracefully into the background as new characters were introduced and took center stage.

One thing is for certain: Regardless of how popular a character was, there was no way to include every single member of SEAL Team Sixteen in each and every one of the books. And even if beloved characters *did* appear, the situation wasn't always the right opportunity to get readers caught up on what was going on in their lives.

Picture a scenario where a SEAL team fast-ropes in to rescue characters who are being held hostage. The SEAL in command does *not* say, "Hi, my name is Lieutenant Mike Muldoon, and by the way, my wife, Joan, and I just had a baby boy, and even though we're not getting much sleep, we're both deliriously happy."

I mean, that's just not gonna happen, right?

And some characters were so . . . strong, shall we say, that it was hard to bring them into a book for a walk-on or extra role—they would tend to take over the scene and then the entire book if I didn't remain vigilant. (I'm talking about you, Sam Starrett!) So I often found myself sending them out of town on some important mission or op just to clear the stage for the newer characters.

Long story short, some years back, I started writing short stories to keep readers up to date as to what was happening in these characters' busy and eventful lives.

But I knew right from the start that I wanted these short stories to have substance. I knew that I didn't want to write "Sam and Alyssa Get a Puppy." Instead, the first short that I wrote was a story in which Sam and Alyssa, newly married, are out on a missing persons case, working together for Troubleshooters Incorporated, when they bump into the victim of a notorious serial killer called "the Dentist."

I called it "When Alyssa and Sam Met the Dentist," and it was more of a day-in-the-life character study of how previously cynical Alyssa is subtly being changed by her recent marriage to optimistic Sam.

This short first appeared in the back of *Flashpoint*, and interestingly, many readers didn't recognize that it was just that—a short story. I got email after email, asking me when the rest of that book about that serial killer was going to come out. (Oops.)

At the same time, I knew that finding evidence of that killer's handiwork was gnawing at Alyssa, so I wasn't surprised when the Dentist came up again, in later Sam and Alyssa short stories (included in this collection, too). And for those readers who are thinking, *The Dentist sounds familiar . . .* , I finally allowed the deadly killer to go head-to-head with Alyssa (and Sam, naturally) in the full-length Troubleshooters novel *Hot Pursuit*.

For those of you who like to know *exactly* how it all fits together, I've included a timeline that allows you to see where each of the stories in this collection falls within the framework of the sixteen published Troubleshooters books, and the two e-published Troubleshooters short stories.

There's also a glossary of terms, FYI, at the back of the book, as well as a special bonus short story called "Shane's Last Stand," which features the Navy SEAL hero of my futuristic paranormal book *Born to Darkness*. (Even in the future, SEALs are still SEALs, and the only easy day was yesterday.)

As always, with all the books that I write, any mistakes made or liberties taken are completely my own.

Suzanne Brockmann
May 12, 2012

TROUBLESHOOTERS SERIES TIMELINE

1999:

When Frank Met Rosie
Timeframe: Thanksgiving Day
Hero: Navy SEAL Chief Frank O'Leary
Heroine: Rosie Marchado

2000:

1. *The Unsung Hero*
Timeframe: August
First Published: June 2000
Hero: Navy SEAL Lt. Tom Paoletti
Heroine: Dr. Kelly Ashton
Storyline: A SEAL recovering from a head injury spots a believed-to-be-dead terrorist in a quiet little New England town.
Secondary Romance: Tom's niece Mallory Paoletti and comic book artist David Sullivan
World War II Subplot: Resistance in Nazi-occupied France, a love triangle between Charles, Joe, and Cybele.

2001:

2. *The Defiant Hero*
Timeframe: Spring

Note: Flashbacks to 1997, with young SEALs Nils,
   Sam, and WildCard
First Published: March 2001
Hero: Navy SEAL Lt. (jg) John "Nils" Nilsson
Heroine: Meg Moore
Storyline: The rescue of Meg's kidnapped grandmother
   and daughter.
Secondary Romance: Navy SEAL Sam Starrett and
   FBI Agent Alyssa Locke
World War II Subplot: The evacuation of Dunkirk (Eve
   and Ralph).

3. *Over the Edge*
Timeframe: Summer
First Published: September 2001
Hero: Navy SEAL Senior Chief Stan Wolchonok
Heroine: Navy Reserve helo pilot Lt. (jg) Teresa Howe
Storyline: The Navy SEAL takedown of a commercial
   airliner hijacked by terrorists.
Note: This book came out two weeks before 9/11.
Secondary Romance: Navy SEAL Sam Starrett and
   FBI Agent Alyssa Locke
World War II Subplot: The Holocaust in Denmark.

4. *Out of Control*
Timeframe: This book was written pre-9/11, and is set
   in that "before" world, even though the action was
   meant to take place in early 2002.
First Published: March 2002
Hero: Navy SEAL Chief Ken "WildCard" Karmody
Heroine: Savannah von Hopf
Storyline: Kenny and Savannah's scramble through the
   Indonesian jungle.
Secondary Romance: Expat David Jones and do-
   gooder Molly Anderson
World War II Subplot: German Americans as spies in
   Nazi Germany (Rose and Hank).

2002:

5. *Into the Night*
Timeframe: Intentionally vague, to catch up to the
    post-9/11 world
First Published: December 2002
Hero: Navy SEAL Lt. (jg) Mike Muldoon
Heroine: Joan DaCosta
Storyline: The terrorist assassination attempt at the
    Coronado Naval Base.
Secondary Romance: Mary Lou Starrett and
    Ihbraham Rahman
World War II Subplot: The battle of Tarawa, and the
    formation of the UDT units, granddaddies to the
    SEALs (Vince and Charlotte).

2003:

6. *Gone Too Far*
Timeframe: June
First Published: July 2003
Hero: Navy SEAL Lt. Roger "Sam" Starrett
Heroine: FBI Agent Alyssa Locke
Storyline: The rescue of Sam's missing daughter.
Secondary Romance: FBI Agent Max Bhagat and for-
    mer hostage Gina Vitagliano
World War II Subplot: Tuskegee Airmen and the
    Women Airforce Service Pilots (Walt and Dot).

When Alyssa and Sam Met the Dentist
Timeframe: Autumn

2004:

7. *Flashpoint*
Timeframe: Summer
First Published: April 2004
Hero: James Nash

Heroine: Tess Bailey
Storyline: The search for a terrorist's missing laptop in an earthquake-ravaged country.
Secondary Relationship: Friendship between Jim Nash and former SEAL Lawrence Decker

Waiting
Main Characters: TS Operative Sam Starrett and the wives of the SEALs of Team Sixteen

2005:

8. Hot Target
Timeframe: Late winter, early spring
First Published: January 2005
Hero: Navy SEAL Chief Cosmo Richter
Heroine: Jane Mercedes Chadwick
Storyline: The protection of a Hollywood producer receiving death threats for making a movie about a gay World War II hero.
Secondary Romance: FBI Agent Jules Cassidy and actor Robin Chadwick
World War II Subplot: Jack and Hal, and the ghost army of the 23rd HQ Special Troops.

9. Breaking Point
Timeframe: Summer
First Published: July 2005
Hero: FBI Team Leader Max Bhagat
Heroine: Gina Vitagliano
Storyline: The rescue of Gina and Molly by unlikely allies Max, Jones, and Jules.
Secondary Romance: Expat David Jones and Molly Anderson

Sam Takes an Assignment in Italy
Timeframe: Post–*Breaking Point*
Main Characters: TS Operative Sam Starrett and FBI
  Agent Jules Cassidy

*When Jenk, Izzy, Gillman, and Lopez Met Tony
Vlachic*
Timeframe: Pre–*Into the Storm*

Interview with Tom and Kelly
Timeframe: December

10. *Into the Storm*
Timeframe: December
First Published: August 2006
Hero: Navy SEAL Petty Officer Mark "Jenk" Jenkins
Heroine: Troubleshooters operative Lindsey Fontaine
Storyline: A combined winter training op with TS Inc.
  and SEAL Team Sixteen gets disrupted by a danger-
  ous serial killer.
Secondary Relationships: Jenk's SEAL friends Izzy,
  Gillman, and Lopez all loudly interact.

2006:

Trapped
Timeframe: Early 2006
Main Characters: TS Operative Alyssa Locke and FBI
  Agent Jules Cassidy

*Conversation with Navy SEALs Mark "Jenk"
Jenkins, Dan Gillman, Jay Lopez, and Irving "Izzy"
Zanella*
Timeframe: Shortly after *Into the Storm*

Interview with Kenny and Savannah
Timeframe: Shortly after *Into the Storm*

11. *Force of Nature*
Timeframe: Summer
First Published: August 2007
Romantic Couple One: PI Ric Alvarado and his gal
    Friday, Annie Dugan
Romantic Couple Two: FBI Agent Jules Cassidy and
    actor Robin Chadwick
Storyline: An investigation into a Florida crime lord
    with terrorist ties.

2007:

12. *All Through the Night*
Timeframe: September through December
First Published: October 2007
Hero: FBI Agent Jules Cassidy
Hero: Actor Robin Chadwick
Storyline: Jules and Robin get married in Massachu-
    setts, and high jinks ensue.
Secondary Romance: Personal assistant Dolphina Patel
    and *Boston Globe* reporter Will Schroeder

E-Short-Story 1: When Tony Met Adam
Timeframe: December 2007 through February 2008
First Published: June 2011
Hero: Navy SEAL Tony Vlachic
Hero: Actor Adam Wyndham
Storyline: A romance celebrating the repeal of *Don't
    Ask, Don't Tell*.

2008:

Home Is Where the Heart Is (Part I and Part II)
Timeframe: Spring
Hero: Reporter Jack Lloyd
Heroine: Army Reserve Sergeant Arlene Schroeder,
    home from Iraq

Note: Arlene is the sister of *Boston Globe* reporter Will Schroeder, and the mother of Maggie, both of whom play major roles in *All Through the Night*.

13. *Into the Fire*

Timeframe: July

First Published: August 2008

Hero: Former TS operative Vinh Murphy

Heroine: Hannah Whitfield

Storyline: Former Marine Vinh Murphy is the prime suspect when the man responsible for his wife Angelina's murder is found dead.

Secondary Relationships: The hardened operatives of TS Inc. are forced to talk to a therapist to finally come to terms with Angelina's death.

14. *Dark of Night*

Timeframe: Summer

First Published: February 2009

Romantic Couple One: TS Operative and former SEAL Lawrence Decker and TS Inc. receptionist Tracy Shapiro

Romantic Couple Two: TS Operatives Dave Malkoff and Sophia Ghaffari

Storyline: TS Inc. goes up against the shadowy Agency when James Nash is targeted for removal.

2009:

15. *Hot Pursuit*

Timeframe: February

First Published: August 2009

Romantic Couple One: TS Operatives Sam Starrett and Alyssa Locke

Romantic Couple Two: Navy SEAL Petty Officer Dan Gillman and Jennilyn LeMay

Storyline: Alyssa is targeted by the dangerous serial killer known as "the Dentist."

A SEAL and Three Babies
Timeframe: Early March
Main Characters: TS Operatives Sam Starrett and Alyssa Locke, and their one-year-old son, Ash; FBI Agent Jules Cassidy and his husband, Robin; FBI Agent Max Bhagat, his wife, Gina, and their children, Emma and Mikey.

16. Breaking the Rules
Timeframe: May 4–9, 2009
First Published: April 2011
Romantic Couple One: Navy SEAL Petty Officer Izzy Zanella and Eden Gillman
Romantic Couple Two: Navy SEAL Petty Officer Dan Gillman and Jennilyn LeMay
Storyline: Mortal frenemies and SEAL teammates Izzy and Dan are forced to work together when Dan's little brother is in danger.

PRESENT DAY:

E-Short-Story 2: Beginnings and Ends
Timeframe: Undetermined
First Published: June 2012
Main Characters: FBI Agent Jules Cassidy and his husband, Robin Chadwick Cassidy
Storyline: Robin's life gets intertwined with that of the closeted movie star he plays on his hit TV show, *Shadowland*, and he and Jules decide it's time to make some changes in their lives.

HEADED FOR TROUBLE

WHEN FRANK MET ROSIE

November 25, 1999
New Orleans, Louisiana

The music made him stop and turn around.

It was just a solo voice—a man singing the richest, bluesiest version of *Silent Night* that Frank O'Leary had ever heard. It drew him closer when he should have headed away from the French Quarter and back toward his hotel.

Where his damn fool of a half brother was no doubt still holding court in the lobby bar. Lord Jesus save him from imbeciles. Of course, he himself could be included in that subset, considering he'd agreed to come to New Orleans for the holiday.

It was their mother who'd been the glue that kept them connected, Frank and Casey. Her constant smile and teasing words lightened the years of bad feelings between brothers who'd been born more than a decade apart. Now, though, they had less than nothing in common.

And yet Frank had come all the way from California on one of the busiest travel days of the year at Casey's request.

Because he'd thought his mother would've wanted him to. Because she'd valued her precious family—her two such different sons—so highly.

Despite being just a few blocks down from the whorehouse-on-heavy-stun dementia of past-midnight

Bourbon Street, this narrow road was deserted. A right turn revealed a street just as empty of tourists, but it definitely brought him closer to that angelic voice. Not like Frank was in any danger from the flesh-and-blood demons who crept out of the rotting woodwork of this city at night, no sir.

With his thrice-broken nose, his hair grown out from his usual no-frills tight and square cut, and his PT-hardened body, he knew he looked like the type most folks crossed the street to avoid.

He looked—as Casey had so often scornfully told him throughout his teenage years—as if he had barely a dime in his jeans pocket. Like a drifter. Like lowlife loser scum. Like his father, who'd cleaned out their mother's bank account when he'd left, back when Frank was nine and Casey was twenty.

The joke was that Casey had asked Frank to today's Thanksgiving dinner to borrow money. He'd lost nearly everything in bad investments. And since he knew that Frank still had his share from the recent sale of their mother's house . . .

And here Frank had thought Casey wanted his company during this difficult holiday season, the first since their mother had passed.

Happy fucking Thanksgiving to you, too, *bro*. Yeah, the real joke here was that Frank had left his true brothers behind in San Diego. His SEAL teammate Sam Starrett was hosting a dinner in the apartment he shared with Johnny Nilsson. He'd even roasted a turkey. Nils and the Card were in charge of the vegetables. Jenkins was handling dessert. Everyone else brought beer.

Instead of settling in for a day of food, friends, and football, Frank had shared a grim meal with Casey and his current wife (was Loreen number three or four?) up in their hotel suite. He'd escaped as quickly as possible after letting Casey know he'd already earmarked their

mama's money—all of it—for something special. A down
payment on a condo or maybe even a boat.

Still, it didn't take Casey long to join him in the bar.
Could Frank maybe cosign a loan? Or let him borrow
just a bit off that down payment . . . ? *No, no, no, don't
answer right away, bro. Just think about it . . .*

Fifteen minutes of listening to his brother regaling the
waitresses with tales of his own magnificence was all he
could endure, and Frank escaped from the hotel bar as
well.

But wandering Bourbon Street had been mildly amus-
ing for only a very short time. Preservation Hall was
already closed up tight and silent, and the bands playing
in the various bars were entertaining only to inebriated
ears. Watching grown men acting like frat boys drinking in the street and gazing with calf eyes at the teenage
whores was flat-out creepy. And then there was that
old woman—probably just an actress wrapped in rags
and wearing stage-makeup warts—who'd first enticed
Frank closer, offering to read his palm, and then, after
only one brief look, had bluntly refused.

She'd shaken her head at him, backing away in alarm.

Which didn't mean a goddamn thing.

Like anyone with eyes in their head and a lick of sense
couldn't tell from looking at him that he lived a dangerous life . . . ?

Frank glanced at his watch. If he knew Sam Starrett,
the meal would have long since been replaced by a deck
of cards and a pile of poker chips. There'd be plenty
more beer, lots of laughter, and music on the boom
box—although nothing that could compare to this solo
voice, the owner of which still eluded him.

Silent Night segued into an *Ave Maria* as sung by
an angel who'd done his share of hard time on this
earth.

Frank rounded the corner, and there the street singer

stood. He was a wiry black man in his late fifties, although, on second glance, he might've been younger. Hard living could've given him that antique veneer a decade or two early. He was standing in a storefront, the windows creating a makeshift acoustical shell that amplified his magical, youthful voice.

Only a few people had gathered to listen to him sing. A group of older folks—three sets of couples, clearly tourists, laden with Mardi Gras beads—used their cameras to snap his picture. A bedraggled young woman stood slightly apart from them, in a sequin top and a tight-fitting black skirt, looking like sex for sale.

The singer's voice faltered, and Frank slowed his steps, shortening his stride as the eight of them turned almost at once to look at him. They shrank away as if they all were fortune-tellers and knew that an anvil was on the verge of falling on top of him, out of the clear blue sky.

Cloudy sky, actually. It was definitely going to rain again tonight.

And not all of them shrank from him. The girl—she didn't look more than seventeen—didn't seem too afraid. Probably because she hadn't yet met her pimp's quota for the night, and saw him as a potential john.

She had to be relatively new to the city, new at her distasteful job. She was still pretty, with long, dark hair and deep brown eyes. Her skin hadn't yet acquired that unmistakable gray pallor caused by substance abuse and nocturnal living. She gave her top a hike northward as she met his gaze and smiled a greeting.

The Red Hat Club and their spouses weren't quite as friendly. They quickly scurried off down the street.

"Sorry, man," Frank told the singer, taking out his wallet and extracting a twenty. "Didn't mean to chase 'em away."

He dropped the bill in the cardboard shoebox being

used in lieu of a hat. The man clearly couldn't afford headwear, dressed as he was in Salvation Army castoffs, T-shirt dirty and torn, feet shoved into sneakers with the toes cut away.

"S'okay," the singer said, still eyeing him warily. "They were twenty-five-centers. It's been that kind of night. Aside from your twenty, I ain't got mor'n a buck seventy-five."

Did he really think . . . ? "I ain't gon' rob you, man," Frank said, slipping easily into the molasses-thick accent of his childhood.

The singer nodded, but didn't seem convinced. "If you did, you wouldn't be the first. Like I said, it's been that kind of night."

"You take requests?" Frank asked.

"For twenty bucks?" The man's lips twisted in what might've passed for a smile. "Son, I'll perform unnatural acts."

Jesus, he wasn't kidding. *"Amazing Grace,"* Frank said, "is what I'm hoping for."

The singer's eyes were dark with understanding as he looked up from his crouch beside his box. His hands were shaking as he slipped the twenty beneath the newspaper that lined the bottom of his container, and Frank knew the man wasn't going to spend that cash on either food or shelter, and wasn't that a crying shame?

"I guess we all need savin' at some point or 'nother," the singer said, straightening back up.

"Yes, sir," Frank agreed. Some more than most. The man closed his eyes, took a deep breath, and started to sing.

It was strange hearing that rich voice coming out of that scrawny, dried-up husk of a body. Clearly the Lord worked in mysterious ways.

Frank closed his eyes, too, letting the familiar words

wash over him, the melody soaring and dipping, carrying out into the unnaturally warm Louisiana night.

He sensed more than heard the girl as she moved to stand beside him, and he mentally inventoried his valuables. Wallet was in his front jeans pocket. It wasn't getting picked without him noticing, that was for damn sure. He wore his dive watch on his left wrist. His hotel keycard was in his back pocket—easy to lose, but not a problem if it got taken. What was she gonna do? Go into the Sheraton and try every room on every floor, looking for the lock it opened? Security would escort her out the back door within thirty seconds.

She shifted slightly, and Frank caught a whiff of her perfume. She actually smelled nice—like vanilla. Mixed, of course, with whiskey. He opened his eyes and as he turned to look down at her—she was about an entire foot shorter than he was—she smiled again.

"He's incredible, huh?" she whispered.

Frank nodded. Up close, she was even prettier than he'd first thought, with clear, perfect skin and lively eyes in a heart-shaped face.

She opened her mouth to speak again, but he spoke first. "Ain't lookin' to get hoovered, Sugar, even by a mouth as pretty as yours. Don't waste your time on me."

She blinked at him, clearly confused. "I'm sorry, I didn't . . . You said, you're not looking to get . . . ?" Ah, shit. Her accent and words were pure well-educated Northerner. Her voice wasn't that of a seventeen-year-old, either. She was closer to ten years older. And Frank could see now that her bedraggled state was merely from being caught in the rain that had poured down a few hours earlier, as if someone had pulled the plug in heaven.

"Sorry," he said quickly. "I thought . . . I was wrong." Just his luck, she wasn't drunk enough to let it slide.

He could see her replaying the words he'd said, trying to figure out the ones she'd missed—or misunderstood.

"Hoovered," she said with a laugh, comprehension dawning. "As in . . . Right. Okay." She quickly turned back to stare, as if fascinated, at the singer, color tingeing her cheeks. "I'm feeling pretty friendly tonight, but not *that* friendly. Wow."

Shit, now *he* was blushing, too. Great. "Sorry," he said again.

She turned to look at him again. "You really thought I was . . . ?" Amazingly, she wasn't offended, just curious. Interested even.

Frank tried to explain. "Most women . . . out alone, this time of night . . ." He shrugged.

She nodded, accepting the misunderstanding as an honest mistake. And if he weren't mistaken, she was more than a little thrilled to have been taken for a prostitute. Go figure.

They stood there then, just listening to the music, to the timeless words. *I once was lost but now I'm found, was blind but now I see . . .*

Silence settled around them as the last notes of the song faded away. The singer didn't open his eyes, he just launched into a bluesy rendition of an old torch song. "Crazy." Another of Frank's mother's favorites.

The girl—woman—standing next to Frank cleared her throat. "See, I lost my jacket," she told him, tucking a strand of hair behind her ear. "I was with a group of friends and . . . It's gone. I don't know where I left it. I went back for it, but . . ." She shrugged, an action which did some amazing things to the plunging neckline of that barely there top.

"They let you come out here, all alone?" Frank had to ask, working to keep his gaze on her pretty face. What kind of foolish friends did she have?

"Of course not. But we'd only gone a block when

Betsy felt sick, so Jenn flagged down a cab. She told the driver to take me to the bar we just left and then right back to our hotel, and the first part of that plan worked. But when I came out, the cab was gone," she reported. "It was a toss-up between staying there and trying to flag another while getting hit on by bozos, or walking back. I opted for walking. I attached myself to that group. They were from Ohio."

"You just let them leave," he pointed out, and it was weird as hell, because as he held her gaze, something shifted in his chest, something massive that hadn't moved in years.

"I definitely look less like a, you know, hooker *with* my jacket on," she told him.

"I *am* sorry," he said again, "that I said what I said . . ."

"You reminded me of my best friend's cousin," she said. "Billy. When you walked up, for a second I thought you were him. Which didn't make sense, but . . . He was Marine Recon. What are you? Navy, right?"

How the hell did she know? None of his tattoos showed.

She pointed to his dive watch. "I used to work for a catalog company, and we sold much cheaper versions. Lots of knockoff K-Bar knives, too. And chain mail. You ever need chain mail, I can hook you up with a supplier."

Frank laughed at that. "Thanks." Chain mail. "I probably won't . . ." He shook his head.

"You never know," she said, a sparkle in her eyes. Sparkle and spark.

"I pretty much do." He smiled back. And had to ask. "So, you and, uh, Billy, um . . . ?"

"A thing of the past," she informed him. "And yes, it was tragic. He broke my heart—he went and married someone else. Of course, I was twelve, so within a week I'd moved on to Chandler from *Friends*."

Frank laughed. "Ah."

"How long have you been out of the service?" the woman asked, but didn't wait for him to answer. She somehow managed to read his eyes or maybe his mind. "You're not out—you're still in."

Frank nodded. "You really should've stayed with that group from Ohio."

"And missed the chance to be mistaken for a lady of the evening?"

"What if I was dangerous?" he asked, and there it was again. That spark of heat between them.

"Why *Amazing Grace*?" she countered.

Frank just looked at her, using silence to let her know that he wasn't going to let her change the subject. Damn, but she was pretty, with those dark brown eyes that shone with intelligence, even though she'd clearly had too much to drink. But she met his gaze steadily, refusing to be intimidated, just letting the singer's beautiful voice wash over them. *Crazy for crying and crazy for trying . . .*

Finally, he spoke. "Got a thing for livin' dangerously?" he drawled, purposely leaning heavily on his accent. But even though her cheeks again flushed, this time she didn't look away.

"Actually, no," she admitted. "I've always been careful. Sometimes too careful, I think."

Frank had always scoffed at the idea of love at first sight. How stupid was that? Giving your heart based only on the way a woman looked, without getting to know her . . . ? But as he held this girl's gaze, he felt that same seismic shift in his chest that he'd felt before. "No such thing as too careful."

"Yeah," she said, dead serious. "There is. If I'd left with the Ohio squad, I would've regretted it. Badly.

Maybe I'm crazy, but when I saw you . . ." Her voice trailed off, and she finally looked away. Laughed. "I am crazy. I must be. I just . . . I didn't want to regret not meeting you. Your turn to embarrass yourself. Why *Amazing Grace*?"

"My mother passed last spring." The words left his mouth as if on their own volition. What the hell . . . ? There were members of his SEAL team whom he hadn't yet told of her death, and here he was, telling this stranger.

A stranger who'd just looked him in the eye and admitted that she was willing to risk her own personal safety just to meet him.

Like he was something special, like she'd seen his aura or some kind of halo hanging over his head. Right.

My mother passed last spring really wasn't a complete answer to *Why* Amazing Grace? but somehow she understood. Completely.

"Oh, wow," she said, her eyes sympathetic. "Happy Thanksgiving, huh? It must've been such a hard day for you."

Frank felt himself nod. Whatever it was that had shifted in his chest had moved to his throat. He tried to swallow it back down, but it was lodged there. She put her hand on his arm, her fingers cool and soft against his skin. "I'm so sorry."

She meant it. Frank didn't know what to say.

Across the street, the singer finished his song. He started packing up his box. "Sorry, folks. Gotta run. Shelter starts filling this time of night, weather like this. If I wait too long, I won't get a bed."

Frank hadn't noticed until now, but it had started, again, to rain. It was coming down faster now. Harder.

The singer clutched his box to his chest. "Rosie, can I walk you to your hotel?" he asked.

Rosie. She only briefly glanced away from Frank as she answered the man. "No thanks, Odell. I'm okay."

The singer—Odell—still didn't trust Frank, eyeing him, edging closer, as if he could do some serious damage to the SEAL, who had way more than a hundred pounds on him. "You sure?"

"Thank you, but yes." Rosie was sure.

And as the skies opened up, Odell was gone.

Rosie looked up into the deluge and just laughed. She must've been even more drunk than Frank had thought, so he grabbed her by the hand and pulled her, and together they ran for shelter.

It was pointless—they were already soaked—running wouldn't keep them from getting any more wet. Still, the sound of her laughter made him smile, and—go figure—he was laughing, too, when she finally pulled him into a narrow doorway.

She was breathless and soaked. Her face wasn't all that was glistening wet, but her smile was so damn infectious as they stood there, squeezed together in a space where he'd have barely fit on his own. She was warm and soft against him, the neckline of that clingy top truly amazing from his vantage point.

"This seems like a good time for introductions," she told him. "I'm Rosie Marchado. I'm from Hartford. In Connecticut."

"Frank O'Leary," he said. He couldn't look down into her face without getting an eyeful of her sonnet-worthy cleavage. Sweet Jesus, he loved full-figured women.

"Do you want to . . . ," she started, then stopped. She made an embarrassed face. "God, I've never done this before. You're going to think that I'm . . ." She took a deep breath, which completely renewed his faith in a higher power. "I really never, ever do this, but do you want to . . ."

She didn't hesitate for more than a second or two, but that was all the time Frank needed to fill in the blank.

Have sex, right here in this shadowy doorway. He would kiss her, his hands sweeping her skirt up, her leg wrapping around him as they strained to get closer, even closer. . . .

She was going to ask him for it, and he was going to have to turn her down because she was drunk, except, damn, he couldn't think of anything or anyone he'd rather do.

But then she finished her question with, "Maybe go get some coffee? With me?"

At first her words just didn't make sense.

She wanted hot, steaming . . .

Coffee.

She was looking up at him, her lower lip caught between her perfect teeth. She was feeling trepidation both at the fact that she'd been so bold as to suggest to a near stranger that they go get coffee, and because she thought he might actually say no.

Frank started to laugh. "I know a place we can go." He took her by the hand, and once again pulled her out with him, into the rain.

* * *

They talked.

All night.

And by the time Frank walked Rosie back to her hotel in the French Quarter, he knew that even though she'd given him her phone number—in Hartford freakin' Connecticut—he wasn't going to call her.

He liked her too damn much.

She'd told him about her fiancé. Ex-fiancé. The sumbitch had dumped her two months before their wedding because—the asshole had claimed—their lives together would be too boring.

Boring? In what dimension? She was funny and sweet and smart and—God *damn!*—sexy as all get out. The entire time they sat there, sipping their coffee and talking themselves hoarse, he couldn't stop thinking about how perfect and soft her lips would feel if he kissed her.

But when he'd told her—just a little—about being a SEAL, about being stationed in San Diego, about going TDY in places where American service persons weren't exactly welcome, Frank knew that even though she claimed to be looking for excitement, hooking up with a man like him, who risked his life as a matter of course, would be too much for her.

Oh, she didn't say it in so many words. And, in fact, it was just after that that she'd given him her business card with her personal phone number in curvy handwriting on the back.

But Hartford to San Diego . . . ? The sheer distance alone howled of unpreventable disaster. And now here they were, with dawn lighting the sky behind them. Standing just outside the ornate gilded doors of her hotel.

"So," Rosie said.

Yeah. *So.* Her flight home wasn't until that evening. She didn't *have* to run upstairs to pack. Not right away.

But she was tired. He might've been used to going without sleep for long periods of time, but she was unable to hide her obvious fatigue.

Still, she didn't move any closer to that fancy door.

She was looking, too, as if she wanted something more from him than a handshake and a *Nice to meet you.*

But no way was he kissing her. No way was he stepping hip deep into *that* temptation. Except, damn, he wanted to, and he knew she knew because he could not, for the life of him, stop staring at her mouth.

"Do you want," she started, and he knew she wasn't going to invite him to her room—she had roommates. That just wasn't going to happen. Not tonight.

Not ever.

"I better go." He cut her off, unwilling or maybe just plain unable to turn down whatever she was about to offer.

But she spoke over him. "—to meet for a late lunch?"

"I can't," he said. It wasn't a lie. "My flight's at oh-eight-thirty."

"Oh," she said. "Wow. Well, then, you better . . ."

"Go," he agreed, yet still stood there, like a fool. Wishing for things he couldn't have. Knowing that he had to turn and walk away. He had to go back to the Sheraton and pack—and toss her business card into the trash can under the bathroom counter.

"I know you aren't going to call me," she said softly. "It's okay. Don't feel bad. I know that . . . Well, maybe in another lifetime, you know? I just . . . I loved last night. I loved meeting you."

She touched him then, only briefly, her fingers cool against his face, and then she was gone, the gilded door shutting silently behind her.

It was for the best. It was definitely for the best. Those words drummed through Frank's head as he passed the park where artists and vendors, palm readers and bead sellers had been set up, even after dark, even in the rain. It was empty now, littered with trash from the hardcore partying of the previous night.

It was for the best. For the best.

Mother*fucking* fool, mother*fucking* fool. . . .

Frank violently kicked garbage—plastic beer cups—out of his way. One wasn't quite empty and it flew through the air, nearly hitting a woman who still sat by the park's wall, raincoat up and over her head.

Her wooden sign was still out: *Palms read, five dollars. Blind Maggie Sees the Truth* was lettered in smaller print beneath the picture of a hand. She started awake— she'd been asleep sitting there—and even though she wore dark glasses, she turned and looked directly at Frank.

"You don't have much time," she said, her voice raspy, maybe from age or from sleeping in the rain, but probably from sleeping on the street in the rain at her advanced age.

"Not interested, ma'am." Frank slowed down, but only to press his spare change and a few loose dollar bills into her hand.

But she caught his wrist, running gnarled fingers across his palm. "She loves you."

For an old woman, she had a grip of steel. Frank could have pulled free, but not without knocking her out of her seat and dragging her down the street.

"You just met," the old woman—Blind Maggie, presumably—insisted. "Her eyes . . . She has such beautiful eyes."

As did nearly all the women on the planet. Frank was not impressed.

"She sees you," Maggie intoned. "She loves you already—and you would walk away from such a gift?"

It was foolish. He was a fool. He should have thanked her for her advice. She would have let him go if he'd told her he believed her, and that he was going to get her five-dollar payment out from his wallet. The dead last thing he should have done was argue.

"She deserves better," Frank said.

And just like that, the old woman kicked him—ow, Jesus! Right on the shin.

"Fool!" she used the same word he'd been using to

chastise himself. "What's better than loving and being loved?"

She'd let him go in the course of delivering a kick with that much force, and he backed away.

For a blind woman—right—she tracked his movement with unerring accuracy as he turned and saw—thank you, Lord—the Sheraton sign. His hotel wasn't close, but it wasn't that far either.

"You'll break her heart!" Maggie shouted at him. "You're going to break her heart!"

Frank turned the corner, but she kept on shouting. "You love her, too, and you didn't even kiss her goodbye!"

And he stopped. Just like that. *Fool.* He was *such* a fool. Love her, too? He didn't know. Was that what this was, this tight feeling in his chest, this odd grief at the idea of not seeing Rosie again, Rosie whom he barely even knew. Except . . .

He knew her.

They'd talked for hours, as if they'd been friends for years. He'd told her secrets, things he'd never told anyone else. She'd made him laugh, made him dream of a life he'd never dared dream of before as he'd lost himself in her beautiful dark brown eyes.

And just like that, Frank started running.

Not toward the Sheraton. Away from it.

Toward Rosie's hotel.

He was out of breath and sweating when he pushed his way into the lobby, and the clerk at the front desk looked up in alarm.

"House phone?" Frank panted, and the man pointed to a telephone farther down the counter.

Frank picked it up and dialed zero. "Connect me to Rosie Marchado's room," he said when the operator picked up.

There was a pause. "I'm sorry, sir"—words he didn't want to hear—"we have no guests named Marchado."

Perfect. She was staying with friends and had obviously registered under one of their names.

As Frank hung up, he saw in the mirror that two of the bellhops—big, burly fellows—had come to surround him. Shit. Now he wouldn't even be able to sit in the lobby, hoping that she'd come downstairs early, in the few minutes he had left before he had to catch his own flight out.

"I'm not here to make trouble, boys," Frank told them, turning around nice and slow, keeping his hands up and in sight.

But the bigger bellhop was smiling. "Chief O'Leary?" he asked.

Frank blinked. What the . . . ?

"I served twelve years in the regular Navy," the man said. He was more overweight than muscular, Frank saw now. "I always admired you SEALs." He cleared his throat, holding out an envelope. "Miss Rosie asked me to give this to you. She said you'd be coming by."

Frank took it. Opened it.

Rosie had written him a note in her neat, clear hand. *Suite 312* was all it said. Short and sweet and all he needed to know.

He ran for the elevator, pushed the button. It took too damn long, so he searched for and found the sign for the stairs. He took them up, three at a time.

And there it was. Suite 312. He knocked, knowing that he was probably going to wake up her friends, but he didn't give a good goddamn. He knocked again, even louder, and the door opened.

Rosie stood there, and for several seconds, neither of them moved. And then they both did, both at once, and she was in his arms and Jesus Lord save him, he was finally kissing her.

She was sweetness and fire, kissing him back so fiercely, that his heart damn near exploded in his chest.

When he finally pulled away, breathless and dizzy, she was laughing and maybe even crying a little, too.

"I've never done anything even remotely like this before," Rosie told him. "I just . . . I don't do this."

Frank didn't either. Never before this. And probably, in all honesty, never again. "I have to go," he told her. Words she'd hear from him again and again, unless she came to her senses in the next few hours, days, weeks, *months*. It was quite probably going to be *months* before he could arrange a trip to Hartford to see her again. And it would take him far longer, unless he broke into that savings account where he'd stashed his inheritance from his mother—all nine thousand dollars of it.

Still, he kissed Rosie again, longer, slower, deeper this time, loving the way she melted into his arms.

"My email address is on my business card," she whispered. "Write me, okay?"

"This is crazy," he said, touching the softness of her cheek, trying to memorize her face, her eyes.

She laughed up at him. "Good crazy," she told him. "*Really* good crazy."

He kissed her again, both cursing and grateful for her roommates. If they'd been in her hotel room instead of out here in the hall, their clothes would already be off. And if there was one thing he was certain of, it was that she deserved better than a five-minute fuck, culminating with him running out the door to hail a cab, hauling up the zipper on his fly, shoes in his hands.

But Lord help him, because what he wanted and what he *wanted* were not the same thing.

And she was thinking along the same lines. "Do you want . . . ?"

He waited, sure this time that she was not going to offer him coffee.

"I could . . ." She cleared her throat. "Come with you to your, um, hotel and . . . help you pack your suitcase?"

She actually blushed because they both knew damn well that neither of them would pack any kind of suitcase if they went back to his room. Not that he even had a suitcase. He always traveled with his seabag, a duffel that he could just throw everything into—clean clothes and dirty laundry mixed together, because who the hell cared?

But the thing in his chest was swelling even larger. It was way past his throat now. It pushed on the backs of his eyes, making him feel as if—sweet Jesus—as if he might actually start bawling like a baby. Because what she was telling him was . . .

"You're that sure about me?" he asked, his voice coming out no louder than a whisper. She nodded. She was.

"Let me grab my sneakers," she told him now, disappearing to do just that.

Sneakers. With sneakers on her feet, they'd both be able to run much farther and faster. They could get to the Sheraton in enough time to spend *ten* minutes . . .

"We should wait," Frank heard himself saying. "I want to wait."

She was back in a sneaker-clad flash, looking at him as if he were from Mars, so he tried to explain.

"I want to do this right," he told her. "How about we meet for Christmas? Right back here, in New Orleans." He could take her to dinner someplace elegant and romantic. Someplace with dancing and champagne. And only then would they go back to the hotel, where they'd make love—slowly, tenderly—all night long.

"I'd love to meet you for Christmas," she told him. "And you're right. We *should* wait."

And there they stood, staring at each other.

Rosie held out her hand.

Frank took it.

And together, Rosie's laughter wrapping around them both, they ran for the stairs.

THOUGHTS ON
WHEN FRANK MET ROSIE

It was originally my intention to write only lighthearted stories using popular characters in the Troubleshooters series—and in "When Frank Met Rosie," I did neither. I mean, Frank O'Leary . . . ?

Not exactly winning popularity contests among readers, probably because the man is dead, killed in a terrorist attack in a hotel lobby in *Over the Edge*.

That's the book, remember, where SEAL Team Sixteen goes to dangerous Kazbekistan to participate in the takedown of a commercial airliner that has been hijacked by terrorists.

At the time I was writing *OTE*, I purposely chose to kill off Frank for a number of reasons—the first being that someone needed to die. I wanted to make sure that my readers understood how dangerous K-stan was. It's a fact that SEALs put their lives on the line all the time, as do all of our servicemen and -women. And it's also a fact that people die serving our country. This was the third book in the series. It was, I felt, time for casualties.

Okay, so I could've killed off anyone—it didn't *have* to be Frank. But it *did* have to be one of SEAL Team Sixteen's snipers. See, I wanted a reason for FBI agent (and former Navy sharpshooter extraordinaire) Alyssa Locke to actively take part in the takedown of the hijacked plane. As a point-of-view character, I wanted Alyssa to move from her role as observer to that of shooter.

Now, instead of killing Frank, I could've killed Duke

Jefferson, who was also a sniper. But I'd only just introduced the Duke in *Over the Edge*. Killing a brand-new character wouldn't have had the same impact on readers as killing an established one. And thus, I found myself eyeing Frank O'Leary. Frank was the perfect character to kill. (Remember, I made this choice long before I wrote the short story you just read!) I'd used his name in a number of books, but I hadn't spent much time and page space letting readers truly know who he was. I'd revealed that he was a sniper, and he was laconic, and very little else. Killing Frank wouldn't have been as devastating to readers as killing off a more established character such as WildCard Karmody would have been. And yet, killing Frank was guaranteed to be way more powerful than killing off a stranger such as the Duke.

So Frank got his pink slip. So to speak.

So there it was, and there I was.

Years later.

Summer, 2006.

And I'm wandering around my office, aware that I'd promised readers that my website countdown to *Into the Storm,* where this story first appeared, would include a collection of short stories featuring Troubleshooters series characters, knowing that sooner or later I'd have to get my butt into the chair in front of my computer and start writing.

But Frank O'Leary wouldn't stop haunting me. I couldn't *not* write his story. The man just wouldn't leave me alone.

It's going to sound for a second as if I'm completely changing the subject, but I'm not. See, a few years ago, my editor went to France on vacation and visited the site of the most famous D-Day ever—the WWII Allied invasion of the beach at Normandy. She brought photos back with her, and I was struck by the rows and rows and rows of crosses and Stars of David that marked the graves of the American servicemen who fell in that deadly battle. They stretch out, in a field there in France, as far as the eye can see.

Each one of those markers is a life lost. Each one of those markers signifies a family and friends who mourned the loss of a loved one—a son, a brother, a buddy, a husband—forever gone. It was hard for me not to well up with tears as I looked at those photographs. It's been more than sixty years since those courageous men died, but I am still grateful and awed and devastated by their sacrifice.

Body counts are part of war. But numbers are cold and hard to comprehend. What does it mean, 9,387— the number of Americans buried so many years ago, in that cemetery in France?

9,387 Americans who never came home. 9,387 lives that did not continue.

9,387 Rosies.

Frankly, I don't know what makes me more sad— thinking that each and every one of the brave men and woman who have died serving this country had their own Rosie, who grieves for them, or thinking that they hadn't lived long enough to find their Rosie yet.

So I sat down and wrote "When Frank Met Rosie" because, since we went to war in Afghanistan and Iraq, there have been many thousands more Franks and Rosies. As of July 2012, as I update this piece, the number of servicemen and -women who have died in Afghanistan and Iraq is 6,527. That number may have grown by the time you read these words. 6,527 should not just be a number that makes us shake our head in remorse as we go about our daily lives. Those 6,527 are people who loved and were loved. They are—each and every one of them—stories cut tragically short.

Frank really wanted me to write his story—the good part. The part that happened *before* he lay dying in helo pilot Teri Howe's arms on that hotel lobby floor. Before he knew that that fortune-teller was right—that he *was* going to break Rosie's heart.

The most important part of Frank's story was that he didn't wait.

He ran—at full speed—into a relationship with a terrific woman who saw him clearly and loved him for who he was. Thank goodness for that because, even though he didn't know it, the blind palm reader hit the nail on the head—he was almost out of time.

Life is way too short, and Frank and Rosie embraced it—and each other—completely.

Since I've written his story, Frank O'Leary doesn't haunt me as much anymore. Oh, he'll pop in from time to time—he wants me to write a major lottery win for Rosie. And he's starting to nudge me to introduce her as a character in the main series of books. He's getting tired of her being so lonely. He also hopes that you enjoyed reading about the start of the very best part of his too-short life.

When Alyssa and Sam Met the Dentist

Autumn 2003
This story takes place after
Gone Too Far *and before* **Flashpoint**.

Sam was hovering.

He'd already made up a multitude of excuses to come into the bathroom while Alyssa was in the shower, and now, while she brushed her teeth, he lurked just outside the door.

She'd scared him tonight.

They took turns when out on assignment. Tonight, Sam had been on lookout, hiding on the hillside, watching for headlights that would announce an approaching car, as Alyssa jimmied the cheap lock on the door to Steve Hathaway's ramshackle cabin.

The place had been deserted. In fact, this entire part of the county was deserted—they were at least forty miles west of the booming metropolis of New Hope, in northern New Hampshire, population 473 at the height of ski season.

Getting inside that cabin undetected had been laughably easy.

Alyssa now dried her face on the plush resort towel as Sam checked up on her for the twenty-seventh time since they'd returned to their suite here in the ski lodge.

"I'm really okay," she told him.

"I know," he said.

Sam bent over backward to make sure he never said

anything that might make her think he doubted her ability to take care of herself.

Earlier tonight, when she'd pushed open that cabin door, switched on her penlight and gone inside, Sam had spoken into his radio from his perch on the hill.

"Lys, I can't see you." He'd worked hard to keep his voice sounding calm, relaxed. Filled with Texas. Because he knew that *she* knew he dropped his honeyed drawl when he was stressed. "Talk to me."

She'd flashed her little light across the walls and floors, giving him a running commentary. "I'm in a room with a bed, no other furniture. Just piles of trash—classic love shack. It smells like old socks and mildew, with a dash of overflowing septic tank."

"Yum."

"Yeah." She'd sifted through one of the garbage piles with her foot. It was mostly paper—newspapers, empty food boxes, stacks of junk mail. "Honestly, Sam, I can't imagine Amanda Timberman being caught dead here. Even for some of Stevie Hathaway's golden-tan pretty-boy ski-hero booty."

"What's in the other room?" Sam had asked.

"Looks like a combination living area and kitchen," she'd reported, opening up the kitchen cabinets, looking for . . . what? She wasn't even sure. "Sink, stove, refrigerator . . ."

Alyssa pulled herself out of the memory and back to the pristine warmth of the lodge bathroom. "I wish they made some kind of nostril brush—you know, like a toothbrush only smaller," she told Sam now. "I can't get that awful smell out of my nose."

He leapt into action. "Whiskey'll take care of that."

She followed him into the other room. She didn't particularly want a drink, but he seemed so glad to have found a way to help, she didn't want to stop him.

As Sam opened the minibar, she wandered toward the

balcony window, where the pink of dawn was lighting the sky to the east. Glasses clinked, ice tinkled.

"Here." He handed her a glass. "It'll make you stop smelling it." He corrected himself. "Her." He tried again. "Death."

Just a few hours ago, during dinner, this had felt more like a vacation than a paid job. It was, at the very least, a silver bullet assignment. She and Sam had been forced to stay in this four-star ski lodge with room service, balcony views of gorgeous autumn sunsets, and chocolates on the pillows.

They'd been assigned to find twenty-five-year-old Amanda Timberman, who'd vacationed at the New Hope Ski Lodge a few short weeks before her disappearance.

Lucas Timberman, the young woman's father, was a total pit bull when it came to place the blame on Randy Shahar—Amanda's ex-fiancé. He claimed Shahar, born in Saudi Arabia, had killed his daughter after she'd discovered he was part of an al-Qaeda terrorist cell.

Shahar—who had moved to the U.S. when he was four months old—had come to Troubleshooters Incorporated, hoping they could locate Amanda. A former chief in the U.S. Navy Special Boat Squadrons, he now ran a fleet of whale-watching vessels out of Provincetown, Massachusetts.

Timberman's accusations were bad for business.

As if it weren't hard enough to be an Arab American business owner after 9/11.

Finding a missing person wasn't the sort of job that Troubleshooters Inc. usually took on. The company specialized in security—personal and corporate—with a leaning toward counterterrorism. But Tom Paoletti, the former commanding officer of SEAL Team Sixteen who owned and ran TS Inc., was friends with Shahar.

Tom had not only taken the assignment, but he'd given it to Alyssa Locke, his second-in-command.

Formerly an FBI agent, and before that an officer in the Navy herself, when Alyssa had taken this job with Tom Paoletti, she'd permanently partnered up with Navy SEAL Sam Starrett.

In more ways than one.

A few months ago, she'd married the man—a fact that still seemed surreal.

That she was married at all was odd enough. But that she'd married a textbook alpha male . . .

Sam—her husband—was standing in front of her now, looking hopefully at her empty glass. A man of action, he liked having something to do. "You want another?"

"No," she said. "Thanks, but . . ."

"Didn't help, huh?"

She shook her head.

He pushed a strand of hair back behind her ear. It always amazed her that someone with such big hands—and an ability to put his fist through a wall when provoked—could have such a light touch. "Another might help you sleep."

Again, she shook her head. "Tom said he'd call after he spoke to Randy. I want to be coherent."

"I could talk to him," Sam volunteered.

"I know," Alyssa said. "Thanks. But . . ." Sam hadn't looked inside that refrigerator.

Her cell phone rang, and she opened it. "Locke."

"What time is it there?"

That wasn't Tom Paoletti's voice. It was . . . "Jules?"

"It's nearly three A.M. here, which means it's not quite six there. Aren't you allowed to answer your phone with *Alyssa* at least from, say, two to six A.M.?"

"It's Jules," Alyssa told Sam. She and Jules Cassidy had been playing phone tag for weeks now. It was exactly her former-FBI-partner and best friend's MO to call in the middle of the night after being frustrated by voice mail.

"Are you—honest to God—in a town called No Hope?" Jules asked. "Because I got this weird message from SpongeBob, and it sure as hell sounded like he said you were in No Hope, New Hampshire, and all I could think was *shit*. No Hope High School . . ."

"You called Jules?" Alyssa asked Sam.

"No Hope Hospital," Jules continued.

Sam lifted a shoulder. "It's been a rough night. I thought you might want to talk to him."

"I'm really okay," she said again.

"I know."

"No Hope Hair Salon . . ."

"It's *New* Hope," she told Jules as she sank down onto the leather sofa, one leg tucked up beneath her.

"New Hope Hair Salon—that's almost as good." His voice changed. "You okay, sweetie?"

Sam sat down on the other end of the couch and put his feet up on the coffee table, his long legs stretched out in front of him. He was trying hard not to look worried.

"We've been looking for this woman, Amanda, and we found her tonight. In the refrigerator of an abandoned cabin. She'd been there for six months and . . . Whoever killed her had . . ." Alyssa had to stop, take a deep breath.

Sam reached over and put his hand on her foot.

"He mutilated her," she said. "It was . . . gruesome and surprising, and . . ." Sam's gaze was as warm and solid as his hand. She was, in truth, talking to him. "I think I'm embarrassed. My reaction to seeing her was . . ."

She'd actually screamed. Only her years of training had kept her from running from the cabin after opening that refrigerator door. Or maybe it had been the lightheadedness and suddenly blurred vision that kept her glued to the spot.

"I almost lost it," she said. "I actually had to put my head between my knees." All the while unable to say anything more than *Oh, shit, oh, shit* . . .

Which had sent Sam running down the mountain, racing to her unnecessary rescue.

Or maybe it had been necessary. She'd been beyond glad to see him, to feel his arms around her. She'd done everything but burst into girlish tears.

"I mean, come on," Alyssa told Jules. "What's that about? I've seen murder victims before. This is nothing new."

But Sam shook his head. "You were caught off-guard. We both were. We were sure she was still alive."

They'd spent dinner trying to guess where Hathaway and Amanda had gone.

Such optimism was new for Alyssa. In the past, she'd always been a worst-case-scenario thinker. Anyone who'd been missing for six whole months *had* to be dead. But this time, she had been positive that they'd find Amanda by finding Hathaway. Instead . . .

The FBI agents heloed in from the Boston office were convinced that Amanda was the latest victim of a serial killer they'd been tracking for years. The Bureau was excited because, even though Steve Hathaway was an alias, for the first time they believed they finally had a photo of the man they were after, thanks to Randy Shahar.

"I liked her—Amanda," Alyssa told both Sam and Jules. Although she'd never met the woman, she'd read her diaries and talked with her friends. "I thought she'd found true love. I thought she was hiding from her father because she knew he'd be mad that she'd married the ski bum instead of the businessman. I actually pictured her with Hathaway in some little house with a white picket fence, living happily ever after." Instead, he'd probably made a necklace with her teeth. "God."

She looked up at Sam and told Jules, "Two months of marriage to Pollyanna here, and I've already moved into Sunnybrook Farm."

Jules didn't laugh. Instead, he sounded wistful. "That must be nice."

"Yeah, it is," Alyssa said. Sam was shaking his head over his new nickname. "It's scary, though. The potential for disappointment can be pretty high." As opposed to always expecting to be disappointed. "Look, Jules, I have to go. Thanks for calling."

"Anytime, sweets. Give Pollyanna a big, wet, sloppy kiss for me."

"I will." She hung up the phone.

"You know he's going to call me that from now on," Sam said. "For the rest of my life. And, by the way, it's Rebecca who lives at Sunnybrook Farm. As opposed to Laura Ingalls Wilder, who lives in that little house on the prairie. Pollyanna lives . . . Shit, I have no idea where Pollyanna lives."

"Come here," Alyssa said, moving toward him, meeting him halfway, in the middle of the couch. He put his arms around her, so that she was leaning back against him, her head beneath his chin.

Outside the window, dawn was putting on quite a show.

"Are you going to be able to sleep?" he asked. "Ever?"

She laughed, except it came out sounding like a sob, and his arms tightened around her. "I keep thinking, if only . . ."

"Don't," he said. He kissed the top of her head. "Just don't."

"I can't help it," she said. "I hate it when the bad guy wins."

"I know. But they're going to catch this one now," Sam said.

"I hope so."

"They will." He kissed her again. The way he put it, it was a *when*, not an *if*. He had no doubts whatsoever. For Sam, the future was filled with possibilities, not possible disappointments.

"Nice, huh?" he said as, outside the window, the brilliant colors of dawn—a new day—streaked the sky.

"Yeah," Alyssa said, loving the feeling of his arms around her. It was very nice, indeed.

Waiting

2005
This story takes place sometime after
Flashpoint *and before* **Breaking Point.**

Sam Starrett's daughter had finally surrendered and fallen asleep when the telephone rang.

He closed her bedroom door as silently as possible and raced down the hall toward the living room, where he'd last seen the cordless phone.

Yesterday, three-and-a-half-year-old Haley had missed her nap, and their dinner had been loud and far more tearful than dinosaur-shaped mac-and-cheese warranted. Apparently, without an afternoon rest, having to choose between green beans and peas as a side dish was a tragic dilemma of astronomical proportions.

Sam, always good at creative solutions, thought he'd solved the problem by heating up both vegetables.

At which point Haley wept because the spoon she wanted to use was in the dishwasher.

It was then that Sam understood. As a former Navy SEAL and one of the top counterterrorism experts currently working in the private sector, he recognized that he was caught in the dread no-win scenario. He realized that even if he hand-washed the spoon, there would be something wrong with the fork, or the color of the napkin, or maybe even the brand of Parmesan cheese he and his wife, Alyssa, kept in their fridge.

It was obvious that the real problem wasn't with the

peas or the spoon or the cheese. Haley missed her mother—Sam's ex-wife, Mary Lou—and that, plus lack of nap, had locked them into orbit around the Planet of Inconsolable Unhappiness.

Sam could totally relate. He, himself, was struggling hard to keep from joining his daughter there because Mary Lou wasn't the only one out of town. Just over a week ago, Alyssa had gone OCONUS.

A diplomat on a peacekeeping mission to Kazbekistan— a third world terrorist hotbed nicknamed "the Pit"—had contacted Troubleshooters Incorporated, the private security company where Sam and Alyssa both worked. Former senator Eugene Ryan was adamant about not showing up in the battle-weary country surrounded by heavily armed, dangerous-looking bruisers as guards. At the same time, he wisely didn't want to go in without adequate protection.

And so he'd requested Alyssa join his security team.

In a country that wasn't exactly known for its equal rights, no one would expect a woman to be an expert sharpshooter and total kickass bodyguard despite her lack of height and bulk.

Sam had desperately wanted to go along—but his goal was not to keep Ryan safe. No, he wanted to watch his wife's six. And he was the exact physical type that the former senator didn't want along for the ride. Not to mention the fact that he'd promised his ex-wife that he'd watch Haley this week . . .

He'd driven Lys to the airport and kissed her good-bye, working overtime to keep her from noticing his tightly gritted teeth.

It had to happen sooner or later, but as he'd watched her walk into the terminal, he had to admit that he'd been hoping for much, much later. But here it was. For the first time since they were married, Alyssa was off on a dangerous assignment without him. And it would be another week, at least, before she came safely home.

So last night, as the green beans and peas were both heating in the microwave, Sam had sat down with Haley on the floor of the kitchen and told her it was obvious there was nothing to do but go on and have a good ol' cry.

"Why are *you* crying?" she'd asked.

"Wah," he'd said. "The Dallas Cowboys lost the football game last week."

His pretend sobs had made her giggle, at least for a little while.

Still, the entire rest of the evening had been filled with the potential for an all-out meltdown.

The first few days had been fun. An entire week at Daddy's was a novelty for Haley, who'd never spent more than a weekend away from her mother. Sam knew it had been exciting for her, too, to look at the pictures from the brochure and imagine Momma and her new husband having a romantic vacation aboard a cruise ship.

As for Sam, he'd appreciated the distraction—what was Alyssa doing right now? Was she in danger? Was he going to have to wait another five days before she had a chance to call him again?—as he took his tiny blond daughter to the zoo and over to Old Town San Diego.

But today, over their Cap'n Crunch and orange juice, Sam and Haley had started counting the days on the calendar—four—until Mary Lou came back home.

Four days was definitely doable, provided they didn't miss any more of those very important naps.

Provided Sam could convince Haley to fall asleep. He'd just sat with her for more than an hour, holding her hand.

The phone shrilled again as Sam searched for it among the pile of toy cars and dolls on the living room rug. He loved his little daughter dearly, but please sweet Jesus, don't let her wake up yet.

He managed to find and grab the cordless phone before it completed that second ring. "Sam Starrett." Shoot, he must be tired. This was his home phone, and here the correct greeting was *Hello*.

The woman on the other end didn't seem to mind. "Please hold for Mr. Cassidy," she said.

Well, la di dah. Lookie who got himself a secretary.

Sam had left a message for Jules Cassidy just yesterday, asking for an update in the FBI's search for the serial killer known as "the Dentist." Just over a year ago, he and Lys had handled a missing person case that hadn't ended happily. They'd found the young woman they were searching for—or rather, they'd found what was left of her after the Dentist worked her over.

They'd also discovered that the Dentist had been posing as a ski instructor in New Hampshire, using the alias Steve Hathaway.

Alyssa—normally tough as nails—had been unusually upset when they'd found the body, even though the murder had occurred six months earlier. She'd taken it personally—so Sam had started getting regular updates on the case from Jules, her friend and former partner from her FBI days.

It was obvious to Sam that after seeing that dead girl, Lys wanted to kick the Dentist's ass straight to hell where he belonged. She was afraid—and rightly so—that it was just a matter of time before the killer targeted his next victim.

After months of no progress, a man had recently surfaced in a resort town in Colorado who fit Hathaway's description. Sam was hoping the FBI agents working the case would locate the Dentist's grisly souvenirs from his victims and have enough evidence to take him into custody before Alyssa returned.

Giving her that news would be a wonderful welcome-home present—a thought that made him smile. Forget about flowers and chocolate. His wife wanted a psycho-killer behind bars.

She was different from most other women, no doubt about that. Which was not to say she didn't love choco-late. . . .

Ah yes, Sam missed her very much.

The line clicked, and Jules finally came on. "Sam."

"Hey," Sam greeted him, genuinely glad to hear Jules's voice. Five years ago, if someone had told him that he'd be happily married to his old nemesis Alyssa Locke, and best friends with *her* best friend—an openly gay man—Sam would've laughed his ass off. But obviously a lot could happen in five years. "Thanks for calling me back, *Mister* Cassidy."

There was the briefest pause, then Jules said, "I guess you're not watching TV."

"What? No. I've got Haley for the week and anything besides *Sesame Street* is too intense for her," Sam said as he now began searching for the remote control beneath the Spider-Man and Powerpuff Girls coloring books that covered his coffee table. Haley got night-mares. It was Big Bird or a Disney DVD. Although it was possible that too much Big Bird was now giving Sam nightmares.

When he actually slept, that is.

"Sam, hang on a sec." Jules put his hand over the receiver as he spoke to someone else on his end. Usually irreverent and upbeat, he sounded serious. Hell, he was calling Sam *Sam* instead of SpongeBob or Pollyanna or one of those other humiliating nicknames that he usu-ally used.

"What happened?" Sam asked as Jules came back on the phone. He answered his own question. "Another dead woman without teeth in Colorado."

"This isn't about the Dentist," Jules told him as Sam found the remote and aimed it at the TV. "Listen, do yourself a favor and don't turn on the news."

Too late. Sam had already flipped to CNN where . . .

"Oh, shit," he breathed, sitting down heavily on the sofa.

Peacekeeper Attacked was the headline that hung over the anchor's right shoulder, along with a picture of Eugene Ryan. ". . . in northern Kazbekistan, where the former senator's helicopter was believed to have been shot down."

Oh, God, no.

"We just received confirmation," Jules told him, "that one of Eugene Ryan's helicopters was hit by a shoulder-fired missile, just north of Ikrimah, which is a city in the northern province of—"

"I know where Ikrimah is," Sam interrupted him. "*One* of . . . ?" How many helos were transporting Ryan's delegation? Jesus, he couldn't breathe.

On the TV, the news anchor was now delivering a fluff piece on a pie-eating contest, a big smile on his face.

"One of two," Jules delivered the grim news as Sam hit the mute. Which meant there was a fifty/fifty chance Lys was on the helicopter that went down.

In flames.

"Before we lost radio contact," Jules continued, "the second chopper reported that there were definitely casualties, but we don't know how many and we don't know who."

"Before," Sam repeated, "you *lost radio contact . . . ?*"

"I am *so* sorry," Jules started, but Sam cut him off.

"Fuck *sorry!*" Sam winced, looking toward the room where Haley was sleeping. He lowered his voice, but it came out no less intense. "I don't want *sorry*. I want the information that you've—"

"We don't *have* any information," Jules raised his

voice to talk over him. "All we have is speculation. Rumors. You know as well as I do what good that—"

"What are the rumors?" Sam asked.

"Sam," Jules said. "You *know* rumors are just—"

"Did the second helo go down, too?" Sam had to know.

"No," Jules said, but then added, "Not exactly. What we think happened, and sweetie, breathe. This is mostly guesswork. Even though we have a few people who claim to be eyewitnesses, we have only their word that they were actually there. So yeah, they reported that after the first chopper crashed, the second swung back around to assist the survivors. According to these unreliable sources, it apparently landed, going out of view, behind several buildings. Then, allegedly, there was a second big explosion."

"And?" Sam asked tightly.

"And nothing," Jules said. "It's all speculation. You know as well as I do that this could be nothing more than one of the local warlords planting disinformation—"

"There was an *and* in your voice," Sam insisted. "God damn it, Jules, tell me all of it."

Jules exhaled hard. "The attack happened shortly before sunset. There've been unconfirmed reports of a fierce firefight in that area pretty much all night."

Sam was going to be sick. "So, best-case scenario is that my wife is on the ground in a hostile part of Kaz-fucking-bekistan, engaged in a gun battle with people who don't just want to kill her for being American, but who want to kill her slowly, on camera, broadcast over the Internet."

Worst case was that Alyssa was already dead—that she had been dead for hours.

"Who's going in after them?" Sam demanded.

"I don't know," Jules said. "Look, I'm going to make

some phone calls, see what I can find out, okay? It may take me a while."

"Jules," Sam started, but he didn't have to say it. Jules said it for him.

"I'll call you back as soon as I hear anything. Good news *or* bad."

"Thanks." As Sam hung up the phone, the news anchor made a joke about a pop star who was getting married. It was absolutely surreal.

How could anyone laugh when Alyssa might be dead?

He turned off the TV, but then turned it back on, flipping to the other news stations and then back, hoping for something, anything that would let him see just what Alyssa was up against.

If there were any way to survive this, Lys would find it. Of that Sam had absolutely no doubt. She was strong, she was skilled, and she had the heart of a warrior.

But if her team was badly outnumbered by their attackers, if it was a handful against several hundred, they would soon be overpowered. And all of the skill, strength, and heart in the world wouldn't keep her alive.

* * *

Sam splashed water on his face, then dried it with his towel. It was one of the blue ones that he and Alyssa had picked out when they'd moved into this little house together, a few weeks before their wedding.

"Blue is all about serenity and tranquility," she'd told him as they stood in the department store, when he'd suggested they get brown because it would hide the dirt and stains.

But she was serious, which had surprised him. And as they'd decorated their house she'd paid a lot of attention, for someone so down to earth and practical, to the mood created by color, as well as to something called feng shui. Which was all about furniture placement and good vibes and all kinds of touchy-feelie New Age voodoo.

Of course, maybe there was something to that feng shui crap, because Sam had never been happier and more at peace in his entire life than he had this past year, living here.

Then again, he'd be beyond ecstatic living in a cardboard box, as long as Alyssa was with him.

Please, God, keep her safe.

Sam took a deep breath, then opened the bathroom door.

The phone rang again, and Joan DaCosta, the wife of SEAL Team Sixteen's Lieutenant Mike Muldoon, picked it up out in the living room.

As the news of the downed choppers spread, friends and relatives were calling him to find out details and offer their support. But it had quickly gotten overwhelming. "I'm sure Alyssa's all right. I'm sure she's fine," they reassured him. But they wanted him to say it back to them, too.

And truthfully, as optimistic as he usually was, in this case, he wasn't sure about anything. And no one *really* wanted to hear how he was scared shitless, and that this sitting still and waiting for news was driving him freaking nuts.

No one, that is, except for Joan and Savannah and Meg, the long-suffering wives of his three best friends from his days as a Navy SEAL.

Meg Nilsson—Johnny's wife—had been the first to arrive. She'd just opened his front door and walked inside his house, God bless her, announcing, "Hey, it's only me. I didn't ring the bell—I didn't want you to think I was someone bringing you bad news."

She'd brought her two daughters—Amy, a teenager

from her first marriage, and four-year-old Robin, who had Johnny's eyes.

Amy possessed a maturity and sensitivity far beyond her years. She'd ushered both Robin and Haley outside, where she kept them occupied and entertained. Even now, hours later, Sam could hear their laughter from the backyard.

Shortly after Meg arrived, Chief Ken "WildCard" Karmody's wife, Savannah, pulled into the driveway. Mikey's Joan was right behind her.

They'd each given him a hug and told him they weren't going to let him go through this alone.

"Joan'll let me know if it's Jules on the phone, right?" Sam asked now, as he went back into the kitchen, where Meg and Savannah were sitting together at the table.

At first glance they seemed to be unlikely friends.

Savannah was a high-powered attorney who had just made partner and opened a law office in San Diego, after years of a bicoastal marriage. She came from money and worked not because she had to, but because she wanted to. Sam suspected that, if and when the time came to start a family with Kenny, she would throw herself into it with the same wholehearted devotion.

Kind of the way Meg did. A brunette to Savannah's elf-princess blonde, Meg Nilsson worked part-time from a home office. Her standard uniform was very different from Van's lawyer clothes—T-shirts and shorts, sneakers on her feet—better for chasing after little Robbie.

And yet Savannah and Meg *were* friends. They both loved their husbands—who willingly traveled to war zones and other places that were hazardous to one's health.

They both knew that their husbands might be injured or even killed in the line of duty at any given moment.

They knew what it felt like to carry around that anxiety, to live for those overseas phone calls that usually came in the middle of the night: *I'm sorry it's so late, but I have cell service—it's weak, but it's there—and I'm not sure when I'll get it again* . . .

Four days ago, before the helo crash, he'd gotten a call like that from Alyssa. And for five minutes while he spoke to her, he could breathe again. She had been safe, and he knew it.

For those five minutes.

It ended far too quickly, and as soon as he hung up the phone the anxiety came screaming back.

Alyssa was scheduled to be away for just a short amount of time. SEALs, however, often went out for months. Sam absolutely couldn't imagine living like this for more than a few weeks.

"Jules said it would be a while before he called again," Meg gently reminded him.

"Have you tried cleaning the refrigerator?" Savannah suggested. "I've found it helps a little if you just keep moving."

Sam sat down, wearily rubbing his forehead. Jesus, his head ached. "I did the fridge the night Alyssa's flight left," he said on an exhale. "Then, in the morning, I took an ax, went out in the yard and removed this old stump we'd been talking about getting rid of." He'd chopped the crap out of it in about four hours.

"I usually stick to cleaning out closets." Savannah was impressed. "I've never tried anything that involves an ax."

"I have," Meg said dryly. "Don't bother. It doesn't help."

Nothing helped.

"If you want," Savannah suggested, "we could help you organize your closets. It'll keep you busy. And you'll also win big bonus points when Alyssa comes back."

When Alyssa comes back. They were sitting there, all

three of them, pretending that *if Alyssa comes back* wasn't what she really meant.

God, he hated this. But the alternative was sitting in his kitchen by himself. Or trying to fool Haley into thinking everything was all right, and sneaking into the bedroom every ten minutes to turn on CNN, see if there was any new information that made it to the cable news station first.

So he told Savannah, "I did the closets on the second night. It took a while, but I wasn't going to sleep, so . . ."

"It's amazing, isn't it?" Meg asked, clearly working to keep the conversation going. "Just how much junk two people can accumulate in a short amount of time . . . ?"

"Yeah," he agreed. "I found this old hat—a baseball cap—that I thought I lost years ago and—" He broke off. "I can't do this. I'm sorry, I can't stand it. I'm just sitting here, so freaking helpless—I can't do a thing to help her. Even if I got on a plane . . ." It would take him at least forty-eight hours to get to Ikrimah. He closed his eyes. "Right now, she could be dying. Right now. Right *now*. And I can't help her."

Meg took his hand. "I know," she said quietly. "It's hard, isn't it?"

Sam looked at her, and he knew that *she* knew exactly what he was feeling. "How many times have you done this?" he asked.

"Thought John might not be coming home?" she clarified. She didn't wait for him to respond. "There've been, oh, I guess three or four times somewhat similar to this situation. But, you know, every time he's out there and there's some news report about a helicopter crash or a suicide bomber or . . ." She laughed as she shook her head. "Believe me, there's a lot of prayer involved when you're married to a SEAL."

"And a lot of really clean refrigerators," Savannah added.

"Pristine closets."

"Well gardened yards."

"You see, John knows where he is when he's on an op," Meg told Sam. "He knows when he's safe and when he's at risk. But all I know is he's somewhere dangerous and . . ." She shrugged. "It sucks."

No kidding. "I had no idea," Sam admitted. "Before this, I just . . ." He shook his head. When he'd gone wheels up with the team he'd understood that it was no picnic for the wives, girlfriends, and significant others they left behind. But he'd had no clue just how awful it could be.

Joan appeared in the doorway, cordless phone in her hands. "That was Mike," she told them. "The team's training exercise'll be over in an hour. He and John and Ken'll bring dinner when they come."

The phone rang again, and Joan retreated toward the living room. "Starrett and Locke residence," Sam heard her say. But then she gasped. "Oh, my God!"

Sam was up and out of his chair, and he nearly collided with her as she came racing back into the kitchen, thrusting the phone at him.

"Jules," he said as he clasped it to his ear. Please God, let this be good news. "What's the word?"

"It's not Jules," Joan said, but he waved for her to be quiet, because all he could hear was static, and then . . .

"Sam, it's me. I'm all right," Alyssa said—beautiful, wonderful, vibrant, and so-very-alive Alyssa—her voice suddenly clear as day.

"It's Lys," Joan announced, which was good because try as he might, Sam couldn't get the words out.

"Ah, Jesus, thank you, God" was all he could manage, and even that was little more than a whisper.

Meg and Savannah both leapt to their feet. Meg pulled one of the kitchen chairs behind him, and Savannah tugged him back into it, Joan pushing his head down between his knees—as if they thought he might actually faint.

"Hey!" But, shit, he *was* dizzy and on the verge of falling out of the chair, so maybe they were onto something there. But before he could thank them, they all left, hurrying out into the backyard to give him privacy.

"The SAS came in and . . . Gordon MacKenzie, remember him?" Alyssa asked. "His team pulled us out. He remembers you. He wants to know what you think of his SAS boys now."

Gordon MacKenzie . . . ?

"Gordie told me his SAS team did some training exercises with SEAL Team Sixteen, back a few years," Alyssa continued as Sam desperately tried to regain his equilibrium. "He said they learned a lot from you—that you used to rate them on a scale from one to ten. But you never gave them anything higher than an eight."

Yeah, he remembered that. MacKenzie had gotten in his face and accused him of being a hardnosed asshole. Actually *arsehole* was what he'd said in his quaint Scottish accent. Sam had countered by standing his ground and saying he'd give them a ten when they fucking deserved a ten. And no sooner. Maybe they'd earn it next year, he'd told MacKenzie when the exercise had ended.

"Sam, are you still there? Can you hear me?" Alyssa was saying through the phone.

"Yeah," he said. "Yes. Lys, are you really all right?" Frickin' Gordie MacKenzie's team had helped save Alyssa's life. Next time he saw the dour bastard, he'd kiss him on the mouth. "Where are you?"

"The helo just landed on an aircraft carrier," she said. "We're safe." She sounded exhausted, and she exhaled hard. "Those of us who made it out alive."

"Are you hurt?" he asked, heart in his throat.

"Just a little tired," she told him—she always had been the queen of understatement. "Well, yeah, okay, I could use a few stitches—just a few, don't get upset, I'm fine. We're pretty dehydrated, though. They've got us all on IV drips."

"I am so freaking glad to hear your voice," he told her, and she laughed. "You have no idea."

"Yeah," she said. "Actually, I do. Although, don't be jealous. I have to admit, as glad as I am to talk to you, I was even more glad to hear Gordie MacKenzie's voice this morning."

No kidding. "Tell Gordie that I love him," Sam said.

Alyssa laughed again. "Those aren't the three little words he's longing to hear from you, Sam. Seriously, what they did was . . . It was remarkably courageous. We were trapped and . . . I honestly didn't think anyone was coming for us—that anyone would be able to . . . I thought . . . It was bad," she said quietly.

Sam had to put his head back down between his knees. Alyssa, who never gave up, who wouldn't dream of quitting, had honestly thought she wasn't going to survive.

"He doesn't need me to give him a ten," Sam told her. "He knows."

"Still . . ." There was a storm of static. ". . . ignal's fading—I have to go. Sam—"

"I love you," Sam told her. *Thank God, thank God, thank God . . .*

"I know." Alyssa's voice was fading in and out, but he could still make out her words. "There was a point where it would have been easier to, you know, just . . . have it over and done, but . . ."

"Thank you," he said, hoping she could still hear him. "For not giving up."

"How could I?" She sounded as if she were a million miles away. "You were with me, you know. Every minute. I could feel you by my side." Sam could just barely hear her laughter over the static. "Ready to give me shit if I so much as faltered. Gordie told me you have a permanent spot on his shoulder, too—whispering into his ear. And here you thought you were taking it easy, sitting around the kitchen with your feet up."

Taking it easy. She had no idea.

"I love you," he heard her say right before his phone beeped.

He looked at it and yeah, the signal was gone.

Sitting around the kitchen . . . He'd been on dozens of dangerous missions. He'd risked his life more times than he could count.

None of it had been as hard as the past few hours.

Sam dialed Jules Cassidy's phone number, left a brief message. "Alyssa called. She's all right."

Through the kitchen window he could see Meg and Joan and Savannah out in the backyard with Haley and the other girls.

Sam punched Johnny Nilsson's cell number into his phone. The SEAL lieutenant was still out on a training exercise, so he left a voice mail. "Alyssa's safe. I just got off the phone with her. But that's not the only reason I'm calling. I think it would be smart if you brought your wife an armload of flowers when you came home," he told his friend. "Tell Mike and Kenny, too. Not just tonight, but every night for the rest of your lives."

* * *

It was already a half hour past Haley's bedtime when Sam sat on the edge of her bed. He'd promised she could watch a little bit of the football game with him, only it had started later than he'd thought.

"You want Duck or Hippo in there with you tonight?" His daughter frowned, and he quickly added, "Or both, on account of it being a special occasion."

"Because Alyssa's okay?" Haley asked.

"Yeah," he said, smiling into her anxious blue eyes. "And because she'll be home the same day as your momma."

Haley nodded, taking that in. "Amy said we had to stay outside in case you wanted to cry and say bad words," she told him. "Did you?"

"I think I said a few," Sam admitted. "And, yeah, I might've cried a little."

Haley nodded, so seriously. "If you want, I could put my fingers in my ears, like when the fire truck goes by."

Sam struggled to understand. "You mean . . . so you won't have to hear me cry? Hale, I'm not going to—"

"In case you say more bad words," she explained.

"I won't," he told her, struggling now not to laugh. "How about giving me a hug and kiss good night, Cookie Monster?"

"Sometimes there's nothing to do but have a good ol' cry," she said, repeating his words from the night before. "If you want, I could cry, too."

"No." Sam smoothed back her hair and kissed her on the cheek. "Thank you, but no." He tucked both Duck and Hippo in with her.

"If you want," Haley suggested, clinging to his fingers, "I could hold your hand. Keep you company until you fall asleep. I'm not very tired."

But her eyes were all but rolling back in her head. Amy had done quite a job, running Haley back and forth across the yard playing tag and Red Light Green Light and Follow the Leader and other games Sam didn't even know the names of.

He'd keep that in mind tomorrow. Maybe they'd take a ride over to Coronado, buy a kite, and run up and down the beach a few thousand times.

"I love you, Hale," he whispered, but she was already asleep.

Sam left her door open a crack and went into the living room, where he turned on the TV and watched the football game right to the bitter end.

He then watched the news, where the anchors solemnly reported that five members of Eugene Ryan's delegation to Kazbekistan had died when their helo was shot down.

Five families had gotten the kind of phone call he'd been dreading. They had been given the message Meg and Savannah and all of the other wives of the SEALs in Team Sixteen prayed they'd never receive.

Their husband, wife, son, or daughter was never coming home.

It was entirely possible that any tears that Sam may have shed were the result of the Cowboys losing the game.

But probably not.

Sam Takes an Assignment in Italy

2005
This story takes place some time after
Breaking Point *and before* **Into the Storm.**

"Why," Sam bitched into his cell phone on Tuesday night, "did Tom have to send *me* out here?"

His wife, Alyssa, didn't answer, because she wasn't on the other end. She was out handling a real case—an *important* case—so he was just leaving voice mail.

A known sex offender had gone missing. The man's sister had hired Troubleshooters Incorporated to find him before he hurt anyone else. Alyssa had taken the assignment and was in Richmond, Virginia, tracking him down.

Meanwhile Sam sat here, halfway around the world, the newest poster child for Murphy's Law. *Whatever can go wrong, will go wrong.*

And oh, how it had.

And you there, trying to glass-half-full this disaster? It's obviously not painful enough for you, so let Mr. Murphy supersize it, 'kay?

No doubt about it, Murphy had been riding Sam's ass from the moment he'd kissed Alyssa goodbye far too many weeks ago. This so-called easy assignment setting up security at a corporate honcho's big fat Italian wedding had turned into a nightmare. Four days had turned into a week, and then that week had turned into an unbelievable three.

Yeah sure, the little coastal town was beautiful—all blue sky and ocean, gorgeous beaches, bright sunshine. Yeah sure, Sam was making a fortune for Tom Paoletti's security company—and yeah, all right, he'd earned himself one hell of a bonus for his trouble, too—but come *on*.

The inefficiency of the honcho's staff was mindnumbing. Sam could have made bricks by hand and constructed a wall around the wedding chapel himself in the time it took them just to make the decision to set up a temporary chain-link fence and then hide it with a decorative one.

First the ceremony was going to be held indoors. Then out. Then in. Then on the beach. Each time the location shifted, Sam reworked the details that would keep the VIPs safe and the paparazzi at bay. He hadn't written this many reports since college.

And then—God please help him—there were the bridesmaids from hell. Four spoiled daughters of either the bride or the groom—this was a third or fourth marriage for the client, Sam had lost count—they all had far too much time on their hands. Ashley, Heather, Sabrina, and Chloe.

Ashley and Chloe were the worst. They followed Sam constantly, refusing to let him be. He'd flashed his wedding ring and mentioned his wife when they were first introduced. When they hadn't seemed to get the hint, he'd flat-out told them that he loved Alyssa more than life itself. He'd even showed them a photo of her, but they just did not let up.

Which led to tonight's phone call and Sam's desperate plea for Alyssa to hurry up and find the man she was looking for, get her butt on a plane, and join him.

"It's like trying to work in the middle of a *Girls Gone Wild* video," he complained, and of course, again, she said nothing because she wasn't there.

"I miss you, Lys," he whispered, which was, in fact,

his biggest problem. He could handle an entire army of Ashleys and Chloes. He could rewrite a report for the hundredth time if he had to. He could attend dozens more meetings that redefined *boring*.

What he couldn't do was survive too many more mornings waking up thousands of miles away from the woman that he loved. And it wasn't just that he missed her in his bed. He missed her smile, her voice, her very presence in his life.

"Please come and save me," he begged and cut the connection.

* * *

Wednesday brought more perfect weather—and another teeth-gritting delay in the impending nuptials. Chloe informed him over breakfast that the wedding had now been moved to Sunday—just a day later than Saturday, but still.

She also told him that her father would be out of touch until Thursday morning—which left Sam with just enough time to *not* be able to squeeze in a round-trip to Richmond.

Of course, if he'd been told about this yesterday morning, he could have made it there and back.

Sam worked off his frustration—or tried to anyway—with a ten-mile run. It was nearly noon before he returned to the resort.

He was drenched with perspiration, his hair literally dripping with sweat. He would have stuck to the shade and gone straight up to his room without talking to anyone, except there was some sort of commotion by the pool.

The hellsmaids—three of them anyway; Chloe was AWOL—were giving their full, shrill attention to a man dressed in a snugly fitting blue T-shirt and linen pants. He was height-challenged, with dark hair and . . .

"Hey, sweetie," he said as he spotted Sam dripping on the stone walkway beneath the arches, turning to greet him with a wide smile. "Rumor has it you need some TLC."

Alyssa apparently couldn't make it here to Italy, but she'd called their good friend and her former partner in the FBI, Jules Cassidy, as a stand-in.

He came right over and gave Sam a hug, despite the high sweat and slime factor. In fact, Jules gave him a big hug. A much, much, *much* too long of a hug.

For once, Heather, Ashley, and Sabrina were wide-eyed and silent, staring at them, definitely wondering . . .

So Sam cleared his throat. "It's good to see you," he told Jules. Which was no lie. But when he cleared his throat again and gruffly added, "Sweetie," it definitely boosted any potential misperceptions.

Jules laughed his ass off, of course. "Alyssa is going to love hearing about this," he whispered as he hugged Sam again.

Yeah, she would. Provided they would ever be in the same country at the same time again.

* * *

"I was in Dubai," Jules said, as Sam pulled two bottles of cold water from his suite's kitchen fridge. He tossed one to Jules. "Thanks. It's not *quite* the same neighborhood, but close enough. Closer than Richmond. I had some time off coming, so . . . Here I am."

"Checking up on me." Sam toasted him then took a long swig from his bottle.

"Absolutely not," Jules said. Up close, the FBI agent looked tired. His usually bright smile even seemed a touch forced. He sank into one of the leather armchairs in the suite's sitting area. "Your wife trusts you completely. Although, that *Girls Gone Wild* comment? It was probably not her most favorite thing she's ever heard you say."

"I was trying to get a rise out of her. And no offense," Sam said, half-sitting on the desk where his laptop was out and open, "but I was kind of hoping she'd be the one to show."

"She sounded pretty pissed off when I spoke to her," Jules reported. "This guy she's looking for? He knows she's looking. He's been messing with her. Playing games."

"Thanks. I love hearing that." Sam's blood pressure was up so high, his ears were ringing. "Motherfucker's a sex offender."

"And if Alyssa were ten years old, she'd be in danger," Jules reassured him. "She finally called in for backup, by the way. Lindsey and . . . damn, I'm blanking on his name . . . former CIA . . . ?"

"Dave Malkoff," Sam supplied the name of the Troubleshooters' operative.

"That's him." Jules glanced at his watch. "They're probably in Richmond with Alyssa right now, cuffing the guy."

"Good." Which meant Alyssa could be *here* by tomorrow night.

"Yeah, you're way too happy at that news," Jules said. "You haven't checked your email, have you?"

Sam shifted his laptop so he could see the screen, jumped on line and . . . Sure enough, there was an email from Alyssa. Subject: *I'm needed in San Diego.* "No. No, no, no . . ."

He clicked on it, skimmed it. The good news was that she, Lindsey, and Dave had indeed caught the game-playing sex offender. The bad news was that their boss,

Tom Paoletti, had another assignment waiting for Alyssa. Which meant it would be . . . *What?*

"She's going OCONUS," Sam told Jules, using the military term for outside of the United States. "Unless I can somehow get home by Friday morning, it's going to be another two weeks—at least—before I see her." She'd added a P.S. that Sam didn't understand. *"Tell Jules that Dave's a maybe?* What does that mean?"

Jules took another swig from his water bottle. "Don't get too excited, because I haven't cleared it yet with Tom. Or Max. I have to wait a few more hours before I call either of them. But if they give me the thumbs-up, I'll be able to hang here, hold down the fort for you, until a replacement arrives. Alyssa told me she was going to ask Dave Malkoff."

Sam shook his head. "As an FBI agent, you can't—"

"I won't," Jules said. "You just told me the wedding's not until Sunday, and the client's gone until Thursday. Dave—or someone else—will definitely be here before then. I'm just going to hang here, pass along the message that you had to leave, that your replacement is on his way. I'm not getting paid, I'm just doing you a favor."

It was one hell of a big-ass favor. "You don't get much vacation time," Sam pointed out. "Wouldn't you rather, I don't know, go on a cruise?"

"With who?" Jules gazed at him. "Ben?" He rolled his eyes as he shook his head. "Just take a shower, let's go get lunch. If you really want to hear it, I'll tell you the whole terrible Ben story. But I definitely need nourishment first."

* * *

"He did what?" Sam said.

"Brought his beard," Jules repeated. He leaned back

to let the waiter take his plate. They sat in a little out-door restaurant, overlooking the harbor below. The food had been unbelievable, the owner himself coming out of the kitchen to make sure everything was to their liking. "*Beard* is slang for a woman who pretends to be a closeted gay man's wife or girlfriend. Ben's beard is named Amanda. She's his roommate. His own parents actually think she's his fiancée."

Sam struggled to comprehend. "So, this guy lives with a woman, except he's gay and . . . she's okay with that?"

"She's not really his fiancée. They have separate bed-rooms," Jules told him. "She's a grad student—they're friends from high school. Plus, he lets her live in his condo for free."

Sam had to make sure he understood. "So Amanda helps Ben fool everyone into thinking he's straight."

Jules nodded. "*Don't ask, don't tell*—I think you've probably heard of the policy? It sounds so innocuous, but it forces servicemen and -women into the closet. They have to hide who they are, pretend to be some-thing they're not. It's okay to be gay in the military, as long as no one knows." He was disgusted. "Ben takes Amanda to all kind of functions—including this date he had, with me."

"It was really a date?" Sam asked, as the waiter poured them each a cup of coffee. Alyssa had told him that when it came to dating, Jules was remarkably gun-shy—and yeah, okay that was probably an unfor-tunate expression to use.

But Alyssa's going theory was that Jules was still hung up on some actor he'd met out in Los Angeles—Robin something. The SOB had hurt Jules badly—their rela-tionship had been a total train wreck. Still, Lys had been urging her old friend to get back into circulation. This Marine captain, Ben, had been calling him for a while—apparently Jules had finally taken that first-date step.

"Ben calls and goes, *Hey, how are you? I just got back from overseas. I was wondering if you wanted to get together, maybe have dinner at my place?*" Jules reported. "I wasn't ready for that. So I suggested we meet at a restaurant. It wasn't even downtown. It was suburban and discreet, and . . . he brought Amanda anyway. So we all sit down to dinner and it's way weird. I mean, she was nice, but, what the hell . . . ? She finally gets up to, you know, hit the ladies' room, and Ben goes, *I'm career military. This is how I've made it work.* He knew I was freaked out. He said, *You should've come over. It's easier, more comfortable*, and I said, *Not for me.* I said, *I'm not climbing into your closet with you,* and . . . that was that. I haven't seen him since." He paused. "The stupid thing is, I really like him. The *really* stupid thing? I'd be genuinely upset if he resigned his commission. The Marines need more officers like Ben."

"I'm sorry it didn't work out," Sam said.

"Thanks."

They sat in silence for a moment.

"Thing is, I'm thinking about doing it." Jules finally spoke. "Calling him and . . . You know, maybe if it's just sex, it won't bother me. As much. You know, keeping it on the down-low."

Sam took a sip of his coffee, choosing his words carefully. "I guess whether or not you decide to do that should really depend on what you want. If it's sex . . ."

"Who doesn't want sex?" Jules pointed out.

"If it's *just* sex," Sam said, "there's a waiter over there who's been checking you out." Part of him could not believe he was having this conversation. "Personally, I don't think it's a good idea, hooking up with some stranger . . ."

At least Jules wouldn't get the guy pregnant. Years ago, Sam had had sex with a stranger—a bar bunny— and he now had a daughter, Haley, and an ex-wife, Mary Lou. Talk about careless mistakes. Although Haley was definitely the best mistake he'd ever made. She was a real peach of a kid. It had all worked out in the end, but for years it had been bad. He'd messed up his life, along with Mary Lou's, Haley's, and even Alyssa's.

"Ben's not a stranger," Jules pointed out, taking out his wallet and paying the bill.

"What happens when you fall in love with him?" Sam asked. It was another question that he couldn't believe he was asking. Still, the words needed to be said. "You know, I should pay that."

Jules shook his head to both the question and the offer. "That won't happen." He said it with such finality and stood up as punctuation. "Let's get back. I want to make those phone calls."

"How much do I owe you?" Sam persisted, opening his own wallet.

Jules waved him off. "It's on me."

"You come out here to do me a favor, *and* you pay for lunch . . . ?"

"You have no idea how much I appreciate your friendship," Jules said.

Sam held out several bills. "Yeah, actually I do," he said. "It's probably as much as I appreciate yours."

Jules couldn't just take the money and be done with it. He had to go and hug Sam. "Thanks."

Of course, now the gay waiter was checking Sam out, too. He even followed them out into the square as they headed up the road.

Which turned out to be provident, since they hadn't gone far before a group of men, ranging in ages from teens to much older, blocked their path. They were scowling and grim, and their postures were clearly meant to menace.

Jules stepped in front of Sam, his body language relaxed, a smile on his face. "Good afternoon, gentlemen," he said in close to perfect Italian. "Is there a problem?"

Sam counted them quickly. There were nine, but only three—red shirt, goatee, and tattoo—looked capable of holding their own in a brawl.

Tattoo let out a stream of Italian that was far too rapid-fire for Sam to understand. He definitely caught the words *Rome* and *the Pope* along with what sounded like negative language. He wasn't quite sure what the man was saying, but there was no mistaking his intention when he roughly shoved Jules.

And just like that, the talking was over. Well, almost over. "I got Tattoo and Red Shirt," Jules announced in English, as he effortlessly took down the man who'd shoved him.

That left Goatee for Sam. But ouch, the man had a fishing knife. Sam quickly adiosed it, breaking more than a few fingers in the process.

That was all it took. Goatee ran home, crying for his mommy, eating the dust of the rest of the gang. They'd all long since am-scrayed, except for the delusional man in the red shirt, who actually still believed he could get a piece of Jules.

The FBI agent was subcompact and had a far better fashion sense than Alyssa, but he knew how to bring it in hand-to-hand combat. He fought with an efficiency of movement that Sam admired. It was beautiful, actually. Jules fought with his brain, unlike Red Shirt, who'd let loose his inner Neanderthal, swinging blindly, flailing mindlessly—making himself good and winded in the process.

Jules, on the other hand, was breathing about as hard as he'd been during lunch.

Red Shirt came at him one too many times, and Jules dodged him yet again, this time tripping him on his way past, using an expertly placed elbow to help the man greet the ground that much harder. He didn't get back up.

The gay waiter, meanwhile, had run to get the entire serving staff of the restaurant, including the owner.

As Sam watched, Jules turned to face this new threat, ready to take them all out if necessary. But—again, since his brain was fully functioning—he immediately recognized them for what they were. The cavalry come to save them. Not that they'd needed it.

The owner of the restaurant spoke fluent English. "This is not the first time such an outrage has happened here. Such anti-American sentiment is not helpful to our town. Tourism is down as it is."

Anti-*American*? Not anti-gay?

The man ushered them into his kitchen, ordering his staff to bring the first-aid kit and ice for Jules's raw knuckles. Sam looked at Jules, but he was playing right along, talking about the anti-American protests in Greece and even Dubai, as he helped Sam over to a table and pushed him into a chair.

It was then Sam realized he was bleeding. He'd gotten cut by that knife.

It wasn't too much more than a scratch, but the restaurant owner—who was also the chef—wasn't about to let them leave without cleaning them up. And feeding them a sampling of all his desserts, which was fine by Sam.

The man even drove them back to the resort in his little Mini. It was only then, after they said their good-byes, as they headed down the pathway past the pool, that Sam asked, "Anti-American?"

But Jules's phone rang. It was his boss's administrative assistant, Laronda. It was okay with Max if Jules wanted to take a few more days off. Which meant . . .

"Let's get you a flight home," Jules said.

But Sam shook his head. "Anti-American, my ass. I've been here for weeks. That was not about us being American. That was about you being gay. I'm not leaving you here alone."

Jules rolled his eyes. "That's ridiculous."

Sam held out his bandaged hand. "No, it's not."

"Yes, it is."

This was going nowhere fast, but Sam couldn't let it go. "Jules—"

"Don't you get it?" Jules asked, leading the way up the stairs to Sam's hotel suite. "This is my life. I could be jumped, beaten, and, yeah, even killed for being gay—not just here, but in any town in virtually any country in the world. Particularly in the United States, by the way. Are you going to follow me home to DC, Sam? Lots of hate crimes happen there, you know."

"Then maybe *you* should have a beard." Sam knew as soon as the words left his mouth that it was the wrong thing to say. But then he unlocked the door to his suite, and the situation went from bad to worse.

Chloe, dressed in only a pair of leopard-print thong panties and some very high heels, was dancing to music on the radio while fixing herself a drink at his wet bar.

A drink? Another drink. Clearly, she'd had quite a few already. "There you are," she said, as she caught sight of Sam. "I've been waiting for you."

Once again, Jules stepped in front of Sam. "You must be Chloe. I *love* your shoes."

She grabbed—apparently just as Jules had hoped she would—for her robe. In fact, he even helped her into it. "Pack," he ordered Sam over his shoulder, as he led Chloe out onto the balcony. "You remind me of Scarlett Johansson," Sam heard him saying to the girl. "You

must get that all the time—you *don't*? Really? You look
a *lot* like her . . ."

*   *   *

Sam was almost completely packed, but he wasn't going
anywhere without Jules. He stood in the bathroom. It
didn't make sense to pack up his toilet kit, only to un-
pack it again tonight when he went to bed. His clothes
were no problem. He could easily live out of his suitcase.
He'd look slightly more rumpled than usual, but . . .

"I got you on the four o'clock flight to London." Jules
stood in the door.

Sam looked at him in the mirror. "I'm not leaving you
behind."

Jules nodded. "I appreciate your loyalty, but Chloe
had a little confession that, well, she asked me to share
with you."

Sam waited.

"The bride and groom have apparently eloped," Jules
told him. "The wedding party is indefinitely postponed.
Your services are no longer needed—as of last night, as
a matter of fact."

"*What?*"

"Apparently Chloe neglected to tell her sisters about
this, too. She wanted to stay a few extra days, and . . .
She's young and misdirected. Apparently she's got quite
the crush on you, cowboy."

Sam used one arm to sweep what Jules would call his
"products" off the sink counter and into his bag. "The
four o'clock to London will only get me home in time if
nothing goes wrong," he said tightly. No delays, no canceled flights, no screwups between connecting flights.
"And I'm still not leaving unless you've got a flight out
of here, too."

"Yeah, about that," Jules said. "Confession part two.

Apparently she hired those men to, well, as she put it, make me go away."

Sam looked at him. "Young, misdirected—and vicious."

"She is a little socially disengaged," Jules said. "But she's leaving, too. With her sisters. I thought I'd hang for a few days. Maybe get to know Paolo a little better."

"Paolo?" Sam asked.

"He owns that restaurant," Jules admitted. "While you were washing out that cut on your hand, we got to talking and . . . he, um, offered to give me cooking lessons."

Sam laughed. He hadn't even realized that the restaurant owner—an older man with gray at his temples, good-looking in an Italian Tom Hanks kind of way—was gay. "That's a new way of saying it." He sobered fast. "Are you sure you want to . . . ?"

"Sweetie, the only thing I'm *absolutely* sure about is that I don't want a beard," Jules said.

"I shouldn't have said that," Sam told his friend. "I didn't mean it. But I worry about you."

"I know. I forgive you. I just . . . I want a relationship with someone like Paolo who's not afraid to be himself," Jules said. "God, I really want someone I'm in such a hurry to go home to that I'll pack in that horrific way that you just did." He laughed, but then sobered. "You know, before? When you asked me what I want? I want what you have with Alyssa, Sam. I want what Max has with Gina, what Jack has with Scott. I won't have that with Ben. *Or* with Robin, who's in fucking London right now promoting his latest movie, so I'm *not* going to London with you, even if it's only to catch a flight to New York, thanks but no thanks."

Maybe Alyssa was right. It sure seemed that all roads led back to this Robin guy.

"I remember," Sam said, "being in love with Alyssa,

but she didn't want anything to do with me. I was so desperate not to think about her, and . . . Nobody could compete. Messing around with other women didn't help. It only made me miss her more. Plus the other women usually ended up hurt, which sucked."

"I hear what you're saying." Jules nodded. "And I appreciate your candor. But you need to go, or you're going to miss that plane."

Sam grabbed his bags. Opened the door. "Thanks again for everything."

"I'll give you a call in a coupla days," Jules said. "Kiss the shit out of Alyssa for me, okay?"

Sam laughed. "Absolutely."

* * *

Alyssa wasn't waiting for him at LAX. She was in San Diego, at the Troubleshooters Incorporated office, organizing the gear her team—Sam included—would need for this next assignment. It was cold where they were going, and they'd need to stay hidden, which meant camping without the benefit of fire.

Freeze-your-balls-off-style camping was definitely not Sam's favorite thing to do, but this time, he absolutely couldn't wait. A pup tent, a two-person thermal sleeping bag, and his incredible woman . . .

Yeah, he'd find a way to keep plenty warm.

Traffic was heavy, not just on the Five, but off it as well. He finally arrived, and, yes. There she was, in the parking lot. His wife. Working to fit three truckloads of supplies into two tiny packing crates. And getting the job done with room to spare.

Sam just stood there for a moment, watching her, just letting his heart swell. Her dark hair was long enough to pull back into a ponytail, but tendrils escaped, curling around her face. She was, without a doubt, the most beautiful woman in the entire world, even without any makeup, dressed down in forest cammie-print BDUs and lumberjack boots for two weeks of stomping around in the woods.

She was using her former-naval-officer voice— no-nonsense with a hint of dominatrix. But then she turned and saw him, and smiled. When she spoke again, her voice was honey. "Sam. You made it."

"Thanks to Jules," he said. She seemed happy to just stand there and look at him, too. He was grinning at her like an idiot.

"He called me," she said. "Told me all about the thong incident. Poor Chloe."

"Poor *Chloe*?" Sam protested. "What about poor me?"

"Poor Sam, having such a *trying* few weeks, in the most beautiful part of Italy, with naked women throwing themselves at you." She was trying to sound sarcastic, but her amusement bubbled through. She mocked him even more. "It must've been terrible, like . . . like . . . working in a *Girls Gone Wild* video!"

That was it for the just-let-me-look-at-you part of their long-awaited reunion. Sam dropped his bag and went for her. She met him more than halfway. He knew she'd missed him badly, too, because she didn't even bother to look around to see who might be watching them—they were, after all, at work. But she didn't care.

She just kissed him, and as he kissed the shit out of her, he thought of Jules, of how lonely he was. *You asked me what I want? I want what you have with Alyssa . . .*

It didn't matter to Sam where they slept tonight—in their own bed, or in a five-star hotel, or even in a tent. As long as Alyssa was beside him, Sam was home.

When Jenk, Izzy, Gillman, and Lopez Met Tony Vlachic

2005
This story takes place slightly before Into the Storm.

"Weirdest lesbian encounter ever," Izzy said as he dealt the cards around the desk that he'd helped Mark Jenkins move into the middle of the shabby motel room. "This girl comes up to me. I'm in a bar in Boulder, Colorado, and she is unbelievably beautiful. I'm talking a fifty on a scale of one to ten. Seriously Victoria's Secret gorgeous. Long dark hair, a face like Natalie Portman, a body like a porn star."

Gillman rolled his eyes. "You are so full of shit."

They'd been garrisoned in some low-rent places before, but this one, remote and located in a town that shut down and went to bed at 2030 every night, was about as nasty as Jenk had ever seen.

It did, however, include the essentials: a bathroom, a shower, beds to sleep in, an air conditioner that wheezed and chugged as it cooled down the room, a deck of cards, and a mini-fridge filled with beer.

So okay, the cards were Jenk's and the mini-fridge was Gillman's—one of those insulated coolers you could carry in your truck and plug in when you reached your destination.

Izzy turned to Jenk, injury in his voice and on his

face. "You didn't hear me strapping on the bullshit meter when Fishboy here was telling his lesbian supermodels-in-the-airport story, did you?"

Jenk had just been dealt three aces—his best hand all night. There was actually a chance he'd win back the money he'd lost over the past few hours. "Let's just play cards."

Now Izzy's disgusted exhale was for Jenk.

Jay Lopez, as usual, tried to restore harmony. "So she's beautiful and she comes up to you, and says . . . ?"

"*I need a huge favor.* And I'm thinking, *Well, it's your lucky night, because I've got a huge favor,*" Izzy told them. "Only I managed to not say that. Probably because she was stupifyingly beautiful. I think what I ended up saying was *Durh . . . ?* And I probably enhanced it with a little drool, you know, on my chin."

Izzy took two cards from Lopez, dealing him two new ones. Danny Gillman took only one—which meant he either had a great hand or he was bluffing.

Jenk stared at him, willing him to do it. Scratch his chin with the back of his hand. Gillman did it every time he bluffed—it was the most obvious tell in the history of mankind.

But Gillman didn't move, because at the start of the game, Izzy Zanella had let it slip that Gillman *had* a tell.

In true Izzy fashion, he'd refused to share with Gillman exactly what that tell was. And no one else was going to let on that they knew, so Gillman had sat nearly stone-still for the entire game, terrified that, by moving, he'd subconsciously and inadvertently activate his tell.

He was stone-still, that is, except when Izzy pissed him off. Or when he tried to piss off Izzy in return.

Of course, for the first time in all their years of poker playing, Gillman was winning. Big.

"I'm doomed." Tony Vlachic, aka Chickie, aka the

New Guy, didn't have a tell. He simply announced whenever his hand sucked. This was his first time playing poker with them, and he'd good-naturedly put up with all of their crap. He had a Pepsi in front of him because they wouldn't let him have a beer, insisting he was too young.

"Maybe next year, when you turn thirteen," Izzy had told him.

Now Chick took another slug of his soda and traded the limit—three cards.

"She goes, *I told my brother you were my boyfriend. Will you help me fool him into thinking we've been together for a while?*" Izzy scooped up Jenk's two discards and gave him two replacements to go with his trio of aces and . . .

A four and a seven, both hearts. Crap. Jenk kept his face carefully blank as Izzy traded three of his own cards for three new ones.

"And that, boys and girls," Izzy continued with his story, "was when she kissed me."

"Yeah, right," Gillman scoffed.

"She *did*," Izzy countered. "Chickie was there. Tell 'em, Chick."

Tony looked up from frowning at his no doubt unbelievably crappy hand. "She definitely kissed him," he verified. "For close to three minutes, without coming up for air."

"And when she finally does surface," Izzy said, "she goes, *Do you have a car, because I really need a ride.* So I tell her, yeah, I got a truck, is that okay? And she's like, *You really don't mind?* And something's up—I mean, besides the obvious—because she's got tears in her eyes and she's kind of shaking, and that was when I knew. I mean, I'm a good kisser, but . . . So we go out to my truck, and she tells me she's gay, that her parents sent her to this rehablike place to make her straight, and she had to pretend she was 'cured' in order to get out. The brother follows her around, making it impossible for her to see her girlfriend, who, by the way, is also gorgeous. Long story short, I drove them both to Vegas. I get email from them every now and then. But Maddy, she's the one with the brother, right before she gets out of the car in Nevada, she goes, *I'm definitely gay. Because if kissing you didn't turn me straight, nothing will.*"

"Really," Gillman said, clearly not believing him. "If I emailed her and asked, she'd tell me that wasn't just something you made up?"

Chick raised the bet ten dollars. Was he really going to attempt to bluff after looking at his hand as if it was something he found at the bottom of a year-old pile of dirty laundry?

"Why would I make that up?" Izzy asked as Lopez folded. "Now if I told you that with Maddy and Peg, I'd enjoyed the best three-way I've had in years . . ."

"Yeah, like you've had a lot of three-ways," Gillman scoffed, raising the bid even higher. He didn't look at any of them, definitely afraid his tell was something they'd see in his eyes. He looked at the pile of cash in front of him, or his cards. Nowhere else.

"What, Gilligan, you haven't?" Izzy countered, using Gillman's least-hated nickname. When Izzy called the other SEAL *Fishboy*, that really pissed him off. "Not on the isle, with Ginger and Mary Ann?"

"We're not talking about me, asshole."

Jenk knew that the not-looking-at-anyone thing was pretty much a tell in and of itself. If Gillman had a great hand, why would he be worried about giving that away? Unless he was bluffing about bluffing, so that Jenk would see his raise and . . .

"Not even with Thurston and Lovey?" Izzy just did not know when to let a subject drop. Gilligan was going to knock the table over, and they'd have to start the hand again. Of course, maybe that would be a good thing.

"Just shut up."

"You know, it's okay that you haven't—"

Jenk cut in. "I have," he said. "And it was kind of weird. The other guy had a really hairy back." Yeah, *that* had caught their attention. Even Gillman was staring at him. Chickie was the only one who didn't look up. "I'm kidding," he told them.

"You scared me for a second there, M." Izzy tossed his cards down. "I'm out. Too rich for my blood," he told Gillman, adding, "Even though it's obvious as shit that you're bluffing."

Gillman refused to take that particular bait, his eyes solidly back on his cards.

It was down to Jenk and Chickie, and it was Jenk's turn to play. See Gillman's bid, *raise* Gillman's bid, or fold . . .

Chick's phone must've vibrated. "Shit, sorry, I gotta take this call," he announced, standing up and going out onto the motel driveway, which was fine with Jenk. It gave him a little extra stall-time to try to psych Gillman out.

Jenk leaned back in his chair. With enough time and a little effort—keep talking on the phone, Vlachic— maybe he could get Gillman to forget about the poker game. "My weirdest lesbian encounter was when I spent Christmas with three drag queens."

Gillman looked up again at that. Eye contact. He immediately looked back down, but it was definitely a start. "Drag queens can't be lesbians. Drag queens are guys."

"But they refer to each other as *she*," Jenk pointed out. "And if they're into each other . . ."

"Whoa, good point," Izzy said. "So it's a lesbianish

thing on the surface, except they're really chicks with dicks. As opposed to guys with a surprise."

"Guys with a . . ." Now Gillman made eye contact with Izzy. He had to in order to give him a properly disdainful WTF look.

"A female cross-dresser," Jenk explained.

"There's no such thing," Gillman said. He actually put down his cards. "I mean, yeah, maybe back in the nineteenth century, when women had to wear hoop-skirts, sure, but nowadays women wear pants all the time."

"There's pants," Lopez said, "and there's *pants*."

Gillman wasn't convinced. "But—"

Izzy cut him off. "They exist, Wendy. Take my word for it."

"Wendy?" Now Lopez was confused.

"I think it's a Peter Pan reference," Jenk told him.

Gillman was easily outraged, especially by statements made by Zanella. It was interesting, this intense rivalry or personality clash or whatever it was between the two men. Jenk had been out in the real world, on dangerous ops, with both of them; they worked together in perfect harmony, no hint of any animosity, cogs in a well-oiled machine. But during R&R . . . Look out.

"Now you're saying *Wendy* was a cross-dresser?" Gillman challenged Izzy.

Iz laughed his frustration and disbelief. "I'm saying you're a fucking idiot, and that yes, there are female cross-dressers here where *I* live, outside of Never-never-land."

"What, do you know this because you're one of them?" Gillman asked, and Jenk cringed because Izzy unfolded, rising to his feet.

But he just stood there, all six plus feet of him, towering over the table. "Yeah, Dan," he deadpanned. "I'm a woman. And this girl needs to whiz, wicked bad." He disappeared into the bathroom.

Jenk exchanged a look with Lopez. *Well, that happened.* Or, more accurately, *didn't* happen. He raised his voice slightly so that Izzy could hear him through the bathroom door. "You know, my three drag queens were at least as tall as you."

Gillman, the fucking idiot indeed, actually looked disappointed that the conversation, so to speak, hadn't been taken outside. He also looked as if he'd completely forgotten about their card game. That was good, and Jenk wanted to continue keeping him distracted. "So I was around eleven years old, it was Christmas Eve. New York was getting hit with the worst snowstorm in something like a hundred years. It was really coming down—like somebody-better-go-find-Rudolph bad. And my dad, as usual, had waited until the last minute to get a gift for my mother—that was his MO. He swore to me, every year, that she would like her present better if he could find it on sale. I was pretty sure she would like it better if it didn't *suck* because he'd gotten it five minutes before the stores closed on Christmas Eve, but he was convinced he was right."

Across the table, Gillman was engaged. "My dad used to do that, too. Mom had this scary *I can't believe you spent our money on this piece of shit* smile that she gave him almost every Christmas morning."

"So it's four in the afternoon on Christmas Eve," Jenk continued, "and there's already a foot of snow, and my dad and I are in the Honda—Mom's always been into high gas mileage vehicles, so no SUV or truck for us. We're spinning in circles down Route 35, which is okay, because no one else is crazy enough to be out on the road. We finally reach the Jefferson Valley Mall, and to my dad's complete horror, it's dark. The whole mall closed early because of the weather. On Christmas

Eve. So we head into Yorktown Heights, but the only store open is this convenience store, over by the motel. But Dad's desperate, so in we go. And let me tell you, the gift selection was grim. On top of that, the clerk says, *Computers are down, no credit card sales.* But my dad has cash, and he's trying to choose between these tacky votive candles, a Yankees mouse pad, and this disposable toilet bowl brush, and I know he's in serious trouble. I mean, I'm only eleven, but even back then I understand that you don't buy your wife a disposable toilet brush for Christmas. Unless you don't want to get any until Memorial Day."

"Unless, she's got, like, a toilet bowl fetish," Izzy suggested, emerging from the bathroom.

"Have you met Jenk's mom?" Lopez asked him.

"No," Izzy said. "Have you?" He turned to Jenk. "I'm jealous. You bring Lopez home to meet the 'rents, but you don't bring me? What am I to you? Just some cheap, easy plaything that you use and discard?"

"So I'm trying to talk my father into the certificate-for-a-romantic-weekend idea," Jenk spoke over him, because sometimes it was best just to ignore Izzy. "I'm telling him there's a program on our new home computer that he can use to make it look like he spent hours designing it. Plus Mom will love the idea. My ulterior motive, of course, is to be allowed to stay home alone with Ginny, my older sister—who had some extremely hot friends."

"Ginny's pretty hot herself." Izzy turned to Gilligan. "You ever meet Ginny?"

"Yeah, once," he said, and it was clear he wouldn't have used the word *hot* to describe her. "She came to San Diego. She was kind of, well . . . large. I mean, short, like Jenk, but . . . round. No offense, Jenkins."

"Yeah," Izzy said. "No offense, Jenkins, but Gilligan thinks your sister is freaking fat."

"She *was* pregnant," Lopez pointed out, ever the voice of calm.

"She was?" Gillman looked to Jenk for confirmation. "I didn't know she was married."

"Yeah. Gin's got three kids," Jenk said. He put his cards down on the table and, stretching, stood up. Chickie was still out in the driveway. Jenk could see him through the window, pacing back and forth out there as he spoke on his phone.

"Wow," Gillman said.

Jenk opened the mini-fridge and pulled out another beer.

"Wow," Izzy echoed. "For someone with three kids, she's not just hot, she's freaking hot."

Jenk popped the top and held the bottle out to Gillman. Who took it, alleluia, and took a long swig. "Iz?"

"Nah, I'm good," Izzy said.

"Jay?"

"Thanks." Lopez drained his bottle, and Jenk traded him for a new one, putting the empty in the growing pile with the others.

"So we're in this store," Jenk continued his story, "and these three huge woman—I mean they were really tall. They come in, and they're dusting the snow off their coats and their hair, and they're really disappointed at the no credit card news. One of them—Sherilee—overhears my conversation with my dad."

"Sherilee," Izzy repeated.

"Sherilee, Rhonda, and Marcia," Jenk said, sitting back at the table. "Sherilee goes, *Last-minute Christmas shopping?* And my dad takes, like, four steps back. He's staring, and I think it's because, well, he's height-challenged like me, and this woman is about six four. She's also wearing a tiara. How many women shop at the SuperQuick in a tiara? She goes, *Not to be pushy, but I make jewelry.* And I'm looking at that tiara, thinking, *No way*. But she calls one of her friends over, pulls back the other woman's sleeve. And there's this bracelet that looks as if it were made for my mom. It was silver and turquoise and . . . It was beautiful. It was beyond perfect. And my dad, he's clearly freaked out, but he has to ask. *How much?* She looks at me, she looks at him, says, *A hundred dollars*. She hands it to Dad to look at more closely. Dad goes, *Fifty*. She says *Cash?* And he takes out his wallet. And she says to her friends, *Go, girls*. And they start gathering armloads of chips and Yodels—there's not a lot of real food in that store. Turns out the trains stopped running, so here they are, at the Yorktown Heights Motel, with three dollars cash between the three of them. If my dad hadn't bought that bracelet, they wouldn't have been able to buy anything to eat until the computers came back on line. And from the way the lights were flickering, it wasn't going to be soon."

The door opened, and Chickie came back into the room. But he looked as if someone had jammed a pole up his ass. He made a beeline for the cooler, grabbing another Pepsi, before disappearing into the bathroom.

"So I'm talking to them," Jenk continued, "and they're really nice. They're actresses, and they do a cabaret show, traveling around the country. Marcia plays the piano, and they all sing. And I'm looking at those bags of popcorn they're holding, thinking about the lousy Christmas Eve dinner they're going to have, so I say, *Why don't you come have dinner with us?* And my dad kind of freezes, and I don't know why. We've always had a strays-and-orphans policy at our house—there's always someone from outside of the family at our holiday meals. So I say to my dad, *You know Mom won't mind*. And Sherilee says, *Thank you, honey, you're so sweet, but . . . we'll be just fine*. And Dad's got the bracelet in one hand, and me in the other and he drags me out the door.

"It wasn't until we were in the car, when he goes, *Mark. Those are men in women's clothes.* I think I actually argued with him. You know, *Why would men wear women's clothes?* I remember him saying, *Because they want to.* And I just didn't get it, but I was a kid, so it didn't freak me out the way it did my dad. I mean, I thought it was crazy, but if they wanted to wear high heels, it was fine with me. And I said, *But they're nice. Mom would love them.* And he didn't say anything. He didn't pull out of the parking lot either. We just sat there, in the car, watching them through the store windows. They were probably trying to decide which brand of beef jerky was the most edible. And I said, *It's Christmas. And they saved your butt.* And he's all pissed, but he hands me the bracelet for my mother, huffing and puffing as he's getting out of the car, muttering to himself about stupid kids and stupid ideas. But he goes back into the store, and when he comes out, Sherilee, Rhonda, and Marcia are with him. We all pile into the Honda, and with the extra weight we don't skid once on our way home.

"It was a great Christmas," Jenk told them as Chick came out of the bathroom and rejoined them at the table. "Mom loved the bracelet, and we had our own personal cabaret show. And maybe I was wrong—I was only eleven—but it sure seemed like Rhonda and Marcia had a thing for each other. Thus, my most interesting lesbian encounter."

"Can we please finish this hand?" Young Vlachic had definitely just had a *Dear John* phone call. He looked at Jenk. "Will you fucking do something besides talk?"

Ouch. Jenk let the harsh words roll off his back, considering the circumstances, as, across the table, Gillman picked up his cards and . . .

He scratched his chin with the back of his hand.

Yes! He was bluffing. Or . . . was he? Gillman also sent Jenk what could only be described as a furtive look. It was over almost before it started, but Jenk saw it.

Except it was clearly intended for Jenk to see, which meant . . .

"I'm in," Jenk decided, tossing his money into the pile in the center of the table. Gillman was back to not looking anywhere but at his cards.

"How much to call?" Chickie grimly asked.

"Twenty-six dollars," Lopez said in a voice that recommended Chick fold.

"No, it's only sixteen to him," Izzy said. "Vlachic was the genius who raised the bet ten fricking bucks in the first place."

Chickie put in the cash. And sure enough, Gillman revealed that he was holding a whole lotta nothing. Total train wreck. The highest card was, appropriately, a jack.

"Nice attempt to bluff," Jenk told him, revealing his three aces. "But you know, you tried just a little too hard. You were too obvious with your eyes and—" He was already reaching for the pot when Izzy stopped him.

"Dude." Izzy pointed at the cards Chickie was lovingly placing on the table.

Holy crap.

It wasn't just a winning hand. It was a kickass, once-in-a-lifetime, mother-of-God *miracle* of a winning hand. A straight flush; spades, Queen high. Even Lopez sat forward and stared.

"No fucking way." Gillman was the first to overcome the shock and put voice to their disbelief. "Dude. You took three cards."

"I guess I'm just lucky," Chick said in that same grim

voice. But then he looked up and smiled, and Jenk knew they'd all been conned. By the twelve-year-old new guy. Who'd gone through BUD/S and was probably closer to twenty-three—and completely capable of conning the unconnable. Yeah, Chick was lucky as hell, but he'd totally fooled them into thinking he still held a crappy hand.

"Who was on the phone?" Jenk asked, suddenly suspicious.

"No one," Chick admitted, starting to put the huge pile of bills and coins into neatly organized stacks. "You just seemed as if you needed a little more time to decide to stay in."

"Brilliantly done," Jenk said.

"What I said before," Vlachic started to explain. "I didn't mean—"

"I know," Jenk reassured him. "It was a nice touch. Very authentic."

"Thanks," Chick said. "That means a lot, coming from you."

Jenk was the team's best liar, which meant that he also had the most accurate bullshit meter. Although it was entirely possible that he was now the team's *second* best liar.

"Hey, Iz." Jenk turned to Zanella. He didn't need to say anything more, since Izzy was on the same wavelength.

As Lopez shuffled the deck, Izzy took a beer from the fridge. He opened it. "Welcome to the team," he said.

And handed it to Chickie.

INTERVIEW WITH TOM AND KELLY

December 2005
This story takes place around the same time as
Into the Storm.

"I got the word just before noon," Tom said, laughter dancing in his eyes as he held his seven-month-old son, Charlie, on his shoulder. "I was no longer needed, so I managed to get a seat on a commercial flight home that left at two fifteen."

"The assignment was really just saber-rattling," Kelly interjected, reaching out to wipe their baby's chin as we sat in Tom's home office in San Diego.

Well, actually, *they* sat in San Diego. I was in front of my computer, in *my* office, writing this scene. But, shhh. Don't tell them that. I'm not sure they know they're fictional characters. Tom Paoletti is the former CO of SEAL Team Sixteen and the current owner of Troubleshooters Incorporated, a private security firm. Dr. Kelly Ashton Paoletti is his wife.

Kelly continued. "He was brought in to stand there and look important and, I don't know, scary, I guess."

"Am I scary?" Tom asked his son. He made a face that was nowhere near scary and the baby chortled with laughter. "I think that's a solid no."

"He can be *very* scary," Kelly told me, laughing too. "Don't let him fool you. Anyway, the point is that he finally called to tell me he was coming home, which was wonderful news. He'd been gone for nearly three weeks.

That's the longest he's been away since Charlie was born."

"Yeah, I missed you pretty badly," Tom said to Charlie. "And I missed your mommy, too." He looked at me. "But everything fell perfectly into place. Like someone waved a magic wand and made it all easy."

So okay, I was wrong. Tom clearly knew he was a character and that I was his writer.

Still, I shook my head at his unspoken question. It wasn't me who'd made things easy for him. I like to challenge my characters, throw them into situations that are difficult—just to see what they'll do, how they'll react.

"That seat on the plane—there was only one left, but it was mine," Tom continued. He obviously didn't believe me. "I was flying into Germany, where I'd catch a connecting flight to New York, and on to San Diego. Again, I got the last seat on *that* flight, too. Then when I was packing, the zipper on my bag broke. I was ready to leave everything behind, just take my laptop, but I got a new bag at a store that was right in the hotel lobby. Of course, it was pink, with a picture of Minnie Mouse on it. Thanks so much for that."

Again, I shook my head. It really wasn't me. I'd spent the past few months writing *Into the Storm*, Navy SEAL Mark Jenkins's story.

"And then there was the taxi," Kelly prompted him.

"Yeah," Tom said. "The entire three weeks I'm in Kazabek, it's impossible to get a cab, but suddenly one's available. I just opened the door and got in. Traffic was usually terrible, but we made it to the airport early. I checked in, everything was great. I got on the plane, and they were actually giving out free drinks and real sandwiches—when does that ever happen? We had a delay before takeoff, but even that was okay. We managed to make up the time while we were in the air. We landed in Germany, and I had just enough time to make it to the gate and . . ." He shook his head ruefully. "I didn't get on the plane."

"What happened?" I asked, looking to Kelly. But she was watching Tom holding Charlie, her eyes soft. No doubt about it, she loved her two men.

"There was this kid," Tom said, but then he corrected himself. "A young man. In an Army uniform. Corporal Tyrell Richards. He was standing near the gate, clearly anxious. And he's looking at me like I'm the grim reaper as I approach. I'm a little late, but I can still make the flight. And as I hand my boarding pass to the man behind the counter, he turns to Richards and says, *That's it, we're full. No standbys.* The look on that kid's face was . . ." He shook his head.

"So Tom asked him where he's from," Kelly told me. "He says Hartford, Connecticut. He's only got a few more days of leave. He was trying to get home to see his wife, meet his daughter. *Meet.* She was Charlie's age. Can you imagine? He hadn't been home in a year."

I shook my head. No, I couldn't imagine.

"So Tom gave him his seat," Kelly continued.

I turned to look at him.

"It really wasn't that big a deal." Tom was embarrassed.

"It probably was to Tyrell Richards," I pointed out.

"And it *definitely* was to Tyrell's wife," Kelly agreed.

Again, Tom shrugged. "It was the least I could do. Hey, champ, you tired?"

In his arms, the baby was starting to fuss. He rubbed his eyes.

Kelly scooped him up. "Nap time," she announced. "It was nice to see you, Suz," she said to me as she and Charlie left the room.

Tom and I sat in silence for a moment, just looking at each other.

"So it took me three days to get home," he told me.

"All that good luck? Instantly gone. I missed my connecting flight to California out of New York, ended up in Dallas for twenty-three hours, two of 'em spent sitting on the runway. Wasn't *that* fun? Still, it was worth it. We got the nicest note from Tyrell's wife." Tom's smile widened. "I also got something of a hero's welcome home. Have I mentioned that nap time is my new favorite time of day? I just wish Charlie'd stay asleep a *little* longer. And I think he's starting to teethe, so he hasn't been falling asleep as quickly anymore. Hint, hint?"

I laughed. Message received.

"That was just the funniest thing," Kelly said as she came back into the room. "Charlie fell right to sleep. He never does that. Although, sometimes babies reach a certain age, and they suddenly nap like clockwork."

"He'll probably sleep through the night now, too," I said.

"Oh, wouldn't *that* be nice?"

"It certainly will be," Tom said with a smile, pulling his wife onto his lap.

"Hey!" She laughed, glancing over at me.

"Suz was just leaving," Tom told her. He kissed her and snapped his fingers, and the scene faded to black.

TRAPPED

Early 2006
This story takes place shortly after Into the Storm, *and before* Force of Nature.

Nachtgarten Army Base, Germany

CHAPTER ONE

"So," Jules Cassidy said, as he tried to cover his best friend and former FBI partner Alyssa Locke more completely with his body. Her leg had been broken in the blast that had trapped them here, and she drew in a sharp breath at the contact, but otherwise didn't complain. "I finally got some last Thursday night. Go, me."

She laughed her surprise, her voice rich in the pitch darkness. "Get out of here."

"Sweetie, I would if I could, and I'd take you with me, too." Jules quipped as he flipped on his flashlight, because . . . why not? It was possible their lives were going to end before its batteries wore out. Might as well enjoy the light while they still had eyes with which to see.

"Ben?" Alyssa asked.

"No," Jules said tartly. "Some stranger that I picked up in a bar. What kind of slut do you think I am? Of course, Ben. God."

"About time, my no-longer-celibate brothah," she said.

There was both pain and worry in her eyes, and Jules knew he should continue to try keeping things light, for both of their sakes, but . . .

"Yeah, I don't know," he admitted. "I'm feeling . . . oddly ambiguous about the whole thing." Especially after the surprise weekend visit from his mother.

"Ben's really sweet," Alyssa commented from beneath him.

"Yes, he is." He'd pulled her as far as he could into the corner of this shallow subterranean room that seemed to be the most structurally sound, behind a pile of bricks and rubble as they waited for the bomb's timer to count down the last ninety seconds of a five-minute delay.

Please, sweet baby Jesus, don't let this be their final last ninety seconds. If this didn't work, if they died here tonight, Alyssa's husband, former Navy SEAL and total Texas cowboy Sam Starrett, was going to follow Jules up to heaven and kick his ass—right in front of St. Peter and God and Jimmy Stewart and whoever else saintly and pure was standing beside the pearly gates.

And please, Jesus, as long as Jules was making a list of demands, let Sam survive the altercation with the terrorists who'd planted this bomb that was about to explode. Wherever the cowboy-booted one was, please keep him safe, too . . .

"I don't know what's wrong with me," Jules admitted to the woman who'd been one of his best friends for years, because although light banter was preferred at times like this, an honest heart-to-heart was better than silently wondering about the fate of the other members of the Troubleshooters team. Sam wasn't the only one out there—Tess, Sophia, and Lindsey were in potential danger from the bad guys, too. "Why haven't I fallen madly in love with him? The whole time we were . . .

together—and it wasn't just Thursday, it was Friday night, too—I was . . . I don't know. Waiting for the choir of angels to start to sing." He laughed his disgust. "Have I mentioned that Ben's into country music? Some of it's not awful—I'll admit that. Some of it's . . . Okay, I'll be generous and use the word *good*. But *some* of it . . . ? Kill me now."

That was probably not the right thing to say while waiting for a bomb to go off, but Alyssa either ignored it or didn't notice.

"Okay, so he's not perfect," Alyssa said. "No one is. Sam's certainly not." She swore sharply. "If he gets himself killed tonight . . ."

"Sam'll be all right," Jules reassured her with a hug—careful, though, of her leg. "He's probably going insane, wondering where we are. So tell me this. If Sam's so imperfect, what would you change about him to make *him* better?"

Alyssa shook her head. "Nothing," she admitted.

"Sometimes imperfect *is* perfect," Jules philosophized. "It's a personal thing. Sam, with all of his imperfections—things that would drive *me* mad—is perfect for *you*."

"So what would you change about Ben?"

Jules didn't have to think about that one. "His parents don't know he's gay," he reminded her. "And then there's that whole *don't ask, don't tell* bullshit . . ."

Their entire relationship would have to be secret. Jules had worked hard his entire life to be open and out about his being gay. This would be a significant step backward—right into Ben's closet. And the man didn't even have a walk-in.

"I think it's a good thing then," Alyssa decided. "A sign of maturity. You know—that you're being cautious with him. You're taking things slowly. You're not just giving your heart away indiscriminately." *The way you usually do.* She left that part unsaid, because she knew she didn't have to remind him.

"So . . . you're advocating casual sex?" Jules needled her. "Ow!"

She'd pinched him. "Don't be an idiot. It's kinda obvious your thing with Ben is serious—it has been for a while—even as . . . sex-free as it's been. Up to now. But there's no law saying that you have to plan to spend the entire rest of your life with every single person that you . . . make the magic with."

"I know," Jules said. And he did know. The concept, however, was easier for him in theory. He'd been friends with Alyssa for a long time, and she was well aware of his tendency to start planning a lifetime commitment ceremony within moments of a new relationship's first intimate encounter. He was a romantic. A hopeless one. In some circles, though, that was considered a strength, not a weakness. "I'm just . . . I'm tired of not being a *we.* And here's Ben, who's made a point of making sure I know he's looking for something real, and . . ."

So what did Jules go and do after spending a few very *we*-ish nights with the man? He ran away to Germany to help Alyssa and Sam with a Troubleshooters Incorporated op that was probably now going to get them all killed.

All but Ben, who was back in DC.

For now.

In a matter of months, his Marine unit was heading back to Iraq. And wouldn't *that* move their relationship to an entirely new level of crapitation? Provided, of course, that Jules survived the next few seconds. . . .

"What are *you* looking for?" Alyssa asked him.

But before he could answer and say that he didn't know—which wasn't really a lie—the timer buzzed and the bomb went off.

CHAPTER TWO

An hour earlier . . .

As far as distractions went, this was working.

Mostly.

Slogging through an ancient drainage pipe beneath a military installation made it very hard to think about anything besides the horrific smell.

At least they weren't up to their ankles or knees in water. There were occasional puddles, but it was mostly just mud beneath their feet. At least Jules hoped it was mud.

He crept along, just in front of Alyssa, who was team leader for this little Troubleshooters Incorporated op, venturing into the bowels beneath a U.S. Army barracks that had been built here in Nachtgarten, Germany, just after World War II. The barracks had been built then, that is. This drainage system looked—and smelled—as if parts of it dated back to the days of the Roman Empire.

On point was Lindsey Jenkins, a tiny slip of an Asian American woman with mad tracking skills and a total kickass attitude—thanks in part to her years with the LAPD. Apparently, she'd committed to memory the blueprint of the maze of tunnels, and she moved surely and silently, leading the way through the dimness, proving to the world that size didn't matter.

Which was something of Jules's own mantra, since he was no hulking giant himself. He still sometimes shopped in the teen boys department in order to find T-shirts that fit him snugly enough to wear clubbing—not that he'd actually *gone* to a dance club in the past few years. . . .

But here and now, compared to Lindsey, who could move as if she had a note from her doctor excusing her from the laws of gravity, he felt oafish and noisy.

And freaking envious.

Lindsey was the relatively recent bride of Petty Officer Mark Jenkins, an adorable Navy SEAL who'd gotten leave from Iraq in order to meet her here in Germany. Her new husband's transport flight had been delayed, however, and he'd shown up at their hotel just as the entire Troubleshooters team had met in the lobby for breakfast.

Needless to say, Lindsey and Mark had not joined them for the meal. The SEAL had soul-kissed his spouse, right there in the lobby, thrown her over his shoulder, and carried her into the elevator—and that was the last anyone had seen of either of them until they'd all met for this op at 2300.

But no one had teased her about it. Too many of them knew what it was like to have or be a spouse in the military. Time with one's partner was precious—and too-often infrequent.

And *that* made Jules think of Ben, which was exactly what he didn't want to be thinking about . . .

Wait, Lindsey hand-signaled now, then vanished ahead into a part of the tunnel that didn't have dim moonlight shining in through heavy cast-iron drainage grates.

Two other Troubleshooters operatives, curly-haired computer specialist Tess Bailey and elegantly blond Sophia Ghaffari, who was clearly in training or at least a bright green rookie, hung back, obeying Lindsey's command, while Jules and Alyssa continued to guard their six.

Even though it was unlikely that there was anything down here to guard them against.

Their mission was to prove that the Nachtgarten barracks were vulnerable to terrorist attack via these illprotected tunnels that wound beneath the entire city. Because—as if the idea of tunnels that crisscrossed beneath the military base wasn't enough of a threat—there was also a no-longer-used, buried and long-forgotten massive oil tank that sat, still two-thirds full, just beneath the facility's main housing.

With some correctly placed C4, aided by that enormous tank of oil, any terrorist with a little Internet-acquired know-how could create an explosion that would take down the multistory building and make the Khobar Towers bombing look like child's play.

And as far as the Internet went . . .

Alyssa and Sam, acting as agents for the country's most elite personal security team, Troubleshooters Incorporated, had written and submitted a detailed report on this installation months ago. They'd outlined, quite specifically, the dangers of what they believed to be a serious threat, due to that very oil tank.

But after the powers-that-be thanked them for their time, absolutely nothing was done to safeguard the lives of the thousands of servicemen and -women quartered at the base.

And *then,* a few short days ago, Jules had found out that Sam and Alyssa's top secret report had actually circulated the White House via nonsecure email—which meant that the barracks at Nachtgarten were now even *more* vulnerable. The report, which mentioned the long-forgotten oil tank, had floated about on the Internet for a solid week before anyone noticed it contained classified information.

Jules had taken the news of the leak up the chain of command to his boss in the FBI, Max Bhagat, who'd been furious about the security breach—enough to get Admiral Chip Crowley involved.

Crowley, a Navy SEAL himself, was a man of action, and before Jules had even left Max's office, a task force had been formed and Troubleshooters Incorporated once again had been hired. This time they were to play the part of the "red cell" in a mock attack of the military base.

Their job was to get, covertly, into Nachtgarten and once again find said oil tank—which was supposedly "too costly to locate and remove," and, also according to the geniuses in charge, "too difficult to locate to create any real threat to the army personnel housed therein."

Yeah, maybe it had been too difficult to locate *until some bureaucrat wrote an email about it, attached Sam and Alyssa's report, and then freaking sent it to all their friends* . . .

God. Nothing pissed Jules off more than stupidity.

Hopefully, after tonight's exercise—complete with weapons that fired only rubber bullets, and *Hey, Nachtgarten security teams, you think that might be a hint that some war-gaming might be going on tonight?*—the stupidity would finally end.

There was, of course, no guarantee of that.

But the Troubleshooters red cell had been ordered to plant a "bomb" atop that oil tank—which would hopefully help wake people up. They weren't going to use real explosives, of course. Instead, they would affix to the tank an electronic device that was the equivalent weight of the C4 needed in an attempt to take down the building. With this device and a nifty computer program that would receive and read the box's signal, analysts would be able to accurately measure the amount of oil that remained in the tank, as well as the effect of an explosion on the barracks above.

Jules had seen this particular computer program in action before. It would create a simulation of the size and strength of the fictional blast, as well as estimate damage and predict body count. It would also—nifty little thing—translate it all into an outrageously huge dollar amount for those bottomline thinkers who believed that removing an obsolete oil tank was a tad too costly.

But all of that was going to happen *after* the team found the tank and slogged their way back to the much fresher air of the decaying riverfront warehouse, where they'd accessed this gross-as-shit drainage system.

Yes, this was *so* much fun.

Lindsey must've returned from her scouting trip, because Tess signaled them forward and they began to move into a part of the tunnel that was pitch-black. It seemed endless, but finally, ahead of them, was another stretch where the moonlight shone in.

And okay, yeah, actually? If he could ignore the malodorous stench? This *was* kind of fun in a twisted way. Jules wasn't quite sure if the idea was Alyssa's or that of the Troubleshooters CO, Tom Paoletti, but one thing he certainly *was* enjoying was the fact that this particular red cell was manned only by women.

Well, except for Jules, who was really only there as an observer.

Still, it felt very *Charlie's Angels,* which appealed to his inner 1970s-era pop-culture-loving child.

As for his role of observer, he was here because Alyssa had insisted. She'd known how *completely* freaked out he'd been by his mother's weekend visit. Lys had wanted both to hold his hand and to distract him from the craziness that had gone down last Saturday and Sunday.

The funny part of *that* was that Jules hadn't yet told her about last Thursday's and Friday's drama. God, had that all really been just a few short days ago? He glanced at his watch. It was currently early A.M. Wednesday. Which meant it was now only two days until Friday—which was when he and Ben had planned to hook up again.

Yikes.

And wasn't *that* just peachy keen?

Jules should have been feeling anticipation. He was a fan of anticipation when it came to things like food. And sex.

Instead, what he felt, felt an awful lot like dread. And guilt. Yup, the guilt sure was a nice touch, swirling around on the top of his mix of emotions about the entire fiasco—last weekend included.

Jules had actually taken the weekend-in-question off because his mother had called to say she was coming to DC to see him. She and her second husband, Phil, lived in Hawaii in a house overlooking the ocean, and Jules usually went there to visit. That was a no-brainer. In the vacation boxing ring, Hawaii could take out DC with one solid uppercut, every single time.

And yet his mother had flown all the way to the East Coast, nearly out of the blue and completely Phil-less, which made the trip seem all the more odd. But when everything was said and done, *odd* wasn't even close to describing the weekend.

Jules's mom had completely caught him off-guard with her news that she and Phil were getting divorced.

And—although *she* didn't put it into such glaringly harsh plain-speak—their split was because of Jules. Phil had finally admitted to feeling that their relationship was strained due to his discomfort with Jules's sexual orientation. He'd actually sent away for literature on a variety of ex-gay ministries—programs that Jules could enter to be "fixed" and turned straight.

Linda Cassidy—she'd kept Jules's father's name, even after remarrying—had immediately "fixed" her ailing marriage by lancing the two-hundred-pound boil that was Phil.

Jules had never really liked the guy, but it had broken his heart to see his mother cry. Especially when she admitted how much she missed his father, who'd been dead now for close to twenty years.

Alyssa touched Jules now—just a hand on his shoulder. They were being silent, so she didn't say anything, but it was clear that she knew exactly where his thoughts had gone.

She shook her head, as if to say *Don't you be thinking about that right now . . .*

Jules forced a smile as he met her eyes in the dim light. *So . . . I finally had sex with someone who's not Adam. How about that? About freaking time, huh?* What was wrong with him that he finally got the courage to confess *that* breaking news to his best friend now, when they both needed to remain completely silent?

Yup, he was a total headcase, no doubt about them apples.

But then Tess, who was in front of them, lifted her hand, signaling *stop*, *quiet* and then *down*.

Crap.

Jules faded back with Alyssa, even farther into the shadows, getting even more intimate with the stankarific dankness that hugged the tunnel's sides and floor.

They waited there, silent and still—until Lindsey beamed herself back, directly in front of them. And okay, it was probable that she hadn't actually used Starfleet technology to get from point A to point B. She'd probably used her feet and walked it, but she'd done so both silently and invisibly. It was damned impressive.

She crouched next to Alyssa, and, as soundlessly as possible, gave her report.

"We're not alone down here. Someone else came through, maybe an hour ago," she said. "Five of 'em, probably all male, carrying heavy packs and all going in the same direction. They came in via a different tunnel, but merged with our route about twenty feet back from where we are right now. I followed their trail for about half a klick and the good news is that they went past the turnoff to the oil tank. They either missed it or . . ." She shook her head.

"The bad news?" Alyssa asked.

"The way they went? It dead ends. There's no access to the surface—no way out of here."

Which meant, whoever they were, they were down here still.

"Is it possible they're a second red cell?" Tess asked. She and Sophia had approached in order to hear Lindsey's report.

Alyssa shook her head. "We're not the ones being tested here. Tom would've told me if he were going to do that."

"Could it be a security patrol from Nachtgarten?" Sophia asked.

"If so," Alyssa asked, "why not guard the tank?"

"They may not know where it is," Jules reminded her.

She looked at him sharply, and it was clear from the expression on her face that she was having a big *eureka* moment. But being Alyssa, she could tell from wherever she was in A-ha! Land, that Jules hadn't yet reached the same thrilling conclusion. So she explained. "They'll know exactly where the tank is after we lead them to it—and put what's essentially a homing beacon directly on top of it."

Jesus yikes. *That* would be very, *very* ungood.

"Break radio silence," Alyssa ordered Tess, who was carrying their radio. Being a red cell, i.e. a group of make-believe and not necessarily wealthy terrorists, they'd been outfitted with less-than-high-tech gear. Instead of equipping each of them with radio headsets, they'd been given a single crappy Vietnam-era radio.

Tess fired it up, but then frowned. She fiddled with it, then frowned again. "Signal's being jammed."

Shit.

It was looking more and more likely that their unexpected company hadn't come down here to play games. It was probable their mystery five had real C4 in their backpacks, and real bullets instead of rubber ones in their guns.

And the consequences of their actions would result in real, horrific death and destruction as opposed to the computer-simulated kind.

Alyssa reached for her cell phone—they all did. Jules's phone had zero bars. No signal. Not down here in the first level of hell. "Anyone?" Alyssa asked. Tess, Lindsey, and Sophia also shook their heads after checking their phones. Nope.

Alyssa met Jules's gaze. "Fall back," she ordered. "We're going out the way we came in. Lindsey, take the radio and run ahead. As soon as you can get a signal, I want an order going out to evacuate the barracks."

Lindsey vanished as Alyssa looked at Jules and the two remaining Troubleshooters operatives. "Let's move."

CHAPTER THREE

"Whoa," Dave said, leaning in closer to squint at his laptop's screen as he sat at the dining table in the hotel suite they'd designated as the temporary Troubleshooters headquarters in Nachtgarten. "That's . . . very weird."

"What is?" Sam Starrett asked, because knowing Dave, he'd tell Sam anyway. He didn't look up from surfing the TV channels, looking for something even vaguely entertaining and stopping on SpongeBob SquarePants—in German. That was kind of cool. *Guten Tag, Patrick. Wie geht's?*

"I'm getting a signal," Dave reported. "But . . ." He hunched over his computer, fingers flying across his keyboard.

Dave Malkoff was something of an oddball. He'd

been working for Tommy Paoletti's Troubleshooters Incorporated since nearly its inception, yet remained adamant about not wanting to be a team leader, which was fine but a little mystifying to Sam.

A former CIA operative, Dave sometimes took himself—and life—a smidge too seriously. He was one of those guys whose intellect was too big for his own good. He'd aced every test he'd ever taken—and a hell of a lot of good that had done him when it came down to real life.

He didn't seem to have any family, and although he appeared to be friends with the incredibly beautiful Sophia Ghaffari, he wasn't friends in the *Hey, mind if I drop by so we can lick chocolate off each other* sense of the word.

And it was pretty obvious to Sam that Dave wished it were otherwise.

Jimmy Nash, a nutjob in his own right, was convinced that Dave was like the guy in that movie—a forty-year-old virgin—but Sam seriously doubted that. Although he wouldn't be at all surprised to find out that old Dave hadn't done the deed yet this decade.

It was, after all, only 2006. No need to rush things.

"Whoa," Dave said again. "Alyssa definitely just activated the box."

Sam looked up from the TV at the mention of his wife's name. He looked at his watch, too. It was a little too early for her team to have reached the location of the oil tank. No way. Maybe if they'd been moving at a dead run, but . . . That wasn't the plan. They couldn't have gotten there yet.

"But it's completely in the wrong place," Dave added.

Sam moved his feet from the top of the desk to the floor. "Why would she do that?" he asked, standing up and moving across the suite, to look over Dave's shoulder at his computer screen. His wife—their team leader—

knew exactly where that oil tank was. "Maybe the box got switched on accidentally."

Dave scratched his head. "I doubt it, sir. There's a code she's got to punch in to unlock the system. It couldn't have been just bumped and turned on without *some*one knowing."

"Is there a system malfunction?" Sam asked. "On our end?" His voice sounded terse, almost sharp, to his own ears, but Dave didn't so much as flinch.

And indeed, there was concern in Dave's eyes, too, as he glanced at Sam. "No, sir," he answered unequivocally but then backpedaled. "I mean, okay. Yeah. I suppose there could be, but . . ." He was shaking his head. "No."

The hair on the back of Sam's neck was standing up. Through the years, both as a SEAL and as an operative for Troubleshooters Incorporated, he'd learned to trust his gut instincts—or at least take them extremely seriously. He picked up the hotel phone, dialed Jimmy's room number.

"Nash," the man answered after only one ring.

He'd been on edge all night, hyper-aware that his fiancée, Tess Bailey, was out there in the world, without him tagging along as backup. Sam had finally sent him to his own hotel room.

"I need you back in here," Sam ordered. "Decker, too. And see if Mark Jenkins is still in Lindsey's room." He hung up without waiting for Jimmy to respond.

"They're definitely a half a klick from the tank," Dave reported as he checked and rechecked both his computer and the program he was running.

There was a rap on the door, and Sam opened it. It was Nash—with Deck right behind him.

"Situation, sir?" asked Decker, who'd once been a chief in the SEALs. It was hard for him not to address the former naval officers in Troubleshooters with formality. In the same way, it was equally difficult for Sam and Tom not to call Deck *Chief,* especially in times of high stress.

"Alyssa activated the box in the wrong location," Dave repeated the little that they knew, as Mark Jenkins, too, came into the hotel room, "and we don't know why."

Enough was enough. "Game over," Sam said. "I'm calling this bullshit. Deck, get on the horn with the officer in charge over at Nachtgarten. Dave, break radio silence and raise Alyssa. I want to talk to her."

If this meant that they needed to reschedule this drill, take a do-over on a different night, so be it.

Jenkins looked as if he'd rolled right out of bed, but he was waking up fast. He was still a SEAL with Sam's old team—Sixteen. In fact, he'd served with both Sam and Tommy Paoletti, often as a radioman.

"I'm not getting through," Dave reported, and Sam met Jenk's gaze.

Sam nodded at the SEAL's silent question. "Let Jenkins try," he ordered.

One good thing about Dave—there was absolutely no ego involved in anything he did. He relinquished control of their radio without a single word of argument, moving back to his computer.

"Captain O'Reilly over at Nachtgarten insists that all possible entries into the drainage system are under armed guard," Decker reported.

"Tell O'Reilly he's a fucking idiot," Sam shot back, "and that our team is already beneath his fucking base."

Deck, being a former chief, spoke fluent officer. "With all due respect, sir," Sam heard him paraphrase the message into the phone, "we'll need to verify—"

"Can't reach our red cell, sir," Jenk announced, pulling Sam's attention away. "Signal's being jammed, somewhere on their end."

What the fuck?

"Dave, call Tommy Paoletti with a code red," Sam ordered as he broke open the suitcases that were stacked in the corner. Even when they went overseas on a training op or security drill, Troubleshooters Incorporated traveled with enough weapons and equipment to handle an unexpected emergency. "Jenk, I want to know who's jamming the radio signal and exactly where it's coming from. Deck and Nash, gear up. You're with me."

"I'm coming, too," Jenkins said, grabbing both a weapon and ammunition.

As did Dave.

"I need you on your computer," Sam told him.

"You'll have me on my computer," Dave told him, readying his equipment for travel, even as he got through to Paoletti on his cell phone. "Commander. Code red. Evacuate the barracks. Sam's pulling the plug on the exercise. We're unable to make contact with our red cell, and we're preparing to go in after them . . ."

If this turned out to be a whole lot of nothing, Sam was going to hear about it until the end of time. But he was okay with that. Please God, let this be a simple communications or computer malfunction.

He didn't often call upon a higher power for help. But he sent up another quick prayer as he led the other men out of the hotel room and down the stairs. Please God, help Alyssa keep her team safe. And God? Thank you for making Linda Cassidy see the light last weekend, and break up with her dickhead of a second husband, giving her son the impetus to fly here to Germany with them, and to be with Alyssa right now.

No doubt about it. If Alyssa were in trouble and Sam couldn't be guarding her six, he'd want Jules Cassidy by her side.

Jules would die for her.

Of course, the flipside was that Alyssa would also die for Jules.

Sam kicked up his speed, breaking into a run as he went out the door into the hotel's parking garage.

Chapter Four

Three men with M60 machine guns had set an ambush along the route leading out of the tunnel.

Jules and the Angels didn't walk into it, thanks to Lindsey's extraordinary tracking skills. She'd picked up the fresh trail—three men, carrying heavy gear—atop the tracks they themselves had made coming in. That the three men had M60s wasn't deduced from the fact that they wore American running shoes. Nor was it divined from the lengths of their strides.

No, Lindsey had crept toward them, wearing her cloak of invisibility, and she'd gotten a visual of those three weapons—machine guns that were capable of turning human beings into some serious hamburger.

She'd also used her cell phone to snap a few photos of the men who were holding those M60s, zeroing in, in particular, on a swastika-and-flame-motif tattoo that they all proudly wore. From this, Jules was able to identify them as members of the New Reich, a particularly loathsome, hatred-spewing group of Neo-Nazis, based out of Dresden.

It was also clear from the symbols in Farsi that the NR had made on the tunnel walls in green fluorescent paint—go figure—that they wanted it to look as if the attack had been made by a local group of Iranian refugees.

Intolerant people could really suck.

But for every Neo-Nazi asshole that was out there, messing up the world with his backward thinking and his stupid plan to kill thousands of American servicemen and -women in order to fuel hatred of innocent people who had nowhere else to go . . . For every one of them, there was an Alyssa or a Lindsey or a Tess or a Sophia. Ready to fight—and die—for justice and tolerance, ready to right wrongs and bring the real truth to light.

Alyssa came back toward the shadows where Jules was waiting, not far from where they'd activated the electronic device.

"They're coming," she told him.

Which meant that she'd been right.

Apparently, about an hour before Jules, Alyssa, and her red cell had accessed the tunnels via that riverfront warehouse, ten members of the New Reich had entered the same drainage system via an as-yet-unknown means. The NR had traveled along a different route in the tunnel system from Alyssa and her team. But the two paths had crossed as they drew closer to the area where the oil tank was buried.

At that point, five of the NR members headed toward the tank, going past it to hide, waiting for the Troubleshooters to arrive and essentially attach a homing beacon to the damn thing.

Three men had hidden near where the two paths met, waiting until the red cell had gone past. They had gone back to set up that M60 ambush on the very route Alyssa's team would be using to exit the tunnels.

Two others had set up a similar ambush along the tunnel they themselves had used to get in.

Alyssa had hoped that they could escape the way the NR had entered, since their own path was now blocked, and had given the order to fall back along that route. They'd all followed Lindsey, but they hadn't gone far before she'd signaled them to stop, and reported this second ambush site.

In short, they were trapped.

Jules knew that *trapped* wasn't one of Alyssa's happy-fun-time words. He also knew that she was worried about Sam. They'd been down here in these tunnels too long without radio or cell phone contact with the support team on the surface. Sam was, at times, a Neanderthal, but he *could* be patient, and he definitely trusted Alyssa to keep herself and her team safe. Still, Jules knew the man, and it wouldn't be too much longer before Sam called off the drill and came down here, in search of them.

At which point he would run right into that first ambush. It was true, the M60s were pointing in the wrong direction, but they were easy enough to turn around. And Sam and every member of his rescue team could well be killed.

Knowing that there was a time limitation and no real way to communicate with Sam and the support team, Alyssa had decided to give the New Reich what they wanted.

Sort of.

She'd sent Sophia, Tess, and Lindsey to try to find a third and alternative exit and to see if they could find a jam-free place to use their radio or cell phones. And then she'd placed the signal box in a shallow room off the main tunnel, a full half-klick from both the tank and the barracks. At which point, she'd programmed in the code and turned the beacon on.

Come to Mommy and Daddy, you darling little Neo-Nazis. . . .

The plan was to let the NR "find" the buried "oil tank"—or at least the signal box that supposedly sat atop it. In theory, they would set their bomb, turn on its timer, and they would leave.

This was, after all, not a group that was big into suicide attacks. Jules was pretty certain that there *would* be a timer. And it would be set with sufficient time to allow them to make a getaway.

They'd scamper out of the tunnels, taking their machine-gun-wielding buddies with them.

At which point Alyssa and Jules would creep out from their hidey-hole in the corner of the room, take a gander at the bomb, see if there was a quick, easy, and *certain* way to defuse it, and then either do so or run like hell.

If it blew, it could take out part of the drainage system, causing a cave-in. But without the oil from the tank to fuel it, it wouldn't do much more than that.

Jules hoped.

"Here they come," Alyssa breathed again. And indeed, there they came.

CHAPTER FIVE

The base commander finally began the evacuation of the barracks.

About fucking time.

But no one with the authority to give an official go-ahead seemed able to grasp the meaning of Sam's report that there were three unknown, unidentified men, armed with three M60 machine guns, positioned about point-five klicks inside the riverside entrance that Alyssa and her team had used to access the tunnels.

The unknowns had had their backs to the Troubleshooters support team that went down there for a quick sneak-and-peek. They'd had no idea the Troubleshooters were there, and it wouldn't take much for them to continue to not know they were there—right up until the moment their weapons fell from their lifeless fingers.

The key word being *lifeless*.

But Captain O'Reilly, the OIC for the mock attack, didn't want the Troubleshooters to use deadly force.

He'd actually suggested that they go down there and shout a warning, maybe start a dialogue.

Deck was on the phone with the captain right now, suggesting that the word of the day be *covert*. Shouting a warning meant that those three unidentified men with very big weapons would then know that the good guys were there. If shots were fired—and they would be—that would ruin Sam's chances to infiltrate farther into the tunnels, see how many *additional* men with big weapons might be down there—maybe already having taken certain American hostages. . . .

"Sir." Mark Jenkins had news for him. "We've located the origination point of the frequency jamming. It's down a parallel tunnel. Dave's pulled up a schematic— shortest route is past the three-man ambush."

"Let me see," Sam said.

Dave turned his computer to give him a better look at a screen that was a confusing jumble of lines and blotches.

"Point to it," Sam ordered, and Dave complied, which really didn't help him that much.

"Is it inside the confines of the base?" Sam asked.

Dave was a smart guy, a graduate of some fancy Ivy League school. He knew exactly why Sam was asking that, and, as he met Sam's gaze, it was clear that he knew if any bad shit happened in the next few moments, he'd be blamed for providing faulty information. Still he didn't hesitate. "Yes, sir, it certainly looks to be."

"Thank you," Sam said. Finally. Something they could work with. He took Decker's phone from him, handing him his own cell. "Get me Tom Paoletti," he ordered Deck, even as he put the former chief's phone to his ear.

"They may not even have real bullets," Captain O'Reilly was saying, of the three men in the tunnel. "If you can prove that they do—"

Yeah, by having them unload a full banana clip in their direction? Thanks a bunch, Captain Kangaroo. Maybe you should actually spend some time in Iraq, grow a little battlefield perspective.

"—perhaps then we can consider additional measures," O'Reilly continued.

"There are at least three fully armed unknowns in that tunnel," Sam reiterated. "They're screwing with our radio signal, and we've located the source of that jamming—it's inside the gates of the base. I'm calling this what it is, Captain—a terrorist attack on a U.S. military installation. We're going in. With force."

"Mr. Starrett," O'Reilly responded, heavy on that *mister*. "I don't have the authority to allow you to do that."

Sam was ready to tell O'Reilly to blow him when Jimmy Nash reappeared. Sam hadn't noticed when the Troubleshooters operative had disappeared, but Nash certainly registered on his attention-meter now, considering that the crazy son-of-a-bitch's clothing had been sprayed with what looked like blood. He was cleaning off a K-bar knife and the look in his eyes was one Sam had seen a time or two in his own bathroom mirror.

"The tunnel's clear," he reported as he put a handful of extremely non-rubber bullets onto the table in front of him.

Jesus Christ. Three against one, yet Nash had done the job silently, without getting so much as winded. Except, wait, he *was* a little winded, and some of the blood on his shirt was his own.

"Your arm's bleeding," Deck told Nash.

He barely glanced at it. "Just a ding."

O'Reilly was still sputtering on his end of the phone, so Sam just spoke over him. "The bullets are real, the tunnel's been cleared. We're going in—"

It was then, before Sam could end the conversation with a cheery "fuck you," that a bomb went off, shaking the very foundation of the warehouse he was standing in.

O'Reilly even felt it on his end. "What the hell was that?"

Sam didn't answer. He'd already hung up and was down in the tunnel, shouting orders. "Jenkins and Decker—find the radio jammer and make it stop. Dave and Nash—" Crazy and Crazier "—you're with me!"

CHAPTER SIX

Alyssa was hurt. Badly.

As the dust settled around them, Jules had been able to tell with only a glance that her lower leg was broken.

She was tough, though, focusing on him, urgency in her voice. "Jules. Are you all right?"

"Yeah." He was. It seemed impossible, so he checked himself again. He'd hit his head and his ears were ringing from the roar of the explosion, but he was, miraculously, all in one piece—no unwanted piercings of metal or chunks of stone protruding from him.

The man that the Neo-Nazis had left for dead was, indeed, dead on the floor, his head at an unnatural angle, his hair singed, his face burned from the blast.

Alyssa pulled herself into a sitting position. "The bomb?"

And that would be a *second* bomb to which she was referring.

"They set a timer for five minutes," Jules reported as he ran his flashlight over it. "Four minutes and twenty-two seconds now." Dang, but there was a lot of C4 attached to those blasting caps. He looked at the jerry-rigged thing more closely, wishing Jazz Jacquette were here. The XO of SEAL Team Sixteen wasn't just a wizard when it came to blowing things up. He was also an expert in keeping bad things like this one from going *boom.*

"Which way is out?" Alyssa asked, still focused on the run-like-hell part of their plan. It had been a good idea—before complications such as broken legs and blasted-shut passageways had come into play.

Jules gave her the bad news point-blank, shining his flashlight onto the pile of rubble that had once been the way out of this shallow room just off the tunnel. "That way."

"Plan B?" she asked.

"Grab some wires and pull?" he suggested.

She shifted herself closer, which had to have hurt her leg like hell. As Jules watched, she took note of the amount of explosives that the New Reich had left behind.

This was a tad surreal. Yes, there was a timer on the bomb, as Jules had expected. But he hadn't considered the fact that if the NR was aiming to frame an Iranian group, to make it look as if said group adhered to fundamentalist crazy-ass thinking, then they would have to leave a "suicide bomber" behind.

A man that the NR leader addressed as Heinrich was that unlucky soul. One minute he'd been laughing and joking with the others as they'd set their bomb in place. The next, he'd been elbowed in the nose and kneed in the balls, and left retching and bleeding on the tunnel floor as his esteemed leader had placed a second, smaller bomb and run away. The det-cord on *that* piece of work had given the NR mere moments of lead time to run, but the amount of C4 had been far less. Still, the bomb had gone off with an earthshaking boom, caving in part of the tunnel, and effectively trapping them all here.

Not that the New Reich had known Jules and Alyssa were in here. No, their intention had been to trap old dead Heinrich. They'd probably already planted a Koran and a pledge to al-Qaeda in his apartment, for the authorities to find.

"Don't pull that wire," Alyssa warned Jules now. "Look—it's booby trapped. If you pull it . . ."

"I won't," Jules said.

But shit. They had only three minutes and fifty-seven seconds.

"Okay," he said, as the sound of machine-gun fire penetrated their enforced seclusion, as beside him, Alyssa tensed. "Here's what we're going to do . . ."

CHAPTER SEVEN

The firefight was over before it started.

The enemy, whoever they were with their fucking swastika tattoos, couldn't shoot for shit. Three were dead, and one was on his stomach, hands on his head in surrender, shitting his pants and crying like a baby.

"Take him to the surface," Sam ordered Dave, because he didn't quite trust that crazy Jimmy Nash and his K-bar would get the son-of-a-bitch up there alive.

Besides, Jim was already shouting for his freckle-faced fiancée. Damn. That was a match Sam didn't really understand. It was like Little Mary Sunshine hooking up with Count Dracula. "Tess!"

The sound of machine-gun fire echoed from a distant tunnel—Sam could only hope it was Jenkins and Decker taking out whoever was jamming their radio frequencies.

"Jim!" That was Tess, shouting back. "I'm all right!"

Sam shouted now, too. So much for needing the radio . . . "Is Alyssa with you?"

"No!"

"Alyssa and Jules were going to try to defuse the bomb." *Jesus.* Lindsey Jenkins—Mark's wife—was suddenly right there, in front of him, concern in her brown eyes. She was scary good at that ninja shit. "The second bomb," she clarified.

Oh, good. There were *two* bombs . . . ?

"So they hid near where they planted the box. Down this way," she told him, and he followed her farther into the tunnel, Nash on his heels. She glanced at them over her shoulder. "The second bomb's significantly bigger. I saw it as the tangos were carrying it in. It has a five-minute timer." She looked at her watch. "A minute thirty-two left, and counting. Alyssa and Jules are trapped in with it."

Once again, Sam kicked it up into a full-speed run. It didn't take long for them to reach the spot. A haze of dust was still in the air from the recent blast. Debris filled the passageway, keeping Alyssa and Jules from getting free, keeping Sam from his wife.

"Get back," he ordered as he shone his flashlight on the walls and ceiling. Structurally, the tunnel still seemed sound. But if there was a second bomb, even bigger . . .

"Fifty-seven seconds," Lindsey announced as no one obeyed Sam. They all got to work and helped him dig—Nash and Lindsey and Tess and Sophia and Jenk and Decker—heaving the bigger stones and chunks of brick out of his way, using their bare hands to scoop away any loose dirt.

As Lindsey kept her countdown going, Sam felt sick because he knew he wasn't going to make it, he wasn't going to break through in time . . .

"Ten seconds," Lindsey said, and he just kept digging. "Six . . . Five . . ."

Nash and Decker each took one of his arms and hustled him back to a safe distance, with the others. No . . .

"Three," Lindsey said. "Two . . ."

"Please God, let Lindsey be wrong," Sophia breathed the words they all were thinking.

"One," Lindsey said.

Silence. And more silence.

Sam kept his eyes shut, not daring to hope . . .

Boom.

The blast was far noisier than it felt. It didn't shake the ground or even rain dust and dirt on their heads. Of course, they weren't trapped in a small area with it. His wife and best friend could well have just been turned into grease smears on the tunnel floor.

"Help me," Sam said, his voice rough, as he again started to dig.

No one said a word. They just silently got to work. Dave was back by then, too, and he joined in. *Please God, please God, please God, please God* . . .

"I think I'm through," Jenkins said, and sure enough, there was a small hole.

"Alyssa!" Sam shouted through it. He could smell smoke and . . . see light? There was light on the other side, and it wasn't fire from the blast.

"Sam!" That was Jules's voice. "Are you all right?"

Was *he* all right? "Yeah, is Alyssa with you?" Sam reached his hand through the hole, which was crazy—he should have been using it to keep digging. But, God, he just wanted contact.

"She's here," Jules told him—words that made him sag with relief. "She's hurt, but she's gonna be all right . . ."

CHAPTER EIGHT

"Thank God . . ."

Jules closed his eyes as he clasped Sam's hand through the hole in the rubble. Thank God, indeed.

"How badly hurt?" Sam asked.

"Her leg's broken," Jules told him, "just above the ankle. I don't want to move her. She's back aways, along the far wall. It's pretty smoky in here—we could both use some water . . ."

"Someone get me water," Sam shouted from his side of the rubble.

"She's very happy to hear your voice," Jules told his friend. "We both are. Did you get 'em all? It was the New Reich, Starrett. There were at least ten of them—that we knew about. You need to be careful—they're armed with—"

"We got 'em all," Sam assured him. "How badly is Lys's leg broken?"

"She'll need a team of medics—a stretcher to get her out," Jules told the former SEAL.

"I will not," she shouted from across the dusty little room.

Sam laughed. "We'll see about that."

"I can hear you."

"I love you," Sam called to her. That shut her up.

"Any other casualties on our side?" Jules asked, bracing himself for bad news.

"Nothing serious," Sam said the words both he and Alyssa were hoping to hear. "Jimmy Nash got what some folks might call cut, but what he calls a ding—a knife slice in the fleshy part of his arm. But everyone else is okay. Tess is going to bring Jim to the surface to meet the ambulances after we dig you out. Other than that . . . We've got guards posted, reinforcements and medics both on their way."

"There's a shitload of explosives in here," Jules told him. "We couldn't keep the bomb from going off, but we removed as much of the C4 from the timer as we could." C4 was like putty—he and Alyssa had pretty much pulled the bomb apart, then put the part with the timer and the blasting caps as far away from them and the rest of the C4 as they possibly could. It had gone off with a percussive bang, but had done little damage.

"I've got some under my fingernails. I'm going to set off all kinds of alarms when I try to fly home."

Sam laughed. "We'll get you a special Navy SEAL manicure, but first let's get you out of here," he said. "Move back and just . . . sit tight."

"Thanks, SpongeBob," Jules told his friend.

"Thank *you,* for staying with Alyssa," Sam said quietly.

"Like I'd leave her," Jules scoffed.

"My point exactly," Sam said. "You're a good friend."

And okay. Jules had to clear his throat repeatedly as he returned to Alyssa. And it wasn't just from the dust and smoke that still hung in the air.

She was actually crying, which she rarely ever did, tears making streaks down her face.

"Hurts, huh?" Jules sat down next to her and gave her his hand to hold. Now that dying was off the table, he knew she was starting to feel as if she had a broken leg.

She took his hand. Yow. She had some grip there.

"Actually," she told him, "I'm feeling really good." Jules nodded.

"You know what I want?" he said, answering the question that she'd asked just moments before the second bomb had gone off. "I want what you have with Sam. I want someone who won't freak out when I have a night like tonight. I want trust and respect and . . . I want someone who'll say *I love you* in front of a crowd of co-workers and friends."

She wiped her face as she laughed. "Yeah, that's pretty nice to hear, huh?"

"Yes, it is," Jules said. "I want to meet someone," he continued, "and not think . . . *maybe.* I want to meet him, I want to look into his eyes, and think, *Yes.* I don't want to have to wonder. I want to know, right away, that he's the one."

Alyssa was silent. "Unfortunately, sweetie, life's not a Disney cartoon," she finally said.

Jules laughed. "No shit, Cinderella."

She looked at him. "You know, when I first met Sam . . . Jules, sometimes you meet someone, and you think, *Please God, not him*."

She laughed, but Jules was silent. He knew, too well, what *that* was like . . .

"And then," Alyssa continued, "you go from *no*, to *maybe* . . . And then, eventually to *yes*. After, you know, you force yourself to admit that you might've been wrong about him."

"What if you're not wrong?" Jules asked her quietly. "What if you know that he can crush your heart and . . . destroy you?"

She brought his hand to her mouth and kissed him. She knew full well that he wasn't talking about Ben. He was talking about Robin—the one man he'd been unable to forget.

Jesus, it had been years since Jules had so much as *seen* Robin, and he was still thinking, *Please God, not him* . . .

"Then you settle for the *maybe* that you've got right now," Alyssa told him gently. "Ben may not be able to tell you that he loves you, not in front of his Marines, but . . . that *could* change. The same way that the *maybe* you're feeling could change to a full-throttle *yes*. And if it doesn't . . . Well, at least you tried, right?"

"Tried what?" Sam appeared in front of them—having dug his way through the rubble, probably by chewing it into molecules with his teeth. He was covered with dust, and was sweaty as hell, but he kissed Alyssa on the mouth. "What are we talking about?" he asked as he handed each of them a bottle of water, then turned his full attention to Alyssa's broken leg. He didn't cut her pants leg open, probably because he could see it was holding the broken bone in place.

Jules knew right then that Sam was eager to get Alyssa out of there—he didn't want to wait for the medics to arrive.

"I was just telling Lys that I'm going to sign up for one of those ex-gay camps and then steal her away from you," Jules told him.

Sam looked up at him askance. "That shit doesn't work."

"I know. I'm kidding," Jules said. He looked at Alyssa. "Sam loses his sense of humor when you almost die."

"Besides, Squidward," Sam spoke over him as he gently lifted Alyssa into his arms, careful not to jar her injury, "we like you just the way you are."

"Told you I wasn't leaving here on a stretcher," Alyssa said as her husband carefully carried her out.

Leaving Jules alone with his doubts—his unsatisfactory *maybe*s.

And wasn't that the way the story always ended? He was like that guy in that old song—alone again, naturally.

But then Sam gave a shout from out in the tunnel. "Cassidy. Move your ass. We're waiting on you." In the romance department, Jules's life may have been a *maybe,* but as far as his friends went, Jules had himself a rock-solid *yes.*

"I'm right behind you, SpongeBob," Jules shouted back, then followed his two best friends out of the tunnel and up into the clean, crisp, star- and promise-filled night.

Maybe he could live for a while with *maybe.*

At the very least, it *was* worth a try.

Conversation with Navy SEALs Mark "Jenk" Jenkins, Dan Gillman, Jay Lopez, and Irving "Izzy" Zanella

2006
This story is set shortly after Into the Storm.

IZZY: (coming into the room) Was *too.*

GILLMAN: (following him, along with Jenk and Lopez) Was *not.*

IZZY: Was *too.*

GILLMAN: Was *not.*

JENK: Guys. Knock it off. Seriously. Don't piss Suz off. She'll be in here any second.

IZZY: I'm not afraid of her. She's just a writer.

LOPEZ: (exchanging a look with Jenk) *Just* a writer. She's *our* writer.

IZZY: Dude, I make her laugh. She likes me.

LOPEZ: Look, if you want my advice, don't do anything to catch her attention. I mean, yes, it worked out well for Jenkins. He got his happy ending in this latest book, but . . .

JENK: What if she decides you're the next Sam Starrett?

LOPEZ: Five, count 'em, five books of torment. You definitely don't want that. So just do what I do. Don't say too much. Just hang in the background, steady and reliable. (Puts his fingers to his lips) Shhhh.

GILLMAN: But on the flip side, what does that get

you? You're, like, number twenty on her list of heroes for upcoming books.

JENK: Here's how you know you're gonna be the hero of her next book. Ready for this?

(They nod.)

JENK: You stop having sex.

GILLMAN: (laughing) What? No way.

JENK: Yeah. No more flings, no more two-weekers, and *definitely* no one-nighters. You gotta earn the right to find your soulmate, and the first thing that vanishes is the urge to tomcat. It's kind of weird actually.

IZZY: So, in other words, you meet some gorgeous woman at a bar and she lets you know she's available, and you end up going home early and watching *American Idol* on TV, alone in your apartment?

JENK: Pretty much.

GILLMAN: God, you scared me for a minute there. I thought you meant that you stop having sex entirely. Like forever. I mean, I thought that was the point of being the hero in a romance novel. You meet this woman who's perfect for you and then you have a lot of sex and get married at the end.

JENK: Yeah, except for the internal conflict, which is a total pain in the ass. And except for the part where you don't really have a lot of sex. You have *great* sex, but it can't really be defined as a lot until the book ends. I mean, these are romantic suspenses—there's a lot of plot.

LOPEZ: Like I said. Shhhh. I'm dating someone right now that Suz doesn't even know about. I want to keep it that way. It's a comfortable arrangement, no crises, no conflict. Much better than getting caught up in a five-book story arc like Starrett was.

IZZY: (uneasy) So how do you know if Suz is planning

to toss you into one of those story arcs? I mean, shit. We were all major characters in *Into the Storm*.

GILLMAN: Obviously, Jenk's safe. But damn, I could be in serious trouble. I've got a major crush on Sophia Ghaffari.

IZZY: (scoffing) Yeah, like you're going to be the hero of *her* book. Two words. Dream on, fool.

GILLMAN: Two words—

JENK: Guys. Stop.

LOPEZ: I know I'm not the hero of the next book because Minnie's cooking dinner for me right now.

IZZY: Minnie?

LOPEZ: Shhh. I shouldn't have said her name. Bad karma.

GILLMAN: Someone light a match.

IZZY: (to Lopez) You're actually dating a woman named *Minnie*?

JENK: (to Gillman) He didn't fart, he just said her name.

GILLMAN: I thought it might help.

LOPEZ: Make fun of me all you want, Zanella. You just wish you were getting some of her manicotti tonight.

GILLMAN: (cracking up) I've heard it called a lot of things . . .

IZZY: Back on topic. This story arc thing . . .

JENK: I think you're in trouble if you appear in a book, and you're not the hero, but you're something that Suz calls a point of view character.

IZZY: What the fuck is that?

LOPEZ: It's like Sam Starrett in *The Defiant Hero* and *Over the Edge*. Part of the story is told from his point of view, like he's describing what's happening in those particular scenes.

JENK: Only he's not the hero of those books, like I was in *Into the Storm*.

GILLMAN: I think I'm safe.

LOPEZ: Me too.

(They look at Izzy.)

IZZY: I'm totally fucked. In the really not good way.

SUZ: (entering the room) Hey, guys. Thanks for dropping by today. I'm sorry to do this to you, but I really only have about two minutes. I'm doing an online chat, and I've got to run, but—

IZZY: Am I your next Sam Starrett?

SUZ: Well, Izzy, you know there's really only *one* Sam Starrett, so—

IZZY: You know what I mean. Am I in one of those story arc things? Five books of torment . . . ?

SUZ: Let's just say that I have plans for *all* of you. I don't want to make you any promises, because it could turn out to be seven books of torment and then you'll be mad at me. Madder. (to Lopez) Hey, Jay, how's Minnie? I heard she just got a terrific job offer in New York City.

LOPEZ: Ah, crap.

SUZ: Oh, come on. Don't you want excitement and passion? Don't you want to fall in love with that one person that you absolutely can't live without?

LOPEZ: I kind of liked manicotti and clean laundry.

SUZ: Don't be a baby. Learn to cook and buy a washer and dryer. (to Jenk) Are you happy? Tell them how happy you are.

JENK: I am almost insanely happy.

SUZ: (to the others) See? I gotta run. Later, guys. Thanks again for stopping by.

IZZY: (calling after her) But Jenk didn't have five books of . . . (to Jenk, because she's gone) What does five books translate to, time-wise?

JENK: Two, three years. But I'm pretty sure she was looking right at you when she said it was going to be seven books of torment.

GILLMAN: (to Izzy) Dude, you're screwed.

IZZY: Well . . . you are, too.

GILLMAN: No, I'm not.

IZZY: Yeah, you are.

GILLMAN: Not like you.

JENK: Guys. Stop. (He closes the door tightly behind them.)

INTERVIEW WITH KENNY AND SAVANNAH

Early 2006
This takes place shortly after Into the Storm.

"So what's been going on in your lives?" I asked, as we all sat down in my office.

Navy SEAL Chief Ken Karmody was dressed for work, which today meant desert-print cammie BDUs. He was going to spend the afternoon crawling around in the San Borrego desert, trying out some new gear.

"You want to tell her?" Savannah asked him.

"Tell me what?" I looked from one to the other.

Savannah was wearing a T-shirt and jeans, sneakers on her feet. It didn't surprise me—she'd been dressing far more casually since she'd met and married Ken. Her blond hair was cut short and it wisped around her face. She looked far more like a college student than a high-powered attorney.

"Van had a little bit of a meltdown the other day," Ken admitted.

I looked to her for confirmation, and she nodded, wincing slightly, embarrassment on her pretty face. "It was more like a big meltdown."

"No, it wasn't," her husband scoffed. "Believe me, from someone who's had big meltdowns a time or two—yours was very small."

"A time or two," I repeated. "More like ten."

He laughed because he knew what I was thinking. No doubt he, too, was remembering the night he drove his car onto his ex-girlfriend's lawn, music blaring from his stereo speakers, drunk out of his mind, hoping she'd take him back. Fortunately for him, she hadn't, leaving him solidly single when Savannah came along.

"They all happened years ago," Savannah pointed out.

But there had been a more recent incident—back when Ken was living in San Diego, and Savannah was still living in New York. They'd met in the middle, in Dallas or Denver, as often as they could, but spent far too many weeks apart.

It was hard for both of them—newly married, living on different coasts. Especially since Ken frequently went overseas with SEAL Team Sixteen. Days off for either of them were few and far between.

"Remember that time," Ken told Savannah, "that you came to San Diego to surprise me, only I went to New York to surprise you?"

Savannah laughed. "Like I'm ever going to forget?" Shaking her head, she turned to me. "I walked into our house in San Diego at about three A.M. The place was quiet, it was obvious Ken was asleep, so I didn't turn on the lights. It was a surprise—my being there. I was supposed to be in New York at some legal thing, a conference that was canceled. So I went into the bedroom, got undressed, climbed into bed and—" She cracked up.

"I had given my keys to Sam and his wife, Alyssa," Ken said, far less amused. "They were painting their house, and the fumes were intense, so . . . I figured since Van and I weren't going to be there, they could sleep at our place. Meanwhile, I was in New York, wondering where my wife was at three o'clock in the morning."

"Having a ménage à trois with your best friend and his wife." Savannah laughed. "The look on Sam's face when he turned on the light . . . And Alyssa . . . !" She howled. "She got a little mad at Sam because she thought he was enjoying himself too much."

"Yeah, I bet he was." Ken was pretending to be disgruntled, but he clearly thought it was funny, too.

"It was so embarrassing." Savannah covered her face with her hands. "And can you imagine being Sam, and waking up with some strange woman pawing at you?"

"You don't paw," Kenny said.

"Yeah, well . . ." Mischief danced in her eyes. "I now know Sam Starrett a little too well."

"Imagine if you'd climbed into Alyssa's side of the bed," Ken said. He grinned, and did a pretty horrendous Groucho Marx imitation. "I've actually spent quite a lot of time imagining that."

Savannah kicked his boot with her sneaker. "That's awful. I probably would've thought you were cheating on me. I mean, when I grabbed Sam, I knew right away that he wasn't you. But if I'd climbed into bed and found a woman there . . . I would've had a heart attack. I would've died of shock. Instantly." She looked at me. "Ken would never be unfaithful. There are few things I'm certain of in life, but that's one of them."

Ken took her hand, bringing it to his lips. "Thanks, babe," he said, his eyes soft.

She smiled at him, and for a moment, I wasn't even there in the room.

But I cleared my throat and brought them back on track. "We were talking about Ken's meltdown."

"Okay," he said. "So Van's having her comedy of errors in San Diego. Meanwhile, I'm in her less-crowded apartment in Manhattan, with an armload of flowers." He shook his head. "I knew immediately what had happened. I saw some memo about the conference being canceled. I saw her notes about her flight to San Diego. And I just lost it. I just . . . sat down on the floor and, well, I cried."

This was clearly the first time Savannah had heard this. Her eyes were wide. "Oh, Kenny."

"I missed you so much," he admitted. "It was killing me, not seeing you."

"That was the same weekend you started talking about moving to New York," she realized. She turned to me. "I couldn't believe he was serious. Leave the SEALs? I went home and started packing. I couldn't let him do that. I couldn't."

"She actually talked the partners in her firm into opening a San Diego branch," Ken told me. "The woman has balls."

"But now I've gone and quit," Savannah said. She turned a little pale. "Oh, my God, I've actually quit."

"She's running for office," Ken announced. "For Congress."

"We haven't decided that yet," she warned him.

He was unperturbed. "Yeah, we have. You want to run, you're running. You're sick of sitting around, watching civil rights erode. What am I fighting for, you know? It drives her nuts, so she's running."

"I have some clients who are Arab Americans," Savannah explained. "These are good people, but they happen to have the same name as someone on the terrorist watch list. Turns out my phones have been tapped. My office was searched."

"She actually stood on a table in a restaurant," Ken said admiringly, "and gave her first campaign speech."

"I had my meltdown at the Café Bistro," she admitted to me.

"You got a standing O," her husband said.

"I kind of did," she told me, as if she still couldn't quite believe it.

"She's running. And she's going to win." Ken stood up. "We've got to go, babe. I don't want to be late."

"Thanks for stopping by," I told them, standing too, and giving them both a hug and kiss.

Savannah gave me an extra squeeze. "Thank you so much for writing Kenny into my life," she whispered.

I just smiled and waved goodbye. I was having too much fun picturing Ken Karmody as first husband of U.S. President Savannah von Hopf.

Now *there* was a story that would be fun to write . . .

Home Is Where the Heart Is

PART I

Spring 2008
This story takes place several months after
All Through the Night, *and several months before*
Into the Fire.

Chapter One

It was surreal, being home.

Of course, this apartment wasn't really home. It was kind of half-home, but half-not, which added to the weirdness.

When Arlene Schroeder's reserve unit had gotten called up, she'd given some of her furniture to her brother, Will, but had put most of it into storage, into a self-service garage-sized room.

For twelve dollars a month—special military rate, set up by a friend of a friend—the antique desk and bed-frame her grandmother bequeathed her, her dresser and formal dining room set, all of her books and clothes, and her precious box with Maggie's baby shoes would be safe and dry and waiting for her, upon her return from Iraq.

Over the long months—two separate tours—that

she'd been gone, she'd frequently wished she'd been able to put her now-thirteen-year-old daughter into similar storage. Instead, Mags had moved in with Will.

Instead, she'd kept growing and had gotten even taller than Arlene, beginning the permanent transformation from sweet-faced child to this remarkably self-reliant, beautiful young woman who now stood in the kitchen of Will's shabby Newton apartment, cutting vegetables for some kind of exotic, Indian-spiced dish that she was cooking for dinner.

Arlene's baby girl was cooking dinner.

She wasn't just cooking dinner, she was cooking dinner while wearing a bra.

As Arlene watched, Maggie added the vegetables to what looked like some kind of dangerously delicious stewing chicken, and put the cover securely on the pot. "In an hour, when the dinger dings," her daughter commanded, "turn on this burner over here. When the water boils, add the rice, lower the heat and—"

"I know—" How to cook rice. Arlene bit back the words that were coming out of her mouth much too sharply. It wasn't Maggie's fault that she felt like an outsider here, like a stranger in a strange land.

"It's basmati," Maggie told her as if that meant something special. "It only needs to simmer for fifteen, sixteen minutes, okay?"

She was so excited that Arlene was home, so excited to be showing off her cooking skills—skills she'd needed to develop because her mother had been sent to serve for much longer than they'd all expected, way over on the other side of the world. She was showing off the skills she'd learned from Will's latest girlfriend, who no doubt had also taken Maggie bra shopping.

Will's latest girlfriend with the ridiculous name— Dolphina—who was petite and perfect, like some Bollywood movie star with her long, shimmering, straight dark hair, her perfect, freckle-free skin, and her big, brown Bambi eyes.

Every other word out of Maggie's mouth was *Dolphina*. Dolphina said this and Dolphina said that and, God, Arlene was beyond grateful that Maggie was happy and healthy and that she clearly felt loved and supported, particularly while her mother was stuck in a place where death by mortar fire was common and unpredictable, but *enough* already.

"Go to your rehearsal," Arlene quietly told her daughter now. "I got the rice—I'll make us a salad, too."

Maggie hugged her, giving her a noogie atop her head—the way Arlene used to do to her. "Little Mommy," she teased.

"Go," Arlene ordered in her best military sergeant, afraid Mags would see the sudden rush of tears to her eyes. She didn't want her daughter to be taller than she was. She wanted her monkey-girl back, but that Maggie was gone forever—the anxious little girl she'd left behind when she boarded that first troop transport all those endless months ago. Arlene had done her duty and gone to Iraq—and she'd lost those last precious few moments of Maggie's too short childhood. She'd sacrificed those last few chances spent with her daughter curled up, gangly arms and legs and all, on her lap. A lap which now felt achingly empty.

"I'll call if I'm going to be late." Maggie grabbed her bookbag and her jacket and bounded out the apartment door.

Leaving Arlene alone for the first time since Maggie and Will had met her plane at Logan, yesterday morning.

Will and the perfect Dolphina were having dinner out tonight. That had been Dolphina's idea—arranged to give Maggie some alone time with her mom. Yeah, didn't it figure? The betch was as nice as she was beautiful and smart.

She also had the extremely glamorous job of personal assistant to a movie star. Well, TV star now. Actor Robin Chadwick Cassidy and his FBI agent husband Jules lived in a chichi part of Boston. Maggie and Will both had visited them at their town house. Many times.

Arlene paced Will's little living room, pretending to look at the photos and artwork on her older brother's walls, but in truth restless—and not quite sure what to do with herself. In Iraq, she was either working or sleeping. Mostly working. If she ever found herself with two full hours on her hands, she'd immediately retreat to her quarters and fall unconscious on her bunk.

After first hitting the computer tent, waiting on line to connect to the Internet, to send her daily, cheerful "everything's all right" email to Maggie and Will. Even if—as was so often the case—she wasn't feeling cheerful or as if anything there in the sandbox was good or right.

She circled the room one more time before deciding to go out for a walk—something she'd never been able to do in besieged Baghdad—when the doorbell buzzed.

She glanced through the door's peephole, certain it was one of the neighbors, or maybe the FedEx delivery person. Will was writing a book, collaborating with a former special forces soldier who lived in Florida, who preferred working with hard copies. As a result, Will now knew all of the various delivery people by their first names.

But the man standing in the hall wasn't wearing a delivery uniform. And he certainly wasn't old Mrs. D'Oretti from next door.

It was Jack Lloyd—but it was a Jack Lloyd the likes of which Arlene hadn't seen very often.

Instead of his usual sneakers and jeans, shabby

button-down shirt, sleeves rolled up, tie loose around his neck, this alternate-universe Jack Lloyd was wearing a suit.

A very nice suit that fit his tall, lean frame very, very well.

Last time she'd seen the man in a suit had been that night that . . .

Arlene opened the door. "Will's not here," she said in lieu of proper greeting. *Hey, Jack, how are you? It's been a long time. Two years, three months, and nineteen days, in fact. You never did return my phone call—and I really was only calling to find out if you'd found my favorite pair of panties in the mess we'd made of your bedroom, that night you rocked my world three different times.*

"Yeah, I know," Jack said, in his familiar whiskey-flavored voice. "I'm not here to see Will."

She'd always thought that that was stupid—voices couldn't have flavors. But then she'd met Jack.

"I'm kinda here to see you," he told her, actually physically bracing himself—as if he expected her to slam the door in his face.

Or maybe it was his eyes that reminded her of whiskey—an intoxicating swirl of brown and gold, in a face that wasn't exactly handsome, yet still managed to make women swoon in the street as he passed by. It was his smile. Boyish. Mischievous. Warm. Inclusive. When Jack Lloyd smiled, even the wary way he was smiling now, it made people feel as if he were sharing a private joke, only with them.

And yes, she *was* standing there, transfixed, like some hapless rodent mesmerized by a king cobra.

She found her voice, which, if it had a flavor, would no doubt be something stupid, like mustard. The bland yellow kind. Not the spicy brown stuff that you got in a good New York–style deli.

"It's really not a good time," Arlene told him, even as he pushed past her and walked into the apartment. Which was when her famous redhead's temper flared. "I have *nothing* to say to you, Jack. And there's absolutely nothing that you could say to me that would—"

"Maggie emailed me, about a month ago," Jack told her, which worked to shut her up. *Maggie* emailed him? "She said you were coming home, but only for a short time—that you were going to have to go back almost immediately. What's up with that?"

Arlene struggled to make sense of his words. Maggie *emailed* him? His smile was gone, and his eyes were void of amusement—this wasn't some big funny that he was trying to pull on her, the way he and Will used to do, back when they were in college and she was barely older than Maggie was now. She focused on his question, and tried to explain. "It's a new program. We get to come home for a relatively brief visit, with the understanding that we'll have significantly longer than the usual six months between our next tours. People were running into trouble in terms of finding short-term employment, knowing they were going to redeploy, so . . ." She shook her head. "Why did Maggie email you?"

"She doesn't want you going back to Iraq," Jack informed her—as if Arlene didn't know that. "And she's a pretty smart kid. She figured out a way that you won't have to."

Oh, Maggie. She shook her head. "There's no way that—"

Jack cut her off. "Yeah, actually, Leen, there is. I did some research, and Maggie's right. Regulation 635-200. You won't go back. In fact, you can get out for good." He cleared his throat. "If you're pregnant."

And there they stood, in Will's living room—Arlene stunned into silence, Jack waiting, patiently, for her to regain use of her vocal cords.

Pregnant?

"Oh, God," Arlene said. "Please tell me that Maggie didn't—"

"Yep. She did." He smiled, but it was tight. "It was one hell of an email. Thank God I was sitting down at the time."

She knew the feeling. Her world had tilted, and she now fumbled for a seat. "I'm so sorry. Oh, my God, she is so dead."

Jack sat on the other end of the sofa—her sofa that had once filled the tiny Cambridge apartment that she'd shared with a much shorter Maggie. He sank back into the soft cushions, yet still managed to look too big to fit there comfortably. "Give her a break, Leen. She doesn't want you coming home in a box."

"How did she . . . ?"

It didn't make sense. Maggie had never known about the night—singular—that Arlene had spent with Jack. It had happened while the girl was visiting her grandparents. And God knows Arlene had never spoken of it to anyone, never so much as whispered Jack's name in Maggie's presence.

But her brother and Jack were close—although no longer as close as they'd been as roommates at Boston University. They both currently worked as reporters for the *Boston Globe,* so it made sense that Maggie would've met Jack at *some* point, but still . . .

"I met Maggie at the wedding," Jack explained. "Robin and Jules. Last December? I told her I knew you, and . . ." He shrugged. "I kinda let slip the fact that you and I had, um, a thing."

"A thing," Arlene repeated.

"Yeah," Jack admitted, making an *oops* face. "And I also may have said something about, you know, about my, well, kinda still having a thing. You know. For you."

CHAPTER TWO

Jack was totally screwing this up. Considering he was an award-winning journalist, he'd just delivered the lamest, vaguest declaration of love in the entire history of the world.

And he could see from the disbelief in Arlene's eyes that she was seconds from losing it and kicking his well-dressed ass out the door.

"You *told* my *daughter*—"

"That I haven't been able to stop thinking about you," he finished for her, afraid to be more precise in defining exactly what he was feeling and had felt for going on over a decade now, because it was clear that Arlene wasn't going to fall into his open arms in the immediate future. He'd had that chance, two years ago, and had completely blown it back then. "Yes. We were talking and . . . I wanted to know how you were."

"I'm fine, thanks," she shot back, "although still missing my favorite pair of underpants."

And there it was—the moment of truth. "Okay," Jack said, trying to sound matter-of-fact and calm. "Good. Let's put everything out on the table. Let's talk about that night. I want to tell you about what happened to me the day after."

She shook her head vehemently. "Let's not. Let's stay on topic and . . ." He could practically see the wheels turning in her head. "Will told me he saved your life," she said. "Last November. That you were in Afghanistan and—"

"He's got nothing to do with this." Jack knew where she was going. She assumed Will was the mastermind of this crazy plot. Truth was, he hadn't even mentioned it to Will. Probably because Will would have shut it down, fast, and Jack had had this completely insane spark of hope that Arlene would welcome the chance to stay home—after getting over the initial shock that her daughter had approached Jack for stud services. "This was all Maggie's idea."

Arlene wasn't convinced. "Why are you dressed up?" she asked suspiciously.

He looked down at his wool-covered legs, at the bright silk of his tie. "I wanted to, I don't know." He shrugged. "Look nice?"

"So that I'd have sex with you," she concluded. Good old point-blank Arlene. Why couldn't he be attracted to the shy, reserved type? "You wore it because you were wearing a suit that night."

He had been. That night.

He'd just won an award for a newspaper story he'd written on the health-care crisis. He'd been giddy, not just from the award, but because he was being recognized for writing about something that mattered.

After the award dinner, purely by chance, he'd run into Arlene downtown, near Copley Square, getting out of work from what she said was a temporary second job, filling in for a waitress friend at a local restaurant. *She'd* been wearing jeans and a clingy tank top, sandals on her feet, her red curls loose around her shoulders, her smile filled with sunlight and . . .

But Jack couldn't for the life of him remember the underwear she'd had on that incredible night. Black or purple. He'd have thought the color would have been permanently burned into his brain. Black—or purple—against the paleness of her smooth, perfect skin, as she'd tumbled back with him, onto his bed.

As he'd done what he'd been dying to do for years and years and *years*—to bury himself inside of her, to see her beautiful hair spilled across his pillows, to know that the smile that sparkled in her eyes was just for him.

Her eyes weren't sparkling now. In fact, they were narrowed. She was looking pretty grim. And tired.

Haunted, no doubt, from all she'd done and seen over the past long months, living in a war zone.

And Jack knew that if he had any chance at all here, it would come because he told her the truth, so he said, "Yeah. I wore the suit because you told me that night that I looked good in a suit, that it made you want to, you know, take *off* my suit and—"

"I remember what I said," she cut him off, then swore, because her redhead's complexion made it impossible for her to hide a blush. Yeah, she not only remembered what she'd said, she obviously remembered what they'd done after she'd said it.

Jack remembered, too. Vividly. In glorious Technicolor. Except for the color-of-her-panties part.

"I didn't call you back," he told her quietly, "because Becca threatened to kill herself. I made a really bad mistake, a few nights before you and I hooked up. She came over to my place, and . . . I thought it was . . . you know, once more for old times' sake? It was stupid. *I* was stupid—I'll be the first to admit that. I should have known better. But then when she . . ." It had been a nightmare—his ex-wife's phone calls, her threats, his fear that she just might be crazy enough to do it. His twisted reasoning that she truly must've still loved him . . . "She's the mother of my kids, Leen. I thought I needed to give it one more shot—regardless of what I really wanted. Which absolutely was you."

She didn't believe him. He could tell from the way she was nodding. "You could have written a note. Sent my panties back."

Crap. "Would you believe me if I told you I wanted to keep them?"

She laughed in his face. "For Becca to find? No."

"Yeah, that would've been bad," he admitted. "But I did. Want to keep them. That's not why I didn't send them to you, though. It's actually . . ." He just had to say it. "See, I, um, found *two* on my floor. Black and purple. I didn't know which was—"

"That," Arlene interrupted him, standing up and crossing toward the door, "I believe."

Jack stayed in his seat, determined that she hear him out. "The others were Becca's, and . . . I swear, Arlene, that night? I was certain my marriage was over and done. We'd been separated for six *months*. I spoke to a lawyer earlier that week—"

"Thanks for dropping by."

He tried a new tack. "Maggie says you're home only for a month."

She opened the door. "Perhaps I wasn't clear enough. It's time for you to go."

"You know, if we worked hard at it, I'm pretty sure I could get you pregnant in that timeframe."

"Joke's over, Jack." Arlene was getting seriously pissed.

But he still didn't move. He couldn't. He wouldn't. "I should have called you," he said. "I was wrong, and I regret it. If I could do it over, and do it differently, I would. I would call you and I would explain, and I would . . ." He had to clear his throat. He closed his eyes and he just said it. "I would tell you how much that night meant to me, and how badly I wanted to have other nights, just like it, for the next fifty years."

She shook her head, unrelenting, but then said, "You broke up with Becca a year ago. It never occurred to you to call me then?"

Hope shifted inside of him, just the slightest spark of life inside a miniscule seed, ready, with the least bit of encouragement, to grow. She'd obviously kept track of him. Asked Will for information.

"You were seeing what's-his-name," he pointed out. "Peter. The idiot."

"If you thought he was such an idiot," she countered, hands on her hips, "why not kick down my door and—"

"I thought you were in love with him. Will told me it was serious."

She laughed her surprise, turning it into a scoff. "It wasn't."

"Yeah, well, Will told me it was." Jack was unable to hide his frustration. "He told me you were happy and I . . ." He held her gaze, imploring her to believe him. "I wanted you to be happy, Leen, so I stayed away."

That shut her up. In fact, she shut the open door, too, coming back to stand in the middle of the living room. But now her arms were folded across her chest—he was far from winning.

"So when you found out that Peter was a thing of the past," she finally said, "you immediately emailed me . . . ? Except, wait, you didn't."

"I found out that Peter was a thing of the past," he told her, a touch testily himself, "when Maggie emailed *me,* asking if I was interested in *knocking* you *up.*" He glanced at his watch. "She's going to call, in about two minutes, to tell you to have dinner without her—that her rehearsal's going to run late."

Arlene was horrified. "You didn't actually tell her that you'd—"

"Yeah, right."

She was apparently unable to process sarcasm right at that moment, so he clarified. "Of course I didn't. But I did tell her I was going to come here and . . ." The ring he'd bought was burning a hole in his inside pocket, but he wasn't supposed to throw the damn thing at her. He was supposed to go heavy on the romance, get down on his knees. No, there was a time and place for everything, and that ring box was staying deep in his pocket. At least for now. "Talk to you," he finished, since she was waiting, impatiently for the end of his sentence.

"Hey, how are you. It's been a while. Let's have sex so I can get you pregnant, because a thirteen-year-old thought that would be a good idea."

Okay. Apparently he was wrong. Arlene was completely capable of dishing out the sarcasm, even if she wasn't able to take it.

"No, actually, my plan was to say, *Hey, how are you? It's been a while. I'm still as crazy about you as I've always been and for the first time in what feels like forever we're both single at the same time, so what do you say we put a new spin on the relationship thing and see if we can't get it to work by getting married—to each other this time.*"

And that had done it—Jack had completely stunned her. He'd managed to stun himself, too, having all but resolved, mere seconds ago, not to mention the M-word.

But now that he had, he might as well go big. He reached into his jacket pocket for the ring box, opened it, and set it on the coffee table, in front of her.

She slowly lowered herself into Will's ugly-ass Barca-Lounger, her eyes huge in her too-thin but still-beautiful face. She didn't say anything, she just stared at him.

And okay. If he were going to be rejected, he might as well make his humiliation complete. He got down on his knees on the carpeting in front of her and took her hand. Her fingers were cold as he interlaced them with his own. "Marry me, Arlene," he whispered.

"That's crazy," she breathed, but she didn't look away. And he knew, just from gazing into her beautiful eyes, that she was still as attracted to him as he was to her. That spark they'd flamed to an inferno on that amazing, unforgettable night was still ready to ignite. "*You're* crazy."

Jack shook his head. "All these years, our timing's been off—"

"And you don't think it's a little off *now?*"

"No," he said. "I think it's perfect."

"In less than four weeks, I'm going back to Iraq."

"Maybe not," he pointed out.

"No," she argued. "I am. I definitely am."

"Arlene—"

"Jack." She was holding tightly to his hands now as if trying to squeeze some sense into him. She was gazing into his eyes, too, to make him understand. "I have to. If I don't go back, they'll send someone else. Someone who hasn't been as well trained, someone who hasn't learned how to keep the kids in my unit safe. And even if that didn't matter to me . . . ? God, I'm not sure I even want to have another baby. And I'm certainly not having one unless I'm married to someone I *know* is going to be there for the next twenty years."

He opened his mouth to speak and she cut him off again. "I'm not going to have a baby just to . . . have a baby. So, nice try. Good attempt. I don't know what Will is blackmailing you with, but you can tell him you did your best."

"Leenie—"

"Shhh." She reached out and brushed his hair back from his face, her fingers cool against his skin. "Let it go, Jack. That night? The sex was great, but . . ." She shook her head. "We'd drive each other nuts."

It was then that the phone rang—Maggie, right on schedule.

Arlene let go of Jack's hands, and pushed herself out of the chair, stepping over him to go into the kitchen. She picked up the phone and didn't even bother to say hello. "You get your butt home, young lady. Right now."

She didn't wait to hear any excuses or counter-arguments. She just hung up the phone with some force.

"You should *definitely* not be here when she gets back," she called to Jack.

CHAPTER THREE

"Huh," Robin said. "That was weird."

As Jules Cassidy inched his way out of the busy air-port parking lot, he glanced at his husband of less than a year, who was staring at his cell phone, his movie-star-perfect brow furrowed in puzzlement.

Robin's hair was jarhead short. Apparently Joe Laughlin, the character—a closeted gay A-list actor—he played on his hit cable-TV series, *Shadowland,* was "starring" in a war movie as an enlisted Marine.

As usual, Robin had been nervous about Jules's reaction to the crew cut, since he'd had it buzzed while Jules was away. But, also as usual, Jules loved it, just as he'd loved every haircut and style—long, short, in-between and a multitude of colors—that Robin had ever had.

His spouse was freakin' gorgeous—*and* a full triple screaming-bejeezus hot. And it had been eons since Jules had kissed the man, let alone . . .

The car in front of him was stopped by the car in front of *them,* and on and on it went, out of Jules's line of sight, and probably all of the way out of Logan and right to the front steps of their South End of Boston home. Still he tried to mind-control the car at the front of this mess, no matter that it was miles away, willing whoever-it-was to put the pedal to the metal.

"I just called Will's, to see if Dolphina was there," Robin was explaining, "and I'm pretty sure Maggie's mother answered."

"Arlene, right?" Jules said, as the solid, endless min-ute they'd been sitting in this exact spot turned to two and began working its way to three. "Does she go by Bristol, or—"

"She's Schroeder, like Will," Robin reported.

Jules nodded. That was what he'd thought. Ted Bris-tol, Maggie's dad, not only lived across the country in

Seattle, but, according to Will, was a textbook functioning alcoholic. Despite being capable of holding a job
and paying his rent, his was not the household that
Arlene had wanted Maggie to live in for a week, let
alone a year.

Years plural, now—because Arlene was being sent
back to Iraq for her third tour. Which made Jules's im-
patience about the traffic seem petty and selfish, but for
the love of God, was he the only one here who was in a
hurry to get home?

"She didn't sound happy," Robin was telling Jules
now—she being Arlene, whom he'd just spoken to on
the phone. "And she didn't wait to find out that I wasn't
Maggie before she *young-ladied* me and ordered my
butt home."

"You better call back." Jules was in four-weeks-and-
three-days of a hurry to get home, to be accurate. Which
was four weeks longer than he'd expected to be gone
when he'd packed his carry-on bag last month.

Yeah, kids. Last *month.*

His meeting in Washington had turned into a meeting
in London, which had morphed into an FBI assignment
in Afghanistan. Which was not the kind of place where
Robin could join him for a long weekend.

Jules had more than half expected Robin to meet him
here at the airport with a limousine and driver. If he
had, this traffic wouldn't matter. They'd be in the back,
with music playing and the privacy shield up.

"I'm getting one of those circuit's-busy signals,"
Robin reported, and then smiled ruefully as he met
Jules's gaze, as he accurately read Jules's mind. "Sorry
about—"

"It's all right." Jules took his life partner's hand, intertwined their fingers. Robin had broken the no-limo
news to him mere seconds after they'd first embraced.

I couldn't get a limo at such short notice, but Jesus, I'm glad you're home.

Jules had laughed at the time, thinking that Robin was just being Robin—the king of immediate gratification. When it came to expressing the physical side of their love, *here and now* was Robin's mission statement, and Jules often found himself being coerced into receiving and/or giving some of that immediate gratification at times he normally would have considered inappropriate.

In the middle of the day, when they were already both late for work.

In the bathroom at a friend's house, during a party.

In the back of a limo.

And okay, *coerced* wasn't really the right word. He'd never needed much convincing. Still, as Robin often pointed out, Jules always had been something of a Yankee in terms of his definition of *inappropriate*.

Had been.

But right now, as they sat and sat and sat in traffic, Jules realized that somewhere over the past year or so, the idea of sex—with his wonderful, fabulous, lovely husband—in the very private back of a limo had become not only entirely appropriate but eagerly anticipated.

"God, babe, I missed you," Robin breathed, as Jules lost himself in the warm ocean-blueness of his eyes.

And even though kissing this man to whom he was legally wed could be dangerous while trapped in a parking lot with lots of other cars and drivers who were also trapped and no doubt angry at the world, Jules leaned forward and caught Robin's mouth with his.

Because, fuck it. They kept a tire iron under the front seat, and Jules and Robin both knew how to use it. Not only that, but there were additional items that could be used as weapons in the back of the car. A military entrenching tool, with a little shovel that unfolded, which was allegedly kept in the car in case they got stuck in snow and ice, but was heavy and could do some serious damage if slammed into an attacker's face. Plus he had his sidearm. Yeah, it was locked in a travel case but he could open it quickly enough and *what* was wrong with this world that he was sitting here, mentally taking inventory of weapons that he might need to defend both Robin and himself, merely for publicly expressing their eternal, committed love?

Jules shut off his internal FBI agent—well, as much of it as he could—and cleared his mind of everything but the softness of Robin's lips, the sweetness of his mouth, the love he could practically taste, and God *damn,* it was good to be home.

Chapter Four

"I mean it, Jack." Arlene came out of the kitchen, temper blazing. "You do *not* want to be here when Maggie gets home."

Jack settled back in the chair she'd recently vacated, ready to argue, but the phone rang again.

Arlene was still holding the cordless handset, and she forcefully clicked it to *talk,* and put it to her ear. "I don't care if your rehearsal's not over yet, you *get* yourself *home.*" She looked surprised, then, as she listened to whoever was on the other end of the phone—it was probably not Maggie, judging from the heightened color along her delicate cheekbones.

She was beautiful, and Jack knew full well that the gorgeous red hair and charming freckles, the big green eyes and gracefully shaped mouth, and the lithe, athletic body were just the outer package. He'd fallen in love with the funny, sharp-witted, often sarcastic, sometimes tough, and always kind girl—and yes, Leenie had been a girl when he'd fallen for her.

And Jack had been an idiot, because he'd run away from her, because along with everything that he found attractive about her, she was also messily emotional, always getting into trouble, too much of a tomboy, too freaking independent, and yet way too vulnerable and shockingly naive.

And instead of waiting for her to grow up, and then kissing the hell out of her and marrying her ass, he'd convinced himself that Becca—cool, aloof, mature, with handbags that always matched her expensive shoes—was the kind of woman he should want.

Should.

But didn't.

Yes, he was an idiot.

"I'm so sorry," Arlene was saying into the phone. "No, Dolphina's not here. She and Will were going to dinner—she was going to meet him downtown at the *Globe* office and . . ." She cleared her throat. "I have to tell you how much I enjoyed *Rip Tide*. And *American Hero*. I think that one's still my favorite. You were amazing."

Okay. That had to be Robin Chadwick Cassidy on the other end of the phone. And now Arlene's cheeks were tinged with color for an entirely different reason, her anger at her daughter momentarily forgotten as she had a fangrrl moment.

And as she continued to speak to the movie star, she smiled, which made her look young and sweet, and Jack's heart lurched in his chest, and he knew—without a doubt—that he was *not* going to leave here without at least a promise that she'd think about giving the two of them a solid try.

"Okay, maybe the ring was too much too soon," Jack

told her as she hung up the phone. "We've got a month. Let's see each other."

"See?" she asked, eyebrows raised. "Or have sex?"

"The two are not mutually exclusive," he pointed out. "Frankly, I'd like very much to take you to dinner every night and then back to my place to—"

"And you seriously think it's just the *ring* that's too much too soon?"

"I'm just saying," Jack confessed. "If I had my way, we'd be on a plane to Vegas tonight and you'd be my wife before I—"

"Stop." She cut him off again.

"I know the attraction's still there," Jack pushed harder. "You can pretend all you want that it's not, but I know, Arlene, so—"

"I'm not denying the attraction. I'm just . . ."

"What?"

"The timing's not right." But now Arlene wouldn't meet his gaze. In fact, she turned away. "I need to call Maggie, and tell her to get home."

"You want to take it slowly," Jack persisted. "We'll take it slowly. Although not too slowly, because you've only got a month and—"

But Arlene had apparently dialed Maggie's cell phone, and she now spoke to the girl. "Get home."

Jack could hear the higher-pitched sound of Maggie's voice, coming through the speaker of the phone. Arlene cut her off. "This isn't a game, Maggie. This is my life. *And* Jack's life. And you had no business . . ." She shook her head. "No. *No*. I'm *not* going to argue with you. You get home and—No, you can't speak to Jack," she exhaled on something that sounded like laughter but was, in fact, disbelief. "Get. Home. *Now*."

She cut the connection, turned back and aimed her fury at Jack. But it was mixed with despair and that was what came out when she spoke. "Please," she begged him. "Please. Just . . . go."

He nodded and got to his feet. "Can I see you tomorrow?" he asked. "See. Not have sex. Although do let me know if you change your mind."

The look she gave him was so black, he immediately backpedaled. "I'll stop with the teasing," he said. "I'm kidding when I say things like that, okay?"

She shook her head, half laughing again, but also rolling her eyes in exasperation. "There's no point in—"

"Spending a pleasant afternoon with a friend," he finished for her. "There's always a point to that. Let's have lunch. We can drive out to Baldwin's Bridge, eat down by the marina."

"Don't you work?" she asked.

"All the time," Jack said. "In fact, I'm writing an article on Governor Patrick's reinstatement of the Massachusetts Film Council. I'll finish it tonight, have tomorrow completely free. Come on. We can walk on the beach, stick our feet in the ocean."

She was wavering. "I don't know. . . ."

"Say yes," he whispered, his hope growing into something real, taking root in his stomach, in his soul. It was that hope that made him reach for her, and he slid his hand into her hair, his palm brushing the smoothness of her cheek, her curls soft between his fingers as he held her there, leaning in to caress her lips with his own in the briefest of kisses.

He wanted, more than anything, to crush her against him, to kiss her the way he'd kissed her that magic night in Copley Square.

But he didn't. He stepped back. He let her go.

"I'll call you later," he said. And he made himself walk out the door.

CHAPTER FIVE

Jack had left that stupid diamond ring behind.

As Arlene stood in Will's living room, waiting for Maggie to come home, she knew she couldn't leave that jeweler's box sitting there, open like that. It would only fuel her daughter's fantasy.

And at the same time, she didn't want to touch it.

She didn't want to get a closer look, and be tempted to do something stupid.

Like try it on.

She picked it up, briskly snapped it shut and was trying to figure out where to stash it when the door buzzer sounded again.

She jammed it into one of the deep recesses of her slouchy, oversized carry-all, then went to the door, hoping that Maggie had again forgotten her keys, but knowing that . . .

Yeah. It was Jack standing out there again. No doubt he'd come back for his ring.

But when she opened the door, he apologized.

"Sorry to . . . I just, uh, I wasn't even down the stairs when Maggie called. She asked me to give you a message—to tell you that she's not coming home, and I told her I wouldn't, that she was going to have to talk to you herself . . . ? But then she texted me and . . ."

He held out his phone.

Maybe mom wont have 2 go back if *I* get pregnant. Tell her ill b back in the morning.

Arlene shifted her horrified gaze from Jack's phone to his worried eyes. "Oh, shit," she said, as he tried calling Maggie back.

He shook his head—she wasn't picking up. "She's not serious," he reassured Arlene. "We'll find her—we should start by calling her friends."

But Arlene shook her head. "I don't . . . Her friends—they're just names to me. I don't have . . ."

"I'll call Will and Dolphina." Jack flipped through his phone's address book. "We're going to find her, Leen. She's just . . . This is a threat—her way of holding her breath till she gets what she wants."

"You don't know her," she said, and as the words left her mouth, her heart clenched because the truth was, Arlene didn't know her own daughter anymore.

"You gonna let me in?" Jack asked, and as she stepped back, opening the door wider, she felt the last of her control slip and she burst into tears.

CHAPTER SIX

Before tonight, Jack had never seen Arlene Schroeder cry. Not like this, with deep, body-shaking sobs, as if her world were coming to an end.

He'd seen her damn near frothing at the mouth with anger. He'd seen her frustrated and humiliated and joyful and proud and giddy with laughter. He'd seen her fight not to cry, furtively wiping away any moisture, so that no one could see her tears.

He'd seen her green eyes filled with passion and, damnit, love—that *was* love he'd seen that night as she'd pulled his head down to kiss him, their bodies moving, straining together.

"I got maybe thirty seconds, Lloyd, so make it fast or I'll talk to you later." Will's voice was loud and clear through Jack's phone.

"I'm at your place," Jack informed Arlene's brother as he put his arms around her still-shaking shoulders. "Maggie's in trouble. Arlene's melting down. You and Dolph need to get over here—now."

He didn't let his old friend reply, he just hung up his

phone, tossing the damn thing onto the rug, so he could wrap himself more completely around Arlene.

Who slapped him away. "Don't touch me!" She was now trying—and coming close to succeeding—to stop her tears, to jam her emotional outburst back inside. But the look on her face broke his heart, and he couldn't keep himself from reaching for her again.

"We'll find her," he promised her again. "Will and Dolphina are on their way home. We'll make a list of all of Maggie's friends—"

Again, she pushed him away, striding into the living room where a box of tissues sat on Will's computer desk. "None of whom I've met. Lizzie, Beth, Paloma, Inez, Keisha, Jason, Mike." She blew her nose forcefully. "I don't even know their last names."

"Will and Dolphina will know."

"I'm her mother." Despite her best efforts, Arlene's tears again overflowed. "I should know. I should be here."

"Yeah," Jack said. "You should."

And there they stood, looking at each other.

"I don't want to go back," Arlene whispered. The tip of her nose was pink, which made her attempts to wipe away her tears rather useless. But she straightened her shoulders and kept her lower lip from trembling. "But I have to. I made a promise."

"But when's your debt repaid?" Jack asked her quietly. "This war's gone on too long. And I've read the reports. Your being over there—*our* being over there . . . It isn't making things safer here, for Maggie, for any of us. How do you reconcile that?"

"I don't," Arlene admitted. "And I hate being there. I *hate* it, Jack. But I made a promise. If called upon, I would serve."

"The government made a promise to you that they haven't kept," he pointed out.

"That's a matter of opinion," she countered. "For the sole sake of argument, let's assume—I don't believe you are, but let's assume—you're right. They broke their promise, not just to me, but to everyone in the Reserves and the National Guard, by extending our tours, by creating the stop-loss program that says we can't leave, even if we want to. Okay, great. It sucks. I'm with you there. But nearly everyone overseas has someone who is growing up without them, Jack. Everyone has someone they miss with all of their heart. Every one of us wants to come home." She shook her head. "I made a promise to serve," she said again, her green eyes filled with conviction.

And now Jack was the one fighting his tears. He held out his hand to this woman who awed him despite their disagreement, this woman who took the lofty ideas of honor and duty and lived them, every day, with every breath she took.

"Will and Dolphina will be here soon," he tried to reassure her. "We'll find Maggie."

"And then what?" Arlene asked, sadness in her eyes. "After we find her? How do I make her understand that I have to go back?"

CHAPTER SEVEN

They were four blocks from home, stopped at a traffic light, when Robin's cell phone rang.

"Hey, thanks for calling me back," he said, and Jules knew it was Dolphina, his personal assistant, on the other end. "You changed the password on the office computer without telling me—" He laughed. "No, I'm not going to go in there and mess up your organizational— No, I just needed to check my schedule because I got asked to fill in, last minute, as the host of Sundance Channel's indy film awards and . . . Yeah. No, Art called me directly. They called him and . . . It's two weeks from Saturday and . . . *Yeah,* I want to do it."

The light turned green and Jules tried not to burn rubber as he hit the gas.

But then Robin said, "Oh, crap. She's not serious, is she?"

Jules glanced at Robin, who mouthed the word *Maggie,* then *We need to go to Will's,* then said into the phone, "No, we're still in the car. No. No, Dolph. Really. Jules won't mind—he loves Maggie, too. This falls under *emergency.* The more people you've got looking for her, the better. We'll be right there." He snapped his phone shut as their driveway came into view.

And Jules did indeed love Maggie, too, but *damn.*

"What's going on?" he asked as he drove past their house and headed west, to Newton.

Chapter Eight

Will and Dolphina were helping—and yet really not helping.

Jack watched Arlene as Will pulled a list of Maggie's friends—full names, cell phone numbers, parents' names and phone numbers and addresses—up on his computer. She was beyond grateful that her brother had kept such close tabs on Maggie while she was gone, but Jack knew that she also hated the fact that Will had the information that she clearly felt she should've known.

They went down the list quickly—with Will and Arlene calling the parents and Dolphina, who'd recently taken Maggie and her friends out for pizza and a movie, calling the kids.

Jack took the opportunity to send another text to Maggie. He'd been firing them off ever since he'd gotten her alarming message, hoping to get a response.

Halfway down the list, Jules and Robin Cassidy showed up and joined the effort—Robin helping with the calls, and Jules doing his best to hack into Maggie's email account out on the living room computer.

But none of Maggie's friends knew where the girl was. Even more disturbing was the fact that there had been no play rehearsal scheduled for today.

"When did she start lying?" Arlene asked her brother, who shook his head.

"Maggie doesn't lie," Will said.

"Well, she did today," Arlene pointed out sharply. "Clearly you've been setting a *great* example."

"You have no idea how hard it is." Dolphina was quick to defend Will. "How hard Will works to—"

"*I* have no idea how *hard* it is?" Arlene bristled, her fear for Maggie combining with her frustration and, yes, her jealousy, and expressing itself as anger at Dolphina—this stranger who she felt knew her daughter better than she did.

Jack was on the verge of throwing himself on that grenade when Robin beat him to it. The movie star slipped into the seat next to Arlene at the kitchen table.

"She's an amazing kid," Robin told her. "I think we're all in agreement about that, all right? And okay, maybe she went a little too far, drama-wise, tonight. A little too *Parent Trap,* but you've got to give her props for creativity. And you've got to love her ability to hope. She still believes in fairy-tale happily-ever-afters, but she's also willing to fight—a little dirty, okay, that's true—but remember she's trying to win that perfect happy ending. Not just for you, Arlene, but for herself, too."

And the last of Arlene's anger deflated, leaving behind only sadness. "I'm sorry," she said to Dolphina. "I really do appreciate everything you've done for Maggie. I do. I just—"

"It's okay," the younger woman reassured her. "I can't imagine how difficult it must be for you. I do know how rough it is for Maggie, though. I can tell you with complete conviction that she would *never* do something like this when you're gone. She lives each day, trying so hard to make you proud of her. She's careful never to do anything that might even remotely get you upset. She doesn't want you distracted when you're out there."

"She crosses off the days on the calendar," Will quietly told his sister, coming out of Maggie's tiny bedroom, holding a *Battlestar Galactica* calendar—Lieutenant Starbuck on the front in a devil-may-care pose. "Like she's in prison, counting down the hours until the end of her sentence—until the day you get to come home. Only here it is. You're finally home. And look." He opened the calendar to May—holy shit, was it already May?

"She's still crossing off the days," Will continued, "but now she's counting down to the day that you're going to leave again. You're safe—but it's not going to last. There's an end date, Leenie, and she's gotta be dreading it. God knows I am."

"Let me tell you what it's like," Robin told Arlene, taking her hands because, once again, her eyes had filled with tears. "Jules just spent over a week in Afghanistan, and while he was gone, Arlene, I swear to God, I didn't breathe. There was not a single second of that entire time that I wasn't hyper-aware that he was someplace dangerous. I didn't even escape it at night, because when I finally did fall asleep? I dreamed about him being in danger. Eight days, and I'm ready to tear my hair out." He touched the top of his head. "Not that there's a lot left right now to tear, but you know what I mean."

As Jack watched, she nodded.

"And I was in Kabul, which is a relatively safe part of the country," Jules said, and they all looked up to see him standing in the doorway, a piece of paper in his hands. He held it up. "Got her. According to an email she sent at 1500 this afternoon, her partner in crime is someone named Lizzie. She's over at her house."

"Liz Milton," Dolphina said, whipping out her cell phone and dialing. "That girl lied, right to my face."

"Wait," Arlene stopped her. "Maggie told me about Lizzie in one of her emails. Doesn't she live nearby?" She looked from Dolphina to Will.

Will answered, "Her parents have a condo across the street."

"I don't want to call and have Maggie leave and go somewhere else." Arlene turned to Dolphina, and swallowed the last of the lingering jealousy she had to be feeling for the younger woman. "Please, she admires you so much. Will you go over there, and . . . and talk to her?"

Dolphina nodded. "Of course."

"It might not be a bad idea," Will suggested, "for you to go, too. Meet Lizzie's parents."

"I want to get Maggie safely home first," Arlene said. "Believe me, I'll be meeting Lizzie's parents in the very near future."

"Maybe Jules should go with Dolphina," Robin suggested. "In case Maggie's uncooperative. He could play the FBI card."

Jules was shaking his head. "I'm not here in an official capacity," he said as Jack opened his cell phone, checking to see if Maggie had texted him back. His last text should have elicited *some* kind of response from her.

"Yeah, but Lizzie and Mags don't know that," Robin countered.

"I've kinda already played that card," Jack spoke up,

and everyone turned to look at him. "I've been texting Maggie," he explained, "telling her that she better get home, stat, or else—" but he didn't get any further, because the front door opened, and Maggie herself burst into the apartment, followed by a dark-haired girl who no doubt was Lizzie.

"It's all my fault," Maggie announced. "Don't arrest Will."

"No one's going to . . ." *arrest me,* Will started to say, but Jack kicked him in the ankle. "Ow!"

Jules Cassidy was on the ball, good man. "It's lucky you came back when you did," he told the girl in what had to be his official FBI agent voice, crisp and cool. "Or I would have had to bring Will in."

"For what?" Lizzie apparently wasn't as gullible as Maggie, attitude dripping off of her. "No one's done anything wrong."

"For neglect of a minor," Jack supplied the made-up excuse he'd texted to Maggie several minutes earlier, before Jules could answer.

Lizzie crossed her arms. "Then maybe you should arrest Maggie's mom. Talk about *neglect.*"

Ouch. Arlene flinched as if the girl had struck her across the face.

Maggie looked stricken, too. "No," she told her friend, "you don't understand."

"She's never home," Lizzie argued. "You know, this is the first time I've *met* your mom? I mean, God, Mag, your mother's supposed to take care of *you,* and all I ever see is you taking care of her, sending her packages, worrying about her . . ."

"You don't *understand,*" Maggie said again.

"You're my best friend, and you live your life in total terror," Lizzie said just as hotly. She turned to Arlene. "No one should have to live that way. You joined the Reserves, not the Army. This wasn't supposed to be your career, and you shouldn't have to go back. And you *don't* have to. All you have to do is—"

"Lizzie," Maggie said. "Stop."

"Have a baby," Lizzie finished.

"It was stupid," Maggie told her friend, "thinking I could set my mom up with Jack, thinking she would just . . . fall in love with him." She turned to her mother, with tears in her eyes. "I'm sorry."

"You don't need to be in love to make a baby," Lizzie said, disgust in her voice. "My little brother's proof of that. People have kids for stupid reasons all the time. Why not have one for a *good* reason?"

"Liz, just go home." Maggie was defeated. "You're making things worse."

"If you die," Lizzie told Arlene, "*when* you die, you won't have to be here to see what it does to Maggie. Or maybe you'll come home without your legs, and Maggie will have to take care of you for the rest of her life and—"

"Lizzie, go home!" Maggie shouted.

And everyone leapt into action. Dolphina grabbed the outspoken Lizzie with one hand and Will with the other. "Will and I are going to walk you across the street."

Jules and Robin were right behind them, going out the door. "Call if you need anything," Robin told Arlene, who wasn't paying anyone any attention. She was looking at her daughter, tears in her eyes.

Jack alone hesitated as the door closed behind them all.

"I'm so sorry, Mommy." Maggie started to cry. "Liz doesn't understand. Her parents are rich. They don't—"

"It's okay, baby." Arlene wrapped her arms around her daughter.

"And I'm sorry about emailing Jack," Maggie said through her tears. "He was just so nice when I met him at the wedding. When he talked about you, and he told me he's been madly in love with you since you were like, sixteen, and all I could think was . . ."

Maggie kept talking, her words punctuated by her sobs, but Jack stopped paying attention to what she was saying, because Arlene lifted her head and looked at him, surprise in her eyes. Surprise and disbelief.

Great.

Yeah, it was definitely time to go.

But now Maggie was speaking directly to him, pulling free from Arlene to face him. "I'm so sorry," she told him, tears running down her face. "I just wanted . . ."

"It's okay, honey," he told her. "I know. I got a little caught up in the fantasy, too. But you can't just snap your fingers and make someone change everything they believe in. Your mom, she's one of the heroes and . . . I had a shot at making her fall in love with me a few years ago, and I screwed it up. I wish I hadn't, because I'm pretty sure that I could've talked her into marrying me and . . . Having a baby right now might've been the right choice for all of us." He shook his head. "But she and I, we're both different people now and . . . And you can't just make someone fall in love with you, especially after letting them down in the past. Life doesn't work that way."

Maggie nodded, subdued. "I know."

Arlene spoke. "You've really been in love with me for seventeen years?" She was standing with her arms crossed, looking at him as if he were roadkill.

"Something like that," he said, through a mouth that was suddenly dry. "I know you don't believe me, but—"

"It never occurred to you to *tell* me that? To say the words? *Hey, Arlene. How have you been? I'm kinda in love with you . . . ?*"

Yeah, like he was going to walk in here, cut open his

chest and toss his heart onto the floor? "I asked you to marry me."

"Out of pity," she countered.

"What? No," Jack said. "I asked for the reason most men propose marriage to the woman that they . . ." He had to clear his throat, and even then the word came out on a croak. "Love."

"You asked her to marry you, but you didn't tell her you love her?" Maggie was deeply unimpressed. "What are you, an idiot?"

"Apparently," Jack said.

Maggie turned to her mother. "He loves you. Madly. He told me. I asked him how he knew it was really love, and he told me he knows because he's felt it forever and it won't go away. He said he dreams about you, and that's the only time he's ever really happy and—"

"Maggie." Jack cut her off. "That doesn't change anything. Except it maybe makes me feel like even more of a loser—"

"Because you love my mom?" Maggie asked. "Why?"

"Because I'm nearly forty years old," he told her, a tad impatiently, "and I should know when it's time to give up and go home." He met Arlene's eyes again. "But every time I look at you," he whispered, "I find myself thinking, *How can I leave when I'm already home?*" He took a deep breath, and said it. "I love you, Leenie. I always have, and I always will."

CHAPTER NINE

Arlene Schroeder had gotten pregnant when she was nineteen, and had married her college boyfriend, Ted, even though she knew it would never—could never—work out.

But he was Maggie's father, and she'd tried, for years, to make it work.

Tried and failed.

But she'd learned a lot from the experience. First and foremost, she'd learned that one person, working alone, couldn't possibly make a relationship succeed. It needed, she suspected, to be a joint effort, a combined endeavor.

And she'd learned that there needed to be a whole hell of a lot more than sexual attraction to make a romance last. Respect, honesty, and friendship were key ingredients to a deep, abiding love.

But here she was, standing in the apartment her brother shared with her daughter, gazing into the eyes of a man who claimed he loved her, a man she'd loved for damn near forever, too. Loved, but didn't really respect or trust.

But as she stood there, with Maggie watching, wide-eyed, Jack got back on his knees.

"Marry me," he begged her. "Not because I want to get you pregnant—although that's definitely on my wanna-do list. But marry me because I love you, because I've always loved you. Marry me because I just can't shake the sense that you've always loved me, too. If you really, truly feel that you've got to go back to Iraq, well, okay. I don't agree with you. I don't think we should've gone there in the first place, and I think the sooner everyone comes home, the better. But if you think otherwise, for whatever reason? I respect you, and I respect your choices. I'm going to be scared shit-less until you come home, and you goddamn better email me every freaking day, but don't *not* marry me, Leen, just because you're doing something hard. If I'm wrong, and you don't love me, not even a little? That's why you shouldn't marry me, but on the other hand, I've been here on my knees more than once tonight. Obviously pride's not a big thing for me, so feel free to marry me out of pity. I'd be good with that."

As Arlene gazed into Jack Lloyd's whiskey-colored

eyes, she could feel Maggie slipping back, out of the room, into the kitchen.

"Don't go far," she called to her daughter. "You and I have a *lot* more to talk about before this day is behind us."

"I know," Maggie called back, resignation in her voice. "I thought maybe it would be a good idea if we all had dinner. I'm starting the rice and setting the table."

The hope radiating off of Jack was so palpable Arlene could practically smell it. Or maybe that was Maggie's hope she was getting a whiff of.

"Get up," Arlene told him.

He shook his head. "I'm fine down here."

"Hey, Jack," Maggie called from the kitchen. "Do you like ranch or Italian on your salad?"

"Jack can't stay," Arlene called. "He's got an article he needs to finish writing tonight because we're going to drive up to the North Shore to have lunch tomorrow."

Jack's smile was like sunshine. "So no to a lifetime, but yes to lunch." He nodded. "Okay. I'm going to call it a victory. A small one, yes, but that's good enough for me—for now."

Arlene held out her hand to pull him to his feet, but once he was up, he didn't let her go. He tugged her close enough to reach out with his other hand and push her hair back from her face, his fingers warm as he tucked her curls behind her ear.

"Thank you," he said. "I'll see you tomorrow. How about I pick you up at nine?"

Arlene had to laugh. "For lunch?"

"Gotta get there early to get a table on the deck," Jack told her. "I'll bring coffee for the ride. Large, but half decaf, skim milk, one sugar, right?"

She blinked at him. "I can't believe you remember that."

Jack shrugged. "In love with you for seventeen years." He laughed. "That's getting easier to say, which is a little scary, I've got to admit."

And there they stood. Arlene gazed up into his eyes as his familiar smile quirked at the edges of his generous mouth. It was the uncertainty she saw there that made her heart beat harder. As much as he tried to pretend otherwise, he wasn't as cocksure as he often seemed.

"I guess I've kinda gone all in," he told her.

"Dark roast," Arlene said, still holding his gaze, "black, three, count 'em three, Sweet'N Lows. That stuff is going to kill you, Jack."

He laughed, but then narrowed his eyes at her. "So what are you saying?" he asked. "That you've been in love with *me* for seventeen years, too?"

She shook her head *no*. "Twenty," she said and he laughed his surprise. She could tell from the sudden heat in his eyes that he was seconds away from grabbing her and kissing her, so she put her hand on his chest to keep him at a safe arm's length. "But I'm pretty sure I was only in love with the *idea* of you," she admitted. "You know, my big brother's super-hot best friend. I guess I'm willing to take a little time to see how the real you compares."

And with that she took her hand away.

But Jack was wary, clearly afraid to push his luck, so Arlene stood on her toes and brushed the softness of his lips with hers.

"Yesssss."

Jack smiled down at Arlene, the laughter lines around his eyes crinkling. "Was that Maggie or me? Because it was exactly what I was thinking."

She pushed him toward the door. "I'll see you tomorrow."

"Nine o'clock," he verified as he opened the door.

Arlene had to laugh. "Sure. Why not?"

He went through the doorway, but stopped in the hall to look back at her. "Huh," he said. "This is kinda weird. I'm happy, yet I appear to be awake."

It was, without a doubt, one of the sweetest, most romantic things anyone had ever said to her. "See you tomorrow," Arlene said past the lump in her throat.

"Don't be too hard on Maggie," he told her.

And with that, he was gone.

CHAPTER TEN

Robin carried Jules's overnight bag into their house.

"We should make a point to spend more time with Maggie," he told Jules as he followed him into the kitchen. "You know, next month, after Arlene goes back. I'll invite her to the set. It's good to keep busy, be distracted. Not that it really helps—although it does help pass the time."

Jules put the pizza they'd picked up on their way home onto the kitchen counter. "It's still really hard for you, isn't it?" he asked. "When I'm gone."

Robin shrugged. "It is what it is. Although I definitely prefer it when you spend four weeks in California. As opposed to a war zone. That really sucks." He crossed to Jules's side of the center island. "Let's eat. Later."

His smile was pure sex, but Jules had more to say.

"I'm away a lot."

"Yes, you are, babe. Just make sure you keep coming home," Robin said, taking him by the tie and tugging him toward the back staircase that led to their bedroom.

But Jules couldn't promise this man that he'd married that he always *would* come home. Or that it wouldn't be in a body bag.

"I hate the idea that I'm doing to you what Arlene is

doing to Maggie," he admitted, even as he followed Robin up the stairs. "She's got no real choice. But I do."

"No," Robin said, turning to face him, right there on the stairs. "You don't. You wouldn't be happy doing anything else. I would never ask you to—"

"I know." Jules kissed him. "But maybe you shouldn't have to ask."

Robin smiled into Jules's eyes. "You must really love me," he said, and the tenderness on his face took Jules's breath away. "Because we have this exact conversation every time you get back from overseas."

"You know I love you," Jules said just as quietly. "And I hate the idea that something I do makes you miserable."

"So make it up to me." The heat in Robin's eyes made Jules smile.

"You sure we don't have anywhere else to go tonight?" Jules asked. "Anyone else to help rescue? Any other crisis to handle?" As if on cue, his cell phone rang.

He took it out of his pocket to silence it and then, without looking at the caller ID, holding Robin's gaze the entire time, he tossed it into a basket of laundry that was sitting near the bottom of the stairs.

And then there they stood, halfway up the stairs, just gazing at each other.

Robin blinked first. "You better get that," he said. "What if it's Arlene. Or, you know, the President?"

Jules nodded. "Yeah." With a sigh, he went down the stairs, and dug his phone out from the clean towels.

Missed Call, it read. But it was neither Arlene nor the U.S. President. "It was Yashi," he told Robin.

Joe Hirabayashi was one of Jules's subordinates and a good friend. If he truly needed to get in touch with Jules, he would call back. But hopefully not for a while. Still on the stairs, Robin smiled and held out his hand.

Jules took it—and raced him to the top.

Chapter Eleven

Arlene sat on her old sofa in Will's living room, with Maggie's head on her lap.

Her daughter had cried herself dry—they both had—and she now slept, as Arlene ran her fingers through her hair.

They'd discussed quite a few difficult topics—sex being at the top of the list. But as Arlene had hoped, Maggie's threat to get pregnant was just that: a threat. Even with Lizzie's less than spectacular example, Maggie wasn't even close to being ready to become sexually intimate with any of the boys she knew.

Although Arlene did find out that she had a crush on Lizzie's older brother, Mike, who had told Liz that he thought Maggie was pretty. He was a junior in high school, and Arlene absolutely was going to send Will and Jack over to speak to the boy. And okay, yes, not so much speak to him as scare the hell out of him. She made a mental note to talk to Dolphina about him as well, to ask her to keep an eye on things and . . .

God, she didn't want to go back. She wanted to be an active part of her daughter's life.

She and Maggie had talked—for a long, long time—about that, too. About duty and honor and keeping promises.

And then they'd talked about Jack.

"How come you never told me about him?" Maggie asked.

Arlene shook her head. "There was nothing to tell. He was Will's best friend. I was Will's kid sister. And then I met your father . . ." She shrugged.

"Jack told me he cried," Maggie told her. "When he found out you were marrying Daddy."

"Really?" She winced even as the word came out of

her mouth. She sounded like one of Maggie's middle-school friends.

"He told me all these stories about you," Maggie reported. "I talked to him for like two hours at Jules and Robin's wedding. I knew he was totally in love with you even before he said it because he called you music. It was right when I first met him. He goes, *You've got to be Arlene Schroeder's daughter,* and I go, *yeah,* and he goes, *Your mother, she's music.* That was what Will said when he first told me about Dolphina."

"So naturally you email him to see if he'd be interested in being my new baby-daddy."

Maggie avoided eye contact. "I guess . . . I thought it was worth a try. I think it would be cool to have a brother or a sister. I could babysit, help take care of him. Or her." She glanced at Arlene out of the corner of her eyes. "I think Jack would make a great father."

"He's got two sons," Arlene told her. "Luke and Joseph. I think Luke's ten and Joey's seven."

"Sweet," Maggie said with enthusiasm. "We could be like the Brady Bunch. With the new baby, there'd be six of us."

Arlene just looked at her.

"I'm just saying," Maggie said—which was one of Will's expressions. Jack's too, come to think of it.

"What am I going to do with you?" Arlene asked as she ruffled her daughter's unruly curls.

"Tomorrow, nothing," Maggie said with a grin, "because you're having lunch with Ja-ack."

It was obvious that Maggie was ecstatic about that, and Arlene found herself thinking of Jack's parting words. *This is kinda weird. I'm happy, yet I appear to be awake.*

It was *definitely* kinda weird, because the thought of meeting Jack tomorrow made Arlene feel happy, too.

Happy and hopeful, even though, in a month, she *was* going back.

Her head still on Arlene's lap, Maggie stirred, waking just enough to look up at Arlene and murmur, "I love you, Mommy."

Arlene's heart clenched as she smiled down at her daughter. "I love you, too, monkey-girl."

PART II

Chapter Twelve

The day was perfect. The sun sparkled in a brilliant blue sky, and the ocean air was fresh and clean as Jack parked in the lot for the Baldwin's Bridge hotel, which had an awesome restaurant overlooking the water.

They'd talked about his kids nearly the entire ride. Jack had focused—hard—on keeping his hands on the steering wheel and his eyes on the road as he filled Arlene in on the latest exploits of Luke and Joey. After the breakup, the boys had moved with their mom to California, to the little town north of San Francisco where she'd grown up. Becca had done it in part in retaliation, to make it harder for Jack to see his sons; and in part to live closer to her parents, which was not a bad thing considering her still less-than-stellar mental health.

The end result, though, was that Jack saw his kids about as often as Arlene saw Maggie.

"Technically, we share custody," Jack said, trying to keep his voice even as Arlene climbed out of the car and stretched. She was totally killing him—and had been from the moment he'd spotted her, waiting for him on the front steps of Will's apartment building, from the moment her eyes had widened as she'd seen him in the Zipcar, even before she'd smiled.

His mouth had gone dry and his heart had pounded. And *then* she'd gotten into the car and sat there, so close and warm and sweet-smelling, with those long, pale, smooth, gracefully shaped legs.

She was dressed for a warm day at the seaside, in modestly cut shorts and a not-too-snugly-fitting T-shirt, half socks with pom-poms on the back and sneakers on her feet. Despite the soccer-mom look, he couldn't stop thinking about sex. And not just everyday, ordinary, run-of-the-mill sex, but sex with Arlene, which, the one night he'd had it, had nearly blown off the top of his head.

"Although," he continued in that same even voice, because dropping to his knees, weeping, and begging her to skip lunch and just check into the hotel with him was *not* going to achieve more than very shortsighted, non-long-term immediate gratification, "because money's so tight, that translates to me finagling an assignment on the West Coast and then working my ass off to get the story written in half the time humanly possible, so I can spend a few days with my kids."

"We all do what we have to do," Arlene said simply as she gazed back at him over the top of the Zipcar—and Jack knew she was well aware that his driving it meant he no longer owned his own transportation. He, who'd always loved his car, had made the choice to give it up because the cost of garaging it in the city was exorbitant.

"I'd be lying," he told her quietly, "if I didn't mention, right about now, that I've been thinking about relocating out there."

"California," she said as something flickered in her eyes.

Jack nodded. "Maggie, um, suggested it. You know? Like as part of the master plan."

Arlene laughed at that, but it wasn't because she thought it was funny. "Oh, my God." Tears filled her eyes. "She's really willing to give up everything—her friends, her life—"

"Whoa, hold on there, she's not giving up her life," Jack said as he came around the car to pull her roughly into his arms.

She didn't resist. In fact, she clung to him as he closed his eyes and breathed in the sweet scent of her hair.

"What she's got now," he continued, "it's . . . It's a half-life, Leenie. You made a deal, I get it, I do, and your honoring it is admirable, but the sacrifice is Maggie's, too."

"You think I don't know that?" Arlene whispered, and when she lifted her head to look up at him, he knew the next words out of her mouth were going to be a request for him to take her home.

"Here's what we're going to do," he told her, talking quickly, and putting one finger against the softness of her lips when she opened her mouth to speak. "We're not going to talk about this anymore, okay? Not today. Today we're going to have lunch, and we're gonna talk about music and movies and books and even non-war-related politics if we dare, plus I'm gonna tell you how great Maggie is. And the heaviest we'll get is maybe a little strategizing for how to deal with her crazy friend Lizzie and Lizzie's brother Mike—who is, right now, too old for Maggie, but I gotta confess that I relate to him with every screaming cell in my body, because I once had a thing for this really amazing girl who was too young for me."

Arlene smiled just a little at that, and he couldn't resist. He leaned down to kiss her. Gently. As sweetly as he could manage. Still, when he pulled back to look again at her, he knew she could see his desire—he couldn't keep it from showing in his eyes.

It was then that she surprised him.

"Who are we kidding, Jack?" she whispered. "Let's just check into the hotel."

Oh, yes please . . . Jack clenched his teeth over the reply, and instead said, in a voice that needed clearing a few times, "That's not why I brought you here."

She didn't believe him, and the look she gave him made him laugh.

"It's not," he said as he made himself step back from her. He reached for the red-and-white-striped bag on her shoulder. It held her sweatshirt, a Red Sox baseball cap, and a bottle of sunblock—and probably, at the bottom, since it was so heavy, a book or some kind of weapon. A handgun. A Taser. A bottle of mace.

Jack had spent time in both Iraq and Afghanistan, and he knew that most military personnel carried deadly weapons while out and about. It was a hard habit to shake—the sense of insecurity that came from *not* being armed.

And, sure enough, she wouldn't surrender the bag. "I got it," she said.

"Okay," he agreed and took her hand instead. "Let's go have lunch."

CHAPTER THIRTEEN

"I was thinking," Robin said as he sat on the edge of the bed to tie his running shoes. His military-short haircut emphasized the angles of his handsome face and somehow made his already impossibly blue eyes even more strikingly neon when he looked up.

Jules was already dressed for their morning run—a ritual he missed sorely whenever he was gone, even for just an overnight. A ritual he missed among many other "rituals." So to speak. Although, right now he was wishing he hadn't been in such a hurry to get out of bed. It wouldn't have taken much effort on his part to convince Robin to make their morning run an afternoon run.

"What?" Robin said as he smiled up at Jules—who realized he was standing there, just grinning at his husband like the village idiot.

"I'm just really glad to be home," Jules simplified.

"You get any vacation time," Robin asked, holding out his hand, "to make up for the extended trip? I mean, besides today?"

Jules laughed as, instead of his helping to pull Robin to his feet the way he'd expected, Robin pulled him down so that they were both sitting together on the bed, fingers tightly clasped. "I'm sure I'll be able to arrange something," he said. "You thinking western Mass? A little romantic getaway . . . ?"

"Actually," Robin said, "I'm thinking . . . *family* vacation. California."

"California," Jules repeated with a laugh.

Robin's movie-producer sister Jane was married to Cosmo, a chief in Navy SEAL Team Sixteen, and they had a place in Coronado, as well as a house in LA. Vacations spent with them were undeniably action-packed and fun, but far from relaxing. They had a toddler, Billy, who was ridiculously adorable, but who fully embraced the concept of the Terrible Twos.

Cosmo's mom adored Robin and always made a point to visit simultaneously. She was great, but she brought her own level of pandemonium to the noisy chaos with her need to play show tunes at astonishingly high decibel levels at least several times each day.

Family vacations were undeniably enjoyable, but they were never restful—or even remotely romantic.

"I was thinking," Robin said again, "that we could

bring Dolphina and Maggie with us. Will, too, if he can get the time off. I'm talking, of course, after Arlene goes. Back."

It was not lost on Jules—the way he said *back,* with that hesitation in front of it and the expression on his face that telegraphed the fact that the word left a bad taste in his mouth.

This past month, particularly the week-plus that Jules had been in Afghanistan, had been *very* hard on Robin. And Maggie, who loved her mom, would be facing similar fears and worries—for far longer than a month.

Taking the girl to California with them wouldn't merely be a diversion. It also was, on Robin's part, a conscious effort to grow Maggie's support group. It would help her, immensely, to let her spend some significant time with Jane, whose Navy SEAL husband constantly went into dangerous hotspots. It would be priceless for the girl to meet the entire group of SEALs' wives, who would share their methods for coping. Plus, Maggie would return to Boston with a whole long list of new friends to email and call—friends who knew *exactly* what she was going through while her mother finished up her current tour of duty.

In his head, Jules ran quickly down the list of SEAL wives who, along with Jane, lived out in California: Kelly, Meg, Teri, Savannah. Joan came and went, and would probably make a point to show if a gathering was planned. They were all intelligent, funny, compassionate, strong, determined women—great role models for a teenaged girl. Better yet, they would see a bit of themselves in Maggie and be proactive in maintaining contact by reaching out to her and making sure she knew that she wasn't alone.

It was a brilliant idea—thoughtful and generous and kind.

And Robin was sitting there with trepidation in his eyes, at the idea of asking Jules to sacrifice his hard-earned vacation days. Forget about the fact that Robin was willing to donate some of his own rare days off, as well.

"I love you," Jules told Robin. "Madly. Let's plan this thing."

Robin smiled his delight back at Jules, but then asked, "Are you sure, babe? Somehow we always seem to spend our vacations doing what I want to do." He corrected himself. "I mean, sure, we do little things that you want, like right now, like go for a run, but—"

"Wait a minute," Jules interrupted. "You don't want to go for a run? I thought you wanted to go for a run."

"No, we're definitely going for a run because *you* want to go for a . . ." Robin's voice trailed off. His eyebrows went up as he realized . . . "Whoa, really?" He laughed then added, "What part of *Hey, babe, let's stay in bed a little longer so I can rock your world* did you think I *wouldn't* want to hear?"

Jules laughed, too. "I don't know. You got up. I thought—"

"I had to pee. I come back, you're already getting dressed. I figured, okay, I'd have to wait until after lunch, at which point, by the way, I was very definitely planning to talk you into taking a nap." As Robin spoke he kicked off his sneakers and pulled off his T-shirt and . . . Yup, his shorts went, too.

"Let's run later," Robin added as he grabbed Jules and pulled him back with him into their bed.

"You're full of good ideas today," Jules pointed out after Robin kissed him quite thoroughly.

And then they both stopped talking as Jules got to do *exactly* what he wanted to do on this, his vacation day.

Chapter Fourteen

Lunch was lovely.

The Baldwin's Bridge hotel had outdoor dining on their patio, and Arlene's view of the ocean was spectacular. Especially since it included Jack Lloyd sitting across the table from her. She'd always found him to be extremely easy on the eyes.

He looked up, smiling his thanks as the waiter delivered their check, and she used the opportunity to study him as he read the bill.

His pretty brown hair moved in the warm breeze, and his eyes were more green than golden brown today, matching the faded sage color of his nicely fitted T-shirt.

He'd delivered exactly what he'd promised—conversation that was carefully minefield-free. They'd bounced from a variety of lighthearted topics—including the plan she and Maggie had made over breakfast, to throw a Friday night party at the local laser tag amusement center. The idea being for Arlene to meet Maggie's friends in a low-stress, high-fun social situation. And since Will's apartment was too small for a party of any size . . .

Jack agreed that it was a good idea and a good location, and then suggested that the party was the perfect time and place for him and Will to have a few private words with Mike-the-high-school-junior.

The conversation had moved, then, to other subjects, skimming across them with lightning speed before landing, with both feet, on her job and her life in Iraq. Arlene had backed away from that, rather emphatically, and to her surprise, Jack hadn't pushed—not even a little.

All he said was, "I've been over there, on assignment. And I know it's not the same thing, not even close, but . . . I've seen it. I know what it smells like and . . . If you ever want to talk, you don't have to worry about, you know, shocking me."

She'd nodded and pretended to study the dessert menu, but in truth she couldn't read a word past the blur of tears that had rushed to her eyes. Tears that Jack, in turn, gallantly pretended not to see.

As Arlene now watched him, he dug into the back pocket of his pants for his wallet, from which he extracted a credit card that he slipped into the leather folder with their bill. He held it up for the young waiter to grab on his way past, again smiling his thanks at the intercept, before reaching for his mug to finish off his coffee—milk free, but with three Sweet'N Lows.

He met Arlene's gaze then and gave her a smile that was even warmer than the ones he'd shared with the waiter. "This was great. This was . . . a dream come true."

She had to laugh at that, even as she reached across the table to take his hand. He drew his breath in, as if he were surprised by the sudden contact, and he looked down at their interlaced fingers. When he glanced back up and into her eyes, she could see it again. His desire. It was warm and solid and impossible for him to hide. At least from her.

"I think the dream-come-true part happens next," she told him, and his gaze dropped to her mouth, but only for a second. "Seriously, Jack. I just want to . . . I don't know. Feel good for a little while. And then get back to Newton so I'm there when Maggie gets home from school."

"Getting a hotel room in the afternoon on day two, after not seeing each other for more than two years is *not* what I'd call taking it slowly," he pointed out.

"I'm not going to be home for very long," she countered, holding his gaze.

Jack nodded. "I'd . . . rather spend the time talking. About things that matter."

Laughing, she pulled her hand free. "God, you're a terrible liar."

"I'm not lying," he said, laughing, too, but then immediately amended his declaration. "Well, okay, I'm lying because yes, *yes,* I want to say yes. I want to . . . *Yes.*" He leaned forward and lowered his voice. "But I don't want to screw this up. I am *not* going to screw this up. So yes, I *would* rather talk to you. So how about this? We drive back to Newton, pick up Maggie from school, and then go to the airport where we catch the next flight to Vegas. We can talk all the way there—the flight's about six hours, nonstop. We arrive, you marry me, we have a little celebration dinner, check into a hotel, getting Mags a separate room, and kiss her good night. At which point, I promise, I will make you feel very, *very* good."

"That's insane," Arlene whispered, but she couldn't look away. She just sat there, staring into his eyes, and she could see—she knew—that he wasn't teasing or flirting or pretending. He was dead serious.

"I want you in my life," he said quietly. "So, no. I disagree. It's not insane. It's quite possibly the most sane suggestion I've ever made. Ever."

She shook her head. "I don't know where to start."

But she didn't have to start, because he knew exactly what she was thinking. "You know me," he persisted in that voice that had always flowed over her like velvet. "You've *always* known me. And I should've asked you to marry me, right on the very first day that I met you, because I knew, right then, right at that moment, that with you by my side, my life would be complete."

"Except I was too young," she pointed out tartly, "so saying that, *doing* that, would've meant, what? Three years of celibacy? Instead you opted to spend at least three of those months with Kim Bickford."

"Holy shit." Jack sat back in his seat. "You remember Kim? Jesus, I barely remember her last name."

"She slept with me in my room," Arlene told him, "when you and Will came to visit. It was pretty obvious, pretty quickly, that you weren't dating her for her massive vocabulary. So don't play the our-love-transcends-time-and-space card, okay? It doesn't fly."

"I'm only human," Jack admitted. "I made a lot of mistakes. I won't deny that. Hell, I still make mistakes."

"And it doesn't occur to you that this could be one of them?" she asked. It was her turn to lean forward. "You don't need to marry me to sleep with me, Jack. I'm sitting right here. You don't need to ply me with any bullshit, or even another glass of wine. I'm good to go. A sure thing."

"It's not bullshit," he argued. "I was young. And stupid. God, Leenie, remember that weekend that we played that epic Monopoly game?"

Arlene *did* remember. It was post–Kim Bickford, and Jack and Will alone had come to visit for the weekend.

After the infamous full-family Monopoly match, she'd been unable to sleep, and she'd gone into the kitchen for a snack and found Jack sitting at the island counter, reading a battered economics textbook for a required course that was, as he'd said, "kicking the crap" out of him. They'd started talking. And talking. And were both still awake as the dawn lit the sky.

It was the first of about a dozen similar Saturday nights, before he'd started dating a girl named Shannon West. At which point he completely dropped off the map.

"I was terrified of you," Jack confessed now. "Scared shitless by the way you made me feel. I was afraid of losing, I don't know, my freedom, my youth, which is . . . God, I say it and it sounds so stupid now. But it's true. If I could go back in time, I would've just kept coming over, every single weekend until . . . Ding! You turned eighteen."

Arlene laughed at that. "Just because I'm a sure thing now doesn't mean I was one back then."

"You were in love with me, too," he said quietly, and she was unable to deny it. "All I had to do was wait. But I got scared. And impatient—I'm not going to deny that, either. But I blew it. I know it. And I have regretted it every single day of my life. A day doesn't pass, Arlene, that I don't think about you."

And there they sat. Just looking at each other.

"If we hadn't messed it up, I wouldn't have Maggie," she finally whispered.

"And I wouldn't have Luke and Joe," Jack agreed. "So maybe everything happens for a reason—including my meeting Maggie when I did, at Robin Chadwick's wedding." He smiled then, just a little. "Who would've thought I'd be invited to a gay movie star's wedding? But I was, because of Will, and . . . Here we are. Older. Wiser. But . . . I'm still that kid, Leen—the boy who shared secrets with you in your parents' kitchen. And that girl who stayed up all night to talk to me is still inside of you, I know she is. Only this time around, I'm brave enough to tell you how I feel, that I want you in my life, that I love you. It's always been you. Always."

Oh, God. "But then what?" she asked. "If we go to Las Vegas—God, I can't believe I actually said those words. You know, in the Army, you're supposed to ask permission to get married. There are forms to fill out—"

"I am very good at filling out forms."

"Jack—"

"I'm not asking you to break any rules," he said. "Do you seriously think, with your record, that if you ask to get married, you'd be denied—"

She interrupted him. "Regardless of that, regardless

of . . . anything. Jack, I need to go back. I *have* to go back."

"I get it," he said. "You'll go back. I'm not asking you to not go back. I know what it means and . . . I'm asking you to . . . be with me. Be faithful and, I don't know, email me. And I'll email you, every day. Every hour if you want. Until eventually the Army's done with you—it's going to happen, and then you'll come home."

"And we'll move to California," Arlene pointed out.

Jack shook his head. "Only if you want to."

"How am I going to say no to that, knowing if I do, you won't see your kids?"

"I'll see my kids. I'll find another job," he said, "with better pay."

"You'll give up writing?" she asked, aghast. "That's not—"

"I'm not going to give up writing," he spoke over her. "I'm a writer. I'll always write. But if I have to—" he shrugged "—I'll get a second job to supplement what I earn as a journalist, and I'll be able to fly Luke and Joey out to see me—us—more often." He reached across the table and took both of her hands. "We can make this work, I know we can."

And as she sat there, looking into the warmth of his eyes, she could almost believe him.

"Come on," he said, but his next words weren't *Let's go get that hotel room.* "There's a really great ice cream shop down the street. I'll buy you a cone. We have time for a stroll through town before Maggie gets home from school."

"You want to get ice cream," Arlene felt the need to clarify, as Jack held out his hand and tugged her up from the table. She grabbed her bag and slipped it over her shoulder.

"I *want* to go to Las Vegas and then have sex for a solid month, straight," Jack said, "but buying you ice cream and window shopping with my arm around you sounds really good, too."

Bemused, she let him lead her away from the entrance to the hotel lobby and out into the brilliant sunlight of the early afternoon.

CHAPTER FIFTEEN

They had dinner that night with Maggie, and the sound of Arlene's laughter mingling with her daughter's made Jack smile.

Will and Dolphina purposely made themselves scarce, no doubt taking advantage of Arlene being home to spend some alone time of their own over at Dolphina's apartment.

So Maggie and Arlene and Jack played a board game called Settlers of Catan, in which Maggie kicked their collective ass, but after which she insisted she had homework to do and vanished into her bedroom, closing her door tightly behind her.

It was only then that Jack trusted himself to kiss Arlene because he knew damn well that she wasn't going to sleep with him—not with her teenage daughter awake in the next room. At least not until after they took that trip to Vegas . . .

"You're diabolical," she gasped between kisses, out of breath in the kitchen, as she clung to him. "*Now* you kiss me . . . ?"

"I want you to take me seriously," he told her before he kissed her again.

They eventually moved back into the living room and pretended to watch a movie on TV while, in truth, they made out on the sofa until the light that shone from beneath Maggie's door went out.

At which point, Jack told Arlene he'd pick her up

again at nine the next morning, kissed her good night, and sent himself home.

That next day, her T-shirt was tighter, her shorts were shorter, and he could tell she'd spent some time on her makeup and her hair.

When she got into the Zipcar and he kissed her hello, her hand traveled up his thigh, inside the leg of his shorts. But he caught her wrist, asking, "Is that your way of telling me you're ready to go to Vegas?"

She laughed as she shook her head *no,* but told him, "You know, I *do* take you very seriously."

"Only because I'm not having sex with you," he pointed out. And then he drove them to Concord, where they walked the Minuteman trail until it started to rain, so they ran for the car, and then went to the mall and got tickets to a movie.

The plan was to have popcorn for lunch, but they ignored it—and the movie—and just sat there in the dark, alone in the small theater, kissing and touching like they'd never had a chance to as teenagers.

At least not together.

With incredible restraint, Jack limited himself to second base.

He won the real prize on their way home, when he got her to talk—just a little—about the latest of her friends who had died in Iraq as the result of the blast from an IED. It had been soul-crushingly awful—and just another day in a war zone.

They pulled in front of Will's apartment building as Maggie was walking up the street, coming home from school. And this time, instead of hanging around, having dinner and making Arlene and Maggie laugh, Jack gave them both the excuse that he had to get back to his place in Watertown to work—that he had an assignment to write.

In truth, when he found out that Maggie had plans to

do a homework project over at her friend Keisha's house from seven to ten, he knew he had to stay away.

Jack was, after all, only human. And spending three hours alone with Arlene would require superhuman strength.

Besides, he'd set himself a capitulation date.

Saturday. The night after Maggie's party. If Arlene didn't agree to marry him by Saturday, he'd change the rules of the game. Because enough was enough.

He was in the process of cleaning the hell out of his crappy studio apartment. He'd already spoken to Jules and Robin about taking charge of Maggie for the second half of the weekend, since Will and Dolphina were going to a wedding on Sunday.

But until then, with his incredible restraint, he was showing Arlene, in glorious living Technicolor, that he was one majorly serious mofo.

At least he hoped that was how she was reading it.

Right now, she was looking at him as if he'd completely lost his mind. And as Maggie went into the building, the door swinging shut behind her, Arlene whispered, "She won't be home until ten. I can call Will and make sure—"

Jack stopped her with a kiss. "I love you," he said. "But I gotta go."

"Jack," he heard her say, laughter and bemusement in her voice as he climbed into the Zipcar. He waved at her as he pulled away.

Long-term goals. *Long*-term goals. . . .

He was in this to win it—and Saturday wasn't all that far away.

Chapter Sixteen

The party at Laser-Mania was a huge success.

Maggie's schoolmates were wide-eyed when they

realized that a movie star was one of the guests. They were also astonished at the concept of having the entire huge amusement complex to themselves.

But as Jules well knew, those two things went hand in hand.

"I don't know how to thank you," Arlene said to Jules as they stood at the railing in the spectator loft and watched Robin talk to Maggie and the other kids down on the laser battle course below. The large area had recently been redecorated to look like the hulking remains of a decaying spacecraft—very science fiction, and not at all reminiscent of Iraq. The laser weapons, too, were very ray gun—otherwise Jules was certain that Maggie would've picked another location for their party. "I can't even begin to imagine how much this cost."

"Not as much as you think," Jules reassured her. "And definitely less than bringing security in, to try to protect Robin in a Friday night crowd. He's kind of a hot target—that's just something we live with. The studio knows it, too, and they help pick up the cost of protecting him. It's a worthwhile investment for all parties."

She smiled at that, and it softened the angles of her face, making her look much too young to have a daughter Maggie's age. "You're so lucky," she said. "I mean, to have found him."

"I am," Jules agreed, as down beneath them Robin explained the rules to a game that was really called Balls, but that, for today, he was calling by the more PG-13 name Pairs. "He's amazing."

Teams of two attached themselves together with a harness and a three-foot-long bungee cord. They would then compete in a laser tag game with another likewise-attached team. First team to annihilate the other won. You got more points if both team members survived, but one person standing was okay, too.

But once your teammate was "killed," and her laser

vest lit up, she had to stop and drop, which was limiting for the survivor, who was now attached to a "dead" body.

It was a fun game, even for beginners. And Jules knew that before the evening ended he'd be dragged into it, and forced to handicap himself by doing something ridiculous. Like taking off his boots and limiting himself to firing his laser ray gun with his toes. Or tying his feet together and firing his weapon with his hands behind his back.

Right now Maggie had teamed up with Robin, while a very pretty Asian American girl named Keisha was giggling as she attached herself to the skinny boy named Jason.

Maggie's smile was a little bit forced, and she kept looking over at the door that led into the gaming area, as if she were waiting for someone to come in.

Dolphina and Will were setting up the room where they'd all have pizza—yeah, right, that's what they were doing, alone in there. Arlene's friend Jack had yet to arrive, so maybe Maggie was waiting for him. . . .

But, no. "Maggie's friend Liz isn't here," Jules realized.

Arlene nodded. "Yeah, they had a big fight. Lizzie's pretty volatile." She sighed. "Mags is really upset, and I feel guilty, because I keep thinking maybe it's for the best."

"Look who I found, lurking out in the parking lot."

Arlene practically did a triple-lutz, she turned around so fast. She lit up with a smile that was so wide Jules had to squint at the extreme wattage. And, sure enough, the voice belonged to *Boston Globe* reporter Jack Lloyd. He was with a grim-looking boy who was nearly Jack's height, but half his weight. He was almost as skinny as young Jason.

But he was older than Maggie and her friends. Maybe by as much as four years.

He'd clearly made an effort to look nice. His jeans were clean, and he was wearing a button-down shirt, sleeves rolled to his elbows. His long hair was pulled back into a neat ponytail. But he had the hardened, edgy attitude of a kid who'd often found himself in trouble—and probably not by accident.

Still, Jules had to give the boy credit. He looked Arlene dead in the eye and held out his hand and said, "I'm Mike Milton, Mrs. Bristol."

"Liz's brother," Jack provided, in case they weren't on the same page. He turned to Mike. "And she's Ms. Schroeder. Maggie's name is Bristol, but her mom and dad are no longer married."

"Of course, I knew that, I'm sorry," the kid said. He glanced at Jules, but apparently decided that he didn't need to know who he was, because he turned back to Arlene. "Ms. Schroeder, I came over here tonight because my sister is convinced that you don't want her anywhere near Maggie ever again, and maybe that's the case, but there's really something that you need to know before you make any ultimatums and that's that Liz is the only person Maggie talks to, you know, about your being out there, in danger? And it's really not that Maggie talks to Lizzie, but it's that Liz *makes* Maggie talk. And I can see it—I can see that it helps her. Mags. And I try to get her to talk about it, too, but . . ." He shook his head. "Lizzie's the only one she'll talk to and I know she's not perfect, Lizzie, she's really not even close to perfect, but her friendship with Maggie is . . . It's important to both of them and . . . I wanted you to know that."

It was quite the speech, a little wordy in places, sure—and it would have benefited from more traditional punctuation, which also would have allowed the kid the chance to take a breath.

But as far as heartfelt went, it was a perfect ten, in

Jules's book. And evidently it got high scores in Arlene's, too, because she was now clearly struggling to find her voice to respond.

Jack gave her the time she needed to compose herself by putting a hand on Mike's shoulder and saying, "You were right—that's really important information for Arlene to know."

"Thank you," Arlene added. "I can tell that you . . . care a lot about Maggie."

The boy's attitude shifted into full-on badass, and he laughed his disgust as his entire face shut down. "Perfect, yeah, I should have expected you to go there. Right. I don't know why I bothered—"

"Yeah, you do." Jack cut him off. "And she didn't *go there,* but you sure as hell just did. So why don't you just confess to Maggie's mother that you're smitten, but you know damn well that right now the girl's too young. Cap it off with a little reassurance that you're honorable—"

"I *am* honorable," Mike countered hotly, his chin high. "Not that I expect you to believe me."

"I'd very much like to believe you," Arlene said evenly. "But I don't really know you. So why don't you go home and pick up Lizzie and both come back here so we can all spend some time getting to know each other."

The boy looked at Arlene as if she'd just spoken to him in Chinese.

"Unless you have someplace you need to be," she continued. "In which case, you and Liz can come over for dinner. Maybe tomorrow . . . ?"

"Not tomorrow," Jack said quickly. "We're busy tomorrow. Night."

Arlene looked up at him in surprise. "We're . . . ?"

"Busy. Yes, we are." Jack nodded. For some reason he was unable or unwilling to look at her, his focus on Mike. "How about Sunday. I'll come, too."

The boy was astonished by the invitation, and Jules could tell that he was not the kind of kid who was often astonished. Mike closed his mouth. Opened it again. Closed it again, then cleared his throat. "No," he said. "Well, I mean, yeah. Dinner would, um . . . I know Lizzie would like that and, um, I would. Also. But she's . . . kinda waiting out in the car. See, I thought there might be a chance that Maggie's mom would be . . . at least marginally cool."

Arlene had laced her fingers with Jack's, and she smiled now. "Go and get her. And tell her that Maggie— and I—will be very happy to see her."

Mike nodded. "I can't stay tonight," he said. "I wish I could, but . . . I made a promise I have to keep. If you're serious about dinner, just tell Lizzie when, and . . . I'll be there."

Arlene nodded. "Sunday."

"Or Monday," Jack interjected.

Arlene laughed as she looked at him. "Or, apparently, Monday."

As Mike headed toward the stairs, Arlene murmured to Jack, "Really?"

Jules turned to look over the rail and to watch the game that had started below. Maggie and Robin were kicking ass as their opponents shrieked and laughed.

"I'm still holding out for Vegas," Jack murmured back, as Jules tried not to listen. He wasn't exactly sure what they were talking about, but it didn't take much imagination to guess. "I'm giving you twenty-four more hours."

She laughed again. "I'm not going to Vegas, Jack. Not after you just tipped your hand."

"I'm a terrible negotiator," he agreed. "But I do believe miracles happen every day, and that I'm due for one." He kissed her and changed the subject as he tugged her over to the railing so that they, too, could look down at the action. "So. Mike Milton. A lot less scary than he looks. But definitely damaged goods."

"I have boys just like him in my unit," Arlene said. "Just dying for a little respect, and for someone to treat them decently." She looked up at Jack. "And yet . . ."

"Good cop, bad cop," he told her. "You can deliver the respect and decency. I will pull him aside and let him know that we have a one-strike policy—and that if he touches Maggie inappropriately, I will not hesitate to cut off his balls."

The game ended with the sound of a buzzer, and the door to the playing arena opened.

"Lizzie!" Maggie squealed as the other girl launched herself into the room, and they hugged as if they hadn't seen each other in five years, as Robin unhooked himself from the harness.

Mike stepped in through the door, too, and Maggie went running toward him. He glanced up at Jules, Arlene, and Jack.

"Yes, we are watching you, bucko," Arlene said quietly, even though she was smiling down at him.

He was not a stupid kid. He was well aware. He was also carrying something that he held out to Maggie. When she took it, Jules saw that it was a graphic novel. One of the X-Men anthologies.

Maggie was thrilled. As Mike spoke to her, she hugged the book to her chest and hung on his every word.

"Look at how she looks at him," Arlene murmured. "God help us."

Jack laughed. "Look at how hard he's trying to be cool."

Lizzie came over and tried to pull Maggie away, and Mike laughed. He ruffled his sister's hair, and then did the same to Maggie's before he turned to leave. He looked back, though, right before he went out through the door, and it was clear that he would rather have stayed.

"Gotta love a kid who keeps his promises," Jules pointed out.

"To his fellow gang members?" Arlene wondered aloud. "To his drug dealer? To his pregnant girlfriend?"

Jack laughed again. "We'll ask him at dinner."

"On Monday," she said.

His smile grew broader. "On Monday," he agreed, pulling her close, as Jules escaped downstairs.

CHAPTER SEVENTEEN

Maggie's hands were as big as Arlene's.

It shouldn't have been a shock because she was now taller than Arlene, too.

And yet . . .

Maggie had gotten a green plastic signet-type ring with the face of a leprechaun imprinted on it out of what looked like a giant bubble-gum dispenser. She had been hoping to get the ring that had the head of the not-very-Johnny-Depp-ish pirate, but immediately announced that this was much better. And it became a whole, big, hilarious thing—whoever was deemed the all-star in the current round of Pairs got to wear the ridiculous ring.

And so it passed from hand to hand.

Arlene had had possession of it for a few brief moments before the pizza arrived.

"This actually fits you? On your ring finger?" she asked Maggie as she slipped it on. It fit her perfectly.

Her daughter cheerfully replied, "It's a little tight."

And somehow Jack knew what Arlene was thinking and feeling, because he put his arms around her and gave her a hug, which was comforting and nice.

We. Us. Ours. They'd both been using those words a lot lately, and it didn't feel weird or wrong.

It felt oddly perfect, as if, at long last, the universe had finally been set right.

Even more odd was the fact that Arlene was a little disappointed that Jack had announced his intention to surrender on Saturday night. Despite the sheer impracticality, part of her had been seriously considering taking him up on the craziness of a Las Vegas weekend. But not this weekend, because Maggie was part of her school's Playcrafters group, and they were performing a series of ten-minute plays at a local assisted-living facility on Sunday afternoon. And Arlene wasn't going to miss that.

Not for anything.

As far as her disappointment went, it was very small. Very manageable. It was nicely mixed with her current feeling of breathless anticipation.

After this party was over, she was going to do her best to convince Jack that there was no point at all in waiting for tomorrow night.

Right now the conversation was all about a book called *The Hunger Games.* Will had gotten an early copy from a friend who did a book review blog at the *Boston Globe,* and Maggie had loved it so much that she shared it with all of her friends.

She'd made sure to get it back so that Arlene could read it, too. The copy was coming unglued, the pages rubberbanded together.

Arlene had finished it in one sitting, while Maggie was at school.

"Foxface," Lizzie was saying. "I would totally be Foxface. I would finally have a good reason to use my mad shoplifting skills."

Maggie looked quickly at Arlene. "She's kidding."

Arlene certainly hoped so. Jack was sitting so that his

hand was resting lightly against her back, and she appreciated his solid presence.

"Don't say things like that," Maggie lit into Lizzie. "My mom doesn't know that you're not serious."

"My mother's the shoplifter in the family," Lizzie told Arlene brusquely, with a blunt honesty that was disarming. "She got caught once when my little brother and I were with her and . . ." Her sharply featured face twisted. "Believe me when I tell you I'd starve to death before I ever did anything as moronically stupid as that."

Arlene *did* believe her. "That must've been hard."

"It sucked." Lizzie glanced at Maggie before steadily gazing back into Arlene's eyes. "But there are definitely worse things in life to endure."

"Lizzie," Maggie said, a warning tone in her voice.

"It's okay," Arlene told her daughter, still holding Lizzie's somewhat challenging gaze. "For the record, I liked Foxface a lot." She glanced at Jack who hadn't yet read the book. "I don't want to say more. Spoiler alert."

Jack spoke up. "I guess I gotta read this book."

"Oh, you do," Maggie told him earnestly. "I'll lend it to you."

"I'd love that," Jack said, smiling warmly back at her.

This was weird. This feeling of . . . contentment? Satisfaction? Serenity?

It was a sense of unity, of belonging, of rightness.

Maybe this was what it felt like to have a real family—to have someone, very literally, at her back, not just during bad times, but good times as well. Which was not to say that she and Maggie hadn't been a family, albeit a small one. But it had always felt to her as if it were Arlene and Maggie against the world. With Jack sitting beside her, it felt more as if they were *part* of the world.

The conversation had drifted to the character named Peeta, and Jason was enduring some intense teasing. If

Lizzie was Foxface, and Maggie was the heroic main character named Katniss, then Jason was Peeta. Apparently Lizzie's brother Mike had some competition in the crush-on-Mags department.

Arlene looked at Jack to see if he'd made note of the boy's blushing, but he was frowning.

But only because his phone was buzzing. He'd set it to vibrate, and he now pulled it out of his pocket. "Ah, shit," he said. "I mean, shoot. Sorry. Becca just called me three times in a row."

Arlene laughed. "I think that qualifies for an *ah, shit*," she leaned closer to him to say.

He smiled, but he wasn't happy. "I better take this," he told her as he pushed his chair back from the table.

"Say hi for me," Arlene said, and the face he gave her—*Not a chance in hell* mixed with *Are you freaking kidding?*—made her laugh again.

"I'm in the middle of something important," she heard him say into the phone as he headed for the door to the hallway, "so unless this is an emergency . . ."

Jack put his finger in his ear as he started to push open the door with his shoulder. But then he froze. It was only for an instant before he was moving again, but his body language had changed so dramatically that Arlene was up and out of her chair and heading for him, before the door shut behind him.

As she slipped out into the hall, he was going through his pockets almost frantically, even as he asked, "He's in surgery right now? Who's the doctor?"

He'd found a folded piece of paper to write on, but as he looked at Arlene he said, "Pen, I need a pen."

He always carried one in the back pocket of his jeans—even back when he was in college—and she reached for it, and sure enough it was there.

She uncapped it before she handed it to him, and as he scribbled the name of a doctor and what looked like a hospital onto the paper, he said into the phone, "You seriously left them home alone when Luke was . . . No, I'm not saying it's your fault. How could appendicitis be your fault? I'm just . . . Oh, oh, *that* helps. That's . . . Do we *really* have to do this now? Shouldn't you . . . No, *no*, I'm not saying that! That's not what I—" He took a deep breath and exhaled hard. "Look, I'll call you back with my flight information. Yes. *Yes*." He hung up the phone. "*Jesus!*"

"Luke or Joey?" Arlene asked.

"Luke," he told her, already scrolling through his address book. When he glanced up at her, his eyes were apologetic. "I gotta catch the next flight to San Francisco. World Air flies out of Logan. I have their number in here, somewhere . . ."

"People don't die from appendicitis," she told him.

"Yeah, I know, thank God, right?" Jack said. "But I'm sorry, I still have to go."

He thought she'd said that to . . . "Of *course* you still have to go," Arlene said. "I wasn't . . . That wasn't . . ."

"Where the hell is it?" he asked, frowning at his phone.

Arlene reached into her pocket for her own cell. "I'll get the number from information." She dialed her phone. "World Airlines ticketing," she told the voice system. "Please put the call through."

Jack, meanwhile, had started trying to access his far fancier phone's Internet service. "Shit," he swore as he tried to access the tiny keypad. "Shit. I'm all thumbs."

She'd already been put on hold, so she held out her phone for him. "Trade."

Jack handed his phone over as he took hers, holding it to his ear.

Her Master Sergeant had a similar phone to Jack's, and Arlene knew how to use it. "What are you looking up?" she asked.

"It ruptured," he told her.

Oh, no. She didn't say it aloud, but she didn't have to.

"Yeah. He'd been complaining of stomachaches for weeks," Jack said, but then he pointed to the phone. "Yes, thank you. I need the next available flight to San Francisco. Or LA. I could fly into LA. Or even Sacramento . . . There is?" He looked back at Arlene. "One seat left on a red-eye to San Francisco. It leaves in two hours. I'm going to take it."

"You should," she said, as the Internet revealed that the big danger from a ruptured appendix came from infection after surgery. Peritonitis. And oh, she'd been wrong. People *did* still die from a ruptured appendix.

Jack had dug for his wallet and was giving his credit card information to the airline rep.

He was going to need a ride to the airport, but Arlene didn't have a car. She stepped into the pizza party room, where her brother was completely focused on Dolphina. "Will!" she called.

But it was Jules Cassidy, always vigilant, who looked up and came over.

"What happened?" he asked, and she told him what she knew as she pulled him with her back out into the hallway.

"Robin and I can drive you to the airport," Jules told Jack as he hung up Arlene's phone. "No problem."

"Thank you," Jack said, handing Arlene her phone. "Damnit, I have to leave, like, ten minutes ago."

"I'll get Robin." Jules vanished.

"Luke's going to be okay," Arlene told Jack.

He nodded, but he didn't look convinced.

"Call me when you get there," she said.

"It's going to be late," he said.

"I don't care," Arlene insisted. "Just call me when you land. And again when you get to the hospital. And whenever else you need me."

The muscle was jumping in his jaw. "I will," he said, then he grabbed her and held her close. "Jesus, I'm a total douchebag for thinking this. My kid's in the hospital and I can't stop thinking shit, *shit*, why didn't I check into the Baldwin's Bridge hotel with you when I had the chance?"

She laughed. "You're thinking that because you're human and you know damn well that you were going to get some tonight." She lifted her head to kiss him, and the kiss he gave her back was deliciously loaded with promise. But his worry and fear was back there, too, and she pulled away, because he had to go. "I'll be here when you get back," she promised him in a voice that was breathless.

He kissed her again. "Or you could meet me in Vegas."

"Again with the Vegas thing."

"We'll talk about it," Jack told her.

"Jack." Robin was at the door. "Jules got the car, he's waiting out front."

The trip to the airport was going to take fifteen minutes at best. Longer if there was traffic.

Jack pulled Arlene back with him into the party room. He raised his voice. "Mags, I gotta go."

But Maggie was already standing right there by the door, looking worried. "Jules told me that Becca called and Luke's in the hospital."

"Jack," Robin said again.

"I'll keep you updated," Jack promised Maggie, giving her a hug and Arlene one last glance before he followed Robin back out the door.

Maggie chased after him. "Jack, *wait!*"

Arlene pushed open the door, too, watching as Maggie ran to keep up with Jack.

They were halfway down the hall when something Maggie said made Jack pull up short. Arlene watched as

Maggie stood there, almost nervously turning the green ring around and around on her finger. And Jack gave the girl his full attention as he listened to whatever she was telling him so earnestly. It was clear she was upset as she used the heel of her hand to wipe tears impatiently from her eyes.

Jack, bless him, spoke to her just as seriously, just as earnestly, and completely reassuringly. And then he took Maggie's sweet face in his hands and planted a kiss on her forehead.

And it took Arlene's breath away—watching this man be the kind of father that Maggie'd never had, the kind of father that all little girls deserved in their lives.

Whatever he'd said to Maggie calmed her, and she nodded as he told her something else, and then they both turned, almost at the exact moment, and looked back at Arlene and smiled.

And her heart damn near burst.

Then Maggie stepped back, and Jack was gone.

But then Lizzie appeared, running past Arlene to pull Maggie back with her into the party.

And Arlene knew she was going to have to wait until they got home to ask Maggie what she'd said to Jack, and what he'd told her in response. Except her phone rang, and she saw from the number that it was . . .

"Jack."

"Hey." His warm voice came through the tiny speaker. "Since I'm not driving, I thought I'd call and tell you, well . . ." He exhaled hard. "I'm just going to say it, okay? Maggie was afraid that my having to rush off to California was another ploy of Becca's that would keep you and me apart. And I was sitting here and it suddenly occurred to me that if Mags was worried about that, you might be, too."

Arlene hadn't even considered the possibility. "*Should* I be worried?" she asked.

"No," he said, his voice absolute.

"Then I'm not worried," she told him.

"I love you," he said.

Arlene nodded, even though she knew he couldn't possibly see her. "I love you, too." And then she said words that were even more astonishing—words she truly couldn't believe were coming out of her mouth. "We'll meet you in Vegas, Jack. Maggie and me. After Luke's out of the woods. After Maggie's show on Sunday. Maybe on—"

"Monday," he finished for her, laughing, and she could hear his joy in his voice. "That would be amazingly great."

"Or Tuesday," she said, "provided I can take Maggie out of school."

"I think they'll let her go for her mother's wedding," he said, and the world tilted for her, because it was so surreal. And somehow Jack knew it, because he lowered his voice. "When you start having second thoughts, just remember, Leenie, how many years we've known each other. How good it feels, just to sit together in the same room. How well we fit."

They did fit. But . . . "I still have to go back," she reminded him. "I can't get pregnant. Not . . . yet." Once again, she'd said a word that she would never in a million years have believed that she'd say. But she meant it, because someday—a not-too-distant someday—she could imagine bringing another child into this world. A world that she was going to share with this man who loved her.

Arlene heard Jack smile as he exhaled, as he understood the subtext of what she'd said. "I love you," he said again. Simple. And absolute.

"I know," she said, and it was true. She believed him.

He laughed again. "I gotta go, Han Solo. Although I gotta tell you, you're the only woman on the planet for whom I would willingly play the part of Princess Leia. But my battery's at ten percent and I don't have my charger on me and, shit, I won't have time to get one at the airport."

"Then don't call me when you land," she told him. "Save your phone for an emergency. Call me when you get to the hospital. Whatever time it is. I'll be here."

"I'm counting on it," he said.

And then he was gone.

CHAPTER EIGHTEEN

Jules worked through the weekend, which wasn't as lonely as it sounded, since Boston's Bureau headquarters was a 24/7 kind of operation.

Besides, going in on a Sunday was a fair trade for having the following week off. And it was going to be an awesome week.

When Robin heard about Arlene and Maggie's trip to Las Vegas, he immediately offered to charter a flight out of Logan. It wouldn't cost him anything—he knew a guy who knew a guy, and the first guy owed Robin a major favor. That way, Will, Dolphina, Jules, and Robin could attend the wedding, too.

It wasn't long before Arlene got over her shock at the idea of Robin using up a favor that big on her, and it became a Plan, with a capital P.

Jack's son Luke was recovering from his appendectomy right on schedule—his appendix hadn't ruptured after all, and he was healing nicely from his surgery. The news about the rupture was either a) a mistake or miscommunication from the boy's understandably distraught mother made during a time of great stress, or b) an intentional exaggeration spun to send Jack catapulting across the country at warp speed to his son's hospital bedside, where his ex-wife would also conveniently be waiting and ready to provide comfort of all varieties. Depending upon whether or not Maggie was reporting the incident.

Arlene was decidedly more understanding. It was also obvious that she trusted Jack completely, even while he was in the company of a potentially crazy ex-wife.

But the *real* good news remained the fact that Luke was feeling much better, and that Jack could and would meet them in Vegas on Monday night.

They'd leave Boston on Monday afternoon, after Maggie got her homework assignments from school, fly in, find an all-night chapel for Arlene and Jack to tie the knot, and then bunk at the Bellagio where Robin had a standing invitation to stay whenever he was in town. In fact, all it took was one phone call, and the manager immediately reserved a three-bedroom presidential suite for Robin, as well as a more private honeymoon suite for the happy couple. All of it was on the house, because Robin was just that lovable and charming.

Part B of the Plan was that Will and Dolphina would bring Maggie back to Boston on Tuesday while the newlyweds spent an extra few days in the desert city, no doubt locked together in their room.

Jules would accompany Robin to . . . wherever it was that the Sundance Channel held its impending annual award show. Jules wasn't sure if it was L.A., or maybe somewhere in the Rocky Mountains. It didn't really matter where they went—it was going to be fun.

Of course, Robin could make a trip downtown to pick up the dry cleaning into something wildly entertaining.

Jules's phone rang—his direct line—and he picked it up. It was probably Robin, but he kept his greeting professional. "Cassidy." Besides, he knew that his husband found what he called Jules's "FBI agent mode" to be hot.

But it wasn't Robin on the other end. "Jules? It's Maggie."

It *was* Maggie. That was weird. How had she gotten this number?

"Wow," Jules said, unable to hide his surprise. "Yes, it's me. Hey, Mags. What's up?"

"My mother has to go back early," she said in a voice that was way too tight.

"What?" Jules said, immediately reaching for the remote to turn on the TV in his office. He didn't need to ask where. He knew what she meant.

Back to Iraq.

But the TV flickered on, and he quickly clicked through the various news channels, but they were showing nothing special. No breaking stories, no special reports, no relentless what-if-ing over pictures of some devastation or disaster.

"It's not fair," Maggie said, and he could tell she was fighting tears. "She was supposed to have a full month. This is *bullshit*."

"What happened?" Jules asked, as he went online to check Twitter. Often news came through via the Internet first. But Twitter was quiet, too.

"It's stupid," Maggie told him fiercely. "There was some stupid car accident, and everyone's okay, but one of the NCOs broke her legs and the other one hurt his back, and the *really* stupid part is that in the entire *stupid* Army, there's apparently no one else who can do my mom's job and—" She broke off as Jules heard the murmur of another voice. "I'm talking to Jules and . . . Wait! *Mom!*"

But the phone was apparently snatched out of the girl's hands by her mother. "I am *so* sorry," Arlene said, her voice thick with her apology. "She shouldn't have called you. This is *completely* inappropriate—"

"It's okay," Jules said.

"No," Arlene said. "It is *not*."

He could hear Maggie in the background. "I was just calling him to see if he could give us a ride to the airport, so at least I can have an extra half hour with you instead of having a stupid taxi pick you up!"

"Oh, shit," Jules realized. "Will and Dolphina went to New York." One of Dolphina's many cousins was getting married in a little town just south of Buffalo called Hamburg.

"They must've turned off their phones for the ceremony," Arlene told him. "And even if they turn them on right away, they won't get back here until tonight."

"I'll drive you to the airport," Jules volunteered. "Because Maggie's right. That way she can go, too, and be with you for as long as she possibly can."

"Thank you," Arlene said. "It's too much, but . . . Thank you."

"It's not too much," Jules countered. "Maggie's my friend. *You're* my friend. Friends call friends when they need help."

"When have *you* ever called anyone for help?" Arlene asked.

Jules laughed. "Oh, sweetie, you have *no* idea. Remind me to tell you about the time I was on this godforsaken island in the middle of nowhere, and I actually called . . . certain friends in very high places for some serious help. But let's not get into it now. It's not a story that works well in short form, plus I'd rather find out what's going on with you. There's *really* no one else in the entire U.S. Army who can do your job for a few more weeks, until your leave is up?"

Arlene sighed. "Of course there is. But unit cohesion suffers when new faces are brought in. And when unit cohesion suffers, soldiers—kids—die. I can't—" Her voice broke, but she faltered only slightly before soldiering on. "I can't let that happen. My CO called me directly and asked me to return early. In exchange, she's going to try to see what she can do to get me home for good, as soon as possible."

Jules could hear Maggie clearly in the background. "How could you believe anything *any* of them tells you?"

"I have to go," Arlene spoke over the girl. "If only to help them through the transition." She sighed heavily again. "It's particularly important because everyone's favorite first lieutenant was killed in the same car accident. God, Maggie's right about it being incredibly stupid. Despite all of the snipers and IEDs, Kevin died because a contractor in a semi got stung by some kind of wasp or a bee, and he swerved into oncoming traffic."

"I'm so sorry for the loss of your friend," Jules murmured. "And yeah, it can seem ridiculous. And even arbitrary. A car accident in a war zone . . . ?"

He heard Maggie say something, but this time her words were indiscernible. It was clear, though, that she had started to cry.

"I have to go back, Mag," Arlene told her daughter again. "I wish I didn't have to. I wish I could say no . . ."

"Have you told Jack?" Jules asked quietly.

"Yeah. He ran to the airport, to try to get a flight back to Boston. I don't know if he got one, because his phone died en route, and . . . He's not going to make it anyway, because my flight's at five-thirty."

"Tonight?" Jules asked, his voice betraying his surprise.

"Yes, tonight." Arlene was a little annoyed. "Didn't Will tell me you work with Navy SEALs? They get a call and they go. Immediately. They don't get any time at all to pack or say goodbye."

"Last time I checked, Arlene," Jules said evenly, "you weren't a Navy SEAL."

She laughed, just a little. "I know. And I'm sorry. I'm just . . ."

"I get it," Jules said. "Caught between Iraq and a hard place. Let me talk to Maggie again."

The girl was sniffling as she got back on the phone. "I didn't know that Kevin died."

"I think your mom probably didn't tell you that on purpose," Jules told her. "Look, Mags, here's what I'm going to do, okay? I'm going to pick you and your mother up at around three."

"That's way too early," Maggie protested.

"No, because we'll park, and we'll go inside, all the way to the gate, with her," Jules said. "I have a pass that'll get us into the airport, but you're going to have to go through security, so travel light, okay? Don't bring a jackknife or—"

"I've flown on a plane before, Jules," Maggie said in a prickly tone that was so nearly identical to her mother's that it was almost funny. Almost.

"Well, good," Jules said. "And don't tell your mom, because I might not be able to get it to happen, but I'll make a few calls, see if we can't find out if Jack's a passenger on a Boston-bound flight. Between you and me, I suspect he's already in the air. It's hard to imagine Jack Lloyd being thwarted by dead cell phone batteries."

She laughed at that, but it sounded watery.

"Anyway, *do* tell your mom this," Jules said. "After she boards her flight, I'll take you home and you can hang with Robin. And if she doesn't get in touch with your uncle Will, you are completely welcome to stay with us tonight, or really, as long as you need to."

"Thank you," Maggie said.

"See you in a few hours," Jules told her, but she was silent. "You okay?"

"Yeah," she said, and he could picture her squaring

her narrow shoulders and lifting her chin. "I guess I gotta go help my mom pack."

Chapter Nineteen

The afternoon was a blur.

When Maggie went into the bathroom to take a shower, Arlene used her daughter's phone to call Lizzie's cell, but got bumped to voice mail. So she called the number in Maggie's contact list for Milton, Mike.

Lizzie's scary older brother.

Who picked up immediately. "Maggie? Is everything all right? Are you okay?"

"No," Arlene said, but then quickly said, "Yes. I mean, no, it's not Maggie, and Maggie's okay, but . . ." She quickly explained how she'd first tried calling Lizzie, and then what had happened and how she was going back to Iraq.

He listened quietly, but she heard him sigh.

"I was hoping you could get word to Lizzie," Arlene said, "and then, maybe, both make a point to be somewhere close by for the next few days?"

"Of course," he said. "Look, I know how hard this must be for you, and I know you don't trust me and that dinner you planned was really so that you could interrogate me—"

"She's thirteen," Arlene said.

"You think I don't know that?"

"I think it'll be easy for you to forget."

"I won't," he said. "I gave you my word."

"And I'm holding you to it," Arlene said. "Right now, she needs Lizzie. She needs to feel safe when she's with Lizzie."

"I get it," he said. "I do. And look, I know you have email over there, so why don't you email me." He rattled off a gmail address that included his name and the number of his street address—easy enough to remember. "You can ask me anything or check up on me or . . . whatever."

"Thank you," Arlene said. "I will."

"I'd do anything for Maggie," he said. "And Lizzie really loves her, too. We got your back, Ms. Schroeder. We'll be there for her. Come what may. Shit." He laughed his disgust. "Excuse me. But I *knew* that *Moulin Rouge* was going to somehow come back and bite me on the ass. Maggie and Lizzie watched it, like, twice a week, for about four months. Which of course meant that if I wanted to use the computer, I had to watch it, too. Freaking Ewan McGregor . . ."

From the bathroom, Arlene heard the sound of the shower going off. "Thank you. Again," she said.

"Stay alert out there," he said, adding right before he cut their connection. "Be safe."

Arlene set Maggie's phone on the end table next to the sofa, near where her bags were packed and ready to go.

She caught a glimpse of herself in the mirror that hung next to the front door. Dressed in her BDUs, her pants tucked into the top of her boots, her jacket buttoned to her chin, with her hair tied neatly back, no makeup on her face . . .

She was ready for war.

As she gazed into her own eyes, they welled with tears. And for those few brief moments, before Maggie emerged from the bathroom, Arlene allowed herself to acknowledge the dreadful fact—a terrible possibility—that this might be it for her.

When she said goodbye to her daughter at the airport, it might be for the very last time.

She might never come home again.

But there were tens of thousands of servicemen and -women out there, just like her, who had said goodbye to their sons and daughters, their husbands and wives, their mothers and fathers and families, uncertain as to their own futures. That was always the case when one served one's country.

And until she came home safely—and even if, God forbid, she didn't—she would carry her love for Maggie and Jack and Will and, yes, even Dolphina with her, wherever she went, securely in her heart.

Arlene squared her shoulders and quickly brushed her tears away as the bathroom door opened. She even managed to smile at Maggie, whose own eyes were red.

"Ready?" she asked her daughter, who nodded.

Maggie hefted the larger of Arlene's bags, and together, they went out to the street, to wait for Jules.

CHAPTER TWENTY

Jack sat clutching the armrests in the airplane as it touched down at Logan Airport in Boston.

It was five minutes after five, and Arlene's flight was scheduled to leave in twenty-five minutes—if it hadn't already left early.

He was sitting in the back of the plane, which meant the entire full flight would have to empty before he could start his sprint through the terminal.

He knew that Arlene was flying out through World Airlines. She was taking a flight to New York City, where she'd transfer to another that would go first to Germany.

As the plane taxied to the gate, the intercom clicked on, and Jack focused, hoping to hear which gate that New York flight would be leaving from. But instead, the pilot spoke. "Ladies and gentlemen welcome to Boston where the temperature is a balmy sixty-four degrees. Please remain seated until we get to the gate. And even then, once we arrive, please remain seated and leave the aisle clear until passenger Jack Lloyd deplanes. See, his fiancée is shipping out to Iraq, and if he hurries to gate forty-two, he'll have just enough time to kiss her good-bye."

There was a murmur among the passengers, as Jack closed his eyes and blessed Jules Cassidy—this had the FBI agent's name written all over it.

But then the plane was at the gate, and his seat belt was off and he was on his feet. As he dashed up the aisle, someone began to clap, and the whole plane was applauding like some ridiculous Hollywood romantic comedy.

The flight attendants were smiling at him, and then he was through the door and running full speed up the ramp.

CHAPTER TWENTY-ONE

Arlene sat in the now nearly empty waiting area by gate forty-two, with Maggie on her lap.

"I love you," she told her daughter, who nodded as she clung to Arlene's neck. "But I need you to get off of me now, because I have to give you something."

Maggie wiped her eyes as she slid into the neighboring seat to let Arlene reach into her pants pocket. She pulled out the necklace she'd found on Maggie's dresser. It was long enough to be hidden beneath the neckline of her shirts. And onto it Arlene had put the ring that Jack had brought over to Will's apartment, that very first night he'd rocketed back into her life.

"I don't want to wear this over there," Arlene told Maggie. "So I was hoping that you would wear it for me until I get back."

Maggie's eyes widened. "What if I lose it?"

"You won't," Arlene said as she slipped it around her

daughter's slender neck. "You'll be careful with it. I know you will."

Maggie lifted the ring to look at the diamond as it flashed in the waning afternoon light shining in through the big terminal windows. "I will be careful with it," she promised.

Over at the gate, Jules was deep in discussion with the World Airlines attendant, who was shaking her head. No doubt they'd held the gate for as long as they could. It was time to go.

Jules took out his phone and dialed it, but it was more than apparent now that not only had Jack's phone given up the ghost, but that he wasn't going to make it. Arlene was going to have to say her goodbyes to him via email.

She stood up, and Maggie threw herself into her arms and hugged her tightly. "Be careful of land mines and mortars and snipers and IEDs and truck drivers who are afraid of bees."

Oh, God, now her daughter had yet one more thing to worry about. "I will," Arlene promised. "You be careful of truck drivers who are afraid of bees, too, okay?"

Maggie nodded, getting the message that the accident could just as easily have happened here in Boston. "I love you, Mommy."

"I love you, too, monkey-girl."

"Hey! *Hey! Arlene!*"

They both looked up, and there he was, running toward them.

Jack.

And Maggie gave Arlene a push and it was all she needed to start running, too, toward Jack, and then, God, she was in his arms and he was kissing her.

His mouth was so warm, and he'd been drinking coffee, probably nonstop since he'd caught the plane from California, but he'd made it.

And she didn't ever want to stop kissing him, but she

had to go. And the tears that she always worked so valiantly to hide from Maggie escaped. "I'm so sorry," she told him.

"I know," he said as he turned her so that Maggie couldn't see her, even as she dug through her pockets for a Kleenex. "I'm in love with you, remember? I'm in love with *you*, and if I had to answer the question *What would Arlene do,* I would say that of course you'd go back."

She laughed as she wiped her eyes and blew her nose, as she looked at him, trying to memorize him—his smile, his warmth, the width of his shoulders, the unruly lock of hair that fell into his eyes—for the cold and lonely days and nights she knew were coming.

He was looking at her just as intently, but then he pulled her close and kissed her face, her nose, her cheeks, her mouth, her chin. "Vegas schmegas," he said as he pulled Arlene over to where Maggie was standing near Jules and the woman from the airline. "Mags, can I borrow your lucky ring?"

Maggie clutched the diamond ring that Arlene had just given her, but Jack was pointing toward the kelly green plastic leprechaun that she'd gotten at Laser-Mania.

"I need to borrow it for a few months," Jack added. "I hope that's okay."

Maggie nodded as she handed it to him.

But then Jack's full attention was back on Arlene. And as she gazed up into the warmth of his whiskey-colored eyes, he whispered, "With this ring, I thee wed," as he slipped it onto the ring finger of her left hand.

She laughed both from her surprise and from the power of the emotion that filled her.

"We don't need to be in Vegas to start our lives together," Jack told her. "We don't even need to be together. You're mine now, and Leenie, I'm *all* yours, and when you come back, we'll go and sign whatever papers need to be signed and filed. But that won't change the fact that it starts right now. You and me. Forever."

As Jack kissed Arlene again she heard the attendant from the airline say to Jules, "I'm sorry, sir, the flight is full, otherwise I'd be more than willing to bend the rules."

"How about you let me go on and see if there's someone willing to take the next flight to JFK," Jules suggested, and Arlene knew he was trying to arrange a seat for Jack to go with her, at least as far as New York.

But Jack heard him, too, and he stopped kissing Arlene to say, "No, that's okay. Thank you, Jules, but it's best if I stay here."

With Maggie. He didn't say those words, but he didn't have to. Arlene knew that whatever happened—what was it that Mike Milton had said? That line from that movie? *Come what may* . . .

Come what may, God help her, Jack would be there for Maggie, forever, too.

That vow he'd made may not have been legal, but it was real.

"I'm so sorry, ma'am," the woman from the airline said, and she really was sorry. She actually had tears in her eyes. This was probably the most up-close-and-personal she'd ever been to the reality of a war that was being fought on the other side of the world.

Arlene picked up her carry-on bag, but then she dropped it so that she could hug Jules, and then Jack, and then Maggie one more time.

And then Jules was holding out her bag for her. She slipped its strap over her shoulder as she gave her boarding pass to the woman and started down the ramp. But she turned as she walked, to look back, one last time.

Jack had his arm around Maggie, and Jules was

standing solidly on her other side. "We'll keep the home fires burning," Jack called.

She nodded. "See you soon," she said, and got on the plane.

Epilogue

Sgt. Arlene Schroeder Lloyd received an honorable discharge from the Army in February 2009. She, Jack, Maggie, and three-year-old Ian live in Needham, Massachusetts, in a small house where they are joined several times a year by Jack's sons Luke and Joey.

Jack recently sold his first novel, and has found some significant acclaim as a political blogger for a popular online news site. Arlene works part-time at a little bookstore five minutes from their home.

They are happy, but life is not without turmoil. Especially ever since Mike Milton joined the Marines.

He currently serves in Afghanistan.

And Maggie emails him every day, without fail.

A SEAL and Three Babies

March 2009
This story takes place several weeks after Hot Pursuit, *and a month or so before* Breaking the Rules.

Chapter One

The tiny country of Tarafashir

A narrow portable stairway had been pushed up against the commercial airliner, and the metal pinged and shuddered under Sam Starrett's boots as he squeezed his way down to the airport runway. He had his son, Ash, in one arm, Ash's diaper bag over his shoulder, and not just one but two car seats in the other hand.

They were bulky and awkward, and it was all about getting a good grip—and having large enough hands.

Robin and Jules Cassidy were right behind him, wrestling with the third car seat along with a variety of the group's carry-on bags. Then Sam's wife, Alyssa, muscled down the two strollers they'd need for this monthslong adventure, followed by Max and Gina Bhagat, who carried their freakishly polite three-year-old daughter, and their eight-month-old high-decibel soliloquist son, who was still bewailing the entire traveling team's frustration, discomfort, and bitter disappointment.

This little multifamily outing had quickly turned into a misadventure when their first flight was delayed—

nearly six hours at the gate, and well over two on the tarmac, at J-Effing-K. As a result, they'd arrived in London at WTF o'clock, having missed their connecting flight, an event that had dominoed and created a need to take this latest several-hours-delayed flight which in *turn* had had a mild midair emergency with the electrical system, requiring that they land here, in the tiny country of Tarafashir, still a four-hour crapfest from their final destination.

Sam was well aware that there were definitely worse places to make an unplanned landing—Libya, Pakistan, Kazbekistan, to name a few. At least T-fashir was U.S.-friendly and safe, although mostly piss-poor. The government was a monarchy, and their leader a king who had, at one point, not just been a monk, but, according to legend, a *stoner* monk.

The country's major exports in past decades had been marijuana and opium. And although there was a vaguely successful program in place in which farmers who replaced their crops with soybeans received sufficient food and medical care for their villages, it was clear to Sam, just from looking at the badly patched and pitted runway, that the also-promised modernization of the Tarafashir infrastructure had again been delayed.

Possibly because the entire country still had a raging case of the munchies.

"They're holding our flight to Kabul. Gate one. It's on the other side of the terminal," Max Bhagat announced as he ended his phone call and slipped his cell into the pocket of his jeans before helping Gina juggle their two kids. Mikey, the eight-month-old, was usually as goofily, droolfully cheerful as Sam's son, Ash.

Usually.

Today Mike had fussed and worried his way through the seemingly endless flight, needing all four parental hands to cope. His sister, Emma—age three-going-on-forty—

had been safely tucked in between her Uncle Robin and Uncle Jules. Emma had played for a while with one-year-old Ash—who'd gone into pissed mode, no doubt at Mikey's stellar example, and who had decided he wouldn't even *think* about napping unless he sat on Uncle Robin's lap—until he'd finally fallen unconscious. Ash, that is, not Robin. At which point Em had no doubt spent the remaining hours of the flight discussing the socioeconomic ramifications of *The Cat in the Hat* with her patient pseudo-uncles.

The little girl was freakishly smart, impossibly polite and well-behaved, and way too somber for her own good. Plus, she was a tiny sponge—always, *always* watching and listening to the grown-ups around her.

"Shit." Jules now swore at Max's news about the flight to Kabul, not quite under his breath. He then made a face at Emma, whose brown eyes had become even bigger at his slip.

Sam found that to be one of the biggest discomforts of parenting—the inability to say *shit* in times like these, when a pungent and heartfelt *shit* was clearly needed.

In the past well-over-twenty-four-hours of nonstop, cranky-child-inducing, slow-mo travel, *this* was the one flight they could've stood to miss.

But as Emma giggled at the silly face Jules made, Sam made a note and filed it under *useful information*. The fact that Emma was capable of smiling, let alone giggling, was good to know.

Of course, Uncle Jules was special.

And not just because he was an FBI agent, or because he was fabulous and gay-married to a movie star.

Jules was . . . Jules. One of a kind.

"It's all right, babe," Robin murmured, giving his husband a smile and a nudge with his shoulder. "We always know this might happen, anytime we travel. And it's good. You need to get there."

"Yeah, I know," Jules muttered back on a sigh. "I just wanted . . . at least to be able to say goodbye properly."

"We got time," Sam pointed out. "They're holding the flight."

Max's announcement *was* good news in the big-picture sense—and not entirely unexpected considering that Max, a high-level FBI agent, had the President's private number among his list of contacts on his phone.

Sam turned to look at Alyssa, who took Ash from his arms.

"Mommy wants to say a bad word, too," she told their son, who gave her a drooly smile as he burbled some of his near-perpetual joy back at her, unaware of his own impending misfortune.

Alyssa looked back at Sam then, and he could see her unhappiness. This was the hardest part—she hated this kind of separation. She preferred working *with* him, but she knew damn well that they couldn't both go out into dangerous, terrorist-filled countries. Not together. Not anymore. Because of Ash.

He and his wife risked their lives for a living—that wasn't going to change—but they could no longer risk them both at the same time.

And that sucked.

But it also didn't suck—again, because of Ash.

"We'll be fine," Sam told the woman who was not just the love of his life, but the best team leader he'd ever had. She was commanding, decisive, cool under pressure, compassionate, intelligent, and hot as hell when she barked out orders. Yeah, he was going to miss working with her on this op, too. But he'd survive. "We're gonna be okay."

"I know that." Lys managed a smile as she locked Ash

into the frontpack she wore, so she could carry those strollers while Sam humped it with the car seats and their carry-ons.

Together, with Max and Gina leading the way, with Jules and Robin on their heels, Sam and his family went into the airport's crowded terminal—assuming this rusting and ancient World War II–era Quonset hut could be called a terminal.

It was cooler inside, but only slightly. The building wasn't air conditioned, and the big fans overhead spun slowly, lazily. Sam could see the fading red paint of a sign for gate one on the other side of the structure.

"I just really wanted to help get you settled," Lys told him as they threaded their way through the crowd of locals, most of whom wore the unmistakable white robes that identified them as monks, their shaved heads gleaming in the cheap fluorescent lighting. "And I *really* don't like leaving you here. Tarafashir was *not* part of the plan. *We* shouldn't be the ones to leave first."

"We're gonna be okay," Sam said again. "Our flight's in just a few hours. Those of us who are small will change our diapers, those of us who are bigger will get something to eat that's hopefully neither dog or goat, and we'll all stretch our legs. We'll be fine, and then we'll be in a resort hotel on a private island in the Aegean sea."

Alyssa, Jules, and Max, however, would be *not* in a seaside resort hotel. They'd be in landlocked Afghanistan, sleeping in barracks or maybe even in drafty tents. They'd barely have time, after touching down in Kabul, to grab a meal before they went wheels up again, this time to the first of a half dozen FOBs—remote military forward operating bases in the mountains. The chosen FOBs were all regular stops on the standard USO tour, and the President was determined to visit at least one of them during his upcoming trip.

As members of the special advance advisory team in

charge of providing information to ensure the President's security during his impending visit, they would have to evaluate them all.

Over at gate one, Max had set down the various pieces of luggage he'd been carrying, and was group-hugging his wife and children. It wasn't until he kissed Gina that Sam realized exactly what Jules had said.

I just wanted at least to be able to say goodbye properly.

Jules's wanting to say goodbye properly had nothing to do with time, and everything to do with the fact that while Tarafashir was ruled by a U.S. approved monarch-slash-dictator, and while visiting Americans were treated with respect, the royal family and governing body was socially conservative, and homosexuality was illegal.

And *that* meant that even though Jules and Robin were lawfully wed in the state of Massachusetts, saying goodbye with a PDA more extreme than a handshake was likely to get them thrown into jail.

And that—a goodbye said with a handshake—was *not* okay with Sam.

Not while there was a chance—a slim one, but definitely a chance—that Jules wouldn't return from this mission.

So Sam unloaded the car seats next to Max and Gina, who were still lost in their own private world, and he quickly kissed Alyssa on the mouth. "Don't get on that plane until I get back."

She laughed at that. "I won't, because I'm not taking Ash to Afghanistan."

"Good." He grabbed Jules with one hand, and Robin with the other, and pulled them over toward the obvious international sign for the men's head. The bathroom was a single-seater with a door that didn't lock. Pushing it open, Sam saw that it was, at least, empty.

"Tech check," he said to Jules, who nodded his understanding as he ushered Robin inside, closing the door tightly behind them.

Sam then stood in front of that door, arms folded across his chest, his message clear to everyone despite the potential language barrier: *Find another bathroom. This one's taken.*

Chapter Two

"Tech check?" Robin repeated, confused as Jules closed the men's room door behind them.

No doubt Jules had understood Cowboy Sam's cryptic message, because he was scanning the ceiling and the walls, and even looking along the concrete floor and behind the toilet that hadn't been cleaned. Ever.

"No surveillance cameras," he told Robin. "We're good."

"Ah." *Now* he understood. And it seemed a shame to waste the privacy that Sam had conjured up for them, but there were things Robin needed to say. "I know I'm not supposed to tell you to be careful. I'm supposed to say *be safe*."

"I will be," Jules said as he pulled Robin into his arms. "Both as careful and as safe as I can manage."

Which was great, but in reality, that might not be careful and safe enough to bring him home alive.

Two trips to Afghanistan ago, Jules had come perilously, heart-stoppingly close to coming home in a body bag.

One trip to Afghanistan ago, Robin didn't eat or sleep the entire time that Jules was gone.

"I love you," he managed to say now.

"I don't have to do this," Jules started to tell him, but Robin cut him off.

"Yeah, you do. And I'm gonna be okay. Sam and Gina need me to help with the kids. It's going to be fun."

Jules laughed. "You're a terrible liar."

Robin corrected himself. "It's going to be as fun as it possibly can be."

"Hmmm," Jules said as he looked at Robin.

"Call me," Robin said. "Or email. As often as you can."

"I hate doing this to you. Putting myself in danger. It's not worth—"

"Oh yes it is." Robin cut him off. "It's worth it. *You're* worth it. You're *you*. I love you for being you. Why would I want you to be anyone but who you are?"

Jules's beautiful brown eyes welled with emotion. "God, I love you," he whispered.

"Then kiss me, babe," Robin said. "And then go get on that plane."

And Jules did.

CHAPTER THREE

"I'm sorry, what?" Sam turned to look at Gina, who was the closest thing he had to a languages expert in his current six-person team.

It was a team that consisted of an eight-month-old, a one-year-old, a three-year-old, and two twenty-somethings who were hopelessly in love with their partners—partners who'd recently left for a war zone.

And that meant that Sam's team's major skill sets were eating, pooping, crying, and/or trying not to cry or otherwise appear worried so as not to frighten the super-short team members.

Of course, none of the short people were fooled by the badly hidden stress levels. Certainly not Emma, who was looking pale and was watching Sam glumly with those eyes that reminded him a little too much of her father.

Max had tried to hook up with Alyssa back when Sam was married to his first wife, Mary Lou, and . . . Or maybe it was Alyssa who'd tried to hook up with Max back when Max was trying desperately to keep his distance from Gina because she was nearly twenty years his junior.

It had all been a screaming charlie-foxtrot, and even though Sam had had no right to be jealous, considering he had been married to another woman at the time, seeing Max reminded him of that time of pain. And the fact that mini-Maxine here was the spitting image of her father was vaguely disturbing.

Yeah. This was going to be one long month—not counting the next apparently-destined-to-be-insanely-grueling twenty-four hours of ongoing travel.

"He said our flight's been canceled due to . . ." Gina, who was possibly even paler than her daughter, repeated the heavily accented words uttered by the heavily accented man behind the World Airlines counter.

But it was Robin who understood the last part. "Weather," he inserted. "The incoming flight from Tunisia's been canceled—and that's the plane we were supposed to leave on, so our flight's been canceled, too. The next flight to Athens isn't until . . . *When?*"

Gina leaned toward the counterman, her expression echoing Robin's dismay. "I'm sorry, did you just say *Thursday?*"

It was Monday. Late Monday—almost Tuesday, but still, sadly, Monday.

"Are you freaking kidding me?" Robin's voice went up an octave.

In Sam's arms, Ash started to cry. He may not have understood all of the words, but he clearly got the tone. "Shhh," Sam soothed him, automatically starting to rock. "We're okay. It's okay, Little Bit. We'll figure this out."

Meanwhile, Robin was getting taller, looming over the airline representative. "Oh, no," he said. "No, no. No." He was an actor, and was usually low-key, but in times of stress he was capable of going big with the drama. "Thursday? No. No, no. We'll take your next flight. Tonight. To anywhere."

"Pakistan," the man said. To give him credit, he was trying to be helpful. But he was mostly clueless.

"Except there."

"Libya?"

Gina made a guttural sound of intense pain.

"Or there," Robin said.

"Tomorrow morning," the man told them in the lilting accent that Sam was starting to be able to understand, "we have a flight to Roma. At . . . six-oh-five."

That was only seven hours away. And Rome was marginally closer to Athens. Sam spoke up. "We'll take it."

"But . . . alas, my friends, only two seats are available."

Of course. "Please find the next flight with the number of seats that we need." Sam forced himself to be patient and to not jump over the counter and look at the computer monitor himself.

"Two-seventeen P.M.," the man said but his triumph quickly faded. "But, oh, that takes you back to London."

"London works," Robin said. He looked from Gina to Sam. "I was there just a few months ago. I know a great hotel where they'll upgrade us to the presidential suite. I mean, if it's not occupied. We can take a few days to decompress, take showers please God, get some sleep and some real food, and then, when we're human again, we can get a direct flight to Athens."

"Sounds like a plan to me," Sam said.

"But we'll need to get our luggage now," Gina chimed in, "and the name of a safe hotel near this airport, where we can spend the night."

Sam shook his head. "I know it's not ideal," he told her, "but it's best if we just hunkered down—"

Gina was already shaking her head.

Sam lowered his voice, leaned toward her. "Gina, I know it's not going to be easy to—"

"Oh, God." Gina pivoted and thrust Mikey at Robin. "Take him, take him, *take* him. Emma, stay with Robin and Sam!"

As they all watched—Counterman was wide-eyed, too—Gina bolted for the ladies' room. Halfway there, she realized she wasn't going to make it, so she veered toward a trash can and . . .

A group of about a half a dozen monks had been walking serenely past, but now they all did a very sharp about-face and stepped up their pace, hustling away.

It was almost funny.

But Emma started to cry.

And Sam turned away. He had to. He was a sympathy vomiter—puking people were his kryptonite—and his last few badly cooked and too-greasy meals were flashing before his eyes. That cheeseburger, those onion rings . . . Holy *fuck*, this was going to be bad.

But Robin knew Sam pretty damn well. "Let's get the kids more mobile so I can go help Gina," he said, morphing smoothly from outraged drama queen to calm, efficient team leader, as he handed Mikey off to Sam. "You focus on getting the luggage and some hotel recommendations from Mr. Mumbles."

It was a good idea—at least the part in which Robin played nurse and Sam avoided playing nurse. He burped and tasted fish and chips. "We should stay here, in the airport," Sam started to say, refreshing his grip on both babies.

"That's not an option, Sam," Robin said flatly as he expertly unfolded Gina's double stroller. "Not anymore."

This was going to be noisy. Ash was still in that cry-at-the-drop-of-a-hat place, and Mikey was in full-on pre-wail, having been passed from his mom to Robin to Sam, his mouth in that telltale infinity symbol shape of doom. Putting the boys into the stroller was going to detonate both of them. Guaranteed. But it would free up Sam's hands, and he was going to need his hands while Robin's were full of Gina.

"Have you seen those public bathrooms?" Robin continued. "Forget about the fact that there are probably laws forbidding men going into the ladies' room, I am *not* letting Gina near that toilet. We need two rooms with two private bathrooms, preferably bed bug free but even *that* is negotiable at this point."

Sam had to ask, "Is Gina . . . ?" *Pregnant again?* He didn't say it, but Robin understood.

He made an *I honestly don't know* face as he helped Sam secure both Mikey and Ash with the stroller's seat belts.

"Please God, don't let it be the flu," Sam muttered, and Robin actually laughed.

"Oh, wouldn't *that* be great," he said then raised his voice. "Emma, come here, pumpkin-girl. We're gonna need you to push the scream-team in a big circle, around and around and around our luggage. Can you do that for me, buddy? So I can help your mommy with her tummy ache?"

Emma nodded, still sniffling. "My tummy hurts, too."

"I know, baby," Robin said soothingly. "We're all tired and hungry and a little bit cranky. So why don't you just rock 'em instead. Just back and forth, like this.

Okay? And maybe you could sing them that song I taught you, remember . . . ?"

"We'll need our luggage," Sam told the man behind the counter, raising his voice to be heard over Mike's and Ash's indignation, which was—hallelujah—fading a bit with Emma's help.

The little girl was singing, "All the single ladies, all the single ladies . . ." and Sam turned to give Robin a *really?* look, but Robin was busy tying back Gina's long, dark hair.

Sam swiftly turned back to the counterman. "And the names and numbers of the nearest hotels."

"May I see your luggage tags, sir?"

Sam found his boarding pass and held it out so the man could see the sticker with the info about his checked bags.

The World Airlines rep's fingers clicked on the keyboard, and then he made a sound that Sam didn't want to hear.

It was an *oh*, and it was not a happy *oh*. It was, for sure, a bad news *oh*.

But the man tried to spin it. "It seems your luggage is still in London, sir. But that's good, since you're now *going* to London . . . ?"

God damn it. Sam resisted the urge to put his head down on the counter. But there was one last option they hadn't checked. "Can you look to see if there's any other airline, with enough seats for all of us, flying out of Tarafashir tonight, preferably to Athens or London, but we're open to other possiblities . . . ?"

As the keyboard again clicked, Sam took out his phone and fired off a quick text to Alyssa, updating her as to their snafu.

But then Mikey and Ash's chorus of woe kicked up a notch, and Sam looked over, just in time to see that Emma had stopped singing and rocking them. She stood there, silently staring at him, doing her mini-Max imitation.

And then she puked. She didn't lean over, she didn't otherwise move. She just opened her mouth and out it came, a volcano of nastiness—down her tiny shirt and little jeans, and all over her miniature sneakers.

And Sam knew even as he crushed his instinct to run away and instead leapt toward Emma, to try help the little girl . . .

It was the flu.

They were screwed.

Murphy.

The seventh member of Sam's little team here in Goatfucklandia was Mr. Murphy, whose written-in-stone law was clearly in play.

Whatever can go wrong, will go wrong.

Emma threw up again, this time all over Sam's jeans and boots.

Hoo-yah.

Chapter Four

Afghanistan

The helo ride to the first FOB had been bumpy.

Apparently there was a late spring snowstorm barreling its way into the mountainous region.

Jules was glad that their luggage had been lost because the jacket he'd packed wasn't as warm as this replacement he'd been issued.

Alyssa, however, wasn't as happy as she looked around at the bare bones facilities of the remote camp: the tents, the fort-like walls of the machine gun nests made of concrete and rubble, but mostly rubble.

The desolate, barren surrounding countryside . . .

"He's gotta come *here* first," Alyssa was telling Max

and Commander Lewis Koehl. The CO of SEAL Team Sixteen, Koehl was in on this little recon mission, and three of his men had tagged along as slightly superfluous military might. "Not necessarily *here* here, but whichever operating base is the one that's safest on the day that he arrives. He's gotta land without a fanfare. No Air Force One. In fact, I'd recommend that Air Force One lands very publicly in Germany, to distract and misinform."

"I agree," Max said as Koehl, a man of relatively few words, nodded.

Alyssa continued. "Okay. So POTUS comes in-country on a regular military transport. He's boots-on-the-ground for a nanosecond—less—before he goes directly into the gunship, which brings him out here. And he stays for the shortest amount of time possible." She looked around again, shaking her head, and sighing again. "Even then . . ."

"With all the gunships providing additional security, not to mention the ones transporting the Secret Service detail and the press," Jules pointed out, "we'll be sending out a great, big *We are here, attack us now.*"

"There's not going to be any press," Alyssa said. "Not for this segment of the trip."

"That's good to know," Jules said, then asked, "How come I didn't know that?" He looked at Koehl, who seemed preoccupied, his mind a million miles away. "Did you know that, sir?"

Koehl nodded absently, looking at his watch.

"We limit the visit to five minutes," Max decided. "Get him in and out."

"Or limit the entourage to the size of a normal USO show," Jules suggested. "With SEAL Team Sixteen riding shotgun. And just make sure we have Teams Six and Two locked, loaded, and ready to go, in case there's trouble."

"I say we recommend all of the above," Alyssa said as the first flakes of snow drifted down from the pewter-colored sky.

"Excuse me, sir." A burly red-haired SEAL officer who was nicknamed Big Mac approached Commander Koehl, but then made a point to acknowledge Alyssa, then Jules and Max. "Ma'am. Sirs. I'm sorry to interrupt, but we just got a message that the helo that was supposed to swing past and pick us up has been delayed."

"Delayed," Koehl repeated, suddenly fully alert.

"Yes, sir." The big SEAL's last name was MacInnough. What was his first name? Jules was drawing a blank.

Still, he met Alyssa's eyes, because the subtext of that message was unmistakable. "Cat's on the roof," Jules said.

She smiled at his reference, but it was tight. "Apparently."

"What's on the where?" MacInnough—Alec, his name was Alec—asked as Koehl and Max stomped off to throw their rank and status against the inevitable.

"It's a joke," Jules explained. "A bad one that kind of sums up this delayed-helo situation. I heard it from Sam Starrett, so it's Navy SEAL–approved." He looked at Alyssa. "Should I tell it?"

She smiled, and in full favorite-thing mode, with the snowflakes on her nose and eyelashes, she looked more like a woman ready for a modeling shoot than one with a high-level security clearance and the ability to hit a target with a sniper rifle from ridiculous distances. "If I said no, would that stop you?"

"Probably not." He turned to Alec. "Okay. Guy goes on vacation and asks his friend to house-sit, to feed his elderly cat while he's gone. Coupla days in, he calls the friend to see how it's going, and the guy goes, *Oh, damn, I'm so, so sorry, dude, but your cat died.* And the vacation guy gets upset, of course, I mean, his cat's dead, and he says, *What the hell, Gary*—I guess I've named the house-sitter Gary. *That's not how you tell someone something like that. You ease into it, over the course of several days. Like when I call and say 'How's it going?' you say, 'Well, not great. The cat's on the roof. I'm trying to get him down.' And the next day, I call and you're like, 'Cat's in the tree, now. I'm sorry, man, it's looking bad.' And only then, when I'm psychologically prepared for it, you drop the bomb and tell me the truth.*"

The snow was coming down even harder now, and together they moved toward the main shelter where, yes, they'd be spending the night.

Oh, joy.

"Coupla days later," Jules continued, "guy calls back, and Gary answers the phone, and the guy says, *How's it going?* and Gary says, *Not great. Your grandmother's on the roof.* Bah dump bump."

"That," Alec said, chuckling, "is awesome. And you are completely right. Helo's delayed? The cat is, without a doubt, on the roof—because that helo's not coming. Not today. And? FYI? Last time I was out here at this time of year, and we got weather like this . . . ?"

"This is going to be great," Jules told Alyssa, who actually laughed.

"It started as an ice storm, which knocked out all power and communications," the SEAL informed them. "And then we got about three feet of snow on top of it. Total charlie-foxtrot. We were stuck here for nearly two weeks. They had to airlift in supplies."

"Fantastic," Jules said, as the skies opened up, not just with more snow, but with a very definite wintery-mix of icy rain.

They all ran the last few yards to the shelter, which was warmish and more dry, but smelled like summer camp: a cross between a wet yak and a boys' locker room that hadn't been aired out in a decade or two.

But it could've been worse.

There was coffee brewing, and as Jules pulled Alyssa with him toward the pot and collection of chipped mugs, Alec followed.

"How *is* Sam?" the SEAL asked.

CHAPTER FIVE

Tarafashir

Sam was asleep.

The former SEAL was sprawled out on one of the two rather ratty mattresses that lay directly on the worn hotel room floor, both baby boys fast asleep beside him.

Robin sighed as he did another silent inventory of their bottled water. No matter how many times he counted, he came up with the same number—not enough.

Right about now, they were supposed to have been checked in to their suite at Chez Bella, a lovely, gay-friendly resort in the Greek Isles.

Right about now, Robin was supposed to have helped Sam and Gina get the little ones into their rented cribs, so that the grown-ups could enjoy a lovely room-service dinner on their lovely private balcony that overlooked the very lovely Aegean Sea.

Instead, they were crammed into two dimly lit, seedy adjoining rooms in a run-down fleabag hotel in a third world country that, while pro-American, was extremely anti-woman and decidedly anti-gay.

"One room for the contagious," Sam had announced when they'd checked in at a front desk in a lobby that also apparently served as the local brothel, "and one for the rest of us."

Although, really, the logistics of *that* were challenged when both Gina and Emma needed access to a bathroom at the exact same time.

Robin had played nursemaid while Sam had kept himself and the babies properly distracted. And, eventually, the fireworks had stopped, and their two casualties fell asleep, exhausted, on the ratty mattress in the adjoining dimly lit, seedy room.

Sam then spent the best part of an hour cleaning the bejesus out of both bathrooms and washing out his jeans and Emma's clothes while Robin sang songs and played peek-a-boo with Ash and Mikey.

But now all three were asleep, leaving Robin as last man standing, which meant . . .

"Don't even think about it."

Robin turned to find the former SEAL watching him, apparently not-so-much asleep after all.

"Don't think about what?" Robin asked, injecting a whole load of innocence into his voice. He may have been a crappy liar when talking to Jules, but he was a very good actor, so he now acted like he didn't know what Sam was talking about.

But Sam wasn't fooled. "Leaving the hotel to get supplies," he said, his voice low so as not to wake the babies.

"We're almost out of disposable diapers, we definitely need more bottled water . . ." The front desk only offered beverage choices of beer, wine, and whiskey, along with their main menu consisting of women and children of all ages. "And I don't know about you, but I could use something to eat."

Sam sat up. "Yeah, but you're not the one to go out shopping. Not in this city, by yourself. I think I have some Cheerios in my bag."

"Dry Cheerios," Robin repeated. "Yay, but, no thank you."

Sam shot him a look. "I have powdered milk, too, but I meant for Ash, and even Emma, in the morning, if she's up for it." He pointed with his chin toward the bag that sat on the sad-looking dresser. "I still have some power bars. And chocolate. We can make it—ration the diapers—until we're on the plane tomorrow."

Robin had to laugh, but he did it quietly. "You seriously believe we're leaving tomorrow?"

"Oh, yeah. Come hell or high water, we are getting on that plane." When Sam said it like that, complete with his trademark Texas twang, it rang of absolute-factness.

It would've been so easy to buy into the former SEAL's military-officer-grade conviction. Still, Robin knew better. "The way I figure it, Ashie'll start throwing up some time around four A.M. Or Mikey. Or both of 'em, just to make life interesting. After which it's only a matter of time before you and I fall. We need to have enough food and water here in this room before that happens, because as much as you don't want *me* going out there, I don't want Gina going out there."

"I won't fall," Sam said with that same written-in-stone tone.

"Dream on. You're already looking green," Robin countered.

"I'm not saying I won't lose my lunch. That's coming, believe me, I know that. It's amazing it hasn't happened yet. But what I'm saying is I won't fall when I do. Trust me, I've been sick before while out in the world," Sam told him. *Out in the world* was slang for out on a SEAL mission. "And this situation sucks, for sure, but it's nothing like *that* was. I'll be able to get us the food and water we need."

He said it with that same grim certainty, but Robin was not convinced. "If you're dehydrated and delirious—"

"I won't be."

"—then it's gonna be on me," Robin said. "And I'd rather go out and get the supplies now, rather than having to leave both you and Gina alone with—"

"And I'm saying *no*." Sam held up his hand, his eyes tightly closed, as if he were willing away whatever awfulness he was feeling. Apparently, it didn't work, because he whispered, "Ah, *fuck*," and then scrambled for the bathroom.

"Okay, so I was wrong with my doomsday scenario," Robin admitted, even though there was no way Sam could hear him over the unpleasant noise he was making in that bathroom. "It's not Ash who throws up at four A.M., it's you who yukes at right-now o'clock, followed by Ash and Mike, simultaneously, at four A.M."

Robin checked the babies. They were both sleeping soundly, lying on the firm mattress. He took the pillows and blankets off the bed. It was warm enough in there—understatement, it was a sauna—not to need them. This way, Ash and Mikey would be fine, even if they woke up.

He then checked for his wallet—it was in the back left pocket of his jeans—before moving toward the bathroom, where he expected to see Sam kneeling before the porcelain goddess through the slightly open door. "I'll see if housekeeping has some kind of bucket we can borrow, so you can at least sit out there and keep an eye on—"

But Sam was already standing and rinsing his face from the questionable water coming out of the faucet of the sink.

Robin pushed the door all the way open. "Don't drink any of that," he warned, and Sam shot him a baleful look.

"I'm not an idiot, Boy Wonder."

"For all I know, you're delirious."

"Will you stop with the delirious." Sam wiped his face with a towel, then braced himself on the edge of the sink as he glared into the mirror, as if willing himself to be well enough to run their errands in a strange city in a foreign country in the middle of the very dark and potentially dangerous night.

"I can do this," Robin said.

"What if someone recognizes you?" Sam asked, and the fact that he was no longer flatly saying *no* was a testament to how awful he was feeling.

"Then . . . I'll sign an autograph for them . . . ?"

Sam didn't laugh. "I'll go, and just fucking get this over with."

Robin countered with his own worst-case scenario. "What if you go out, and you stop to puke, and someone thinks you're vulnerable—which you will be, because, hello, you're puking—and they mug you?"

"That'll be their mistake," Sam said.

"Not if they catch you off-guard and knock you unconscious."

"Not gonna happen."

"Your eyes are closed right now," Robin pointed out.

Sam opened them and looked at him. "Because I'm pretty sure *you're* not going to jump me."

Somewhere, in some far corner of the city, a siren started to wail.

"What is *that*?" Robin asked, but Sam shook his head. Fortunately it wasn't close enough to wake Gina, Emma, or the boys.

"Maybe a fire alarm?" Robin suggested.

"Could be," Sam agreed, but he didn't look or sound convinced. "Grab my phone, will you? It should be done charging by now."

Robin went out to where Sam's phone was plugged

into an adapter that was plugged into the outlet in the wall. It was only slightly charged, but he brought it in to Sam anyway.

"Fucking brownout slows everything down," Sam muttered as he straightened up and took it, flipping over to his messages—of which there were apparently none. "Shit, I got no bars, to boot." He tried making a call anyway, but gave up to again grip the sink when it didn't go through. The distant sirens had stopped, which was good. Wasn't it?

"Fahhhk," Sam breathed as Robin returned from plugging the phone back into the charger. "How could there be anything left in my stomach?"

It was a rhetorical question, not meant to be answered. Still . . . "Don't fight it," Robin advised.

Sam shook his head. "See if *your* phone has service," he ordered from between clenched teeth.

"While I do that," Robin said, "you see if it helps to just let go."

To his credit, Sam nodded and growled, "Close the fucking door."

Robin did as he took out his phone and simultaneously checked on the babies, who were no doubt dreaming they were back in the womb—it was that hot and humid in the hotel room.

His phone was useless, no service, no Internet. He tried making a call anyway—to Jules—but it beeped three times and went dark. Of course, that could've been Jules's inability to get a connection wherever he was, so Robin called what he thought of as the Troubleshooters Incorporated hotline. Day or night, it would connect him to whoever was on call at the office where Sam and Alyssa worked. But it, too, beeped and denied.

Robin tried texting Jules. *Now Sam's got the flu, too. Is there anyone local to provide assist? Maybe upgrade*

*us to guest quarters in a private residence? Wishful
thinking on my part? Be safe. We're ok. Love you.*

He pushed *send,* and the message vanished, but his
phone didn't make that satisfying swooshing sound that
meant the text had gone through.

In the bathroom, the dying ogre sounds finally
stopped and the toilet flushed.

Then Sam was back to running the water in the sink.
Still, Robin knocked softly as he opened the bathroom
door.

Sam glanced up. He looked like crap, and now his
hands were shaking as he toweled off his face, but he
said, "That helped."

Robin bit back the *bullshit,* and instead said, "I wish
we could go back in time, and stop ourselves from getting on that flight. We'd already be in London."

Where the concierge knew him by name, thanks to
his fame.

*What else can I get for you, Mr. Chadwick Cassidy?
How else can I help you, Mr. Chadwick Cassidy? Is
there anything else you need, Mr. Chadwick Cassidy?*

Most of the time, the endless fawning and relentless
toadying completely wore Robin out. Right about now,
though, he'd welcome it with open arms.

"We've been in far more uncomfortable spots," Sam
pointed out.

Just a few weeks ago, Jules, Robin, Sam, Alyssa, and
Ash had all been together in New York City, where a
notorious serial killer nicknamed "the Dentist" had
come dangerously close to killing both Jules and Alyssa.

Jules had survived by luck and his own quick thinking, while Sam had saved Alyssa's life by blasting a hole
in the wall of a creepy old town house, and then caving
in the killer's head with a pickax.

Which no doubt still gave him nightmares.

Or . . . maybe not.

Still, Sam was right. That entire experience had been far more *uncomfortable* than this one.

"Continuing to look on the bright side," Robin said now, "we haven't exactly had time to worry about Jules and Alyssa, have we?"

Sam made a vaguely laughter-like sound. "Good point."

Robin returned to troubleshooting their current problem. "We could wake up Gina, have her watch Ash and Mikey," he said. "Fetch her the aforementioned bucket. That way you and I could go on this supply mission together."

"Because you're so big and mean?" Sam asked.

Robin ignored the snark. It was obviously illness-induced. "I'm big enough. And I've played a Navy SEAL," he reminded Sam.

"In a movie."

"But being safe on the street is all about the illusion. The attitude," Robin argued. "If I walk the way you walk, stand the way you stand . . . No one will come close to us. We won't be a target, even when you're ralphing into the ornamental shrubbery."

"If," Sam countered. He had his eyes closed again, his knuckles white as he gripped the sink. "*If* I'm ralphing. Which I won't be."

"When," Robin said. "Here in my reality-based world, which, by the way, is a world where you usually reside, it's *when*."

"I don't want to leave Gina here alone," Sam said.

"So then we're back to my going downstairs and asking one of the ladies of the night to fetch a bucket for you before I go out and . . ." Wait a minute. Wait. A. Minute. The solution, suddenly, was right there. "Eureka!" It was so obvious. "All we need to do is hire a coupla hookers," Robin said triumphantly.

Sam didn't just open his eyes at that. He full-on turned his head.

The WTF look he gave Robin would've been funny if . . . Not *if*. It was definitely funny.

"To get us food and water," Robin explained, laughing. "Obviously they're for hire, right? We just hire them to do what we need instead of the creepy stuff. Of course I'd love it if we could use your credit card instead of mine. Because you know if I use mine, it'll be all over TMZ before you can say *paying for sex*. And Jules's career is . . ."

He didn't finish the sentence, because Sam had made it clear in the past, many times over, that he believed Jules's marriage to Robin had permanently trashed Jules's once gleaming career with the FBI. Of course, Sam had also acknowledged that some things were more important than a man—or a woman's—career.

In the distance, the sirens started up again.

"What *is* that?" Robin asked.

"Try to find an English-speaker," Sam ordered. "And make sure that whoever you hire is well over age eighteen. No twelve-year-olds, as tempting as it'll be to try to save them, or at least give them a respite from their ongoing abuse. Because no one's going to believe us when we say we paid 'em to grocery shop. It's important."

"Understood," Robin said.

"Try to get more than one bucket or pail or even some plastic bags while you're down there," Sam continued, "so we can go mobile when it's time. And make arrangements for a car to pick us up to take us to the airport no later than noon. We *are* gonna be on that plane, I don't give a shit what you think. And find out what the fuck those sirens are about. If we've got bad weather coming, or some kind of, I don't know, tsunami or what have you, I want to know about it."

"Good thinking," Robin said.

"Be back up here within five minutes," Sam continued. "Even if only to check in before going back down again. I don't want you gone for longer than that, at any given time. And, whatever you do, do *not* leave this building. I'm trusting you, Robin. Man to man. Do this right. Don't let me down."

Of all the things Sam might've said . . . "I won't," Robin promised.

He checked the babies one last time—all was still quiet—before he went out the door.

CHAPTER SIX

Afghanistan

The meeting was productive.

Alyssa had taken advantage of the advisory team's being locked in with a squad of soldiers by starting a discussion as to how *they* would set up security for a high-ranking visitor.

The ideas from officers and enlisted alike were flying fast and furious, and Jules was helping Alyssa take notes the good old-fashioned way, with paper and a pen by lantern light, since their cell phone and iPad batteries were nearly depleted, and the FOB's generator was reserved for essential things like keeping the coffee hot.

Max was sitting nearby, observing, listening, trying to appear patient when, in fact, Jules knew he was mentally pacing.

The last message that had come in from Sam was that not only had their flight been delayed, but that Gina had come down with some kind of food poisoning or stomach virus.

Jules knew that *Max* knew that his being over here

was hard for Gina. This entire "vacation" was little more than an endurance test for her. For Robin, too.

And even for Sam.

As a former SEAL and a man of action, it was possible that the role of sitting and waiting was hardest on Sam.

But it was Sam who had suggested the trip, generously offering to babysit not just Ash, Mikey, and Emma, but Robin and Gina, too. His plan was to distract everyone—no doubt himself included—while Alyssa, Max, and Jules were working in a war zone.

But Gina's getting sick was a little *too* distracting. For all of them. Especially Max, who was looking a little green himself.

"Let's take a break for now."

Jules glanced up as Alyssa continued, "We'll have an opportunity later to continue the discussion, so keep those ideas percolating."

Percolating. Good word. He stood up, stretching his legs, and headed for the coffeepot, going only slightly out of his way to pass Max, who had a half-filled mug, surely cold by now, on the table in front of him.

"You want a refill?" Jules asked.

"Yeah, because not sleeping tonight from a caffeine overdose sounds like it'll be so much fun," Max said dryly. But he held the mug, handle out, so that Jules could take it.

"We all know no one's sleeping," Jules countered. "Not until we get the word that their plane's wheels up out of Tarafashir." He took the mug and got in the growing line for coffee.

"*Out* of Tarafashir?" It was Alec MacInnough who was in front of him, and the SEAL officer turned around to tell Jules, "Who wants to leave Tarafashir? Man, what I wouldn't give to be going *in,* with Commander Jacquette and the rest of Team Sixteen."

Jules looked at him through the blear of too many days without any real sleep, and those words didn't make any sense. Until they made too much sense. "Wait a minute. What happened in Tarafashir?"

Alec was a little taken aback by Jules's intensity. "Oh, wow, sorry, man, I thought you knew. I mean, you brought it up, right?" He looked over Jules's shoulder, and Jules turned to see that Alyssa was standing right behind him.

"Why is a SEAL team going to Tarafashir, Lieutenant?" she asked, her voice even, her demeanor calm. Jules knew her well enough to know that her blood pressure was spiking.

"Ma'am, there's a hostage situation at the airport in the capital," Alec reported, looking from Jules to Alyssa and back. "Some kind of terrorist sleeper cell was activated and, well, they attacked. I didn't see the report, I just . . ." He raised his voice. "Jenkins!"

"Yes, sir?" With his freckles and boyish height, Petty Officer Mark Jenkins was older and way more capable than he looked. He appeared at Alec's elbow as if he'd been conjured there, and Alec jumped.

"God damn it," Alec said, "how do you do that?"

"I was standing right here, sir, you just didn't see me."

"What happened in Tarafashir?" Jules spoke over Jenk, even as Alyssa raised her own voice, calling, "Max! Sir, I think you need to hear this!"

And Max joined them as Jenkins, normally upbeat and cheerful, realized that this was personal. "Who's in Tarafashir?" he asked, his face suddenly that of a man with a dozen years of SpecOps experience.

"Sam and Ash," Jules told him. "And—"

"Robin and Gina," Alyssa said.

"My kids, Emma and Mikey, too," Max whispered.

Jenk glanced at Alec. "Sir, maybe there's been more information."

"Yeah." The SEAL officer nodded. "Excuse me, I'll go talk to Lew and request computer access. In the meantime, Jenkins, at least tell them what you know."

"Yes, sir, but it's not much," Jenkins said as Alec went out into the snowstorm, not bothering to grab his coat or a hat. "From what I understand—and you need to know that the report I saw was not verified, but . . . Earlier this evening, a dozen gunmen entered the airport in the capital city of Tarafashir and, without any warning, opened fire. Casualties are believed to be high, but we don't have details, because the tangos are still in possession of the terminal. We *do* know that two planes—both commercial airliners—took off shortly after the attack. F16s have scrambled with the intention of shooting them down if they don't follow radioed instructions and land immediately." He glanced at his dive watch. "It's hard to imagine we haven't already achieved that objective."

"So there was no timeline on the report that you received," Jules clarified, because he knew that Alyssa was thinking the same thing he was: *Please God, let them have left the airport before the bloodshed started.* She was reaching for her phone, no doubt to check what time it had been when Sam had sent his text.

"No, sir," Jenk said. "I'm sorry, sir."

If they could verify that Sam sent his message *after* the devastating attack . . . But in order to prove that, they needed to know when the gunfire had erupted.

Jenk continued, "But surely someone has that information by now."

"They're okay," Jules said, trying to convince himself as well as Alyssa and Max. "You saw the bathrooms in the terminal. If Gina was sick, no way would they spend the night there."

"Sam would want to," Alyssa said.

"But Robin would insist," Jules told her. "And trust

me, sweetie, when he wants to get his way? He gets his way. Sam didn't stand a chance. They're in a hotel. I know it." He looked from Alyssa to Max, trying to impale them with the power of his certainty.

But it was then that Alec MacInnough came rushing back into the shelter, shaking snow and ice off his thick brownish red hair. "Kill the lights," he shouted, and what little light there was was doused, leaving them in pitch darkness.

That couldn't be good. Jules leaned close to Alyssa to mutter, "Chewy, I got a bad feeling about this," just as Alec found them and announced, "Sorry, Internet's down."

Of course it was.

"I need you to bundle up," the SEAL added. "Quickly please."

"Can we send a message via radio? Contact Sam that way?" Alyssa asked, even as she slipped on her newly issued winter-white jacket and pulled on a white wool hat, tucking her dark hair inside.

"Radio's also out—with the wind and the cold and . . ."

Even better.

"Well, it's also probably being jammed, although we haven't verified that," Alec informed them as he led them to the door, but then held out a hand, signaling for them to wait.

"Probably?" Jules repeated, zipping up, while Alec opened the door a crack, peering out.

"We're kind of under attack," the SEAL said.

And . . . *there* it was. The only way this situation could have gone from mere shit creek to full-on paddle-free.

"Kind of." It was Max's turn to be the parrot as he pulled up his hood and tightened it around his unhappy face.

"Definitely," Alec clarified cheerfully. "So far it appears to be somewhere between two and four shooters—snipers. They took out the generator for the other building."

"So we're leaving the shelter and playing the part of the ducks in a row because . . . ?" Jules let his voice trail off.

"We're not going anywhere," Alec said. "Not yet. But we need to be ready."

"Snipers, in this weather?" Crouched next to Jules, Alyssa was incredulous. "With no visibility? Why is anyone going anywhere when we can just hunker down and freeze them out?" She paused. "Unless they're in place to take out squirters."

A squirter was someone who fled from an attack, particularly after the attack objective was bombed and on fire.

"Oh, good," Jules said as he realized this was why MacInnough had them here, by the door. The SEAL was no doubt in charge of keeping the visiting VIPs alive in the coming *mortar attack*.

As Jules looked back into the gloom of the building, he realized that the soldiers who'd been hanging out had put on winter cammie, and were slipping out, locked and loaded, into the night, through various back doors.

"Local command has insisted that the insurgents in this area don't have mortars or even grenades," Max reported tersely. "They claim that they barely have ammunition."

"Clearly they have enough ammunition to take out the generator," Alyssa countered.

"Yeah, and then there's the recent intel about an arms dealer moving into the neighborhood. Along with the info that a local warlord allegedly just traded his three favorite wives for a rocket launcher," the SEAL said. He smiled happily. "Said info is no longer alleged. And—lucky us—we didn't have to go traipsing through the mountains in a blizzard to find the damn thing. He brought it right here, to us. Considerate bastard."

Considerate bastard, indeed.

"How can we help?" Jules said it at the exact same time as Alyssa and Max, but he was the only one who added, "Owe me a Coke."

Chapter Seven

Tarafashir

Robin came back almost immediately.

"It's just me," he said, and it was good that he did, because when Sam heard the key in the lock, he'd immediately ratcheted up his personal defcon level.

"We've got a problem," Robin then said, going over to the carry-on bag and pulling out Alyssa's baby-carrying frontpack. He tossed Sam's larger model over, too, then adjusted the straps of Lys's to make it big enough to fit him, no doubt so that he could carry Mikey hands-free. "We've got to get out of here. Those sirens were a warning about a terrorist attack at the airport. And over at the American Embassy. There's a hostage situation there, too."

Sam curbed the urge to vomit at Robin's news as he slipped on the baby-pack, and picked up his phone. Still no bars.

"Cell towers are down," Robin reported. "At least in this part of town. And this hotel doesn't have a land-line."

"Gina, wake up." Sam went into the other bedroom, where Max's wife was curled around Emma.

The little girl's eyes opened first, so Sam held his hand out to her, his mind racing. They had to leave, but where would they go? He didn't know this part of the city, his GPS wouldn't work with the towers down, he didn't have a weapon, he needed a weapon, there were men with weapons no doubt standing guard outside the airport, which wasn't that far from here. Whatever they had was his for the taking. All he had to do was find a guard or a pair of guards who were isolated from the others. Disarming them and arming himself would be as easy as plucking Uzis from the idiot tree.

Except, Jesus he felt sick.

Sam forced himself to focus on the task at hand. "Em. Come on, hon, I need you to get up and use the bathroom, then I'm going to help you put on your clothes, okay, sweetheart?"

Emma looked down at Gina, who was still sound asleep, then up at Sam again before she nodded and solemnly took Sam's hand.

"Good girl," Sam said as he helped her up. "Need help in there?"

Emma shook her head no, pushing the bathroom door closed behind her.

Gina stirred then, looking up first at him and then over at Robin, who'd come to the doorway, packing a sleepy Mikey into the baby carrier he was now wearing.

"What . . . ?" she said.

"There's been a terrorist attack," Robin said again. He turned to Sam, even as he found several bottles of water. He handed one to Gina before giving the baby a sip from the other. "I was asking the desk clerk about the sirens, and at first he said it was nothing, but there was a TV on, and the news came on and even though it wasn't in English, I could see that there was a problem at the airport, so he told me about it and about the hostage situation at the Embassy, too, but I knew that if I hadn't seen it on TV, he wouldn't've told me. And I also knew—I just *knew*—that if I hadn't played it cool and just been like, *Wow, thanks for the info, I guess we won't go to the airport tomorrow after all, we'll just sleep in and wait for the problem to be resolved,* the entire gang of 'em would've jumped me and tied me up and . . ." He took a deep breath. "We've got to leave— now—and not through that lobby. Because when I turned back to the stairs, one of the women said, *Have a good evening, Mr. Robin, sir.*"

"Shhh-yoot," Sam said, as Gina scrambled into the bathroom, pushing past Emma, who was listening, of course, her eyes wide.

"Yeah," Robin agreed as he handed Emma's still-damp jeans to Sam. "They recognized me. Hey, bunny-girl, let Sam help you get these on, okay?"

"Come here, Em." Sam crouched down next to the little girl. Her life was in his still-trembling hands, and she was looking at him as if she knew it. "We're going to be okay," he told her, told Robin, too. "There's a back stairway, out into the alley." It was possible that it was being guarded, but even if it was, Sam could handle the guards.

Even sick as a dog, he could do this with his eyes closed.

Meanwhile Robin continued, "The people who own this hotel probably have no connection to the terrorists, not politically or religiously, but a guy who pimps out children is gonna see this—me being here—as just another way to make a quick buck. I'm pretty sure he already sent someone over to the airport to try to sell me to the bad guys as the most recognizable hostage in all of Tarafashir. Most recognizable on CNN, that is. Of course, once they realize they have Max Bhagat's wife and kids . . ."

That was going to be a goatfuck of a whole different color.

"That's not going to happen," Sam said. Once out of

this building, they were going to have to get out of the city, too. There were caves in the nearby mountains where they could hide indefinitely. Except, forty miles was "nearby" only to a former SEAL. There was no way Gina was going to manage a four-mile hike, let alone forty miles on foot.

Sam mentally moved on to Plan B: Find a place to hide here in town.

Step one: Find someplace with a working landline, so he could call Lawrence Decker over at Troubleshooters Incorporated. Deck would call in backup, as well as an extraction team. It would be expensive, but Sam didn't give a shit.

"We gonna go?" Emma asked him as she bravely put one chubby little leg and then another into her pants, wincing only slightly. "S'cold."

"Yeah, I bet it feels good since it's so hot in here, huh?" Sam said.

She looked at him, like, *That was stupid, it feels icky and you know it,* but instead asked, "Mama an' Mikey an' Ash an' Unca Wobin gonna come, too?"

"Yes, they are," Sam said as he adjusted the elastic band around her tiny waist. "We're all gonna go together, but we have to be really quiet, okay?"

She nodded, looking up at her little brother, who was fussing in earnest now in Robin's frontpack. "Mikey wants Mama." She looked over toward the bathroom, where Gina had emerged. "Mama, Mikey wants you."

"I should feed him," Gina said staunchly, even though she needed to lean against the doorjamb. "I can feed him while we go." She looked at Robin. "That way you can carry Emma."

"I can carry both of them," Robin said.

"But you can't feed Mikey," Gina argued.

"All we need is to get stopped by the police because

you're breast-feeding in public," Robin said. "Besides, you're probably dehydrated—"

Sam let them duke it out as he went into the other room. He put all the water he could carry into the pockets of his cargo pants and made sure he took his phone charger, too. Still, what he wouldn't give for a weapon, any weapon . . .

He scooped the power bars, powdered milk, and Cheerios from his bag into one of the pillowcases from the bed, making it all easier to carry. Everything else, they'd have to leave behind.

On second thought, he added several disposable diapers.

He then tied the pillowcase to his belt, and lifted a sleeping Ash from the bed. "Time to go."

In the other room, Gina had wrapped one of the white sheets around herself, completely concealing Mikey. She'd draped part of it over her head as well, to cover her hair.

"Mama's a monk," Emma said as Sam stared.

"Yes, she is, isn't she?" he said, and put Ash down on the bed.

" 'Cept she don' have a shiny head."

"That's okay, baby," Robin called quietly from the bathroom. "I'm giving myself a shiny head."

And indeed, Robin was in the bathroom, already a step ahead of Sam, using the ridiculous disposable razor from the hotel's overnight-pack to shave the hair from his head.

"I cut my hair all the time to play a role," Robin said to Sam as he looked into the mirror and attempted to manipulate the razor.

Sam reached to take it from him. "It'll be easier and faster, if I . . ."

"Thanks." Robin sat down on the closed toilet. "I'm

thinking this is probably the most important role of my life. It'll grow back. It grows fast. I'd suggest you do it, too, and Gina, even, but I don't think we have the time. But let's definitely take the razors, in case we land somewhere with running water."

"You'll walk in front," Sam instructed. "Hood back. We'll keep ours up. Stay in the shadows. Like you said, it's all illusion and this one will work." It would have to.

Sweat dripped down Robin's face. "Hurry, man."

"I'm going as fast as I can," Sam said. "I don't want to cut you."

"Should we try to seek sanctuary at a monastery?" Robin asked.

"That's an option," Sam told him. "But our main goal is to find someplace where we can hack into the phone line—the landline. And FYI, I'm going to need you to carry both Ash and—"

"*Fuck! Shit,* turn away, turn away!"

Sam stepped back as Robin stood up, turned around, lifted the toilet seat and, yes. Robin joined the ranks of the extremely ill.

It was too much, too close, too real, too awful, and Sam joined in for the chorus, leaning over the sink. But his contribution was little more than dry heaves, since there was nothing left for his body to expel.

Still, his eyes watered, and his hands shook, and his body strained.

Robin finally flushed. "Sorry. God, I'm so sorry."

"We all knew it was just a matter of time." Sam turned on the water for him.

Robin only briefly splashed his face before returning to sit. "Hurry. Please."

"I'm going to need you to carry both Ash and Emma at first," Sam said, as if there'd been no interruption as he swiftly finished the job and used a towel to wipe the remaining hair from Robin's head and shoulders. "While I make sure there're no guards in the back alley, and dispatch them if there are. Can you—"

Robin didn't hesitate despite his shaking hands and watering eyes. "I can. I will. Whatever you need."

Out in the room, Gina and Emma had managed to gather the other sheets from the beds, and Sam and Robin now wrapped themselves in white, too.

"If I tell you to do something," Sam said, kissing Ash's sweet-smelling little head before handing him over to Robin, who put him into Alyssa's frontpack, "you do it. Is that clear?" He looked from Robin to Gina to Emma, including the little girl.

She nodded as Sam picked her up and handed her to Robin, who was sweating, but still managed to smile at Sam. "Let's do this thing."

Chapter Eight

Afghanistan

"Best way to help," Alec MacInnough told Jules and Max and Alyssa, "is to not get killed. It'll be over before—" He laughed as Commander Lew Koehl came through the door. "Looks like it's already over."

"We got 'em," Koehl said, actually cracking a very satisfied smile.

Max was not as happy. "How long have you known about this?"

"Long enough," Koehl said, "for you to be pissed. *I'd* be pissed if I were you."

"You put my team into danger."

"That's not why I'd be pissed," Koehl countered. "You were never in danger. And even if you were, what? You'd rather we'd sent a USO tour in your place? Your coming out here was necessary. It was business as usual. *I'd* be pissed about the fact that some of our allies are not in truth our allies. The information we share gets shared in turn with the very same people who want to kill our soldiers. *That's* why I'd be pissed. Because we have to pretend to be friends with those who side with our enemies. In order for our diplomats to keep up the charade, you *couldn't* know. You had to be in the dark."

Max was silent.

"I'm okay with being bait under these particular circumstances," Jules said.

"The good news," Koehl told Max, "is that the President never intended to visit a FOB as part of his trip. That was misinformation."

"Oh, thank God for that," Alyssa said.

"So what just happened here?" Max asked. "A team of your SEALs inserted . . . how?"

"HALO jump," Koehl said, which Jules knew stood for High Altitude Low Opening. And *that* meant that a team of SEALs had jumped out of a plane way, *way* high up in the sky, up where they'd needed oxygen masks and tanks to keep from suffocating. And after leaving the plane, they'd gone into freefall for a ridiculously long amount of time, only to open their parachutes relatively close to the ground, under all radar, where they could coast to a landing, undetected.

They'd then, no doubt, dug in despite the bad weather, forming a perimeter around the forward operating base, and waiting for the bad guys to show up with the newly purchased rocket launcher.

At which point, the SEALs crushed them like the amateurs that they were.

Mission accomplished.

"Let's get the generator back on line," Max said. "We need Internet access to—"

"I'm sorry, sir," Koehl said, "that's going to take a while. We had to let them get close enough to take out our SAT towers. And one of their snipers took a very lucky shot at the main generator, and . . . We'll need to wait for the weather to clear before we can switch that out with the backup generator."

Max looked from Alyssa to Jules, and Jules knew that Max was thinking about Gina and his kids, stuck in besieged Tarafashir with Sam and Ash and Robin.

"Sam's the best," Jules reminded him. "And Robin's with him."

This was what it was like to be assigned to one of these remote outposts. Every now and then, in fact, probably more often than not, they'd lose contact with the outside world, and every person stationed here would have absolutely no idea how their loved ones were faring.

And yet they'd put their heads down and do their jobs without complaining.

It was humbling. And inspiring.

"How can we help now?" Jules asked both Koehl and MacInnough. "I imagine guard duty is going to be stepped up over the next few days. And as long as we're here, we're available to assist."

CHAPTER NINE

Tarafashir

"Give me Emma and cover Ash's eyes," Sam gruffly told Robin, who immediately knew that whatever had happened out in that alley, it wasn't going to be pretty.

"Don't look," Sam told Emma as he covered her head with the sheet that Gina had been holding for him while he made sure their path to freedom was clear.

It was now.

Robin was aware of the figure of a man lying face down in a greasy puddle of . . .

It was raining, but not that hard—a light misting that made the empty street seem almost to shine.

"Are you okay?" asked Robin, moving closer to Sam, whose answer was a curt nod and a hard look. *Shhh.*

They had to be silent, and to move as swiftly as possible.

Ash was going for baby-of-the-year award, having fallen back to sleep in the frontpack Robin wore beneath his monk-costume-sheet. Sam, superhuman that he was, was not only carrying Emma beneath his disguise, but was now also helping Gina carry Mikey, with an arm of support around her waist.

The good news was that Gina and Emma were no longer throwing up.

The bad news was that Sam and Robin were going to leave an unmistakable trail behind them.

But Sam was already on top of that, and whenever Robin couldn't take another step farther, Sam seemed to know it, and he steered Robin toward the gutter, which was already disgusting. And when Robin was done, Sam covered up what he'd left behind, which had to be hell for Sam.

But onward they moved, every turn taking them further into the center of the city, and farther from the hotel.

And then, seemingly arbitrarily, Sam stopped them, tucking them more deeply into the shadows by ducking down behind a pile of trash—an old, sodden mattress and broken furniture. Finger to his lips, he set Emma down, wrapping her in the sheet that he took from his shoulders.

Then he turned, giving his attention to a small door

that Robin hadn't even realized was there among the battered bricks of the building's foundation. It was hobbit-sized, made of blistering and warped wood, with a big rusting metal lock sealing it shut.

Sam took out a knife, the blade flashing as it caught a stray bit of light, and Robin realized that he must've taken it from that guard in the alley.

He used it now, not to pick the lock as Robin had first assumed, but instead to pry off a set of hinges that connected the door to the brick wall. The nails popped easily out of the damaged wood, and Sam lifted the entire door from the wall.

And that was why they'd stopped here, at this particular building. It had a seemingly secure door leading into its basement—a door with hinges on the outside.

Sam held up a hand, signaling for them to wait while he went through that door first.

Time seemed to hang as Robin worked his way through a long list of what-if scenarios. What if Sam didn't come back? What if he came back shouting *Run! Run!* What if, while he was gone, someone discovered them, crouching there? What if Ash or Mikey or Emma started to cry? What if Gina passed out—she was looking pretty pale. What if Robin passed out—but he couldn't pass out. He wouldn't. He had to be ready in case Sam came bursting out of that basement, telling them to run.

But then, thank God, Sam appeared in the doorway. He reached his arms out, gesturing for Robin to give him Emma. Gina and Mikey went in next, then Robin passed Ash in to Sam, so that he could muscle the door back into place behind them.

It was dark in there, but Sam used his cell phone as a flashlight, the light from its screen bright enough so Robin could see the rough-hewn walls and the dirt floor, the ancient pipes overhead.

Like most basements around the world, it was cluttered with cast-off and long-forgotten junk. A half a bicycle, a semi-truck tire, a broken cricket bat, a pile of ancient and dust-covered empty bottles, a set of broken and rusty gardening tools, and a whole lot of less easily identifiable trash.

There wasn't much there they could make use of, at least not that Robin could see.

Sam, however, seemed fascinated by what looked like an ancient circuit breaker box in the corner across from a long-cold coal burner—no doubt about it, this place now featured only cold-water flats.

Robin's stomach churned and burbled, and he dug for his own phone to use it to light his way to the far corner of the room, stopping to grab a rusting shovel. But right before he turned away, he realized what it was that Sam was looking at.

Those were *telephone* wires coming into the building—wires that led up through the walls to the various apartments above them.

And as Robin quickly dug a shallow hole in which to place his continuing misery, so to speak, he realized that rescue—via a quick phone call to Troubleshooters Incorporated—was close at hand.

Sure, they were going to have to break into one of the apartments and either use the phone or steal a phone. But that seemed simple enough compared to what they'd already done and where they'd been and—

"Holy fah . . . leh-lah, leh-lah," Sam said.

"What's wrong?" Gina asked.

"No," Sam said. "Nothing's wrong. It's good, in fact, it's great." He laughed. "Someone in the building has a nonsecure wireless network. I don't have phone service, that's still down, but I can use my phone to access the Internet through this open wireless system, and send an email."

"I'll dictate," Robin said, using the shovel to cover up his deposit before he used his cell phone to light his way back to the others. "Dear Dave and/or Decker, Please come and get us ASAP. Love, Sam. P.S. Don't kiss us on the mouth when you greet us because we are fah . . . leh-lah contagious."

"I'm paraphrasing," Sam said dryly. "With luck, they're already looking for us and . . . Yeah, Dave was definitely standing by and thank you sweet baby Jesus. The SEALs have retaken the airport. *And* the Embassy. We're safe, but Dave recommends we stay put, out of sight, until they can send someone out here to pick us up."

"Is there any way we can get a message to Max?" Gina asked, her arms tightly around Mikey and Emma. "He and Alyssa and Jules must be going crazy, worrying about us."

"I'm on it," Sam said, his thumbs flying across his phone's keyboard. He'd put Ash into his frontpack, but after he sent the email, he gave the baby a hug. "You are *such* a good boy," he told his son.

Who mewed once and then vomited down Sam's shirt and jeans.

"Robin," Sam said quietly.

"I'm right here," Robin said. "I'll take him."

"Thank you."

He took the baby, and Sam took the shovel. And ran.

"Shh, it's okay," Robin said, as Ash started to cry. "You're okay, Big Guy. It's four A.M. You're right on schedule. Mikey's next."

"I'm pretty sure Mike had it first," Gina told him. "I thought it was just normal baby spit-up, but in hindsight . . ."

"Really?" Robin said, using a piece of one of the sheets to clean off Ash. "Yay."

CHAPTER TEN

Greek Isles

Jules found Robin sleeping on the beach, beneath an umbrella. "Hey, babe."

Robin sat up so fast he almost fell out of his lounge chair. "Oh, my God! You're here!"

"Yeah, we caught an earlier flight." Jules laughed as Robin enveloped him in a hug and kissed the bejesus out of him.

God, yes, this was exactly what he'd needed . . .

But then Robin pulled back to look at him. "Two *weeks* earlier?" he asked.

"The assignment took less time than we'd originally thought."

Robin ran his hand self-consciously across the dark stubble that covered his head. "I thought I'd have more time to, you know, grow this out."

"It's actually adorable. And amazing," Jules said, "and it makes it kind of impossible to ignore what happened to you, and Gina, and Sam and the kids—God, when we heard, we were sick, we were so worried."

"No, actually, *we* were sick," Robin quipped.

But Jules wasn't ready to laugh. "What a nightmare and Jesus, all I could think was this kind of worrying is what I put you through, this is what I willingly do to you, every time I go out there and put myself in danger."

"No, babe," Robin said, pulling him close and enveloping him in his arms. "No, that's just not true. I mean, yeah, it can be scary, but I know—I *know*, in fact, I've just had the ultimate reminder that you can take care of yourself. I mean, I knew that, I did, but now I *really* know that you're super-safe, as safe as you can possibly be, especially when someone like Sam or Alyssa or Max is by your side. Watching Sam deal with everything and anything that got thrown at us . . . ? He knew exactly what to do, where to go, how to handle it."

"He told Alyssa he couldn't have done it without your help," Jules said, gazing searchingly into Robin's brilliant blue eyes.

Robin smiled and shook his head. "That's just more of Sam being Sam," he said as he held out his hand so that he and Jules could intertwine their fingers as they walked back to the resort. "If he'd had to, he would've figured out a way to carry both me and Gina *and* all three kids."

Jules laughed, because he knew it was true. "The whole stomach flu thing must've killed him. Sympathy vomiter and all."

"He was hurting," Robin agreed. "And yet he won a knife fight. Won in a major way, like, after it was over, he was in possession of the knife and he wasn't the unconscious one."

"That's our Sam," Jules said. "How many stitches?"

"Ten," Robin reported. "Although I had no clue he was hurt, let alone that he needed stitches, until we were in Germany." He narrowed his eyes as he looked at Jules. "Did you need any stitches in the past week and a half?"

Jules shook his head. "Nope. But I caught Mikey's flu."

Robin laughed. "Oh, no."

"Oh, yeah. Max did, too. We passed it along to pretty much all of the FOB. *And* the CO of SEAL Team Sixteen," Jules reported. "He was *really* happy about that. Alyssa's got it now. She was feeling funky on the plane, and soon as we took off . . ." He made a face as he shook his head.

"Ah, God," Robin said. "So she's just at the beginning of it. Poor Sam."

"He's Sam," Jules said. "He'll deal." He smiled at Robin. "But we're here, and we'll definitely help."

FAQs Answered: Interview with Suz

The following is compiled from a series of online interviews. My thanks to all who posed such interesting questions.

Q: You began your career as a romance writer, but now your books are labeled romantic suspense or romantic military action/adventures. Does this influence what you write?

SUZ: No, it doesn't. But I have to admit that I've used labels like those—and even the broader label of "romance novel"—to "get away" with writing exactly what I want to write.

I think labels are something that publishers, booksellers, and even readers use to help them organize the purchase and sales and selection of books. What's this book about? Well, it's about this man who comes to believe that terrorists targeted his ex-wife and daughter. Oh, so it's a thriller. Well, yeah, sort of. Except there's more. Our hero comes face-to-face with a woman he's had a couple of brief but intense affairs with in the past, and as they spend time together, they're finally able to begin to build a real relationship. Oh, so it's a romance. Well, yeah, sort of, except there's more. An awful lot of time is spent on the hero's childhood and . . .

And so on.

You know, the first book in my Troubleshooters series, *The Unsung Hero*, is really a novel about

Charles Ashton, an eighty-something World War II veteran with terminal cancer. This character's story, both his adventures as a downed pilot in Nazi-occupied France and his contemporary struggles with his own impending demise, is the soul of this book.

And yet there's enough going on in the book so that it is a romance. And a military action/adventure.

And there's a sweet secondary romance between two teenagers. And . . . it's a lot of things, all in one book.

I could give you a log line for *The Unsung Hero*: "A Navy SEAL commander recovering from a near-fatal head injury spots a terrorist in his sleepy New England hometown."

Where's the romance? Where's eighty-year-old Charles? Well, they're in there—they're the heart and soul of this book that's most easily labeled a romantic suspense!

Q: What comes to you first, character or story?
SUZ: For me, it's almost always character that comes first. I spend a lot of time writing books with recurring characters—people whose personalities have been solidly established in previous books. I often move former secondary characters into main character roles and devise their story by asking the question, "What type of conflict or situation would push these particular characters beyond their personal edge? How can I make them really suffer?" Because really, the best stories deal with characters who must face their personal vulnerabilities.

Here's an example of what I mean. Say you had a hero who was a mountain climber. You could create a plot that involved him scaling a cliff to save a stranded child. You could throw in an impending thunderstorm—no, make it a hailstorm with high winds. He's got to get up there and rescue that child—no, make her a toddler, trapped with her father who had a heart attack right there on the trail. That could be sort of exciting, right?

Well, no. Because the hero's a mountain climber. It's no big deal for him to scale that cliff. He'll probably yawn while he's doing it.

And the reader will yawn, too.

But what if the hero isn't a mountain climber? What if he's the opposite of a mountain climber—what if he's terrified of heights? I'm talking Jimmy Stewart– level vertigo à la the Hitchcock movie of that very name.

Toss *this* hero into that scenario I sketched out above, and no one's yawning now! When this hero rescues that child, he's not just climbing a cliff, he's facing his demons.

So what I do when I plot my books is figure out who my hero is going to be, what his vulnerabilities are, and what type of situation I can throw him into, to make him really suffer! The same rule applies, of course, to my heroines.

Q: Sam and Alyssa are probably your most popular couple. Where did the idea come from, to stretch their story out over five books?

SUZ: When I outlined Sam and Alyssa's story arc, my intention was to present a traditional romance back-story in "real time."

It's fairly typical to find a book in which the hero and heroine have had a romantic and/or sexual encounter in the past, and have, after that encounter, gone in two different directions. But in the actual book, these two characters come face-to-face again, and are forced to work together and deal with their history, as well as any feelings that are still in play.

With Sam and Alyssa, I wanted to bring my readers along for a ride, having what would typically be that backstory play out over the course of six or seven books, as subplots.

For example, in *The Unsung Hero,* I introduced the two and even though they are minor secondary characters, it's clear that they are throwing sparks and clashing.

In the next book, *The Defiant Hero,* there is a major romantic subplot in which these two characters again clash in a hate/love relationship that explodes, with the help of overindulgence in alcohol, in a one-night stand. Neither character is mature enough to deal with a real relationship, and the morning after is filled with regrets and additional mistakes. At the end of the book, they decide to pretend that night never happened, and go about their separate lives.

The third book, *Over the Edge,* takes place six months later, and the two characters again meet and are forced to work together. Again they clash and spark, and there's another one-night stand. But this time, both are a little bit older and wiser, and they realize there could be something more between them. But the book ends with an external conflict—a girlfriend Sam dated during those six months he and Alyssa spent apart is pregnant and he feels he must "do the right thing" and marry her—that sends the pair in separate directions.

The fourth book, *Out of Control,* has more of a minor subplot from Alyssa's point of view, in which she is attempting to get on with her life. Sam, meanwhile, is trying to make his loveless marriage work for the sake of his new baby.

The fifth book, *Into the Night,* shows Sam trying to make the best of his marriage to a woman he doesn't love, and who truly doesn't love him. In this book, Sam comes to the realization that marriage without love is not "the right thing."

And the sixth book, *Gone Too Far,* is Sam and Alyssa's story. Again, they're thrown together. Sam is single again. Both are even older and wiser, and prove through their journey in the book that they have earned the right to a happy ending—which they achieve at the end of the story.

I outlined Sam and Alyssa's story arc way back after I wrote *The Unsung Hero.* I suspected that telling Sam and Alyssa's story in this manner, in an arc that spread across so many books, would be compelling.

Keep in mind that, up to *Gone Too Far,* Sam and Alyssa's story was told as a subplot in addition to the main plot/main romance of each book. At the time, this was something different from a traditional romance—writing a romantic subplot that ended unhappily or without absolute closure at the book's end. Readers were drawn to this, as I'd hoped!

Q: Were you surprised at the response to Sam and Alyssa's story arc?

SUZ: It was my hope that I'd create a stir with Sam and Alyssa. I'd hoped that people would connect to them—I actually had no idea, though, just how strong that connection would be.

The biggest shock—to me—came when quite a few readers assumed that Sam and Alyssa's story ended with *Over the Edge.* Because in my mind it was so clear that their story was *far* from over.

Q: Which character in the Troubleshooters books (aside from Sam or Alyssa) is the most popular?

SUZ: That would be Jules Cassidy. When I go on book tours, I do a Q&A session at nearly every signing. And one of the first questions asked—it doesn't matter where we are—is "Will we be seeing more of Jules in future books?"

Q: You've been accused of "waving your rainbow flag" in *Hot Target*. Care to comment?

SUZ: I happen to disagree. Yes, this book features Jules Cassidy, who is gay. Yes, this book features other characters who are gay. Yes, this book goes into those characters' backstories (their childhoods, their histories) in some detail—just as I do for all my characters in this book and in every other book I've ever written. And yes, the backstories for these gay characters deal with their coming out—which (as is the case for all gay people) required enormous courage.

I believe strongly that my books are entertainment. I hope you might learn a thing or two while reading them, but first and foremost, my job is to entertain you.

If I'm waving a flag in *Hot Target,* it's the same flag I've always waved in all my books—the American flag. And that's a flag that's supposed to stand for acceptance and understanding. For freedom for *all*—and not just freedom for all Americans, but freedom for all of the diverse and wonderful people living on this planet; freedom to live their lives according to their definitions of freedom. It's a flag that's supposed to stand for real American values like honor and honesty and peace and love and hope.

Q: Readers enjoy the diversity of the characters in your books. Jules is gay, Alyssa is African American,

Lindsey is Asian American, Max's grandfather came from India . . . How hard is it to write those characters?

SUZ: Not hard at all.

Here's the deal: The world I live in, a fairly urban, blue-collar-ish suburb of Boston, is ethnically diverse. I chose to live here, on a busy street with buses running past my house, and neighbors and friends of all different colors, shapes, orientations, and sizes, because I love diversity. I believe it's what makes America great. (I believe that differences of opinion, too, are so important to a true democracy.)

I love meeting people who, on the surface, appear to be different from me. But it never takes long for me to recognize that our similarities far outweigh those superficial differences. Bottom line: People are people. We all tend to want the same big things—love, security, adventure, success, peace of mind.

And yet at the same time, people are individuals. It's important to see people as individuals, without being burdened by the labels and definitions that our society imposes upon them. (Upon us!) Sure, you can define individuals by the color of their skin: a black man, a white woman. Or you can define them by their religion: a Muslim woman, a Jewish man, a Wiccan woman. There are dozens of labels we throw onto people all the time: gay, straight, bi. Democrat, Republican, Independent. New Yorker, Midwesterner, Texan.

What does this mean? To me, I don't see a black straight Christian man who's a Democrat from Chicago.

I see a man.

And that man has dozens upon dozens of individual characteristics—both those superficial yet easily labeled differences, as well as differences such as his love of mocha ice cream (Mocha Ice Cream Lover! There's a label!) and his dislike of peanut butter, his ability to do complicated multiplication in his head, his inability to spell, his fear of tornados, his musical talents, his need to check in on his children before he goes to sleep at night even though he knows they're all right, his undying love for the woman he first met at a party in college that time he was so drunk he threw up on his best friend's shoes and she wouldn't have anything to do with him for months but he knew she was the one so he didn't give up. . . .

If you take the time to look beneath the labels and generalizations, you will always find a person who is more like you than not. (When Sam sat down and talked to Jules—really talked to him—he realized they were more alike than different.)

This is why, to me, things like skin color and background and age differences aren't that big of a deal in terms of a romantic relationship, and why diverse characters aren't hard to write.

Q: Let's talk a little more about that—about looking beneath the labels and generalizations—as well as the facades that people create to hide behind. This seems to be a theme that runs throughout your books.

SUZ: That's absolutely right. One of the themes that I frequently tackle in my books is about how we deal with perception and facades. We present ourselves to the world in a certain way, and people identify us, judge us, and label us. This happens all the time in our society. It's easy, it's quick, and it requires little effort.

My goal with my books is always to grow tolerance and acceptance. To encourage people to look beyond the things that they *expect* to see, to try to see individuals instead of stereotypes.

Sam Starrett, for example, starts out as an alpha male who has some preconceived notions about other people—particularly about Jules Cassidy, who is gay. Sam is a little homophobic and Jules freaks him out. He doesn't see Jules-the-individual, he sees one of those creepy-to-him gay guys.

But at the same time, Alyssa Locke is doing the very same thing to Sam. She sees a white guy from Texas, with his cowboy boots and Texas drawl—a good ol' boy, or a "cracker," if you will. She jumps to some conclusions about him. Redneck. Small-minded, racist . . . When, in truth, he's nothing of the sort.

Throughout Sam's journey in these books, he comes to know Jules. He works with Jules and learns that Jules is worthy of his respect and admiration. He gets to know Jules as an individual, and the two men become friends. Real friends. At the end of the story arc, Sam is no longer homophobic. His ignorance about what being gay means is replaced with understanding—and acceptance and friendship.

Likewise, Alyssa's assumptions are changed as, through her story arc, she discovers who Sam truly is.

Q: But at the same time, Sam has to stop hiding. He has to reveal himself to Alyssa.

SUZ: Yes, he does. You know, I think the ultimate human story is that of finding a true connection with another person—finding real, honest love. The thing about *that* is, in order to find such a real connection, you've got to be willing to reveal yourself completely, which takes true courage.

One of my favorite scenes in a movie is in *Bridget Jones's Diary*, where the Colin Firth character says to Bridget, "I like you very much. Just as you are." What an incredible moment!

We come from a society that infuses us with dissatisfaction and fear. Not only are we taught to believe that we're not good enough, but we're taught that we better pretend to be something better or we will be made fun of, or worse—ignored.

We also, as a society, are quick to label. Like I said earlier, we feel more comfortable putting people into categories—defining people in easy-to-understand ways. She's a lawyer. He's a science teacher. She's Jewish. He's Latino. She's the mother of three. He's a grandfather.

But the labels we give also judge. He's an ex-con—he's dangerous. She's well-endowed—she's a slut. She's blond—she's a ditz . . . etc., etc.

Of course, not all labels and judgments are negative. He's a Harvard grad—he's a good job candidate. She's a nun—she's kind and forgiving. But just like negative assumptions, these positive judgments may or may not be true!

Everyone who lives and breathes and walks the earth—and I'll include my characters in with that group, since I try my best to breathe life into them—has to deal with the labels that others in our society have put on them. They also have to deal with the labels that *they* put onto other people. Plus they have to try to see the truth behind the labels that the rest of the world puts on other people.

And they themselves can take advantage of others' needs to label and define—by playing into others' expectations. For example: Cosmo Richter is a Navy SEAL. He's tall and muscular with exotically colored eyes and striking features. He looks dangerous, and he's quiet—he doesn't talk much.

He also keeps what he's feeling to himself—he's

very private. People look at him and see his lack of reaction and think, *Yikes. He doesn't feel a thing. He's like a dangerous robot.* And Cosmo lets them think that. He finds it's easier to go through life protected by that shield—people who are a little bit afraid of him tend to keep their distance from him. Right?

But what happens when Cosmo finds someone to whom he'd like to get close? What does he have to do to connect with her? He's got to reveal himself, to unpeel.

It's this unpeeling of layers that truly fascinates me—because no two people unpeel the same way. Some reveal themselves voluntarily and hopefully, while others resist, kicking and screaming. Some never really unpeel completely (like Nash in *Flashpoint*)— but they try. And sometimes that's enough for the people who love them—just knowing that they're trying.

VALENTINE'S DAY

AN ESSAY ON NAVY LIFE

Written for Valentine's Day 2002

Traditionally, Valentine's Day is about heart-shaped boxes of candies, romantic cards, a dozen roses, a candle-lit dinner for two . . . All lovely traditions, but face it, they just don't compare to the Valentine's Day gift that the servicemen and -women in the U.S. Armed Forces give—not just to their loved ones but to every American.

My friend Rob is a petty officer in the U.S. Navy, and his ship recently returned to port after six months at sea. He and the rest of the crew spent Thanksgiving and Christmas away from their families. They were all glad to be home in time for Valentine's Day.

Not that they needed Valentine's Day to make their return to port romantic. In fact, recently Rob told me about a particularly sweet Navy ritual called "The First Kiss."

As they approach their home port, all of the married men and women aboard the ship participate in a lottery. And oh, the competition for this is very fierce. Because the winner is the first to disembark, the first to greet—and kiss—his or her spouse after six very long months away from home.

It's the sheer romantic sentimentality of this custom that gets to me. The very first person to set foot on shore isn't chosen by rank or rate or power. That honor is given to someone lucky enough to be married and in love.

This is the big, bad U.S. Navy, an arm of the most powerful military force in the world. And yet everyone— from admirals to seamen recruits—unabashedly recognizes that the most important part of their homecoming lies in the arms of the men and women waiting for them.

But maybe that's not such a surprise. Anyone willing to sacrifice so much to serve their country, to help ensure that America remains the "land of the free" has to have a good understanding of the power of love.

For our servicemen and -women, love isn't about heart-shaped boxes of chocolate.

It's about spending every minute of your long-awaited shore leave desperately trying to find a telephone to call your daughter on her birthday.

Love isn't a candlelit dinner for two, it's a hurried meal at 1530 hours in the mess hall for fifty, because the ship's in hostile waters and you've got to get back on duty.

Love isn't a lacy greeting card, it's moving slowly in the darkness, one careful foot at a time, searching for booby traps in a cave that was once a terrorist hideout in Afghanistan.

Love isn't a dozen roses, it's fifteen dozen nights at sea, sleeping in a rack in a crowded cabin, half a world away from your lover's arms.

Love isn't just the First Kiss—it's *every* kiss that every man and woman in military service willingly gives up when they volunteer. It's every moment away from home and family that they sacrifice for another love— love of country.

And love of freedom.

Happy Valentine's Day to all the servicemen and -women in all branches of the U.S. Military.

Thanks for the terrific gift.

And hurry home.

GLOSSARY OF TROUBLESHOOTERS TERMS

AK-47: An automatic rifle, first manufactured by Kalashnikov in Russia in 1947. Capable of firing 600 rounds per minute.

ALL HANDS: A meeting or an event where attendance is mandatory.

ALPHABET AGENCIES: Slang for government agencies identified by acronyms such as the FBI and CIA.

AO: Area of Operations.

AWOL: Absent WithOut Leave.

BATTALION: A unit of 800 to 1,000 troops.

BDUs: Battle Dress Uniforms.

BUD/S: Basic Underwater Demolition/SEALs. The intensive training all candidates complete in order to become SEALs.

BEQ: Bachelor Enlisteds' Quarters. Housing for unmarried enlisted personnel.

BOQ: Bachelor Officers' Quarters. Housing for unmarried officers.

C4: An easy-to-carry, versatile, pliable plastic explosive with a texture similar to Play-Doh. Lightweight and stable, it can be dropped, shot, and even lit on fire, but it won't explode without a detonator. Often used in place of Sterno to heat coffee. Originally called Composition C, it was developed during World War II by the British.

CAMMIES: Military uniforms in various camouflage print patterns, including woodland, jungle, desert, and urban.

CDRNAVSPECWARCOM: Commander of Naval Special Warfare.

CHARLIE-FOXTROT: Radio call signs for the letters C and F, charlie-foxtrot is a more polite name for clusterfuck. (See also *clusterfuck*.)

CHIT: A permission slip, usually for leave.

CIA: Central Intelligence Agency.

CLUSTERFUCK: A total screwup or disaster, usually caused by incompetence, ignorance, or sheer stupidity. This term makes good use of a word that is a favorite among sailors. (See also *goatfuck*.)

CNO: Chief of Naval Operations.

CO: Commanding Officer. (SEAL Team Sixteen's CO was originally Tom Paoletti. Lt. Commander Lewis Koehl is the current CO of the team.)

COMPANY: A unit of 150 to 200 troops.

COMSPESH: Computer specialist. Tess Bailey is Troubleshooters Incorporated's Comspesh.

CONUS: Continental United States. (See also *OCONUS*.)

COVER: Hat.

DADT: Don't Ask, Don't Tell—a misguided and obsolete law that forced LGBTQ servicemen and -women to lie about their sexual orientation.

DECK: A floor of a building or ship.

DEFCON: DEFense CONdition. The USA's graduated security alert system. DEFCON 1 is the highest level of alert, DEFCON 5 is the lowest.

DIVISION: A unit of 10,000 to 15,000 troops.

DOD: Department of Defense.

DRESS WHITES: The U.S. Navy's white, lightweight summer uniform. Can be the Class-A uniform or Service Dress Whites, or formal attire. Also known as an ice-cream suit.

DZ: Drop Zone.

E&E: Escape and Evasion.

EXFILTRATE: Departure of SEALs, usually with stealth, from an area of operations.

EXTRACTION: To be removed from an area of operations, usually by air. SEALs often extract by sea.

FBI: Federal Bureau of Investigations.

FIREFIGHT: A skirmish involving the exchange of gunfire.

FOB: Forward Operating Base.

FROGMEN: Nickname for U.S. Navy UDT operators. (See also *UDT.*)

GEEDUNK: A vending machine or ship's store selling soda and/or junk food. Geedunk can also be the soda/junk food itself. The name comes from the sound of a can of soda falling from a vending machine.

GOATFUCK: A total screwup, a mission gone bad, a disaster. (See also *clusterfuck.*)

Note from Suz: In compiling and researching this glossary, I think I may have found clues leading us closer to the answer for that timeless question "What is the difference between a goatfuck and a clusterfuck?" I recently found a military definition site that proclaimed the definition of "goat" to be similar to "loser." This site identified a goat as the lowest-ranking man in a group of service personnel, but a goat could also be those officers from the very bottom of a military school's graduating class. (Joke: What do you call a goat who graduates bottom of the class from West Point? You call him "Sir.") So it's possible that a goatfuck is a slightly more inevitable screwup caused by the incompetence or stupidity of the participating officers. But, if goat is interchangeable with loser, then anyone caught in a disastrous situation could, in a true military manner, with glass-half-empty thinking, consider themselves to be the loser or goat who is getting, you know, disastered. Whereas "cluster" seems to imply a more impromptu screwup on a far grander scale . . .

GRINDER: The assembly area at the Coronado Naval Base, designated for PT.

GWOT: Global War on Terror.

HALO JUMP: High Altitude Low Opening parachute jump.

HEAD: Toilet or bathroom onboard a ship.

HELO: Helicopter.

HK-MP4: Heckler & Koch submachine gun—a favorite of the SEALs. A compact 9mm weapon that is reliable even after saltwater immersion.

HK-MP5: Heckler & Koch submachine gun, even smaller than the MP4, also known as a "room broom." Also a 9mm, it's often used for close combat urban situations. Small enough to conceal under a jacket. (If you're a SEAL, that is, but probably not if you're Lindsey Fontaine.)

HOT BUNKING: Sharing a bed, but sleeping at different times. Used in cases of limited billeting or housing, usually onboard a ship. If Sam Starrett and Kenny Karmody were hot bunking, Sam would sleep for the first shift. Kenny would wake him when it was his turn to sleep. Sam would roll out of the bunk and Kenny would roll in—and the bunk would still be hot from Sam's body heat. At the end of World War II, troop transport ships were frequently filled beyond capacity. The men chose to hot bunk or even sleep on deck in order to get home to their families as quickly as possible.

HUMINT: Human Intelligence. Intelligence gathered the old-fashioned way, by using the eyes and ears of human agents, spies, or informants.

ICE CREAM SUIT: Nickname for any white uniform, particularly Navy dress uniforms.

IED: Improvised Explosive Device.

INFILTRATE: Entry by SEALs, usually with stealth, into an area of operations.

INSERTION: To be placed in an area of operations, usually by air. SEALS often insert by sea.

INTEL: Intelligence.

JARHEAD: Nickname for Marines. Also known as Uncle Sam's Misguided Children (USMC).

K-BAR: A very deadly fighting utility knife issued to SEALs. Also known as a KA-BAR knife.

KEVLAR: The material used in bulletproof vests and body armor.

KIA: Killed in Action.

KLICKS OR CLICKS: Kilometers. Military measurement of distance. One klick equals 0.6214 miles.

LZ: Landing Zone.

M16: Nickname for the Colt M16A2 rifle issued to the SEALs. Unloaded, it weighs more than twelve pounds. Fires a small, high velocity bullet, with a range of 460 meters.

MEDAL OF HONOR: Highest military award of the United States.

MEDEVAC: Medical Evacuation, usually by helicopter, to field hospital or aid station.

MESS HALL: Dining facility.

MIA: Missing in Action, usually from a battle situation. If someone is declared MIA, it's not known if they are dead or alive.

MP: Military Police.

MRE: Meal Ready to Eat.

MURPHY'S LAW: "Whatever can go wrong, will go wrong." A good SEAL officer will expect Mr. Murphy to accompany him on every mission, and be prepared for his appearance.

NAVINTEL: Naval Intelligence.

NCO: Non-Commissioned Officer. Senior Chief Stan Wolchonok and Chief Cosmo Richter are both NCOs.

NCONVs: Night vision goggles. (See also *NVGs*.)

NVGs: Night Vision Goggles or Glasses.

O COURSE: Obstacle Course. An important part of BUD/S training.

OC: Officer Candidate. (See also *OCS*.)

OCONUS: Outside the Continental United States. (Pronounced oh-koh-ness.)

OCS: Officers Candidate School. Originally used to train enlisted men for special wartime assignments, it's now a twenty-six-week program for enlisted who want to become commissioned officers. Sam Starrett began his Navy career as an enlisted man. He attended OCS and became an officer.

OFFICERS' COUNTRY: The places where officers work and even live, such as the BOQ. Particularly relevant onboard ship.

OSS: Office of Strategic Services. Developed in 1942, the OSS was an early version of the CIA and Special Forces.

OTS: Officers Training School. (See also *OSC*.)

PITA: Pain In The Ass.

PJ: The nickname for the U.S. Air Force Para-Rescue Jumpers or Parajumpers.

PLATOON: A unit of 30 to 50 troops.

POINT MAN: The SEAL responsible for taking the lead in an advancing squad. The point man will be the first to contact the enemy or trip booby traps. Related terms: On point or taking the point.

PSYOPS: Psychological Operations. The use of propaganda or misinformation to affect the morale of the enemy.

PT: Physical Training.

PUCKER FACTOR: A rating system for fear or tension. A high pucker factor indicates that all muscles are extremely tight.

PX: Post exchange. A store, usually on base, selling general merchandise for servicemen and -women and their families.

REAL WORLD OP: The real thing, as opposed to a training operation.

RECON: Reconnaissance. To investigate, gather information and intel, to scout.

REGIMENT: A unit of 2,500 to 3,500 troops.

RE-UP: To reenlist.

RING OUT: To fail the intensive BUD/S training program. SEAL candidates actually must ring a bell upon their departure, and announce that they are quitting. The majority of all SEAL candidates ring out.

RTO: Radio Telephone Operator.

SAR: Search and Rescue.

SAS: Special Air Service. The United Kingdom's Special Operations Forces.

SATCOM: Satellite Communications.

SEABAG: A duffel bag used by SEALs and sailors.

SEAL: Special Operations force of the U.S. Navy. SEALs operate on SEa, in the Air, and on Land.

SECDEF: Secretary of Defense.

SERE TRAINING: A military program that teaches Survival, Evasion, Resistance, and Escape.

SHORE PATROL: The Navy's version of the MPs or Military Police.

SILVER BULLET ASSIGNMENT: An easy assignment in a comfortable setting, usually given as a reward to deserving personnel.

SITREP: Situation Report.

SNAFU: Situation Normal—All Fucked Up.

SOF: Special Operations Forces, such as SEALs. (Not to be confused with Special Forces. For the difference between Special Operations and Special Forces, see below.)

Q: What's the difference between Special Operations and Special Forces—and how do the SEALs fit in?

SUZ: Special Operations and Special Forces are two very different things. Special Forces go in with lots of firepower, lots of force, lots of noise. Spec Ops is something else entirely. They operate in small, covert groups. In other words, they go in or "insert" silently, get the job done, and leave or "extract" without anyone knowing they've been there. (Or at least not until things start blowing up!) SEALs are the U.S. Navy's contribution to U.S. Special Operations, so they're frequently used when water—oceans, lakes, rivers—is involved.

SOCOM: Special Operations Command.

SOP: Standard Operating Procedure.

SPEC OPS: Special Operations.

SQUAD: A unit of 8 to 15 troops.

STERILE: An item, usually a uniform or a weapon or other gear, that has been stripped of any marking that could attribute it to the U.S. Military. Also known as sanitized.

STERILIZE: To make an item or place sterile. To remove all evidence of occupation or ownership. To sanitize.

TAD: Temporary Additional Duty. The Navy's version (they've always got to be different, don't they?!) of TDY or Temporary Duty.

TANGO: Radio call sign for the letter T. Also nickname for a terrorist.

TDY: Temporary Duty, used by the Army and Air Force. (See also *TAD*.)

UA: Unauthorized Absence. The Navy equivalent to AWOL.

UDT: Underwater Demolition Teams. The World War II granddaddies of the SEALs. Also known as Frogmen.

USO: United Service Organization, established in 1941 to build morale by entertaining servicemen.

WATCH ONE'S SIX: From a clock face position, twelve is immediately in front of you, six is directly behind you. If someone is watching your six, they are watching your back, to help protect you.

WESTPAC: The Western Pacific area of operations. Also used to refer to a tour aboard a Navy ship, usually six months in length. For example, before entering the BUD/S program, Mark Jenkins did two WESTPACs in a row, one aboard the U.S.S. *Enterprise*.

WHEELS UP: Slang for leaving town or going out on a mission. (Example: Jenk grabbed his seabag and ran for his truck after getting the call that Team Sixteen was going wheels up.) Refers to an aircraft lifting off. As the plane heads for cruising altitude, the landing gear, including the wheels, goes up.

WTFO: What the Fuck, Over? A question commonly raised among sailors.

WWII: World War II, the war against the Axis of Germany, Japan, and Italy. It began on September 1, 1939, and ended on August 14, 1945.

XO: Executive Officer. Second in command to the CO or Commanding Officer. Lt. Jazz Jacquette was Lt. Commander Tom Paoletti's XO of SEAL Team Sixteen.

Meet Shane Laughlin, the hero of **Born to Darkness,** *in a special bonus story about his final mission as an officer with SEAL Team Thirteen—the mission that strips him of his command, earns him a dishonorable discharge, and leaves him blacklisted and unlikely to find work in the darkly futuristic world of the mid-twenty-first century.*

BONUS STORY: SHANE'S LAST STAND

By the middle of the twenty-first century, much of the world has changed for the worse. Despite advances in technology, crime has increased, drug use is rampant, and the threat of terrorism hits closer and closer to home. And in the dark days of America's second Great Depression, the divide between the haves and the have-nots continues to grow.

Many things are different in this dark and murky future, but one thing remains the same: Navy SEALs are still Navy SEALs.

And the only easy day was yesterday.

CHAPTER ONE

Something in Shane Laughlin's ankle snapped upon landing.

Or maybe it tore.

Either way, it sent him to the ground, and he bumped and scraped and bounced, jarring the injury over and over as his chute dragged him across the rocky terrain.

Shane bit back a curse. It was the least-graceful landing of his entire military career, and it took everything he'd learned in countless training sessions to get the parachute back under control, even though Magic and Owen both scrambled to help him.

"You okay?" Magic asked, as Owen took possession of all their chutes.

Jesus, Shane's ankle was on fire. What the hell had he

done to himself? Whatever it was, it was bad. Still, he pulled himself to his feet and tried to put weight on it—and would've landed back in the dust had Magic not caught him, the pain making him see actual stars.

But he shook them away, giving Magic an "I'll be fine," because they didn't have time for this. The mission not only required the drop zone be fully sanitized—with the SEAL team's eight chutes rolled into vacuum packs and carried back out—but that it be fully sanitized quickly and quietly. And that meant sitting here shouting *fuck* was not an option.

Regardless of the studies done that proved swearing helped diminish pain.

"Yeah, I think I'll take that as a *no*," Magic said as Shane signaled his senior chief—a height-challenged but wiry fortysomething named Johnny Salantino—who'd made note of the goatfuck in action and was already heading for them.

"Ankle or knee?" Magic continued.

"Ankle." Shane dinged himself again, and again the pain was excruciating. *"Fuck!"*

"You okay there, LT?" the senior asked in his raspy Brooklynese as he crouched down next to Shane.

"Ankle," Magic reported.

"Head count?" Shane asked the senior through gritted teeth.

"Eight. All here, sir, all in one piece. You're our only casualty," the senior replied, then turned to report as Rick Wilkie, the team's hospital corpsman, joined them, "Ankle."

It was un-fucking-believably inconvenient, considering they were in the middle of nowhere. It was a full-on double-fuck of inconvenience since Shane was supposed to be leading his team of SEALs both swiftly and stealthily up the nearby mountain, to a small town where a terrorist leader named Rebekah Suliman, code name Scorpion Four, was enjoying her last supper.

But neither swift nor silent remained part of Shane's current repertoire.

"Don't even think about touching that boot," Shane warned Rick. If he took it off, he'd be in far worse shape. "And keep your syringe away from me. I need a clear head and it doesn't hurt that bad."

Okay, so that was a lie, and they all knew it. But sooner or later, the pain would diminish. Sooner or later, he'd get used to it. Please God, let it be sooner rather than later . . .

"I could give you something local, sir," Rick suggested.

"No, we'll improvise," Magic answered before Shane could respond.

But Shane outranked him. He outranked everyone here on the ground. "Do it," he ordered Rick, pulling up his pant leg to give the medic as much access as he could without that boot coming off.

"With all due respect, LT, you run on this thing, it could end your career," Magic said as the meds Rick injected quickly took the edge off the pain in Shane's ankle, bringing it down to a steady but more-manageable throb.

"I'm not going to plan to run on it," Shane told this man who'd been his confidant and friend since BUD/S training. "But I've gotta be ready. Because I can't stay here."

"I'm going to give you this to hold, sir." Rick handed him a carefully wrapped syringe containing the heavy-duty painkiller. "Let me know if you use it."

"I won't." But Shane pocketed the packet. It could come in handy, in the event they got pinned down and had to remain absolutely silent to keep from being discovered. The last thing he wanted to do was give away their position by breathing too hard.

"What *is* the plan, sir?" the senior asked.

Shane glanced at Magic, who had already shrugged off his pack, and was divvying up the contents, spreading the weight to Owen and the other SEALs. "The plan is to sweep and sterilize the area, and head toward the target," Shane said. This wouldn't be the first time Magic clocked a dozen clicks with Shane leaning heavily on him, or vice versa.

And as much as he hated the fact that he and his injury would handicap his team and slow his men down, putting this entire mission into the extremely capable hands of his senior chief while Shane spent the next two hours miserably stashed behind some brush or in a shallow cave simply wasn't an option.

First of all, there were no caves in this particular region of this country formerly known as Afghanistan, and the sparse bushes wouldn't have hidden a three-year-old, let alone a full-grown man of Shane's height and weight.

And recon patrols came through this area regularly.

Also?

The extraction point—the place where a helo was going to pull them out of this hellhole—was up in the mountains. In order to get there, Shane had to pass the village where Scorpion Four was being feted.

So, nope. There was no quick fix, no easy way out. Shane was destined to be this mission's PITA, this op's representative from Murphyville. *Whatever can go wrong, will go wrong* was Murphy's Law. And he was here as living proof.

But then, as if on cue, Slinger announced, "We got us a tracker, sir."

Apparently Mr. Murphy hadn't pointed his bony finger only in Shane's direction. He'd also tossed an additional monkey wrench into the mix.

"*A tracker?*" Shane repeated, as he let both Rick and the senior help him to his feet. "Just one?"

The lanky SEAL with the good-ol'-boy accent was frowning down at his equipment. "Yeah," Slinger said, "it looks like . . . Wait, I'm gonna calibrate and . . ."

"Don't put weight on it," Magic warned Shane. "You're going to forget and put weight on it." He then added a "Sir," although from the way he said it, the subtext was *asshole*.

"This is fucking weird. It looks like it's five separate trackers, but they're all in a single concentrated area." Slinger, known by his parents as Jeff Campbell, was Shane's gearhead. He was more than a computer specialist—he was practically part cyborg. The equipment that SEAL Team Thirteen was issued was not supposed to be tampered with or adapted in any way, so Slinger used his own, leaving the military-issued gear to Owen, who was this team's second tech, aka the pack mule who carried the crap they never used.

And even though the SEAL team had dropped into an allegedly technologically challenged part of the world, due to the locals' severely limited access to the electrical grid, and even though Owen's military-issued equipment bag didn't contain a tech-sweeper, Slinger had automatically gotten out his mini-tablet-slash-sweeper, and was using it to fully scan the landing zone.

Because Slinger knew Shane. And anyone who knew Shane knew that he verified intel reports—*all* intel reports. When he was out with his team in the very dangerous real world, he refused to assume anything.

If he'd received intel that the sky was blue, he'd verify that, too. Sometimes verification required little more than a quick glance skyward, but more often it required reconnaissance—either technological or the humint kind.

Because their very lives depended upon it. And in the course of his illustrious career, Shane had yet to lose a single man.

"This," Slinger said, "is *mother*fucking strange . . ."

"You're picking up only five trackers?" Shane confirmed. "Total?"

Oftentimes, enemy forces would seed the terrain with nearly invisible miniature tracking devices. Those tiny trackers would become snagged onto pant legs or lodged in the treads of boots or sneakers. But in those cases, the seeding would be extensive, and the entire team would give a positive read.

"Affirmative, LT," Slinger reported as Shane leaned on the senior, his arm around the smaller man's shoulders, so he could move forward. "I'm picking up a small cluster of, yup, five trackers and . . . Shit, sir, it's on me and it's . . ." He cut himself off and thrust his altered mini-tab at Owen. "Effen, take this and see if you can't figure out what-the-fuck."

As the newest member of Shane's team, Jim Owen was considered the FNG, or the f-ing new guy. Magic, who was the king of bestowing nicknames, had started calling him Effen for short, and it had stuck.

As Shane watched, Slinger held out his arms, as if he were going to be wanded by airport security, and Owen ran the sensor over him.

"*That's* weird," Owen said.

"Yeah, right?" Slinger agreed as he unbuttoned and pulled off his overshirt and then his T-shirt beneath.

"How would it have gotten onto your T-shirt, Campbell?" the senior asked, his voice loaded with skepticism.

Owen frowned as he aimed the sensor at the shirts that were now dangling from Slinger's hand. He then brought the sensor back toward Slinger's now-bare chest. "Uh-oh."

Shane braced himself for more bad news.

"What the *fuck*?" Slinger said again, as he took the device from Owen.

Magic moved to look over Slinger's shoulder as both of the tech guys stared down at the readout. "Told you she was too pretty for you, Slingblade," he said, which didn't make sense.

"No fucking *way*." Slinger thrust the sensor back at Owen, then went for his belt, unfastening his pants and pushing them down his legs. Like most of the SEALs in Thirteen, he didn't bother with underwear. And like most of the SEALs in Thirteen, modesty was not an issue for him.

Owen circled Slinger, reaching out with the device to touch the taller SEAL on the lower left side of his back. "I'm reading the entire cluster here," he said, then came around to Slinger's front, same side. "*And* here."

And then Magic's words made too much sense. "The trackers are internal," Shane realized. They were *inside* Campbell. Some beautiful counteragent had fed him . . . What? A cupcake with trackers in the icing? And five of them had managed to not get crushed by his teeth.

It ranked up in un-fucking-believable-land, along with Shane trashing his ankle on a relatively easy jump.

But it meant that they'd just been reduced from a team of eight to six. Or, realistically, even fewer. Son of a *bitch*. The pain in Shane's ankle was now the least of his worries.

"What did you eat?" the senior chief asked Slinger. "Or maybe the more pertinent question is, *where* did you eat?"

"Approximately twelve to fourteen hours ago," Rick chimed in. "Judging from its placement in your lower intestines."

"What the fuck kind of trackers are these, that they could survive stomach acids?" Slinger wondered as he yanked his pants back up.

"Can you somehow jam or alter the frequency of the signal that's being sent out?" Shane asked.

Slinger shook his head. "No, sir. I mean, yes, if it was only one tracker, but I'm pretty sure these have five different frequencies." He looked over at Owen, who still held the device. "Check my math, Effen."

"Five trackers, five frequencies," Owen confirmed for Shane. "Sir, we'd need five different jammers."

And they only had two. Two is one and one is none. It was a Navy SEAL saying from way back, when the Teams had gotten their start during the Vietnam War. Carry two of everything, so that when a piece of equipment failed, the SEALs would have a backup. But here and now, two was as good as none, since two wasn't even close to five.

"Did you have a late lunch in town?" Rick asked, back to trying to figure out where Slinger had gotten tagged.

"No, I had lunch on base." Slinger fastened his belt. "Dinner, too. I didn't eat or drink anything between meals. Water. I had water. Out of a bottle that I also got on base."

So much for the cupcake with icing theory, which meant . . .

"I think maybe the question that needs answering is not *where* or *what* did you eat," Magic said, on the same page as Shane, "but *who*."

Slinger swiftly turned to look hard at Magic, then swore pungently. "Seriously?" he asked as he pulled his T-shirt back on, his movements jerky with his anger. "You *seriously* think . . . ?"

"Hells yeah." Magic turned to Shane. "Yesterday afternoon, while you were having your daily high-maintenance damage-control phone call with Ashley, we went over to the Schnitzel Haus. We've been having these epic pinball battles—me and Sling. They have an old-style machine with the real metal balls and—"

"Get to the point," the senior chief interrupted for Shane, right on cue.

"Yes, Senior, sorry, Senior. The point. Is that Sling got his internally tracked ass, here, picked up by a woman who was gorgeous. Unnaturally so. I'm talking A-list movie-star worthy. Well, maybe more like B-list. I mean, considering it was the middle of the afternoon, and Slinger looks, well, like Slinger. No offense, man."

Slinger just shook his head in disgust.

"Are you sure you didn't eat anything in the bar?" the senior asked. "Peanuts, pretzels—"

"I'm very sure, Senior Chief," Sling said grimly.

"So what are you saying? That she took you to her hotel and . . . ?" Owen's voice trailed off as Slinger turned and just looked at him.

"Oh," Owen said, as light dawned. "*Right.* Sorry. Wow. I mean, not wow but, whoa. I mean—" It took a kick from Magic to shut him up.

Slinger sighed heavily as he looked at Shane. "Sir, I'm truly sorry."

"This is a new one," Shane told him. "For all of us." He turned to Rick, who was sifting through his medical bag. "Is there anything you can give him—"

"I was thinking the same thing, sir," Rick replied, "but . . ." He shook his head. "I mean, what's worse? Having him traceable or having him stop every few minutes with explosive diarrhea? And even then, I can't guarantee all five trackers will be expelled."

That was good to know. Well, it wasn't *good* to know, but it was important information.

"Sir, we need to move," the senior reminded Shane.

"With your injury, our pace is going to be significantly slower than planned."

No shit. Shane looked from the senior back to Slinger. "Sling, I need you to trade equipment bags with Owen."

Slinger sighed again as he nodded. He knew what was coming. "Yes, sir."

"There's another village due west of here. I want you to head in that direction. Let's see who follows you."

Whoever had targeted Slinger with those internal trackers had done it for a reason. Someone wanted to know what Shane's team was doing, where they were going. But whoever that someone was, he or she was forced to use a short-range device instead of more traditional long-range satellite tracking, because this entire area was continuously staticked with SAT interference. All SAT images taken of this entire mountainside would be completely unreadable, and would screw with the signal from Slinger's cluster of trackers. But while long-range tracking wouldn't work, lower-tech short-range would. Ergo it was highly likely that whoever had planted the trackers on the SEAL already had both equipment and personnel here on the ground.

If that was so, the SEALs would find *them* first—after leading them on a wild goose chase.

Shane activated his radio, flipping on his lip mic. "Dexter and Linden," he ordered the two SEALs who'd been silently standing watch ever since this goatfuck began. "Give Slinger a head start, then trail him. I want zero contact with whoever is out there. And watch where you step."

"Aye, aye, Skipper."

They were all aware that this entire region was dotted with abandoned minefields. They'd studied the maps and knew not all were marked as clearly as the land around an abandoned farmhouse that sat just a few clicks to the south.

But chances were, if a building was abandoned, it was not safe to approach.

Shane looked at his remaining men: Magic, Rick, the senior chief, and Owen, who now had Slinger's souped-up mini-tablet in his possession.

"Let's do this," Shane said. "Let's move."

CHAPTER TWO

Their terrorist target was one of a fairly large audience sitting in folding chairs and on mats on the floor, at one end of an ancient Quonset hut dating from the 1940s. The structure had been well cared for and reworked into some kind of school gym. The gym, in turn, was now being used as a makeshift theater.

And that meant that their target was surrounded by civilians, most of whom were children, sitting and watching a performance of Gilbert and Sullivan's *H.M.S. Pinafore*. In a Pashto dialect.

"Their Buttercup's pretty awesome," Magic announced as he crouched down next to Shane, who'd been left in as secure a position as possible with Rick standing guard, hidden on a hillside that overlooked the village.

"And Suliman's definitely in there?"

"I didn't have eyes-on contact myself," Magic told him as he handed Shane the visual imager. It was more than a camera, although it recorded digital images, too. However, it was most useful due to the fact that it utilized face-recognition software to confirm targets like Rebekah Suliman. "But the senior says it's a match."

Shane brought the device up to his eyes, then clicked on the imager's night vision setting, which allowed him to view the images without compromising his pupils' adjustment to the dark. The flexible shield conformed to the shape of his face, keeping even the smallest glow from being seen—even by Magic, who was right beside him.

The senior chief was a firm believer in overkill, and he'd recorded an abundance of digital photos.

The outside of the Quonset hut; the sign for the school, announcing all were welcome, not just boys but also girls; the stage with its crudely assembled set and its crowds of badly costumed, ill-at-ease performers—all children between ages twelve and eighteen.

And there she was. Rebekah Suliman.

The CSO file on Suliman was thin, but the analysts at the U.S. Covert Security Organization ranked the woman not just as a One on the most-wanted list, but as a One-X. Which meant she'd confessed or had been proven—without a doubt—to be responsible for the deaths of hundreds of civilians, including children. That X identified her as someone who had intentionally targeted a school or a bus or the pediatric wing of a hospital. That X meant that Shane's mission was to find her and mark her—and anyone who harbored her—for elimination via stealth missile.

His team was to move in as close as they could, and take pictures that would be used to identify other members of her terrorist cell. Then, after calling in the coordinates, they were to create a perimeter and watch for squirters—those who tried to escape the flames and destruction raining down upon them.

As Shane clicked through the images, he saw that the senior had marked Suliman with an identifying circle in a series of shots of the audience. There were twenty rows of seats set up in two sections with a center aisle, and each section was a dozen seats across. Which meant there were close to five hundred people in that Quonset hut, not including the kids on the crowded stage.

It was mostly a group of women and children watching the performance, with only a sprinkling of men here and there. And even if every single adult in that crowd knew who Suliman was, and were actively harboring her despite her crimes, Shane believed that those kids were innocent.

The day they started targeting schools was the day they should just burn the American flag, because they'd be no better than the scumbag terrorists that they put down.

"How long until the show is over?" Shane asked.

"I . . . don't know it that well," Magic confessed. "I only saw it once, but . . . If I had to guess, I'd say they're probably in the final act."

"So it shouldn't be too much longer." Shane flipped to the next images—closer and closer shots of Suliman, sitting in the third row, second seat in, a big, happy smile on her goddamn, child-murdering terrorist face.

"Yeah, you don't know Gilbert and Sullivan, do you?" Magic said. "That shit can go on and *on*."

In the next slew of images, Suliman turned and leaned down, as if listening to the child—a little boy—who sat in the seat beside her. And then—again in a series of shots that showed the movement in frozen moments— she lifted the boy up so that he was sitting on her lap. With her face close to the child's, she pointed to the stage, and the boy clapped his hands as they both laughed.

Fuck. "The report didn't say she had kids," Shane said tightly.

"Suliman?" Magic said. "She doesn't. Well, she did, but not anymore. They're all dead."

"Maybe . . . nephews and nieces . . . ?" Shane flipped back through the pictures.

"No, they were all killed," Magic said. "Her entire family was blown to hell. That's what makes her so fucking ruthless. She's got no one, Commander. She's no fear and all anger."

Shane turned off the imager and pulled it from his face. "Don't call me that."

"You know you're so there, Laughlin," Magic said. "After this op . . . ? Admiral Crotchkiss is gonna greet the plane himself and plant a great big wet one on you. And then he's going to give you his niece's hand in marriage—oh, wait. What a coincidence! He's already done that."

Magic was convinced that Shane's engagement to Ashley Hotchkiss was the equivalent of an arranged marriage between members of the corporate aristocracy and a young, swiftly rising officer in the U.S. Navy. It was, he insisted, part of an insidious plan to keep the future leaders of the U.S. military securely under corporate control.

But Magic didn't know Ashley as well as Shane did. The idea was ridiculous—that she would marry Shane merely because her father's brother requested it . . . ?

Vibrantly beautiful Ashley, with her gorgeous blue eyes, her classically lovely face, her willowy dancer's body, her sharp intellect, and her keen sense of humor . . . She could have had any man—*any* man—she'd wanted, including a whole pack of powerful officers much higher up the chain of command. But she'd fallen in love with Shane. He'd made damn well sure of it.

"Your bullshit is getting old." Shane now handed his friend the viewer. "Do something useful with your giant brain for a change and look at these images—particularly the ones toward the end. That little boy looks too much like Suliman to not be her kid."

And that meant their job here just got even harder. Because if this boy was Suliman's, Shane couldn't just call in a strike on the home where she was sleeping tonight, because doing so would kill the child, too.

Meanwhile, Magic was flipping through the images. "Dude, what . . . ? Wait . . . No, no, no, this isn't her."

Well, Shane *could* call it in, but he wouldn't, and . . .

"I'm sorry, what?" he asked sharply.

"Jesus, you can be a load," Magic muttered. "We're alone out here, Ricky can't hear us, and yet you *really* need to hear me call you *sir* just because I dissed your fancy-assed girlfriend?"

"Fancy-assed fiancée," Shane corrected him. "And no, dickweed. I was asking because I thought I heard you say—"

"That this isn't Rebekah Suliman? It's not. I don't know who the fuck this is, but it's not her."

"But the face recognition software—"

"Is wrong," Magic finished for him again, still flipping through the images. "I'm gonna reset and run it again and . . . No, it still IDs whoever this is as Suliman, but I'm telling you, bro, it's *not* her." He shut off the viewer and handed it back to Shane. "Your royal majestic lordship sir, maybe you don't remember this, because your soon-to-be uncle-in-law snapped his fingers and got you leave for some party—"

"Ashley's sister's wedding."

"Whatever," Magic said.

"It was a big deal," Shane protested.

"I'm sure it was. But while you were doing the electric slide with old Aunt Edwina, I was loaned out to Team Six. I didn't mention it before now, because it was one of those sneaky, covert, not-to-be-mentioned things. But long very-top-secret story short, I've seen Suliman through a rifle scope."

"I had no idea," Shane said. He wasn't sure what was more surprising—the fact that Magic had gone out with Team Six or the fact that the loquacious SEAL hadn't told Shane about it before now. "How long were you . . . ?"

"It was one very shitty week," Magic said. "I was back on base before you were. Suliman slipped through our fingers, which was doubly disappointing. But I can tell you with absolute authority that this"—he tapped the imager—"is not her. Beeyotch is missing an eye. And I don't care what kind of reconstructive surgery is being done these days in Paris, but even if, by some miracle, she went there and had her face rebuilt, it's *still* not her. Unless they replaced *both* eyes with brown ones, made her ten years younger, a half a foot taller, and gave her a new set of teeth, too."

Shane looked at this man whom he'd trusted, time and again, not just with his life but also the lives of their teammates.

"I suppose the teeth falls under *possible*," Magic went on as he scratched his head. "But if they're going to give her new ones, why make 'em crappy and crooked? And combined with the rest of that shit . . . ?" He shook his head. "Nope." He popped his P—a habit he'd picked up from years of working with Shane. "Not her."

Shane shifted painfully, trying to reach for the bag that held Slinger's equipment. "Let's run the image through a non-gov-issue face-rec program."

"Good idea, and I got it," Magic said, pulling the pack closer. He dug through the nest of wires, looking for the cord that would connect the viewer to Slinger's doctored mini-tab.

But it was then that Shane's radio headset clicked on, and Scotty Linden's rich baritone came over a scrambled channel. He was one of the two SEALs assigned to follow Slinger. "LT, Linden here. Over."

"Gotcha, Scott," Shane said, motioning for Magic to click on his radio headset, too, before he hooked the two pieces of equipment together. "What have you got? Over."

"A six-man team," Scotty reported. "Three are following Slinger, three took off in your direction. Dex is trailing them, I got the others. They're all dressed like locals, but they move like Amurricans. If I had to lay money down, I'd bet CSO. Over."

That didn't make sense. If the U.S. already had a black op group from the elite and highly secretive Covert Security Organization here on the ground, they wouldn't have bothered to send in a team of SEALs.

Unless . . .

"LT," Magic said, his quiet voice not coming through the radio. He'd clicked off his microphone.

Shane looked over to find that Magic had put down the imager. Whatever he'd seen had made him somber.

"Hold on, Linden," Shane said. "Over." He shut off his lip mic, too, and asked Magic, "Who is she?"

"You're gonna hate this, Shane," Magic told him.

Shane nodded. Yep. He already hated it. "Just tell me."

"Slinger's face-rec software IDs her as Tomasin Montague. Her mother was local to this area, her father was French Canadian," Magic reported.

"Why is that name familiar?" Shane asked.

"She's the sole surviving witness," Magic told him, "of the Karachi Massacre."

And . . . there it was.

A year ago, a summit had been scheduled to be held in Karachi, Pakistan, where world leaders were going to discuss the ever-growing, ongoing terrorist threat in the Middle East. But before the talks officially began, a bomb went off, turning the meeting into a bloodbath. Several brutal dictators had been killed—but so had more than a half dozen democratically elected leaders, including the presidents of Germany and Spain.

The U.S. President and his corporate delegation, however, had not yet arrived.

It wasn't long before ugly rumors surfaced, and soon the international media began making accusations that the corporate branch of the U.S. government had been behind the attack. The CEOs in question had spent the past year stridently insisting they were innocent. If only, they claimed, they could locate the young woman alleged to have seen the man who planted the bomb . . . She knew the truth, and she would and could clear their names.

But the woman—Tomasin Montague—had vanished.

But now she'd been found. And Shane and his men hadn't been tasked with putting her and her family into protective custody and delivering her someplace where she'd safely be able to report the truth of what she'd witnessed.

Instead, they'd been told she was a deadly terrorist, and ordered to call in an air strike that would, essentially, wipe out this entire village.

But who had given them this order? Who had altered the face-rec software? Someone very high up the chain of command had to be involved. But how high? And who else knew?

"Shit," Shane said now. He flipped his lip mic back on. "Scotty, I want you to assume these guys are unfriendlies, possibly former CSO now working for the tangos. Copy? Over."

It was too awful to think that they might merely be regular, ordinary—if you could call them that—CSO.

"Copy that, LT," Scott came back. "Holy fuck. Over."

"Have they spotted Slinger?" Shane asked, his mind racing. How was he going to turn this lose-lose scenario into at least a partial win? "Do they know he's alone? Over?"

"Negative," Scotty said. "He's remained out of sight. Over."

"Good. Contact him," Shane ordered. Jesus, maybe— just maybe—this would work. "I don't want them to see him. I want them to think there're seven of him, you copy? And I want him to lead them across the border and then lose them. Stay with them until then, then join him and get to safety. This is a direct order. Over."

"Aye, aye, sir, over."

"Over and out," Shane said. He looked at Magic. "I need you to go find the senior chief and Owen and bring them back here." The conversation he needed to have was not one he wanted to take place over the radio—not even over a scrambled signal. "And give Owen a heads-up. I'm going to ask him to tap into the radio communications between those two rogue teams."

"You don't need Owen," Magic pointed out as he pushed himself to his feet. "You need Slinger for something like that."

But Shane didn't have Slinger. He only had Owen. "I need you back here, too. And bring Rick in when you get here. Oh, and see if you can't scare up changes of clothes for you and the senior and Owen and Rick. I want you to be able to blend in."

"Not for you, too?"

Shane shook his head. "No."

Magic was a smart son of a bitch, and he knew where Shane was heading, and he didn't like it. He crouched down again next to him. "Shane. Please. Whatever you're planning . . . Let *me* take the blame for it."

"And how's that gonna work?" Shane asked. "You, what? Knock me unconscious?"

"I didn't think of that," Magic said, "but . . . Yeah. I could. Do that. Or . . . maybe you hit your head when you hurt your ankle. That's possible."

"Except I've been talking on the radio," Shane pointed out. There would be a record of that.

"Maybe that was during the watchamacallit," Magic said. "The lucid interval."

"And no one's going to be suspicious when I'm in the

hospital and the injury to my head *isn't* severe enough to—"

"Maybe you got better," Magic said, then swore, because he knew how stupid he sounded.

"It's called mutiny. You'll go to prison," Shane said, "and I'll *still* lose my command."

"There's gotta be another way," Magic started.

Shane cut him off. "I gave you an order. Don't make me repeat it."

Magic stood up. "Fuck you, Lieutenant Ass-hat. I'm not letting you do this."

"Yeah, you are," Shane gently told his friend. "Because maybe this is some kind of mistake, the thing with the inaccurate face-rec, and I'll get a medal for saving the day."

"You *seriously* think—"

"No," Shane said. "But I'm going to play it that way, with maybe a little *negative reaction to the pain meds* thrown in for good measure. With luck, I can sell it, and I'll be okay. I'll get through this, too."

Magic didn't believe him. Probably because Shane himself didn't believe it possible. Someone among their superiors had wanted Tomasin Montague dead. And Shane was going to be burned—badly—for his refusal to get the job done.

Still, he pushed, adding, "You know how it works, Dean. The team leader always pays for any mistakes. And if we're both gone, who's going to find out how this happened? Who's going to make sure this doesn't happen again? We didn't work and sweat and bleed to get where we are, only to have them—whoever they are—turn the teams into some kind of goddamn private hit-squad."

Magic shook his head. "Double fuck you, for always being right."

"Go," Shane said.

Magic finally nodded. And turning, he vanished into the shadows of the night.

Shane got busy, taking out the syringe that Rick had given him even as he broke radio silence to contact the SEAL who was following the mysterious team that Scott Linden had said was heading their way. "Laughlin to Dexter. Report in if you can, over."

CHAPTER THREE

"Our intel was incorrect, the target is not here. I'm aborting this mission, and I'm ordering you," Shane said, looking steadily from Rick to Owen to Magic to the senior chief, "to go back over the border, with the rest of the team. With the understanding—"

"With all due respect, sir," Owen interrupted earnestly, looking up from the equipment he was using to try to tap into the mystery team's radio signals. He, like the senior and Rick and Magic, was now dressed like a goat herder—down to the cap that helped cover his face. "We're not leaving you here, alone."

"That's enough," the senior spoke over him, giving the kid his best dead-eye glare.

"With the understanding," Shane repeated, talking over them both, "that you may be delayed by humanitarian efforts to help innocent civilians move to safety in the face of a coming attack from an unknown, unidentified, potentially deadly enemy."

"Jesus, sir, that was a mouthful," the senior said.

"Semantics, Senior Chief," Shane told the older man. "And this is where you say *Aye, aye, sir.* All of you."

They murmured it back to him without a whole hell of a lot of conviction, and he went on. "I'm in command. I made the call to abort, and gave the order. You obeyed said order. If and when you're asked, you'll be telling the truth. These are now simple facts that will protect you."

Because of the SAT signal jamming, there'd be no timeline or record of when the team had left the area. And since Shane alone would remain, and would be picked up by the helicopter at the planned extraction point, he would insist that he'd acted alone in his efforts to save the misidentified woman.

The wording he'd been so careful to use would allow his men to pass lie detector tests, if it came to that.

Except for Magic Kozinski, who knew the truth, but who had the bizarre ability to control his pulse and blood pressure while lying wildly.

They'd all been trained to fool rudimentary lie detectors to some degree. But it was actually kind of freaky how adept Magic was at achieving the necessary calm. In fact, he'd once lowered his pulse to fifty in the middle of a firefight.

So Shane wasn't worried about him, which was a good thing, because Magic knew details, like Tomasin Montague's name. Shane had decided it was best to withhold that information from the rest of the team. The less they knew, the better their chances of surviving the administrative shitstorm hovering on the horizon.

"And what protects you, sir?" Magic asked now. The tone of his *sir* was back to *asshole*. "From the senior corporate officials who want the incorrectly identified target taken out anyway?"

"I'll be okay," Shane said again. Maybe, with Ashley and her powerful father and uncle on his side . . . Maybe he could survive this.

But it really didn't matter. He didn't have a choice.

He wasn't going to give the order to kill an innocent woman.

The senior chief broke the silence. "With all due respect, LT," he said, repeating the very words that he'd glowered at Owen for saying, "we're *not* leaving you here."

Shane was ready for that, too, as he took out the needle and syringe that he'd been hiding up his sleeve. "The pain got too intense, so I—just now, after giving the order to abort this mission—used the meds Rick gave me," he told them as he handed the team's hospital corpsman the syringe he'd in truth emptied while Magic had been fetching the senior and Owen. He'd drained the powerful painkiller into the dusty ground—a fact they all no doubt knew, but couldn't prove, especially since he'd gone to the trouble to make it look as if he'd just given himself the injection.

"I'm gonna need a refill of that," he told Rick, who was carefully disposing of the sharp, "plus several more doses of the local."

"Oh, that's fucking perfect," Magic said crossly. "Make it so you're not only blacklisted, but you walk with a fucking cane for the fucking rest of your fucking life. What is *wrong* with you?"

Shane ignored his friend as Rick looked to the senior chief who, absolutely, would have been instantly in charge had the team's commanding officer really taken that drug. According to the revised military code of 2024, the act of taking a powerful painkiller automatically meant Shane had willingly relinquished his command, due to his being medically unfit to serve. No words to that effect were necessary. It was simply so.

And now, for all intents and purposes, Shane was just another guy that his former team would help, as he—as a civilian—assisted Tomasin Montague and her family.

"Give Lieutenant Laughlin what he needs," the senior ordered Rick gruffly, then shot Magic a "Keep your opinion to yourself, Kozinski."

Shane glanced at his dive watch. He was right on schedule. "I know I'm no longer in command, but we should move into position to intercept, Senior Chief," he said as Rick handed a new packet of wrapped syringes to him and he stashed them in his vest.

They'd all studied the terrain in advance of the op. There were two possible exit routes out of the village and farther up into the mountains. Tomasin Montague and her son would have to take one of them.

The senior chief frowned. Rick and Owen, too, were perplexed.

Magic was the only one who'd caught Shane checking his watch, and because he knew Shane as well as he did, he also knew what was coming.

Boom!

There it was. The first hit of the air strike Shane had called in. He'd radioed the coordinates of that abandoned farmhouse that they'd passed on their way up the mountain.

Boom-bah-dah-boom! Bah-boom! Bah-dah-boom! It sounded like fireworks going off as the land mines that surrounded the farmhouse began exploding, too.

"I had Dex check to make sure the farmhouse was still abandoned," Shane told the senior as he gave himself another healthy dose of the local and pulled himself up to his feet. His ankle still ached like a mother, and it felt weird as shit, but it held his weight. He didn't need Magic's glower and dire words to know that walking on an injury like this could make the damage permanent. But his choices were limited, and he had to do what he had to do. "I figured I might as well take out as much of the minefield as possible—two birds with one stone."

The noise of the attack was like a red alert siren down in the village, and sure enough, from their hillside vantage point, Shane could see a small group of people streaming out of the back of the school's Quonset hut. They moved quickly but carefully, heading toward the steepest of the two paths up the hillside, as if this were something they'd drilled.

"Move into position on both paths," the senior ordered. "In case this is a decoy. Eyes out for our mislabeled former target, ID her, let her pass, but then follow. We'll catch up to her when she's feeling more secure." He looked at Shane, who nodded back.

That was exactly what Shane had intended and planned for. Montague, and the people protecting her, were no doubt frightened by the sound of the nearby bombing. They'd be likely to shoot first, without asking questions, at least at this stage of the game.

"Rick with Kozinski," the senior continued. "Owen and the LT with me."

"I'm sorry, sir," Owen said, looking from Shane to Salantino to Shane and then back, as he corrected himself, "I mean, Senior. But I finally broke into the rogue team's communications, and the order's just gone out to launch a mortar attack."

And there it was. Shane heard it, and he knew his SEALs did, too. The *whump* of a mortar launching was unmistakable, as was the silence that immediately followed. There was no way to know what the target was, because you couldn't hear the damn thing coming.

No whistle, no warning. Just sudden instant death.

But then it hit—a direct blast to the school's Quonset hut—and they all heard that, loud and clear, as the explosion ripped through the night.

The place was still packed with people—mostly children.

Another *whump* followed, and the SEALs all started to run.

"Do whatever you have to, to end those motherfuckers, whoever they are," Shane ordered the senior chief as he scrambled down the hillside, even though he had no right to dispense orders anymore. "Make them stop, then help the wounded! I'll get the woman and her family to safety!"

"Don't you dare get your ass killed by friendlies, LT," the senior shouted back as he headed directly into the kill zone, Rick and Owen on his heels, even as he opened a radio signal to Dex.

"Magic, you're with me," Shane shouted, but the taller SEAL was already at his shoulder.

"My Pashto's shitty, so I'll start with French," Magic said. "Because of the whole Canadian-father thing."

"Just start talking, and don't stop until you're sure they're not going to kill us," Shane said as the group of villagers that were halfway up the steeper of the two trails stopped, turning to watch in horror as yet another mortar hit, and this time a car went up in flames.

And then, because they'd started to move back down the hillside, no doubt going to help the injured escape the fire that was now burning in the school—a move that would mean certain death for Tomasin Montague— Shane didn't just walk toward them on his injured foot.

He full-out ran.

CHAPTER FOUR

Tomasin Montague spoke perfect English.

She also had an escape route planned—but she was unwilling to divulge information about it to two Americans, one of whom was still wearing a military uniform.

Her bodyguards kept their weapons carefully, unswervingly trained on Shane and Magic, and Shane didn't blame them. Were he in her position, he would do the same.

He told her everything.

The assignment he'd been given to take out a wanted terrorist, known for her ruthlessness in killing children.

The realization they'd had that the face-recognition software was intentionally set to deceive them.

Shane's attempt to placate his superiors and buy time to contact and rescue Tomasin and her family by calling in the bombing on the deserted farmhouse down the hillside.

The still unidentified rogue team that launched the mortar attack on the school—an attack that had been silenced, no doubt permanently, by Senior Chief Salantino and the other SEALs.

"It's important," Shane said, as he looked into Tomasin Montague's weary and wary brown eyes, "that this time, when you disappear, you disappear for good. I can help you do that."

She didn't trust him, but she didn't shut him down, so he kept talking.

"I have a friend," he continued, but then corrected himself, because Jean was not anyone's friend. "A contact. In Vienna. He can help you vanish. You and your children." He looked from Tomasin to the little boy she held close to her side, the one from the images, and then to a teenaged girl who was still wearing her costume from the play. She, too, looked a lot like her mother.

One of the guards, the one with the AK-47, murmured something, and even though Shane was no kind of languages expert like Magic, he knew from the tone and the urgency that the man was saying it was time to go.

"You think you can hide," Shane persisted, and the woman looked back at him. "But the people who are after you won't give up. They *will* find you."

"And next time Lieutenant Laughlin won't be there to help you," Magic chimed in. "You have no idea how lucky you are that this man was in command of this mission. *No* idea."

"Jean Reveur," Shane said as Tomasin looked from

Magic to Shane and back again. "You can contact him via his email address. Dreamer19 at qmail dot com. Tell him I sent you. Tell him I'm cashing in the favor he owes me. Tell him after this? We're even."

"You would use up this favor," she said in her gently accented English, "for strangers?"

Magic answered for him. "Yes, ma'am. He would."

"Go," Shane said. "Now. Dreamer19. Qmail. We'll go help the wounded."

The woman nodded, and with her children at her side, she turned to continue up the path into the mountains. The guard with the AK-47 lingered, backing away from Shane and Magic, his weapon still trained on them until he was swallowed by the night.

"Think she'll do it?" Shane asked his friend, who'd already looped Shane's arm up and around his neck, so he'd have to put the least amount of weight on his injured ankle as possible as they scrambled and slid down the steep path to the still-burning Quonset hut.

"Probably not until the news of your court-martial goes public," Magic said helpfully. "Or maybe it'll be the ceremony where they strip you of your rank that'll convince her you're on her side. Particularly if they keep the cameras rolling and catch the part where Ashley returns your engagement ring."

"That's not going to happen. Ashley loves me," Shane said, although even to his own ears he didn't sound completely convinced.

"I know I've given you endless crap about her," Magic grunted as he kept them both from falling as his boots skidded on some loose gravel that bounced down the trail ahead of them. "All my conspiracy theories and predictions of doom? That's just because I'm a jealous piece of shit. She's amazing. And she definitely loves you, man. But Daddy's not going to let her marry you. Not after the CEO-in-Chief chews you up and spits you out. Ashley's got a lot of really great qualities, Shane, but a backbone made of steel isn't one of 'em. You know this as well as I do."

Shane couldn't argue with that.

"She'll cry," Magic continued as they left the hillside behind. "And she'll be heartbroken and devastated. But when it's all said and done, she'll do as she's told."

"I still think I have a chance," Shane started to say.

But Magic wasn't done. "You know, it's not too late for me to—"

"Jesus Christ, just shut it, Kozinski."

But Magic didn't. "Seriously, Shane. With you gone from the Teams, what's the point of my staying? Have you *seen* the new officers in the SpecWarGroup HQ? They haven't gone through BUD/S, but now they're leading SEAL teams? They're not qualified to wipe my ass."

Shane could feel the heat from the fire on his face, hear the screams of the wounded and grieving. "Then I guess you're finally going to have to get your shit together and go through OTS. Make the jump from enlisted to officer."

"Fuck. Me," Magic said. "Can you *see* me in Officers' Training? I won't make it through one week, let alone twenty-six."

"Play your cards right," Shane said, "and maybe *you'll* marry Ashley."

"That's not funny." Magic's voice was tight.

"I know," Shane said. "I'm sorry. You're right."

But then they rounded the corner and found Rick's makeshift triage—which included an area reserved for the unsavable and the already dead.

Magic stopped short. "Fuck. Those bastards killed Buttercup. Shit," he said. "*Shit.*"

Nothing like a dozen dead children as a visual aid to drive Shane's point home. Or two dozen wounded, with more still trapped inside. "You've gotta stay in," Shane said quietly. "Or we'll never find out who's responsible for this."

Magic didn't answer. He also didn't pretend that Shane would stay out here and assist Rick. He just helped him into the burning building and then let him go. Apparently it was okay with him if Shane had to use a cane for the rest of his life, if it meant he'd saved children's lives.

Shane moved past the civilians—mostly women—who were helping with the evacuation. He went right toward the heat of the flames, where he scooped up a little girl who'd been stunned from the blast, who was coughing and vomiting from the thick, toxic smoke. His ankle was starting to scream—the local was wearing off. But he carried her out and gently put her down near Rick, then went back inside for the next, and the next, and the next.

CHAPTER FIVE

The body count included the full six-man rogue team of former CSO agents, or whoever the hell they were.

Senior Chief Salantino hadn't kept anyone alive to ask questions. He'd just dropped them like the terrorist scum they'd proven themselves to be. And he'd made sure the bodies would not be recovered.

He stood now, his clothes covered with blood from nearly twenty-four hours of assisting Rick with emergency medical aid. The SEALs had only left their improvised hospital when word came down that a Corporate Nation Medical Team was on its way, due to arrive within the hour. That meant there'd be CN mediators tagging along, which meant there'd be a full company of contractor-run security forces as well.

And neither Salantino nor Shane wanted to be anywhere in the vicinity when *they* made the scene.

Magic, Owen, Rick, and the senior had to hump it back over the border, on foot, for their story to line up.

Only Shane could wait here for the helo extraction.

But Magic in particular was loathe to leave him there alone.

"Time," the senior said.

"Last chance," Magic told Shane.

Shane held out his hand, well aware that this was the last opportunity he'd have to talk to his friend without others listening in and monitoring every word. At best, for a good long time. At worst, for the rest of his soon-to-be worthless life. "Good luck in OTS, Dean."

Magic clasped Shane's hand. It was more than a handshake. It was a promise. A vow. A pledge.

"You know I'd follow you anywhere, sir." It was the most respectful *sir* Shane had ever heard fall from Magic's irreverent lips. "If you ever need anything. *Any*thing . . ."

"That means a lot to me," Shane said quietly as he released his friend's hand. "Thank you."

Of course Magic couldn't leave it like that. "I fucking hate you, douchebag," he said. "And—fair warning— I just might take you up on that whole marrying-Ashley thing."

Shane laughed as Magic walked away. "Good luck with that, too. And by the way . . . ? She loves me. None of this is over until it's over."

Magic nodded, but when he glanced back at Shane, it was clear in his eyes, and written all over his face. The fat lady had sung, and the curtain was coming down.

And a half hour later, as Shane heard the extraction helo thrumming overhead, as he injected himself—this time for real—with that dose of the heavy-duty painkiller that Rick had given him, he knew it wouldn't be long now before the hammer came down, too.

As the drug dulled his senses and surrounded him with a cushion of warmth and odd indifference, he was pulled aboard the gunship, where the medics immediately went to work on his ankle. And Shane knew they were going above and beyond to keep it from becoming a career-ending injury.

But Magic was right. His superiors up the chain of command were going to crucify him.

It was over.

He was over.

And in the last few moments before Shane succumbed to unconsciousness, he wondered what would become of him, where he would go, what he would do.

As hard as it was going to be to lose Ashley, her impending, inevitable defection would sadden but not crush him.

But losing his command? Being dishonorably discharged?

Being a SEAL was everything to him. It had defined him since he was barely even ten years old. He'd worked, his entire life, to be the best of the best.

Still Shane knew with a certainty that warmed him even more deeply than the drug, that he'd made the right choice, he'd done the right thing. Tomasin was safe. His team was safe.

He might be over.

But he was far from done.

Did Shane sweep you off your feet?
Then you won't want to miss

BORN TO DARKNESS

Read on for an excerpt of this thrilling novel. . . .

Shane was winning when she walked in.

His plan was a simple one: spend a few hours here in this lowlife bar, and win enough money playing pool to take the T down to Copley Square, where there were a cluster of expensive hotels. Hit one of the hotel bars, where the women not only had all of their teeth, but they also had corporate expense accounts and key cards to the comfortable rooms upstairs.

But drinks there were pricey. Shane had spent his remaining fifty-eight seconds at the Kenmore comm-station checking menus, and he knew he'd need at least twenty dollars merely to sit at the bar and nurse a beer. Fifty to buy a lady a drink. And expense account or not, you had to be ready to start the game by buying the lady a drink.

But then *she* walked in—or rather, limped in. She was smaller than the average woman, and slight of build. She'd also injured her foot, probably her ankle, but other than that, she carried herself like an operator. She'd certainly scanned the room like one as she'd come in.

Which was when Shane had gotten a hit from her eyes. They were pale, and he couldn't tell from this distance whether they were blue or green or even a light shade of brown. But the color didn't matter; it was the glimpse he got of the woman within that had made him snap to attention—internally, that is.

She looked right at him, gave him some direct eye contact, then assessed him. She took a very brief second to appreciate his handsome face and trim form, catalogued him, and finally dismissed him.

Of course, he *was* playing the role of the hick just off the turnip truck—he would have dismissed himself, too, had he just walked in.

Shane watched from the corner of his eye as she sat at the bar, shrugged out of her jacket to reveal a black tank top, then pulled off her hat and scarf. She was completely tattoo-free—at least in all of the traditional places that he could currently see.

Her light-colored hair was cut short and was charmingly messed. But it was the back of her neck that killed him. Long and slender and pale, it was so utterly feminine—almost in proud defiance of her masculine clothing choices, her nicely toned shoulders and arms, and her complete and total lack of makeup.

And Shane was instantly intrigued. He found himself restrategizing and forming a very solid Plan B almost before he was aware he was doing it.

Plan A had him missing the next shot—the seven in the side pocket and the four in the corner—which would lead to his opponent, a likable enough local man named Pete, winning the game. After which Shane would proclaim it was Pete's lucky night, and challenge the man to a rematch, double or nothing, all the while seeming to get more and more loaded.

Because Pete was a far better player than he was pretending to be. Pete was hustling *him*, and all of the regulars in this bar knew it, and at that point the bets would start to fly. Shane would drunkenly cover them all, but then would play the next game in earnest, identifying himself as a hustler in kind as he kicked Pete's decent but amateurish ass. He'd then take his fairly won earnings and boogie out of Dodge.

Because if there was one thing Shane had learned from the best pool payer in his SEAL team—an E-6 named Magic Kozinski—it was that you didn't hustle a game and stick around for a victory beer. That could be hazardous to one's health. Resentment would grow. And resentment plus alcohol was never a good mix.

Plan B, however, allowed Shane to stick around. It gave him options.

So he called and then sank both the seven and the four, then called and missed the two, which put the balls on the table into a not-impossible but definitely tricky setup. Which Pete intentionally missed, because making the shot would've ID'd him as the hustler that *he* was.

They finished the game that way—with Pete setting up a bunch of nice, easy shots, and letting Shane win. Which put five dollars into Shane's nearly empty pocket.

Which was enough to buy a lady a drink in a shithole like this.

"You're on fire tonight," Pete said, when Shane didn't do an appropriate asshole-ish victory dance. "How 'bout a rematch, bro?"

And Shane wanted to sit Pete down and give him a crash course in hustling, because this was a beginner's mistake. You never, *ever* suggested the rematch yourself, not if you'd just intentionally lost the game. The mark had to do it, otherwise the hustle was too much of a con. The mark had to think he was going to screw *you* out of your hard-earned pay.

Pete's suggestion made him significantly less likable and more of the kind of sleazebag who deserved his ass handed to him on a platter.

"I don't know, man," Shane said, massaging the muscles at the base of his skull as if he'd had a hard day at the construction site. "You're pretty good. Let me think about it . . . ?"

Pete thankfully didn't push. "I'll be here all night. But, hey, lemme buy you another beer. On account of your winning and all."

Better and better. As long as Pete didn't follow him over to the bar. "Thanks," Shane said. "I'm going to, um, hit the men's and . . ."

But instead of going into the bathroom in the back, he went to the bar and slid up onto one of the stools next to the woman with the pretty eyes. She was drinking whiskey, straight up, and she'd already ordered and paid for her next two glasses—they were lined up in front of her in a very clear message that said, *No, butt-head, you may not buy me a drink.* She'd also purposely left an empty-stool buffer between herself and the other patrons. And the glance she gave Shane as he sat let him know that she would have preferred keeping her personal DMZ intact.

Her eyes were light brown, but she'd flattened them into a very frosty *don't fuck with me,* dead-woman-walking glare. It was a hell of a talent. The first chief Shane had ever worked with in the SEAL teams—Andy Markos, rest his soul—could deliver the same soulless affect. It was scary as shit to be hit with that look. Even to those who knew him well and outranked him.

But here and now, Shane let this woman know that he *wasn't* scared and *didn't* give a shit that she didn't want him sitting there, by giving her an answering smile; letting his eyes twinkle a little, as if they were sharing a private joke.

She broke the eye contact as she shook her head, muttering something that sounded like, "Why do I do this to myself?"

Any conversational opener was a win, so Shane took it for the invitation that it wasn't. "Do what to yourself?"

Another head shake, this one with an eye roll. "Look, I'm not interested."

"Actually, I came over because I saw that you were limping," Shane lied. "You know, when you came in? I trashed my ankle about a year ago. They giving you steroids for the swelling?"

"Really," she said. "You're wasting your time."

She wasn't as pretty as he'd thought she was, from a distance. But she wasn't exactly not-pretty either. Still, her face was a little too square, her nose a little too small and round, her lips a little too narrow. Her short hair wasn't blond as he'd first thought, but rather a bland shade of uninspiring light brown. She was also athletic to the point of near breastlessness. The thug he'd tangled with earlier that evening had had bigger pecs than this woman did beneath her tank top.

But those eyes . . .

They weren't just brown, they were golden brown, with bits of hazel and specks of green and darker brown thrown in for good measure.

They were incredible.

"Be careful if they do," Shane told her. "You know, give you steroids. I had a series of shots that made me feel great. They really helped, but ten months after the last injection, I was still testing positive for performance enhancing drugs. Which was problematic when I tried to earn some easy money cage fighting."

She turned to look at him. "Is that it? You done with your public service announcement?"

He smiled back at her. "Not quite. I did a little research online and found out that that particular drug can stay in your system for as long as eighteen months. I've still got six months to kill."

"Before you can become a cage fighter," she said, with plenty of *yeah, right* scorn in her voice. "Does that usually impress the girls?"

"I've actually never told anyone before," Shane admitted. "You know, that I stooped that low? But it *is* amazing what you'll do when you're broke, isn't it?" He finished his beer and held the empty up toward the bartender, asking for another. "Pete's paying," he told the man then turned back to the woman, who'd gone back to staring at her whiskey. "I'm Shane Laughlin. From San Diego."

She sighed and finished her drink, pushing the empty glass toward the far edge of the bar and pulling her second closer to her and taking a sip.

"So what are you doing in Boston, Shane?" he asked for her, as if she actually cared. "Wow, that's a good question. I'm former Navy. I haven't been out all that long, and I've been having some trouble finding a job. I got a lead on something short term—here in Boston. I actually start tomorrow. How about you? Are you local?"

When she turned and looked at him, her eyes were finally filled with life. It was a life that leaned a little heavy on the anger and disgust, but that was better than that flat nothing she'd given him earlier. "You seriously think I don't know that you're slumming?"

Shane laughed his surprise. "What?"

"You heard what I said and you know what I meant."

"Wow. If anyone's slumming here . . . Did you miss the part of the conversation where I admitted to being the loser who can't find a job?"

"You and how many millions of Americans?" she asked. "Except it's a shocker for you, isn't it, Navy? You've never *not* been in demand—you probably went into the military right out of high school and . . . Plus, you were an officer, right? I can smell it on you." She narrowed her eyes as if his being an officer was a terrible thing.

"Yeah, I was officer." He dropped his biggest bomb. "In the SEAL teams."

She looked him dead in the eye as it bounced. "Big fucking deal, Dixie-Cup. You're out now. Welcome to the real world, where things don't always go your way."

He laughed—because what she'd just said *was* pretty funny. "You obviously have no idea what a SEAL does."

"I don't," she admitted. "No one does. Not since the military entered the government's cone of silence."

"I specialized in things not going my way," Shane told her.

"So why'd you leave, then?" she asked, and when he didn't answer right away, she toasted him with her drink and drained it. "Yeah, that's what I thought."

"I'm proud of what I did—what I was," he said quietly. "Even now. *Especially* now. But you're right— partly right. About the shock. I had no idea how bad *bad* could be, before I was . . . kicked out and blacklisted." Her head came up at that. "So, see, *you're* the one who's slumming. You could get into trouble just for talking to me."

She was looking at him now—really looking. "What exactly did you do?"

Shane looked back at her, directly into those eyes as he thought about his team, about Rick and Owen, about Slinger and Johnny, and yes, Magic, too. . . . "I disobeyed a direct order—which is something I did all the time out in the world, as a SEAL team CO. But this time? It was apparently unforgivable. And that, combined with my need to speak truth, even to power, and my inability to grovel and appropriately kiss ass . . . It got ugly. In the end, someone had to go, so . . ." He shrugged, still convinced after all these hard months that he'd done the right thing. "I was stripped of my rank and command—and dishonorably discharged."

She sat there, gazing at him. His answer had been rather vague and even cryptic, but it was still more than he'd told anyone since it had happened. So he just waited, looking back at her, until she finally asked, "So what do you want from *me*?"

There were so many possible answers to that question, but Shane went with honesty. "I saw you come in and I thought . . . Maybe you're looking for the same thing I am. And since I find you unbelievably attractive . . ."

She smiled at that, and even though it was a rueful smile, it transformed her. "Yeah, actually, you don't. I mean, you think you find me . . . But . . ." She shook her head.

Shane leaned forward. "I'm pretty sure you don't know what I'm thinking." He tried to let her see it in his eyes, though—the fact that he was thinking about how it would feel for both of them with his tongue in her mouth, with her hands in his hair, her legs locked around him as he pushed himself home.

He reached out to touch her—nothing too aggressive or invasive—just the back of one finger against the narrow gracefulness of her wrist.

But just like that, the vaguely fuzzy picture in his head slammed into sharp focus, and she was moving against him, naked in his arms, and, Christ, he was seconds from release as he gazed into her incredible eyes. . . .

Shane sat back so fast that he knocked over his bottle of beer. He fumbled after it, grabbing it and, because it had been nearly full, the foam volcanoed out of the top. He covered it with his mouth, taking a long swig, grateful for the cold liquid, aware as hell that he'd gone from semi-aroused to fully locked and loaded in the beat of a heart.

What the hell?

Yeah, it had been a long time since he'd gotten some, but *damn*.

His nameless new friend had pushed her stool slightly back from the bar—away from him—and she was now frowning down at her injured foot, rotating her ankle.

She then looked up at him, and the world seemed to tilt. Because there was heat in her eyes, too. Heat and surprise and speculation and . . .

Absolute possibility.

"I'm Mac," she told him as she tossed back the remains of her final drink. "And I don't usually do this, but . . . I've got a place, just around the corner."

She was already pulling on her jacket, putting on her scarf and hat.

As if his going with her was a given. As if there were no way in hell that he'd turn her down.

Shane was already off the stool and grabbing his own jacket, as she—Mac—went out the door. Her limp was less pronounced—apparently the whiskey had done her some good. In fact, she was moving pretty quickly. He had to hustle to keep up.

"Hey," he said, as they hit the street, and the bar door closed behind him. "Um, Mac? Maybe we should find, you know, a dealer? I'm not carrying any um . . . So unless you have, you know . . ." He cleared his throat.

She stopped walking and looked up at him. Standing there on the sidewalk, he was aware of how much bigger and taller he was. She was tiny—and significantly younger than he'd thought. More like twenty-two, instead of pushing thirty, the way he'd figured her to be, back in the bar.

Or maybe it was just the glow from the dim streetlight, making her look like youthful beauty and desire personified.

"Why do men have a problem saying *the pill*?" she asked.

Shane laughed. "It's not the words," he told her. "It's the concept. See, what if I'd misunderstood and—"

"You didn't. And FYI, this is Massachusetts. It's still legal here. No need to back-alley it."

"Well, good. But . . . we still need . . . some."

She smiled, and Jesus, she was beautiful. "Don't worry, I got it handled." Her gaze became a once over that was nearly palpable, lingering for a moment on the unmistakable bulge beneath the button-fly of his jeans. She looked back into his eyes. "Or I will, soon enough."

No doubt about it, his luck had changed.

"Please promise that you're not luring me back to your apartment with the intention of locking me in chains and keeping me as your love slave," he said. "Or—wait. Maybe what I really want is for you to promise that you *are*."

She laughed at that. "You're not my type for long-term imprisonment," she told him. But then she stood on her toes, tugging at the front of his jacket so that he leaned down. She was going to kiss him and they both knew it, but she took her time and he let her, just waiting as she looked into his eyes, as she brought her mouth up and softly brushed her lips against his.

Shane closed his eyes—God, it was sweet—as he let himself be kissed again, and then again. And this time, she tasted him, her tongue against his lips. He opened his mouth, and then, Christ, it wasn't sweet, it was pure hunger, white-hot and overwhelming, and he pulled her hard into his arms, even as she clung to him, trying to get even closer.

The world could've exploded around him and he wouldn't have cared. He wouldn't have looked up— wouldn't have stopped kissing her.

And through all the layers of clothing, their jackets, their pants, his shorts, and whatever she had on beneath her cargo BDUs—God, he couldn't wait to find out what she wore for underwear—Shane felt her stomach, warm and taut against his erection, and just that distant contact was enough to bring him teetering dangerously close to the edge.

And by the time he made sense of that information and formed a vaguely coherent thought—holy shit, just kissing this woman was enough to make him crazy—it was almost too late.

Almost. But only because she pulled away from him. She was laughing, her incredible eyes dancing as she looked up at him, as if she knew exactly what he was feeling.

She held out her gloved hand for him, so he took it, and then—bad ankle be damned—she pulled him forward.

And together, they started to run.

If you love the Troubleshooters,
you won't want to miss the action-packed
and achingly romantic new novel
from bestselling author Suzanne Brockmann

DO OR DIE

Available from Ballantine Books
February 2014

And there he was. Ian Dunn. The former prisoner, now an official ex-con. Dressed in jeans and a T-shirt, clunky black boots on his feet. He carried a hooded sweatshirt and a plastic grocery sack that must've held the few personal items he'd had with him in his cell.

He stood there, just looking at them, long after the gate had opened wide enough for him to slip through.

But he didn't move.

And he didn't move.

He looked from Phoebe to Martell Griffin and back, and shook his head, just very slightly, as if they were unruly children who'd bitterly disappointed him.

And if only half of what Phoebe had discovered over the past few hours was true . . . they'd put him in some serious danger, *and* potentially screwed up whatever mission he was currently on.

Martell spoke first, turning to unlock his car with a click and a whoop of his aging anti-theft system. "Come on, Dunn. I'll drive you to a hotel. You'll be safe there. You can take a shower, get something to eat while we talk."

The sound of his voice seemed to unpin Dunn's feet from where they were planted in the dusty ground, and he finally came through the gate, his stride as loose and easy as it had been when he'd walked into the prison interview room. "Yeah, no, I think I'll catch a ride with my cute new lawyer."

Martell laughed and purposely repeated Dunn's words. "Yeah, no, I don't think so."

"You know, maybe that *would* be a good idea,"

Phoebe told Martell. Not only would this prove to Dunn that she was not afraid of him, but it would give them a chance to talk privately. Not that she'd necessarily be able to share anything she learned with Martell, considering client-attorney privileges. Still, she might find out exactly what was going on. As in, who was this Conrad that Dunn had asked about, back in the interview room. She didn't believe his *mutual acquaintance* explanation for one hot second.

"Feel free to follow," Dunn told Martell. "After Pheebs and I talk we'll stop and all have lunch."

And *that* was when Phoebe should have realized that something was up. For him to have gone from a cold *No deal*, back in the prison, to a friendly *Feel free to follow, we'll all have lunch,* was completely ridiculous.

But the reasonableness and ease with which Dunn spoke those words fooled her, and she turned and opened the driver's-side door of her new car.

Phoebe's shiny new car—a gift to herself for nailing the job at the law firm—had a keyless entry that she adored. She no longer had to dig to find her car keys at the bottom of her bag, she just had to touch the handle, and her car door would unlock. Likewise, she just had to toss her bag onto the passenger seat, and the car would sense the presence of the nearby key, and start with a touch of a button.

It was fabulous.

After she unlocked her car, she climbed in behind the wheel. The door hung open as she focused on balancing her bag on the armrest between the two front seats and clearing the wrappings from a quickly grabbed breakfast off the passenger seat, to make room for her newest client.

And this meant that she was completely surprised by what Dunn did next.

He moved inside of the open car door, and she sensed

more than saw his sweatshirt and plastic sack of God-knows-what whizzing past her head as he threw it into the back, as almost simultaneously he put his left hand beneath her thigh, and his right hand between her lower back and the seat.

"Hey!" Phoebe heard herself say as he seemingly effortlessly lifted her up and tossed her over the armrest. She landed butt-first in the passenger seat, her feet tangling with the steering wheel only briefly, because he was there to help her get them free.

Her surprise was echoed by Martell, who shouted, "Dunn! Stop! What the hell!" from the parking lot.

But Ian Dunn was already behind the wheel, door closed and locked, car started and in motion.

"I'll drive, okay?" he said in that very same reasonable, friendly voice, as he peeled away from Martell, a spray of dust and gravel making the other man turn away to protect his eyes.

"No, it is *not* okay!" Phoebe watched out of the back window as Martell sprinted for his own car, no doubt to give chase.

"Better fasten your seat belt," Dunn told her calmly as he gunned it out of the lot and onto the equally ill-repaired road.

"This is *exceedingly* not okay," Phoebe said as she belted herself in, reaching to pull her bag up from the floor, where it had fallen when she'd been jettisoned from the driver's seat. "In fact, this fits the definition of felony kidnapping!"

"Not if you tell me it's okay if I drive," Dunn pointed out, glancing at her as he adjusted the seat, pushing it all the way back, as far as it could go. Even then his legs were clearly too long, and he shifted to get as comfortable as he could.

"I am *not* going to tell you it's okay if you drive," she sputtered, even as she reached one hand into her bag, feeling for . . . "It's my car, and I was driving, and you physically accosted me, which makes it—"

"Kidnapping," he finished for her. "I get it. So have me arrested and send me back to prison. Oh, wait. That's exactly what you *don't* want to do."

"Stop this car," she said, aiming her handgun at him, right through the leather of her bag. "Right now, Mr. Dunn, or I will shoot."

She had to admit that it must've looked ridiculous, like she was only pretending she had a weapon and was in fact doing nothing more than pointing her finger at him. But she knew that getting the Glock out of the bag would mean temporarily not aiming it at him—during which time he could easily take it from her. Even while driving. He was, after all, a former Navy SEAL.

Dunn looked from her face to the bag and back into her eyes before he returned his attention to the road, even as he shook his head. "Nah," he said. "You're not going to shoot me. I mean, seriously, Pheeb, if you were really going to do that, you would've pulled the trigger before I got the car up to speed. You do it now, you'll probably die, too, you know, in the fiery crash? But if it makes you feel better—more in control—by all means, keep your *weapon*"—he made quotation marks with his fingers even as he held onto the steering wheel with the palms of his hands—"securely aimed at me."

"What is *wrong* with you?"

Dunn glanced at her again and sighed. "For starters, my mother was sixteen when I was born, my father barely older. He already had a criminal record, which made it impossible to find work, so he got in too deep with a gang of total, well, assholes, if you'll pardon my French. There's no other word for them, at least not less offensive. Anyway, *that* nearly killed him, but it didn't quite, so now he was a one-legged ex-con—yeah, *that* sucked—who *really* couldn't find a job, so when I was three, he trained me to gain entry of houses through doggy doors—"

"That's *not* what I meant," Phoebe interrupted, but then interrupted herself. "When you were *three*?"

"Well, three and a half," Dunn said as if that were better.

"God! That's child abuse." She caught herself. He was trying to distract her. "What I meant was . . ." She took a deep breath and rephrased. "There's just no way someone in your alleged position wouldn't be grateful to be released early. Therefore you had a reason to want to stay in, which I really hope you will share with me, so I can work with you, and whichever agency you're working for, to find a solution for this problem with Mr. Griffin."

He'd adjusted the rearview mirror, and was now fixing the ones on the side as well. He seemed to be a very good driver, except for the fact that he was going much too fast.

"I'm not working for any agency," he said, completely unapologetically. "Good guess, but no. You're wrong about that. I can't tell you anything more. If I did, well, I'd have to kill you."

He spoke the words so casually, as if he were joking, his eyes on the road in front of them. But just the same, Phoebe knew he meant it at least as a partial threat. An intentional reminder that he was a dangerous man, regardless of the fact that she was the one in possession of a weapon.

"No, you wouldn't have to," she told him, choosing not to let his statement go unchallenged. "As your lawyer, you can tell me anything."

He glanced at her again. "You're not my lawyer."

"Yes, I am."

"No, you're not."

This was petty. And childish. "Yes, Mr. Dunn, I am."

"Really?" he asked. "We're going to keep this up? Because you're not my lawyer, Jerry is."

"I don't have anything else to do while being abducted," she pointed out. "Except defend the fact that, yes, while Mr. Bryant is away, I am your attorney. At least slow down so Mr. Griffin can follow us more easily."

"It's not a fact, because I never agreed to it." Dunn didn't slow down.

"Yes, you did," she countered. "You called me your *cute new lawyer* in the parking lot."

"That was bullshit," he said with another glance at her. "Not the cute part, the lawyer part. You're very cute. But bullshit doesn't count." He added, "I *do* have something else to do right now. I need to use your phone."

She hugged her bag more tightly to her chest. "Am I or am I not your lawyer?" she asked, adding, "No bullshit this time."

Dunn actually laughed. "You're freaking kidding me."

"If you're my client, Mr. Dunn, you can use my phone," she told him as matter-of-factly as she could manage. "If you're my kidnapper, you can't."